ROSINANTI: WRATH OF THE FAITHFUL

The Rosinanti Series: Book Two

By Kevin J. Kessler

ISBN: 1-944985-30-1
ISBN-13: 978-1-944985-30-1

ROSINANTI: WRATH OF THE FAITHFUL

THE ROSINANTI SERIES: BOOK TWO

By Kevin J. Kessler

Lavish Publishing, LLC ~ Midland

Copyright

First Edition
The Rosinanti Series Book 2

Paperback edition
Published in the United States by Lavish Publishing, LLC, Midland, Texas
ISBN-13: 978-1-944985-30-1
ISBN: 1-944985-30-1
Cover Design by: Wycked Ink
Cover Images: Adobe Stock
www.LavishPublishing.com

For Shannon, Who Believed in Magic From the Very Beginning

ACKNOWLEDGEMENTS

As I sit here, prior to undergoing the final round of edits on *Rosinanti: Wrath of The Faithful*, I'm overcome to think of the journey my life has taken in the last year. Publishing the first *Rosinanti*, and *Rosinanti: The Decimation of Casid* felt like a dream come true. They were built upon the foundation of a work I started over 15 years ago. In that time, I was consistently writing and rewriting, and changing things, all built upon that original draft.

Wrath was written in the here and now. Wrath was undertaken knowing everything I've learned in this crazy publishing journey that has swept up my life. Wrath is something I am incredibly proud of.

I have to start off by acknowledging Lavish Publishing once more for making my dreams come true. You folks have allowed me the freedom and flexibility to take this labor of undying love and turn it into a reality that has changed my life. Huge thanks goes out to the three ladies who worked with me on this book, Robin for the amazing editing, Desiree for formatting like a champ, and Lark for yet another home run cover!

To my family: Mom, Dad, Dan Rob, Nana, and Pop, your love and support have meant the world to me. I would be lost without you!

My Beta Team: what can I say? You all have done so much to aid in the creation of this book. Dan Kessler, Chris Doherty, Tim Elbing, Adam Blistein, Kacey Ables, Jenna Famiglietti, Chanell Renea, Chelsea Head, Kyra Dune, and anyone else who has looked at any piece of this manuscript, your feedback has been invaluable!

To Kristin Dutt: My PA, my rock, my reality check, my confidant, my cheerleader, my guardian. I am more grateful for all you do than you can ever know. You're more than a friend, more than a professional colleague. You are family.

To everyone who has enjoyed the Rosinanti Series up to this point: From the bottom of my heart, THANK YOU! You've made my wildest dreams come true. Interacting with you all has been one of the greatest joys of my life. Please continue to reach out. I cherish your opinions, your theories, and your friendship. Please do not be a stranger! Hit me up on Facebook, on Twitter, or wherever I may be!

I hope you all enjoy *Rosinanti: Wrath of The Faithful*. It has been my most sincere honor to create it for you all!

TABLE OF CONTENTS

I: THE DRAGON, UNBOUND

Thunderous beats of leathery wings cast down the air around Kayden Burai's massive form, propelling him ever upwards toward the highest reaches of Terra's atmosphere. He watched from on high, glowing purple eyes ablaze with awe-inspired delight, as the magical energy of the planet floated seamlessly below him in multi-colored wisps of energy. Hovering here, higher than any airship could ever dare climb, Kayden marveled at the rarity of such a spectacle.

For twenty-three years, he had stood rooted to the ground, gazing up at Terra's raw power, as it whirled unattainably far above him. But now, he looked down upon it all. Down upon the energies of the planet that he could call upon at will. Down upon the land itself, which bent to his every whim. At the apex of his dramatic rise into the atmosphere of a world that once chained him, Kayden allowed himself a moment to hover in place. In that solitary second of weightlessness, before the harsh grip of gravity once more seized him, Kayden tensed every rippling muscle of his new body, still marveling at its power and beauty. His first transformation had been so recent that it remained fresh in his mind.

That initial metamorphosis, when he had first shed his mortal human body and took on his true visage, was a moment of rebirth. The dark power which defined his existence was given perfect form in that moment. How had he ever existed as something so small, so helpless? He had once thought himself mighty but, compared to as he was now, the Kayden of old could have been a dust mite. His former life as a human being was so inconsequential to that of the bestial black dragon he had become, which now claimed the very sky as his domain.

Feeling the tug of gravity attempting to pull him back down to the world of human weakness, Kayden tucked his great horned head, and his body followed suit. The black dragon folded his wings and rocketed downward as the wind blew harshly in his face. The air's gentle sting did nothing more than amuse him because its weakness reminded him of Valentean. Oh, how his brother tried, so valiantly, to bring him down during their duel in the Northern Magic. Even with the power of air on his side, Valentean had been completely outmatched. How he had believed he could defeat one such as Kayden was baffling to the ebony goliath.

After all, he thought, *there is no breeze that can move a mountain.*

It had been an entertaining encounter, though. Valentean tried, in vain, to challenge the might of the land with nothing more than wind to aid him. It was laughably pathetic. Kayden's dominance had only increased as they took to the skies, battling as winged dragon-gods. Valentean had been weak, but this was nothing new. Since childhood, Kayden saw his smaller sibling's compassion as a vulnerability. His own mind embraced the raw animalistic thrill of the dragon inside of him, whereas Valentean's deficiency had worked against him once more.

The ability to best his brother spoke volumes about Kayden's new station in life, and the weakness he had cast aside. The memory of that day Valentean managed to defeat him, soundly and publicly, caused him to clench his jaw, and grind his razor-sharp teeth against one another in embarrassment and frustration. In the shadow of his mind's eye, he always saw it: Valentean's bloodied snarl as his fist connected against Kayden's jaw. He recalled his own frustration in the face of his brother's quick defensive tactics. He remembered the taste of blood as Valentean's boot impacted his face. Above all, he could still feel the sting of Valentean's last energy crackling punch which had put Kayden down for the count.

The dark powers within him churned and burned his insides at the memory. As he continued to spin into a controlled dive, Kayden's breath washed out through the gargantuan nostrils of his snout in short, forceful exhalations. He remembered the Tournament of Animus perfectly. He could recall every punch, every kick, and every roar of a crowd which had, of course, favored his brother. Everyone had always taken Valentean's side. Their father coddled him, the royal family doted upon him, and other children flocked to him. Envy twisted Kayden's insides further. The darkness fueled his rage, causing a purple glow to build around his twirling body.

No one ever saw his brother for the aggrandizing egotist that he truly was. All anyone ever noticed was a special young boy, deserving of everyone's attention and adoration. Then, Kayden remembered the day their father had told him that he decided to become Valentean's trainer when *both* twins had avowed themselves to become animus warriors. *Why him?* Kayden thought. *Did I not deserve your blessed training, old man!?*

The glow increased in volume and luminescence until he appeared as a massive purple comet hurtling toward the ground. Their father, their friends, and the people of Kackritta had made their choice. They chose the wrong brother. They looked beyond him to one far inferior.

The darkness within his mind called for blood as repayment for such egregious oversight. The next time they faced one another, there would be blood, carnage, and above all else, finality.

Kayden could still picture Valentean's empowered white eyes, shining like twin beacons and narrowing at him through a miasma of snow in the Northern Magic. He had seen hatred in Valentean's stare on that day, and it was good. He wanted the fool angry. He wanted to prove that Valentean wasn't the pure perfect beacon of light he professed to be. He was flawed the same as any, and he would die at Kayden's hand. In his final agonizing moment, he'd have no choice but to admit he was beaten. Kayden hoped as he watched the light drain from his brother's eyes, he would see there his final, ultimate victory. Valentean would realize that it was Kayden who was superior. It had always been Kayden, and every step they had ever taken was walking them ever closer to this final, ultimate, triumphant, delicious moment of pure unadulterated *vengeance*!

Kayden let out a bestial roar as he released his power in a fury of imagined triumph and righteous anger at the world. The purple streaming, screaming bolt of light that was his body slammed into the ground, upending rock and root and tree in a powerful explosion that decimated the empty countryside.

The chaotic rush of flame was soon reclaimed by stillness and normalcy as silence settled once more. Kayden rose to his feet in the center of a vast circle of barren decimation and clenched his fists at his side. He was human once more, and kept his eyes closed as he adjusted to the harsh change in perspective. The transformation was deflating and jarring. It was as though he were a composer suddenly gone deaf, a painter gone blind. The dominance he felt as a dragon receded into a corner of his mind, and a profound sense of loss struck deep within his heart. But it was only momentary. The guise of a human would have to suffice, for now. Were it his choice, he would never take this weak, wretched form again, but it was *very* much not his choice.

"I see you have been entertaining yourself." The voice was slight, almost meek, but Kayden knew that was intentional. If that voice carried even a fraction of the power that lay beneath it, a mere whisper would crack the planet in two. As mighty as he had felt, astride atop the world, in the face of *her* power, he was naught more than a leaf caught in a tornado. She had seen his temper flare out of control and the senseless damage caused in its wake. How would she react? He often found it impossible to tell. She was something else entirely—not entirely human, but still so much more than he.

Kayden turned slowly, wincing like a child who had been caught breaking the rules. He looked down at her; she barely came up to his chest. Aleksandra was frail and thin, every iota of her visage meticulous, down to the tight black braid, which wound down to a blade-like point at her waist. But her defining feature—a pair of glowing red eyes—narrowed disapprovingly at his actions.

As he opened his mouth to respond, she brought one black gloved hand up and immediately, Kayden's throat closed off. He grasped desperately at his neck, trying to ward off the invisible fingers which obstructed his airway.

He gasped and choked as she slowly raised her arm, inclining one eyebrow at him with silent regard. Kayden felt helpless as his body was effortlessly lifted into the air by an entire meter. He kicked his legs frantically and thrashed.

"I trust this exhibition of infantile ardor has concluded?" she asked simply, her voice low and monotone.

Kayden did not try to speak, he simply gurgled and sputtered and nodded his head furiously.

"Lovely," Aleksandra said, flatly, dropping her hand.

The pressure holding him in place vanished and Kayden collapsed onto his side, gulping breaths of air to his aching lungs.

"Mistress Aleksandra," he said, rising to one knee before the crowned princess of Kackritta. She silenced him with a raised finger, and he complied instantly. Her control over him was absolute. What was even more maddening and terrifying was that this was not even her true body. Aleksandra remained imprisoned in the Northern Magic, confined momentarily in a prison of ice; a parting gift from Valentean and Princess Seraphina, before they had escaped her grasp. What stood before Kayden now was a magically constructed clone made of solid energy. The powerful princess could reach out into the world and control this mystical puppet from her frigid captivity. It was a mere fraction of her power, and it had immobilized him fully. What more could she do when she eventually escaped that prison … what more *would* she do?

"Your dismal justifications do not interest me, Kayden," she said, gazing down at him with that same burning glare. "Camouflage is essential to this leg of our venture, my animus. A black dragon decimating the countryside is sure to attract unwanted attention."

He knew better than to answer. There was no misdirection when she issued a command. If she demanded silence, then he was to fall silent. She suffered not one shred of insubordination.

"Valentean, my sister, and their wretched friend from Lazman are here, on the Eastern Continent, moving ever closer toward our home." Kayden nodded in understanding. "They are a day and a half's march from Kackritta's gates."

She did not sound displeased, and Kayden wondered what exactly they were going to do. Should Valentean and Seraphina rally the armies of Kackritta, and subsequently the rest of the planet, against them, matters could spin from their control. Kayden knew he could face down any foe on Terra, perhaps even an army in his true dragon form. But could even Aleksandra fight the entire world?

"With that in mind, we must make haste," she waved a gloved hand before Kayden, and following a brief glare of crimson light, Aleksandra's floor length black hooded robe was replaced with a shredded green and yellow gown, tarnished with muck and crimson splotches. Her face was covered in grime, bruises, and dried blood. Kayden inclined his head in the form of a silent question. Aleksandra smiled.

"We are going home."

The sun had just set over the horizon. The Kackrittan guard who served as night watchman gazed out over the landscape, eyeing for threats from atop a tall stone guard tower which loomed above the city walls. A veteran of the position, he'd often found his eyes drifting out of focus during these long nightly shifts. All was normally silent upon the countryside. Even the bustling airship traffic, which dotted the skies during the day, lay quiet in the stillness of night.

The watchman found his eyes slowly closing until the sight of movement shook him from his daze. A lone figure atop a white horse clomped slowly toward the city. Taking a small periscope from his belt, the watchman saw the female rider, clad in an emerald dress, laying slumped along the horse's neck. Could it be…?

"Princess Aleksandra!" he screamed, recognizing one of their missing royals. He rushed to the side wall of his tower and rang the alarm bell, alerting the guards who manned the city's drawbridge. "Alert, men!" he called down to them. "The princess! Princess Aleksandra approaches!"

The movement and bustle of the gathered soldiers was instantaneous. The bridge lowered, and as it touched down, an honor guard of five Kackrittan soldiers rode out to meet the princess' steed.

As they carried the bleeding girl in through the gates of the city, the Watchman ran down the long staircase toward a pair of golden-armored elite warriors who hurried forward. A member of the honor guard set the princess on her feet, though she still leaned on his shoulder for support.

"Your highness!" one of the elite's shouted, "we are so relieved to see you return to us! What happened, where is Princess Seraphina?"

All fell silent as the princess looked up at them through puffy, swollen, bruised eyes. She coughed and took a ragged breath. Panic shone within her gaze as she said the name, amidst a terrified sob.

"Valen … Valentean Burai!"

II: HOMECOMING

His legs churned as he sprinted, the countryside blurring past him in a haze of green and brown. He took a full, deep intake of breath, dragging mystical mana energy from the air and filled his body with its tingling, exhilarating rush. Holding the gathered energy within him for a moment, enjoying the sweet intoxicating thrill of its power, he pushed it all out through his legs while simultaneously leaping upward. The mana boosted his already powerful jump and sent him soaring into the clear blue sky.

The wind rushed along his body, cool against his skin, as he hurtled further upwards. Feeling the momentum lag, his eyes began to glow a radiant white as he silently commanded the air to boost him further into the heavens. It instantly obeyed his thoughts and pushed him up at a fierce velocity.

He extended his arms above his head and laughed in excitement. He was actually going to do it this time! His next internal order to the wind was to carry his body forward and allow him to glide on its warm currents. For one blissful instant, he felt free and powerful and at peace for the first time in the two weeks since his life had been completely upended. He scanned the ground below for his companions, and the cradling wind vanished in this single second of distraction.

His eyes grew wide as they reverted to their natural emerald pigmentation. He flailed his arms and legs, attempting to catch himself once more on the air currents he so easily dominated just a moment ago. He screamed and careened toward the unforgiving countryside, which rushed up to meet him. One last desperate plea to the air for aid allowed him to push himself sharply to the left. One final burst of wind altered his trajectory and sent him crashing into the flowing current of the River of Freedom.

As he smashed down through the surface of the water, he instantly felt the liquid move unnaturally around his body. It swirled about him, much as the wind had done only moments before, and pushed him out, back into the sunlight where he crashed on the riverbank, coughing water out of his lungs.

"That was graceful, Val," a soft female voice said with a giggle, just a few meters in front of him. Raising his head, Valentean Burai saw the smirking blue-clad princess he had sworn his life to, smiling at him in gentle amusement. Her arm was still raised in the wake of the spell she had conjured to pull him from the river.

"I had it that time, Sera!" he insisted.

Princess Seraphina shook her head and dropped her arm, brown hair blowing in the afternoon breeze.

"Somehow, I think that when you're trying to fly hundreds of meters in the air, almost doesn't exactly cut it," another voice joined in. The slightest hint of amusement cut through the melancholy air of sadness that had become a constant presence in her tone.

"I will fly, Maura, I have no doubts about it," Valentean replied, gazing with a grin at the blonde-haired girl. Her half smile was the first hint of happiness he had seen in her face since the destruction of her home and murder of her father. Both girls shook their heads at the dripping wet animus warrior, who climbed back to his feet, shaking the water from his ebony hair.

"The last twelve failed attempts don't exactly support your claim," Seraphina said, rising to her feet and stretching her legs. Valentean winked at her, happy to see that, despite everything, through all the dramatic shifts in their lives, he and Seraphina maintained the gentle teasing relationship they had enjoyed since the earliest days of their childhood.

"Can we get moving then?" Maura asked. The echo of that half smile had vanished, and her blue eyes seemed to darken and die once more. Valentean nodded to her, and the last surviving human of the village of Lazman turned and walked away from them.

He sighed in the wake of her exit. Maura's mental state had been weighing heavily on his mind. She had lost so much: her home, her family, any friends she had ever known. But beyond that, she had lost the spark of adventurous fire that once burned so fiercely in her. As he trudged along after her, he felt Seraphina sidle up next to him, slipping her soft hand in his with intertwining fingers.

"Just give her time," she whispered softly before planting a small kiss on his cheek.

Valentean smiled sadly and inclined his head toward hers until they touched. He took a deep breath, drawing strength from this amazing woman and stood back to his full height. The first time they had kissed was still such a recent memory, and with the fate of the entire planet hanging over them, it seemed an inappropriate time to discuss the nature of their relationship. The two had settled into an awkward emotional stalemate, in which they had become more affectionate toward one another, but it had not moved past the occasional hand hold or lengthy embrace.

"She's lost so much at the hands of our … well, Kayden and Aleksandra," he said.

Seraphina gave his hand a reassuring squeeze. The struggle against their fallen siblings had emotionally wrecked the two of them, and Valentean continued to shoulder partial blame for the destruction of Lazman. He kept wondering if there could have been something he might have said or done to turn Kayden from this destructive, blood-soaked path he now walked.

"Nothing that happened is your fault," Seraphina said as if reading his thoughts. "There was nothing you could have done."

"I just wonder if there was..."

"Stop it, Val. You know that what was done can't be changed. You tried everything you could to stop him. Maura forgave you, can't you forgive yourself?"

"Has she, though?" Valentean shook his head. While Maura had ceased being openly hostile toward him, she still tended to keep her distance from the young Rosinanti, as though she feared he would transform once more into the white dragon and tear them all to shreds. "She's scared of me. I feel like she's just trying to honor Aqua by tolerating my presence."

"That's not true," Sera chided quietly. "I don't think there's anyone on Terra who could make that girl do anything she didn't want to."

Valentean nodded thoughtfully and looked over at Seraphina beside him. Her blue gown was torn and filthy, her face caked in dirt and grime. She looked a far cry from a princess, that was for certain. But Seraphina's strength had been shining through since their escape from the Northern Magic. All too often, when Valentean's mind fell to dark places, it had been the princess at his side who pulled him back from the brink of despair with her incurable optimism. Since taking on Aqua's power and becoming Terra's new spirit of order, Seraphina had displayed steadfast confidence in their mission, never wavering for a moment.

Valentean also looked a bit worse for wear since his life was so nearly ended at the hands of Aleksandra. His once pure white animus robes were covered in black scorch marks and tears. Red streaks born of his own blood stained the fabric over his torso. His wounds had long since healed by the power of Aqua's magic, but the blow to his confidence would not be so readily mended. He had thought himself invincible as he stood bathed in the magical energy of the planet, his power unlocked and at his disposal. But despite his newfound might, Aleksandra had utterly thrashed him. It was not even the totality of his loss to the powerful sorceress that so unnerved him, but the ease in which she had dispatched him.

He had put everything he had into those attacks, fought her with every ounce of his newfound strength, and still, she had bested him with no effort. He could remember the terrifying strength in her casual strikes, the blurring speed with which she moved, and the awe-inspiring magic she commanded.

How does one fight something that is unbeatable?

They had sealed her there in the Northern Magic, and in his weaker moments, Valentean almost believed their spell powerful enough to contain her forever. But deep down, he knew Aleksandra would break free. How could she not? Nothing could contain a power of that magnitude indefinitely. He would fight her again, and if he fought her again, he would die. If he died, the world would fall into chaos. There had to be some way to become stronger, some way the spirit of light could equal the spirit of chaos without losing control.

Then he thought back to his encounter with Aurax, the red-skinned Skirlack cleric who had taunted him in Aqua's fountain chamber. He found it odd that a being he had just met could hate him with the extreme vitriol Aurax had demonstrated. That conversation had done nothing more than remind him of all the ways he could fail.

"Stop obsessing," Seraphina scolded, knowing full well the silent war waging within her animus warrior's mind.

He nodded and continued forward, wordless. Today they would arrive in Kackritta at last, and Valentean knew not what would await him there. The people of Terra, and Kackritta in particular, were raised on the belief that the Rosinanti dragons were the ultimate evil. He knew not whether a few simple words from Seraphina could change a millennium of belief.

Then there was the issue of his father, Vahn Burai. What would Valentean say to the man who had raised him, and trained him as an animus warrior? What *could* he say? On the one hand, Valentean wanted to yell at the old man for the decades of lies his childhood had been built upon. Vahn had allowed both he and Kayden to believe themselves to be his biological sons. Bitterness and anger stirred within him in the wake of such a betrayal. But at the same time, Valentean was grateful. Vahn had rescued them, taught them, and loved them as if they were his own. How could Valentean be angry at such kindness?

Seraphina again pulled his mind from these dark musings when she gripped his hand tightly. "Val..." she said, pointing toward the horizon. Squinting against the morning sun, he could just make out the top spire of Kackritta Castle. The vague dots of traveling airships buzzed about the sky, barely discernible from this distance. Valentean flashed her a trepidatious smile. They were home.

Before Valentean could speak, he was startled as Maura cried out. She came running back toward them, daggers drawn. A pair of massive bulky horned monsters chased after her. Valentean recognized them as a pair of potentias creatures. They were quadruped predators that stalked the wilds of Terra. A pair of them had nearly mauled Valentean and Seraphina to death one short week ago, before their ordeal in the Northern Magic.

"You take one, I'll take the other?" Valentean asked.

"Oh? And here I thought I'd have to fight them both." The animus warrior rolled his eyes and dropped into a combat stance. As the first potentias neared him, he reared back one fist and struck the stony monster. With all the strength of his Rosinanti blood, Valentean caved in the side of the creature's face, sending it flying off to the side, rolling uncontrollably across the landscape.

Seraphina gestured toward the flowing River of Freedom beside her as the now familiar blue hue that marked her as the spirit of order spread over her eyes. In accordance with her will, the water leapt from the river and slammed with the force of a tidal wave into the oncoming predator. The potentias stirred painfully at her feet, trying to rise again. Seraphina beckoned to a puddle at her side, calling the water up toward her before she utilized the spark of Valentean's light spirit attached to her soul to freeze it into a jagged ice dagger. She flung the miniature blade through the forehead of the potentias, killing it instantly.

"Are you quite done?" Valentean asked, turning to her.

"Yes, are you?"

"I've been done for a while now. Just waiting for you."

Seraphina smirked at him and made a sweeping motion with her hand. A newly formed puddle jumped up lightly and splashed Valentean in the face. She laughed, holding her stomach as she doubled over.

"Not funny." Valentean wiped the moisture from his eyes. He turned to Maura who had stood safely off to the side. "Are you all right?"

"Yeah, thanks," she replied softly, moving past her two companions without another word.

Valentean grimaced in disappointment.

"Just give her time," Seraphina repeated, laying a hand on his shoulder. Valentean nodded, and they continued onward.

Four hours later, the trio had a full and breathtaking view of Kackritta City. Valentean sighed, so incredibly happy to see his home shining in the daylight once more. Anxiety had been tugging on his mind for most of the week-long trip. But Kackritta City was fine, and it had never looked lovelier. Valentean smiled at the massive red spires of the royal palace that stretched high into the air.

Seraphina beamed up at her home, and relief spread across her face. A long tear cascaded down her cheek. Valentean grabbed her hand with a reassuring squeeze and a smile. Maura gaped open-mouthed at the spectacle of such a massive locale.

"First time seeing the big city?" Valentean asked, hoping to strike up a conversation.

"I've never seen anything like this before," she said, gazing up at the various airships that filled the sky.

"It's even better once you get within the walls and see Kackritta Castle up close." Maura nodded silently. Valentean savored the brief conversation as a small victory. A massive weight lifted from his shoulders as he journeyed toward the homecoming he had looked forward to for so long. He laughed inwardly at the irony of the situation. For his entire life, he dreamt of leaving Kackritta and setting out on a glorious adventure. Now, as he trudged toward his home, he realized just how much he missed this wonderful place.

As the city walls continued to grow before them, Valentean smiled at Seraphina one more time. They were going home at long last. The giant drawbridge began to cascade down at their approach as though it were welcoming them back. For a brief moment, Valentean was at peace. Then, it all came crashing down.

From the city's entrance poured hundreds upon hundreds of armored Kackrittan soldiers. Some sprinted forward, weapons brandished, while others rode forth, mounted on horseback. Low-level infantry soldiers and golden-armored elites charged around them, forming a tight circle. What was happening? Were they going to attack?

As one, the soldiers leveled spears and swords while archers drew back arrows, all pointed threateningly at them. At his side, Maura's hands twitched toward the daggers sheathed at her belt. Valentean shook his head through the cloud of confusion, silently advising her to stand down. She relaxed her hands but remained tense, and at the ready.

Seraphina looked aghast. "What is the meaning of this!?" she demanded, a tone of regal authority dripping from each word. "In the name of your princess, I demand you lower your weapons at once!"

Not a single soldier so much as twitched in response. Valentean took a step toward her, and the entire gathered mass of warriors recoiled. *They know*, he realized with a startled pit of anxiety weighing down his stomach.

The gathering of Kackritta's finest parted to allow a lone black armored horse to gallop forward, upon which sat General Zouka, the commander of Kackritta's military. He brought his steed to a halt before them and glowered down at Valentean through his sunburst orange eyes. Valentean returned the Gorram general's stare, unblinking as he gazed into his scarred face.

"Valentean Burai." He did not shout, but his voice still carried around the vast space. "On this day, in the name of Queen Christina Kackritta of the Kingdom of Kackritta, you have been deemed an enemy of the crown." Valentean's eyes widened, his knees shook. "By the ancient laws of humanity, the lives of all Rosinanti are an abomination, and forfeit. In the name of the crown, we hereby arrest you for the destruction of the village of Lazman and the attempted murder of Princess Aleksandra Kackritta."

"That's a lie, General!" Seraphina exclaimed as she stepped between Zouka and Valentean, arms out to her side as if to shield her animus warrior from this fate. "My sister has betrayed us all! Val is an animus warrior of Kackritta, and he saved our lives."

The general sneered at her. "Princess Seraphina Kackritta, for the crime of harboring and aiding a Rosinanti against your own people, you are hereby placed under arrest by order of the crown!"

Seraphina recoiled as if struck. "I am your princess!" she screamed up at him.

"You are indoctrinated by the magic of the Rosinanti. You are to be brought before your parents and expunged of this foul curse!"

"Wait a minute, I was there..." Maura started to say, before the general's gaze turned to her.

"Maura Lorne, for the crime of harboring and aiding a Rosinanti against your own species, you are hereby placed under arrest by order of the crown!" Maura gasped in appalled shock. Zouka leapt off his horse as the soldiers began to advance. Valentean realized he had to take action.

His eyes exploded with white radiance and a strong gust of wind burst out in all directions, pushing the mass of soldiers back. Zouka, however, advanced unphased and Seraphina shot forth a jagged shard of ice to incapacitate the black-armored Gorram. Zouka unsheathed his massive black stone sword and knocked the projectile away, returning the blade to his back as he charged toward the princess. Valentean leapt at the general. He threw a fast and powerful punch at his face, but the burly Gorram spun out of the way and clasped a massive black-armored hand on the back of Valentean's neck.

Zouka smashed his free fist into the animus warrior's face and sent him soaring backward, rolling to a stop several meters away. Maura rushed in with daggers drawn, taking three slashes that all met nothing but air. Zouka brought one great knee up into her chest and she crumpled in a heap. Seraphina lashed forward, eyes aglow with azure energy. Zouka was at her already, dodging past the jet streams of water she sent flying towards him, and bowling into the princess with his side, sending her smacking into the ground with the force of his girth.

Valentean filled his body with mana and lunged at the Gorram, a blue and white blur amidst the chaotic thrill of the moment. Anger burned within him, and the rage-fueled dragon coiled around his heart screamed for Zouka's head. Just as he was about to throw a fist toward the general's face, Zouka unsheathed his sword and pressed the blade against the back of Maura's neck. Valentean skidded to a stop.

"Stand down, dragon," he commanded.

Valentean gritted his teeth, the dragon within urging him onward, but he bit back on those base desires. He could not risk Maura's life. Seraphina started to rise, but Valentean held his hand aloft, and shook his head, telling her to stay down. She gave him a look of helpless frustration but nodded. Valentean lowered his arms and bowed his head in surrender. The instant he relaxed his defenses Zouka lashed out with a meaty fist, plowing into the side of Valentean's head and rendering him unconscious.

III: IMPRISONED

Valentean awoke with crushing weight pressing on him from all sides, and something restricting the movement of his jaw. He tried to stand, but the monumental force made that impossible. He opened his eyes slowly and found himself in a dimly lit room kneeling on a raised platform. Heavy chains of all sizes weighed down his entire body. They varied from standard shackles to thick mooring chains.

The restraints were locked around his wrists, biceps, ankles, thighs, chest and neck. Each strand of constrictive steel was bolted into the platform. On his jawline hung a sharply angled steel contraption that locked behind his head and held his mouth closed. The device ran past his nose, obstructing the lower half of his face from view behind a mesh of metal. Along the sides of the strange apparatus, he could hear a variety of gears turning, and every time he moved they shifted, whirling faster in response to his struggles.

Valentean tried to call upon the power of the wind to strengthen his body as he struggled against these bindings but felt only the slightest echo of his power. The gears from the steel muzzle began to clank in his ears, and his eyes flickered with white light before the normally intense glow died upon the emerald plains of his irises. What had they done to him? He tried to drag mana energy from the air through the steel mesh covering his nose and mouth. Try as he might, he felt only the incoming rush of air entering his lungs void of the strengthening enriching magical energy he had learned to call upon so many years ago.

“Having trouble?” a steely voice remarked from behind. Valentean tried to turn toward the noise, but could not so much as budge under the cumbersome enormity of his bonds. He could hear heavy, clunking footsteps to his left, and soon the black-armored bulk of General Zouka entered his peripheral vision. The Gorram continued to meander slowly around the captive Rosinanti until he stood in Valentean’s line of sight.

“You may have noticed an inability to call upon that glorious Rosinanti power of yours. I’m sure you’ve realized by now that the muzzle you’re wearing effectively blocks magic; a contraption forged by the mage-smiths of

Grassan. If you ask me, though, it seems a shame to contain something as perfectly beautiful as the elemental power of a dragon-god."

Valentean furrowed his brow at the general. Though his jaw was pressed closed, he managed to part his lips just enough to speak through his teeth. "I didn't destroy Lazman."

"That is not the tale the princess weaves," Zouka responded, folding his arms over his broad chest.

Valentean's eyes bulged in shock. "Aleksandra is here?" The edge of panic rose in his labored speech.

"Indeed, and she spun quite the tale of you and your Rosinanti brother laying waste to the village of Lazman. About how you conspired with the bitter daughter of the mayor to eradicate the home she despised. Also, how you possessed Princess Seraphina with an evil spirit meant to turn her from her own people."

"You can't possibly believe that!" he hissed back at the Gorram.

Zouka scoffed. "Not particularly, no. The princess has chaos in her blood. I have felt it every day since she was a small girl. She tries to hide her ambition from the world, but for one attuned to such things as I, she may as well be shouting her intentions to dominate the whole of Terra."

"You know about the chaos spirit?"

"Oh, I know a great many things, *Rosintai*," Zouka sneered at him, pausing to allow the shock of the moment to settle. "I know exactly what your people were. And I know *exactly* what you are. Enough to know that I never should have been able to render you unconscious with just one punch."

"If you know then why are you helping her?"

"I care nothing for the princess, this kingdom, these people or this war of yours. There is only one thing in all of Terra that I value and seek. It is something you possess. It is something denied to me these many years by the pathetic weakness that is a shared trait of all humanity. A challenge."

Valentean struggled further under the burden of his restraints, meeting Zouka's gaze with an intense glare. "You know what's at stake here and you're actually helping her because … you want to fight me?"

"You above all others should understand my reasoning. We are different from them, boy. You may not have realized it yet, but you are every bit as alone as I am. You are a prince without a people."

"Kackritta is my home. These are my people."

"How delusional. You're an utter fool if you've actually allowed yourself to believe that. These people hate and fear you for no other crime than being what you were born to be. They're tiny and fragile and … pointless." Zouka paced in front of him. "My life ended with my people. There is no purpose in my existence. I have nothing to leave behind but a legacy, and neither do you."

"Then let your legacy be one that means something! Help me! Don't stand against us!" As soon as the word's left Valentean's mouth, Zouka spun to him, smashing his gargantuan fist into the side of the young animus warrior's face. Valentean reeled with the blow, his head snapping back. The dragon within him screeched in rage within the expanse of his mind, and he lunged forward until the chains groaned in protest of his strength. The gears on his facial constraint whirled faster in the wake of gathering energy, snuffing it out until the crushing weight returned.

"Well, now, isn't that interesting," Zouka said, crouching in front of Valentean, bringing his face down centimeters from the muzzle. He stared deeply into the Rosinanti's eyes with intense concentration, as though he were trying to look past the man to see the dragon beneath his skin. "I just struck you with more force than I used to incapacitate you outside of the city. Not only are you still conscious, but you managed to move those restraints."

Valentean noticed that he had, indeed, moved further along the platform in his momentary lust for the general's blood, coming to the limits of the chains' reach.

"Remember that feeling when the hour of our conflict comes. I know that these trappings won't hold you for long. You will escape, and when you do, you will fight me with every ounce of your godly power. I want you uninhibited, void of the pointless compassion that defines your weakness. Fight me, dragon. Fight me and give my life true meaning." The general quickly stood and turned his back.

Valentean stared dumbfounded at him as he rapped on the cell door several times. The sound of locks turning could be heard as the heavy vault-like door swung outward and Zouka disappeared into the darkness.

Maura shifted from her seated position in a dreary, damp prison cell in the depths of Kackritta Castle's dungeon. She had followed Valentean and Seraphina to honor Aqua's final wishes, and where had it gotten her? She thought back to her father, Hehn the Invincible, and the time he had spent in a Karminian prison.

Dad, she thought, *did this feeling of helplessness hit you as well*? She felt utterly powerless as she leaned back against the cold stone wall of her cell. Moving her legs to shake some feeling back into them, she could hear the clinking of chains. The uncomfortable shackles dug into her ankles through the worn leather of her boots. Had it been an entire day since she was tossed in here? Had it been merely hours? Time seemed to have no meaning with the weight of her captivity pressing down. Would there be a trial? Would they allow her to defend herself? Could she tell her side of the story? Or had she been thrown in here to die?

The general had accused her of complacency in the destruction of Lazman. The irony of the situation was rich; to be blamed for the single greatest tragedy of her life. How could anyone come to such an ignorant and ill-informed conclusion?

Her silent inner musings were interrupted by the sound of a key turning in a large iron lock. The snap of her cell door opening held her attention. Dim light filtered in as a lone figure entered through the doorway, shrouded and holding something large against its chest. It left the door slightly ajar and stood silhouetted in the shaft of light like a specter. Maura pressed back further against the wall, her hands twitching, having to ignore the reflex to reach for her confiscated daggers.

"Maura," a soft female voice whispered among the smothering silence. "Dear Maura, I come to help you. To save you."

Maura narrowed her eyes, trying to see this new arrival as she slowly advanced, moving with the cautious trepidation one usually reserved for dealing with an unruly animal. As the thin, frail woman came into view, Maura estimated her to be in her forties. Age lines framed her dull brown eyes and tufts of graying brown hair frizzed around the tight bun she wore on the back of her head.

Against her chest, she held a large red book, nearly the size of her entire torso, which she gripped fiercely with both hands, as though afraid if might fly away on its own. Those hands merited the most attention. They were thin and gaunt, and dug desperately into the soft spongy cover of the massive tome. Maura's eyes settled onto the scarred stump where her middle finger was supposed to be. She remembered well the tale Aleksandra had spun in her father's office just before everything had fallen apart.

"Save me?" Maura scoffed, "I know who you are. You're one of those … hopeful people."

"Faithful," the woman replied, kneeling before Maura and setting the giant book on the ground with an audible thud. "My name is Sophie."

"I've heard your name before." Maura's eyes narrowed in suspicion, remembering the name of Aleksandra's childhood attendant who had inducted her into this inane religion of demon worshippers. "You're that monster's servant-girl."

Sophie's face registered no discernible reaction to the biting comment. "I serve the Herald of the mighty Ignis," she said slowly, the reverence evident in her tone. "I was chosen by our lord many years ago to introduce her chosen prophet onto the path to everlasting glory."

"You mean you tricked a little girl into worshipping a fire demon," Maura retorted, curling her lip.

"I set in motion the destiny of the most important woman in the history of Terra. I opened her eyes, showed her the divine will of the purifying flames. I led her from the lies which time heaped atop the true faith of Terra. I saved her. And she has asked me to save you now, as well."

Maura laughed out loud, a soft humorless chuckle that filled the space between them. "Kiss my ass," she sneered at the frowning attendant.

"Poor child," Sophie said, reaching a hand out to caress Maura's hair. Before the mangled hand could come in contact with her yellow locks, Maura recoiled as if burned and lashed out, trying to grab at Sophie's throat. The older woman jumped back, well out of reach of Maura's frenzied clumsy grasp. She motioned to the book that sat on the floor between them. "Do you know what this is?"

"I don't care."

"This is the Tome of Ignis, our holy text."

"I still don't care," Maura spat, glaring at the red cover. Sophie continued, unhindered by the stinging of Maura's resistance.

"The glorious words of our lord lie within. The text is bound in the flesh of non-believers, written in the blood of the Rosinanti themselves." Maura stared at the book in disgust and recoiled in her revulsion. Sophie opened to the first page, scribbled upon ancient torn sheets in a harsh incomprehensible language. "Shall I begin the reading?"

"No."

"Light and darkness are meaningless," Sophie began, "and the flames of chaos were born unto Terra to combat these falsehoods." Maura turned her face away and groaned, but the attendant would not relent. "The air of the light serves only to fan the inferno which shall burn the land of darkness to ashes."

"You're wasting your time!"

"And so, our lord was born unto a world void of meaning and truth. And thus, did she spread her crimson wings and engulf that world in her cleansing conflagration. But the evil of this world could not be so easily expunged, and the Harbinger was delivered to spread her wickedness throughout the land."

"Are you talking about Aqua?" Maura asked, remembering Aurax's description of her as a harbinger.

Sophie ignored her once more and continued. "The Harbinger poisoned the world with her liquid death, and held back the purity of the blaze for eons…" she continued on and on, passage after passage, for what could easily have been hours. As she read, Maura fell silent, taking her words in and slowly making eye contact with Sophie as she continued to preach. "…the curse of the Shogai holds not only the gifts of the goddess at bay, but also the potential of all humanity. It is through chaos that evolution occurs, through the cleansing fire that the dead and decaying rot is rendered to ash." She paused, looking at Maura with a gentle smile.

"Dear, sweet, Maura, have you understood the words of these passages? Do you comprehend the power behind them, the enormity of the responsibility the Faithful wield in these troubling times?"

"I … I actually do," Maura said, with a small half smile. Sophie took a deep intake of breath.

"I knew you would! And this burden we carry can be yours as well, Maura. You can fight with us against the forces of evil who seek to imprison true divinity and hold Terra back from its greatest potential."

"I never thought of it like that," Maura inclined her head in thought.

"Maura, is it your wish to be reborn in the glorifying flames of chaos? Will you stand with the Faithful and shed the lies of the Harbinger and the Shogai?"

"I don't know if I…"

"Maura, you've heard the words of our faith. You know the truth of them. Your father, your friends, and your home were destroyed as sacrifices to our holy cause. Their deaths had meaning. They were purified in the flames, Maura."

"Yes … the purity of the flames … it's so perfect in its … nothingness," she said, enraptured by Sophie's tale.

"Maura, will you profess your faith to the one true god of Terra?"

"Yes…" Maura said after one long moment of deliberation. "Yes, I will!"

Sophie's smile grew, showing off a mouth filled with perfectly straight white teeth. She reached behind her back and pulled out a long ceremonial knife with runes Maura could never hope to understand burned into the surface of the blade.

"Then you must make your offering, Maura. The offering we have all made to show our love and support of the goddess and her long-suffering children." Sophie held her mangled hand aloft, demonstrating the cost of initiation. Maura stared at it for several moments before slowly extending her shaking left hand, still cuffed at the wrist. Sophie smiled once more and caressed Maura's fingers with her own. "Oh, heavenly mother, shine your blaze down upon your newest disciple. Let her sacrifice enforce your resolve as we wait for the end of the Shogai and the second coming of your holy fury."

She brought the sharpened blade of the knife down, chanting in a coarse harsh hissing language that Maura had never heard before. As the blade neared her flesh, Sophie's chanting increased in intensity, her cadence building until the point of the knife was millimeters from the knuckle of Maura's middle finger. Just as the sharp steel was about to carve through her, Maura withdrew her fingers, wrapped them into a tight fist and lashed out quickly, striking Sophie in the nose.

Aleksandra's attendant fell back, clutching at her face as blood seeped through her fingers. She flailed for a moment before glaring at Maura and reversing her grip on the knife. Maura braced for an attack but instead, Sophie closed her eyes and took a deep calming breath. Blood poured from her nose which now twisted at a sharp angle. Bruising had already begun to sprout beneath both of her eyes.

Sophie took one more long inhalation, placed the knife back onto her belt, and gathered up the massive Tome of Ignis with a grunt of exertion. She smiled once more at Maura; that same infuriating grin she had worn through the entirety of this long encounter.

"I shall return tomorrow for another lesson."

"*Seraphina…*" She heard the voice as though it were coming from a great distance, nearly dying on the breeze before it reached her ears. Seraphina stood alone in a dark room, a vague blue light pulsating on the farthest horizon in the plane of inky blackness that surrounded her.

"Who is there?" she called out, resisting the urge to panic.

"*Don't give in*," the voice said, calm and serene against her increasing dismay. The voice was gentle, filled with compassion but also strength. It was a voice she recognized.

"Aqua," she called out, "is that you?"

"*Remain strong*," the weak voice of her predecessor called out. Seraphina was about to answer when a scorching, burning sensation exploded against her right hand.

She screamed in agony as the dark expanse around her vanished. She found herself on a bed in a bright room surrounded by red robed figures who chanted some unknown, archaic, hissing language.

At her side, she felt a strong grip around her forearm, just above the hand that throbbed with pain. Her screams were muffled as something restricted the movement of her jaw.

She could hear the sound of whirling gears as her face became awash in tears born of agony. The hands of several hooded chanting figures descended to hold her in place.

"She awakens," a voice said from beyond her field of vision as the princess began to thrash.

"Excellent," a familiar voice responded, which cut through the hazy veil of pain. It couldn't be … But, somehow, it was. The hand holding her arm roughly yanked it up and held it aloft for all to see.

"Your holiness, look," the man at her side said. Seraphina saw the mangled, blackened, oozing flesh of her right hand and thrashed against her mysterious captors. She attempted to call upon the power of Order to pull liquid fury from the air to strike out at these faceless forms, but she felt nothing. The whirling of gears increased in speed and a mechanical whine strained against her face.

The pain in her hand was steadily subsiding, and Seraphina gritted her teeth as it passed. The skin on her hand began to heal and regenerate before her eyes, the scorched flesh knitting itself back together and returning to its usual pale pigmentation.

"Even with the force of her magic contained, the Harbinger's power combats the gift of the blaze." That word caught Seraphina's attention. *Harbinger*.

The hands that held her down varied in size and color, but they all had one thing in common: the missing middle finger. It was then that she noticed the room she was being held in. It was her bedchamber in Kackritta Castle. The soft mattress she laid upon was her own.

"Inconceivable," came that unmistakable voice. The two Faithful holding her ankles parted, allowing Aleksandra to approach the foot of her sister's bed, clad in a floor-length red gown trimmed in gold. Seraphina gasped at the sight of her sister, free and glowering down at her, eyebrows furrowed in thought. "Is there no way to expunge this presence?"

"I am confident, Mistress," a voice spoke off from the left, beyond the boundaries of Seraphina's vision. A crouched old woman, clad in the red robes of The Faithful limped up to her bedside and placed a gnarled, spotted, long-nailed hand along Seraphina's brow. She struggled and fought, trying to shake off the unwanted contact, but the Faithful surrounding her renewed their grip.

"What must be done, Finstra?" Aleksandra asked, turning to the woman. The crone waved her other hand over Seraphina's face. The scarred remnant where her middle finger had once been made the princess wince in disgust at this barbaric initiation rite.

"It will not be easy on her. We must fill her with the gifts of the Holy Mother. We must purify your sister with pain and burn the Harbinger from her blood. She may not survive the exorcism. It shall require a hurt unlike anything a human body was meant to endure."

Seraphina's breathing began to grow rapid and desperate. There was no way Aleksandra would actually agree to *torture* her!

"Then it will be done," her sister stated with finality. "She is my blood. She will survive and be purified by the blaze."

Seraphina made eye contact with Aleksandra now, her gaze pleading. "As it shall burn," the elder princess said slowly, intentionally, displaying an iron resolve to her captive sister. They all repeated her words in unison as though it were some mantra of their obscene faith.

"As you command, Mistress," Finstra responded, looking over Seraphina's flesh with a hunger. The princess could see a mania behind the weathered grey eyes of this old woman. She wanted to inflict pain. She was looking forward to it with impatient glee.

"Now leave us," Aleksandra instructed. As one, the Faithful released her limbs and moved from the room with haste at their mistress's command.

Seraphina sat up in her bed, grasping at the whirling constrictive bond upon her face. The steel held fast against her weak struggles and she groaned in exertion and frustration. She glared up at Aleksandra, whose expression softened in the wake of her minions' departure.

"Let me help," Aleksandra said softly, waving a hand before her sister. The gears on her jawline ceased spinning and, after a loud click emanated from the back of her head, the steel muzzle fell from her face onto the mattress. The power of order swelled within Seraphina's body, rejuvenating her.

Blue light exploded from her eyes and the younger princess of Kackritta threw both arms forward, summoning streams of water that hurtled at her older sister.

Aleksandra moved not one centimeter. She raised both hands, conjuring twin fireballs which met Seraphina's attacks, canceling them out in a hiss of rising steam. Her eyes went red, and she extended a hand. Seraphina was thrown forcefully back against the soft mattress, pinned in place and unable to so much as twitch.

"I want to make something perfectly clear to you, sister," she said. "When last we tousled, I was not intending to inflict harm upon you. You saw not a fraction of my power on that day, and I do not think you wish for a demonstration at this moment."

Seraphina relaxed and gazed up, eyes pleading. Aleksandra lowered her arm and the younger princess sat up on the bed, slowly swinging her legs over the side, glaring at her sister. "How are you here?" Seraphina asked suspiciously, bringing a hand up to massage her jaw, which still ached at the memory of that muzzle's oppressive grip.

"Oh, I am not," Aleksandra replied, sitting beside her casually, as though they were discussing afternoon tea. "My body remains where you left me, sister; frozen in place amongst the wasteland of the Northern Magic."

"So, this is a body double," Seraphina surmised.

"Yes, dear one," Aleksandra looked intently at Seraphina. The crimson glow of her eyes vanished until she looked deceptively human once more. "I want you to know that I hold no ill will toward you for your treasonous actions. I understand that you know not what you do." Aleksandra tried to bring a hand forward to touch her, but Seraphina recoiled in horror.

"I knew exactly what I was doing, Aleksandra," she snapped. "I was stopping you from carrying out this insane plot of yours!"

Aleksandra shook her head. "No, sister, that is the presence of the Harbinger's power within you."

"Her name was Aqua!" Seraphina shrieked, rising to her feet. "Don't you dare call her that! She helped us stop you, and we will do it again!"

"Sit down, Seraphina," Aleksandra said, very slowly and very seriously.

"No! I will not just sit here like your obedient little sister while you let your insane followers torture me! I'm not listening to you ever again, Aleksandra! Do you hear me? You've lost me forever with this insanity! Just turn away from it and we can save you from whatever that thing is that they put inside your soul!"

"Enough!" Aleksandra bellowed, rising to her feet as the flaming glow returned to her eyes. She gestured forcefully and Seraphina's body was tossed back onto the bed, landing frozen in a seated position. Once again, Seraphina found herself completely helpless in the grip of her sister's power. "Now, I think we need to tranquilize your hysteria."

Aleksandra rose from the bed and calmly walked across the room, grabbing a small hairbrush from Seraphina's vanity. The spirit of order winced as her insane sibling sat behind her and began moving the brush through her unkempt mop of brown hair, just as she had done when they were children. At one time this action had filled Seraphina with a calming serenity born of sisterly love.

Now. the thought of this twisted demon trying to comfort and bond with her was a perverse unwelcomed experience that made her skin crawl.

"My word, sister," Aleksandra scoffed, "your weeks in the wilderness have left you filthy. Your hair is so knotted."

"Let me go, Aleksandra," Seraphina hissed.

"I could not bear the thought of you traipsing through the untamed wilds with that disgusting Rosinanti as your guide."

"Don't you dare talk about him like that!"

"Such venomous fire in your voice, my dear," Aleksandra commented with mock surprise. "Could it be that you've finally admitted to yourself that you love that creature?"

"He is not a creature," Seraphina grunted, still trying with every iota of her strength to move from the bed.

"He is a beast as twisted and vile as the invasive presence which clings to you now."

"Where is he?"

"Why does it matter? He is where he needs to be, just as you are where you need to be."

"Where is he, Aleksandra?" she insisted once more with desperation in her voice.

Her sister sighed deeply. "Locked in the dungeon's vault, affixed with one of the Grassani-made contraptions which had earlier blocked access to your power." Seraphina's heart nearly broke at the thought of her beloved trapped in that horrible empty cell, muzzled like an animal and powerless. "Have you speculated as to how they function?"

"I want to see him," Seraphina insisted.

"The device is a spell nullifier," Aleksandra explained, ignoring Seraphina's request. "I filled it with a curse that pacifies attack magic, and every time you attempted to cast any kind of offensive enchantment, the magic activated within the device and caused a cessation to your ill-advised hostilities. It is truly a marvel."

"I need to see him!" Seraphina insisted, a tear cascading down her cheek. "Please, sister!"

Aleksandra paused for a moment before she rose, returned the brush to the vanity, and turned to face her seated sister once more. She waved her hand casually and the force holding Seraphina vanished. The younger princess sighed in relief but knew better than to press her luck by attempting to rise again.

"You will see no one until your exorcism is completed. Even mother and father have agreed to keep their distance from you whilst I do what must be done to safeguard your soul."

"You want to torture Aqua's power out of me!" Seraphina exclaimed, panic and anger waging war within her.

"Do not think of it as torture, dear. It is purification by fire. It will be your glorious rebirth. You shall shed the malevolent evil of the Harbinger to be reborn anew into the splendor and prestige of the goddess's blaze."

The air within the chamber rippled and the form of a red-skinned, brown-robed Skirlack cleric appeared behind Aleksandra.

"Aurax," she said before she had even turned to face him. The regality of command once more dripped from her posture and tone. The cleric gave a deep flourishing bow as she affixed him in her sights.

"I do so apologize for the interruption, Mistress," he said, looking up momentarily to sneer in Seraphina's direction. "You sought information regarding the … undertaking, and I wanted to alert you to a new development. Of course, I assume you would prefer this information in less … conflicted company."

"Indeed," Aleksandra responded, turning back to Seraphina as her expression softened. "I must leave you, sister. I do not wish for you to despair concerning the tribulations that await you. Simply understand, as you always have, that I know what is best."

"I'm not going to let you put that muzzle back on me," Seraphina exclaimed, ignoring Aleksandra's ravings.

"Of course not, dear one. I would not dream of subjecting you to such treatment once more. But understand that I cannot have you leaving this room or calling upon that blasphemous power which corrupts you."

A small flame flickered to life in Aleksandra's palm and she flung it toward the ceiling. It grew unfettered until it spilled red-hot scorching fire throughout the chamber. Seraphina screamed in fear and jumped back onto the middle of her bed.

The flames engulfed everything from the walls to the floor and ceiling, stopping just short of the bed, forming an impenetrable barrier of blistering heat. Seraphina coughed and gagged as smoke-ravaged her lungs. She tried to call upon power from the water in the air, but the stifling humidity burned all moisture from the room.

"These flames will keep you in place while I attend to other matters, sister," Aleksandra said, her voice booming above the inferno. "You will be safe on the bed, and these flames will not move beyond this chamber. Now stay put." Aleksandra turned with Aurax and together they walked through the fire, out into the hall.

"Aleksandra!" Seraphina screamed after her retreating sibling. "Aleksandra, please stop this! Please, you have to!" Aleksandra gestured once with a tiny manicured hand and the door to Seraphina's chamber slammed shut, sealing the princess alone amongst the blaze.

IV: A FATHER'S LOVE

Vahn Burai's horse stood hitched by a thick rope to the ground as it gulped water from the small lake where the elite warrior had made camp. It had been nearly two weeks since he had set off on this mission to the village of Lazman in search of his sons.

Vahn had never been an overprotective parent, as he always held faith in the strength of his boys; strength he had trained into their bodies from a very young age. So, when both Valentean and Kayden had been pronounced missing, Vahn feared the worst. He had confessed his suspicions to his old friend, King Roan, one evening as they walked through the palace gardens in the heart of Kackritta Castle.

"I can feel it in my bones, Roan," Vahn had uttered, fully dropping the guise of formality he ordinarily reserved for official reports given within the walls of the king's throne room, "something is wrong."

The king's ruddy bearded face had contorted in thought as the weight of Vahn's words settled around them. "The intuition of a warrior," the king said slowly, "it never fully vanishes does it, old friend? No matter how long we toil about in positions of leadership, far from the battlefield."

"So you've felt it too."

"Indeed, I have. I know it has only been three days since my daughters and your sons were set to return, but something about this situation weighs heavily on my heart."

"So, dispatch a squadron to Lazman," Vahn said, laying a hand on Roan's burly shoulder.

"Vahn, you know I don't have that kind of authority," the king replied sadly, shaking his head, and gazing down at the rosebush before him. Indeed, Vahn knew Roan's title held no official power and was granted to him solely from marriage. He did not carry the blood of the Kackritta family, and thus all official decisions fell on the shoulders of Queen Christina.

"But you've told the queen of these suspicions?"

"I have."

"And she refuses to aid in the search for her own children?" Vahn asked incredulously.

"My wife stated that to send a platoon of Kackrittan soldiers marching on Lazman would be an unwelcomed show of force that may hinder trade negotiations if no problem exists."

"But ... that's madness!"

"I am aware," Roan replied, shaking his head. "But what am I to do, Vahn? She is the queen. The decision is hers and hers alone." Silence settled between the two friends, a cold stillness that echoed around them. These two lifelong warriors, both of them loving fathers, felt powerless in the wake of their queen's command.

"Then I will go," Vahn said.

"What?"

"I will journey to Lazman alone and discover the truth of this matter."

"Vahn, you're no longer a young man. You've retired from active duty. That is a dangerous trip for any man to embark upon alone."

"And yet I must go, Roan," he said slowly, looking his old friend in the eye with a resolve that went far beyond that of a warrior. "That intuition you mentioned earlier, you were wrong about it. That isn't the instincts of a trained warrior alerting you to the danger that has befallen our children; it is a father's love."

Vahn had set out on this solitary journey that very night with the king's personal steed as his mount. He had reached Lazman within one week, the speed of the mighty stallion shocking Vahn as it cut across the landscape of Terra's untamed wilds.

What he found upon his arrival pushed the air from his lungs. Lazman was nothing more than a desolate crater, erased from the world by some terrifying force. The town had been obliterated, along with a percentage of the surrounding mountain range. Were the lives of his sons extinguished in this all-consuming destruction? As he walked through the hole that had once been a village teeming with life, he found something that ignited a spark of hope within his heart.

A small circle of stone road remained untouched by the devastation, as though it had been shielded by something and spared. But how had that happened? Was it even possible? Of course it was. Vahn had learned long ago to stop underestimating the miraculous events that occurred around Valentean and Kayden.

Since the day he had found them lying in that lost mountain cavern, Vahn knew there was something special about his twin sons. He never liked to dwell on these questions for too long, as the potential answers that sprouted within his nervous mind were often terrifying. He always simply thanked the planet itself for the gift of his boys.

But now, in the face of this decimation, Vahn's mind dwelled upon questions he had long since buried within the shadowy recesses of his mind. His boys were not normal human beings. He had suspected as much from the day they entered his life. Those suspicions seemed all but confirmed as he watched them perform feats of dazzling skill during the Tournament of Animus. But whatever his children were, it mattered not. They were his sons, his beloved boys, and he knew in his heart that they still lived.

Vahn sat beside the small fire he had created lakeside, warming his hands in the cool air of the night. His mind drifted back to the many camping trips he had taken with Valentean and Kayden when they were small. It was a simpler time, before talk of animus training, mana, red-eyed sorcerers, and sacred duty had encompassed their lives. In those days, it had been just Vahn, Valentean, and Kayden. They would sit awake together as he taught them the names of the stars. Vahn always kept happy memories such as these alive in his heart. It kept his soul young.

He was so lost in thought that he had not sensed the incoming projectile until it was too late. An arrow fired from the trees behind him flew on a collision course with the aging warrior's heart. Not having enough time to dodge out of the way completely, Vahn managed to intercept the arrow with his forearm. The sharp point of the arrowhead dug through the flesh of his forearm, exploding out the other side and stopping just before his chest.

Not taking even an instant to remove the bloodied barb, Vahn spun to his feet in time to dodge the oncoming rush of three more arrows. He ducked beneath the final projectile and retrieved his sword from the ground beside him, unsheathing it as he moved. His assailants poured from the forest, nearly two dozen strong, all clad in red-hooded robes.

These mystery attackers came in all shapes and sizes, ranging from smaller archers, to sword wielders, to burly warriors brandishing battle axes. Vahn pushed thoughts of starry nights and campfire smiles from his mind, allowing the long retired elite warrior to overtake him and make him a conduit for the art of battle.

"I am Vahn Burai," he said slowly, silently gauging the movements of his foes as they began to encircle him, "elite warrior of the kingdom of Kackritta. I have no quarrel with you, and if you agree to lay down your arms and abandon this ill-advised assault, I can assure you that no harm will befall you."

"We know who you are," one of the sword wielders said, stepping forward and pointing the tip of his blade at Vahn, "father of the Shogai!"

Vahn kept his face void of emotion, maintaining his posture of calm battle superiority, attempting to command the situation despite the massively overwhelming odds he faced. But what on Terra was a *Shogai*? "If you know anything about my sons, now is the time to tell me," he spat back at the speaker.

"Our glorious mistress, the holy prophet of Ignis, has marked you for death in the name of the one true goddess of Terra."

"And who might this mistress of yours be?"

"For the crime of harboring the Shogai, Vahn Burai, you have been marked for death by the Faithful."

"The Faithful? If you seek battle, you've come to the right place," Vahn said, moving the sword before his torso with both hands in a defensive stance. "If you wish to taste steel, step forward and attack me."

The Faithful moved as one, erupting into battle all around him. Immediately, the archers opened fire. Vahn bent his body out of the path of the lethal arrows while deflecting many of those he could not avoid with his blade. The swordsmen met him first, and Vahn engaged them blade to blade. There were ten of them, all young, all fast, and all skilled. Vahn gave ground, knowing the folly of standing tall against such an overwhelming force. In their first pass, he managed to disarm three warriors, two of which he cut down with swipes to the chest and throat, as the archers let loose another volley.

Vahn drew their shots to his advantage, placing the sword wielders between him and the incoming arrows. As his opponents dodged around the assault of their fellows, he cut down two more, wounded one with a glancing slash across the knee, and scored a broad stroke that beheaded another. By this point, the larger axe wielding behemoths had reached his location and Vahn was careful to redirect their attacks rather than meet them head on. The archers ceased firing in the bedlam as it was no longer safe to take a shot at their target whilst he was so entrenched in battle with their comrades. They each drew twin daggers and rushed forward into the fray.

Vahn's universe became a whirlwind of blade and brawn. He dodged nimbly and met or deflected all the strikes he could not avoid. He managed to thin their ranks from two dozen down to thirteen when his age began to catch up with him. He was slowing down and several glancing blows had torn shallow cuts into his arms and legs. He met an overhead swipe of a massive battle axe a fraction of a second too slow and his broadsword flew from his hands, flying into the cracking flame of his campfire.

Vahn rolled to the side to create distance. He met the daggers of a female warrior of the Faithful with a swift kick to the wrist. The short blade flew from her grip and left her ripe for a thrust to the throat from his rigid fingers. She dropped to the ground at his feet. Another assailant came from behind him, sword raised for the kill. Vahn used the pointed tip of the arrow still embedded in his forearm to stab her through the throat before vaulting over her body, enacting a hasty retreat.

There were now eleven left: two axe wielders, three with daggers, and six swordsmen. Vahn panted in exhaustion, his legs shook with exertion. Blood wound down his appendages, born of over a dozen tiny lacerations carved from his flesh. The Faithful advanced on him once more.

Gritting his teeth, Vahn yanked the arrow from his forearm and held it in his right hand. A sword wielder reached him first. As he swung at Vahn, the elite warrior ducked inside his guard and drove the arrow into the young man's throat. As blood spurted from the fatal puncture, Vahn wrenched the sword out of the man's hands and turned to meet the blades of two more swordsmen, whom he cut down swiftly, grabbing a sword from the hands of one of the dying warriors.

Now, with a blade clutched in each hand, Vahn launched himself back into the fray. There were eight remaining. The passage of every second sapped his strength. He would have to be cunning to claim this victory. Vahn slid feet first through the legs of an axe wielder, lashing out with both swords and severing the femoral arteries in the behemoth's legs. He dropped to the ground, bleeding profusely from the surgically precise cuts. Vahn turned from the doomed man, sprang back to his feet, and deflected the strikes of a female dagger wielder and a swordsman.

The male overextended on a swing and Vahn ducked beneath him, driving the points of both swords through his back, wrenching one free to slash across the stomach of the oncoming female. Five were left. The two remaining dagger wielders and two swordsmen attacked together. Vahn parried all of their strikes with his dual blades, whirling them around his body in complex defensive flourishes. He elegantly turned a parry into a strike against the jugular vein of a dagger wielder, who fell to the ground with a crimson spray.

The large man with the battle-axe had arrived at the scene and took a long swipe at Vahn, knocking both of his swords away and sending him rolling to a stop beside his campfire. Rolling to his knees, Vahn retrieved a flaming log from the blaze and hurled it at the hooded head of a swordsman, who screamed as he was engulfed in red fire. Another down. Vahn wiped a film of sweat from his brow and coughed the campfire's smoke from his lungs. He found his weathered old broadsword still lying in the dancing flame. He gripped it by the leather handle and pulled it up, a section of the blade shining red, having super-heated while lying in the fire.

As Vahn met his incoming opponent's sword, sparks flew from the orange glow of his blade, flying into the Faithful warrior's face. He cried out as Vahn slashed and kicked him into the dirt to bleed out. A thin, spry man ran at Vahn with daggers drawn. Vahn caught his charging foe with the tip of his blade, which exploded out through the assailant's back. Vahn threw the young man roughly back, causing him to slide off his sword as a towering axe wielder advanced.

He slashed at Vahn's arms and legs with a flurry of powerful swipes, but the elite warrior could sense victory in the air. He spun beneath a horizontal slash and cut a deep diagonal slice through the back and spine of this last opponent. The axe wielder fell to the ground dead. Vahn pitched forward onto one knee, gasping for some much-needed oxygen, and laid his forehead in the dirt. He took deep, calm, slow breaths to regain control of his limbs, holding them steady, free from the maddening tremor of fatigue. From behind him rose the sound of slow dramatic applause.

"Well done, human," a rich baritone shouted dryly. Vahn whirled, grabbing a discarded dagger from an opponent's corpse and heaved it in the direction of the voice. The blade sailed through the air and passed harmlessly through the body of a thin, red-skinned, black-haired, yellow-eyed creature who smirked humorlessly at him.

"What are you?" Vahn gasped, holding his sword out in front of him.

"Where have my manners gone?" the demon replied, calmly pacing. "I am called Aurax, head cleric of the Skirlack people, the chosen children of Ignis and rightful rulers of this world."

"Is any of that supposed to impress me?"

"I suppose not. You fumble in ignorance, blind to what occurs around you. For over two decades you have unwittingly housed two of the most powerful beings in the history of this planet."

"What do you know of my sons?"

"They are not your sons, fool. You may have tricked yourself into believing that you could raise those creatures as normal human boys. But I have watched you for a very long time, and I know that you have pieced together the truth of their existence. You know exactly what they are. You've known for a very long time."

"They're my sons, and that is all that matters."

"You know that is not the truth of them! Say it, Vahn Burai. Admit it aloud for the first time in your meaningless existence. Speak the truth, the awful reality of what your wretched children truly are!"

Vahn knew the time for pretense had ended. He finally let go of the lies which shielded his mind from the awful truth. He knew what they were. Some part of him had always known. Vahn Burai took a deep, labored breath and spoke the most difficult word he had ever uttered; a stifling admission of the dark truth of his family.

"Rosinanti."

"Excellent," Aurax said as he smiled cruelly at Vahn's pain. "You are not as brainless as the rest of your disgusting species. And, as such, I am sure you've ascertained what occurred in Lazman."

"No, it can't have been…"

"Your sons, free of your influence for the first time, did exactly what they were born to do. Destroy."

"That's not true!"

"Well, not entirely," Aurax said, waving his hand dismissively. "The destruction was caused by only one of them. I'm sure you won't have a hard time drawing a conclusion as to whom I speak."

"Kayden…" Vahn said, choking on grief.

"Bravo, human," he continued. "And, of course, your other son, the Shogai, tried valiantly to save everyone."

"Valentean is alive?"

"Momentarily," Aurax replied, clearly relishing in this moment. "Mistress Aleksandra has marked him for death. He currently lies in the dungeon of Kackritta Castle."

"Aleksandra?" Vahn gasped. What had happened while he was away? He had to get back as soon as possible. Both of his sons needed him.

"Indeed. She is the glorious architect of the destruction you witnessed in Lazman. She allowed your sons to realize the truth of who they are, and she will deliver this world back to my people. I tell you all of this information freely because your life has come to an end, by her holy command." The air distorted around Aurax until he was surrounded by five massive, red-skinned demons, all matching Valentean and Kayden's description of the beast that had attacked Princess Seraphina as a child.

Vahn could barely stand under his own power, and he was grossly outmatched. The creatures advanced with far greater speed than the former elite had thought them capable of, sprinting with the dark swiftness of death itself. As the first monster reached him, Vahn swung weakly at its head. The beast lashed out, striking at his wrists with one meaty fist, throwing the sword from his hands.

The next sensation he felt was that same gargantuan hand punching him in the chest with enough strength to cave in his ribs. Vahn flew backward through the campfire's flames, gazing up through the dancing blaze at the death squad that advanced on him. He could not fight them. Escape was his only chance for survival.

He reached behind his belt for the small bundle of combustible black powder he always kept on his person. As the beasts drew closer to the campfire, Vahn threw the tiny parcel into the flames and closed his eyes. The fire ignited the powder within. A large explosion momentarily blinded the beasts and threw him back toward the edge of the lake. He landed beside his panicked steed, which struggled against the rope that hitched it in place.

Vahn retrieved his fallen sword from the ground and slashed the rope. His momentary distraction had ended and the monsters advanced, determined to halt his escape. Vahn jumped into the saddle and kicked the horse into motion. The royal stallion of Kackritta sprinted with haste born of terror.

The five red-skinned demons attempted to give chase at first. They nearly caught him at one point, but one more kick of his legs gave his steed the energy needed for an additional burst of speed and Vahn Burai escaped into the night.

V: THE PROPHET

The clacking of Aleksandra's heels resounded through the empty hallway of Kackritta Castle's west wing as she walked onward, unfettered and unstoppable. She smiled happily to herself. Everything was progressing as she had foreseen. The pieces of this elegantly performed farce were perfectly in place. Nothing could stop her now, and soon the world would shake in the face of the goddess's power.

Aleksandra had never feared failure. Fear was a foreign concept to the mighty sorceress. She often wondered what it felt like to be afraid. It had been so long since the days of her blind childhood, before her initiation to the one true faith of Terra; the days when she knew the meaning of fear, failure, and rejection.

Before the day of her rebirth, she had simply been a princess. A mortal who clamored for the attention of her mother. In those long-forgotten days, Aleksandra had thought of her mother as the single most important woman in the world.

She scoffed now as she recalled those troubling years. The times she would parade about seeking the love and affection of a mortal woman who placed her crown before her family. Her sainted mother, who believed herself blessed with the gifts of the Sorceress Bakamaya, had often ordered the princess away, having no time to dote upon the affections of a child. She could still remember the sting of denial, the jealous rage of a scorned little girl who came to hate the very kingdom her mother valued over her love.

"Momma!" the four-year-old Aleksandra had yelled happily as she bounded into her parents' throne room. "Momma, guess what?"

Christina stood on the far end of the room, upon the balcony that looked out over the front entrance of Kackritta Castle from on high. The queen did not so much as twitch at her daughter's approach. She remained stationary with her back to the child as she conversed with a number of official looking men in robes of varying color.

The pint-sized princess furrowed her brow at such stinging indifference. She took a deep breath and tromped forward, determined to show her beloved parent what she had discovered today.

"Momma, you have to see this!" she exclaimed again. Once more the queen ignored her frenzied insistence. Had she not heard her? She grabbed a fistful of Christina's green gown and tugged with all her might, tearing a chunk of the expensive fabric with an audible rip. Christina rounded on her daughter, shock and annoyance plastered over her normally gentle, stoic face.

"Aleksandra!" she exclaimed, red flushing her cheeks as the men she had been conversing with awkwardly looked away. "What is the meaning of this intrusion?"

"Momma, I got to show you what I learned to do with ..."

"Enough, Aleksandra!" the exasperated queen said, taking her daughter by the arm and wrenching her back into the room.

The princess looked up at her mother in disappointment and confusion. Why wasn't she excited to hear what Aleksandra had to say? Had she done something wrong? "But Momma I learned how to..."

The queen's hand lashed out with a gentle rap against Aleksandra's mouth. It hardly hurt but it was jarring and unexpected. Tears began to well up within the princess's eyes. "Aleksandra, you are not some doe-eyed child who must be pampered and coddled. As the princess and future queen of this kingdom, you must learn that our life of privilege comes at a cost. We belong to the kingdom, and as such we must face the world with the grace and poise born of the power to rule! I will not have you parading about in such a manner before guests of the crown!" Christina dragged her from the throne room, despositing her daughter in the hallway. As Aleksandra tried to protest, the heavy double doors slammed back into place.

The princess began to sniffle softly. She could just vaguely hear the silky sweet tone her mother used with all outsiders, speaking apologetically for the intrusion. Gazing sadly down at her hand, Aleksandra looked at the tiny button that she carried there. With minimal concentration, it began to levitate, hovering before her eyes.

"Look what I can do, Momma..."

Aleksandra continued toward her destination, attempting to push the memory of that day and that life from her mind. In response to her emotional state, the floor and walls of the west wing began to shake. She stopped abruptly, clenched her jaw and, with eyes shut, tried to block out the painful memories of that sad mortal girl from so long ago. As the princess brought her emotions under control, the quaking of the world around her began to subside.

Careless, she thought. The power of chaos that coursed within her had a tendency to pour out of control when she began to lose her temper. Carrying such a tremendous force was as much as responsibility as it was a gift. In the wrong hands, her explosive energy could be wild, untamable, and unintentionally dangerous.

It was humbling sometimes to realize what she was. She was chosen, raised above the masses, born not only to rule but to herald forth the true sovereign of Terra. As Sophie had instructed her in the tales of Ignis and the Skirlack, she realized how foolish it had been to clamor for her mortal mother's approval. Her true mother, indeed the true mother of all Terrans, was the goddess Ignis. And Aleksandra, above all others, had earned Her holy approval and attention.

Arriving at a weathered set of double doors, Aleksandra gestured forth with one hand and they swung open at her approach. The room that lay beyond was reasonably large and, at one time, had been used to house social gatherings that were not important enough to merit the use of the grand ballroom. It had grown into disrepair during the reign of her mother. The queen felt that gatherings too small for the castle ballroom had no place occurring. But Aleksandra had found a use for it.

The room was filled with red-robed figures of all shapes, sizes, and genders who chanted together in unison, banded together in worship, nearly one hundred strong. As she entered, the chanting ceased. A collective murmur spread throughout the room. As she advanced slowly through the throng of the Faithful, she heard the word "prophet" spoken quite a few times. This was what they had taken to calling her, and the princess reveled in it.

Many reached out hesitantly toward her with the mangled hands that had served as their sacrificial offering to the goddess. She extended her arms and rewarded many of them with a gentle touch from her soft fingers. Their faces came alight with reverie and awe. These were her people, her flock that she had been chosen so long ago to lead. She stepped onto a raised platform at the room's far end and addressed them all.

"Children of the flame," she said, her voice stoic and strong, "I feel humbled to stand before you all, as we gather together to embrace the true destiny of Terra." She could feel a palpable wave of excitement spread throughout the room. "Each day, more of you arrive. Even now, our numbers fill this city by the thousands. Soon Kackritta will be no more, replaced by an empire forged in the flames of chaos, an empire of faith!"

"We are the chosen ones, who have made the sacrifice of blood. And though you, my brethren, stand scarred, the deformity of your offerings are beautiful to my eyes. Were only I able to join you and shed the burden of this hideous camouflage I am forced to wear. But soon the time for hiding will end. Soon the days of our secrecy shall cease, and Kackritta will become so much more than it has ever been. In this place, we establish a temple of true faith. In this place, we begin a blaze that shall cover the whole of Terra in its bursting flame! In this place, the Shogai *will* burn, and from his ashes shall rise the world of the Faithful!"

A resounding cheer erupted from the gathered Faithful. Amidst the throngs of their jubilation, Aleksandra raised her arms toward the sky, palms facing upwards, upon which two balls of red flame burst to life and crackled.

"As it shall burn," she said.

"As it shall burn!" came the triumphant cry of the Faithful, all raising the hands of their offering toward her, palms outstretched as though warming themselves against the heat of her flame.

Some hours later, after much prayer alongside her chosen ones, Aleksandra returned to her bedchamber. As she entered, she could sense the presence of a moderately strong magical being within. It was a presence she had known for many years.

"Mother," she said, nodding in greeting to Queen Christina, who stood across the room awaiting the arrival of her eldest daughter.

"Aleksandra," the queen replied, the hint of a nervous smile tugging at the corners of her mouth.

"What brings you to my chambers? I do hope a summons from you had not gone unrecalled by me."

"No, I ... needed to speak with you, privately."

"Whatever about?" Aleksandra inquired, stepping into the center of the room.

"Your sister…"

"What of her? I am told her treatments go well."

"Your father and I need to see her."

"Whatever for?"

"She is our daughter, as you are!" Tears formed in Christina's eyes, her hands wringing together with nervous energy.

"Oh, Mother, you know that she is possessed by a wicked and dangerous demon. Even with your gift of magic, you would be in terrible danger. The creature that wears her body is not Seraphina. But I will bring her back to us, I promise."

"Yes, but I feel as though I must…"

Aleksandra held up a hand, silencing her mother. "Mother, you must not allow yourself to become so distressed over Seraphina's condition. With my unique gift, we all agreed that I am the most suited to save her from this invasive presence. I have procured experts from around the planet who work with her day and night. Just remember, our life of privilege comes at a cost. We belong to the kingdom, and as such, we must face the world with the grace and poise born of the power to rule!"

"Aleksandra…"

"If there is nothing else to speak of, I must ask you to take your leave, Mother. I grow so weary from the trauma of this unfortunate circumstance."

Christina stared at Aleksandra wide-eyed, as if seeing her for the first time. "Please just bring her back to us," the queen said, struggling to maintain her royal composure as she rushed from the room.

Aleksandra waited until the door to her chamber had fully closed before she allowed a slowly spreading smile born of twisted delicious pleasure to encompass her face. As she turned toward her bed the princess was overcome with a sudden rush of weakness and dizziness. She winced through the whirlwind of unease and cursed under her breath.

As she reached out toward the oaken bedpost for stability, her body quivered before evaporating in a haze of red and black. Suddenly Aleksandra was surrounded by a deep cold, paralyzed by its frigid power. Through glowing red eyes that could not so much as blink, she surveyed the desolate wastes of the Northern Magic from an empowered height.

Her mind screamed in frustration, not accustomed to the weakness born of her containment. She tried in vain to thrash against the bonds of icy magic that kept her rooted in place. Rage blossomed in her heart and small, barely perceivable cracks formed along her hind legs and long dragon tail. Her body was so mighty, capable of so much, but in the wake of her sister and Valentean's combined magic, she had been rendered helpless.

It was a sobering reminder that her power was not without limitations. The strain of reaching across the world to direct her astral essence into a body double was taxing and could not be maintained forever. But she was elated to see that the strength of the spell which rooted her in this place had weakened sufficiently. It would not be long now.

She took a moment to gather the chaos magic that churned within her and reached out once more into the world. For a moment, she saw only darkness, but soon after a brief flash of red she stood once more in her bed chamber in Kackritta Castle, refreshed and in full control.

"Are you all right, Mistress?" she heard a voice ask from her window. Looking over, she saw the black clad form of Kayden crouched on her windowsill. He had seen her in a moment of weakness. She knew he had been gauging her strength for weeks now, looking for any flaw in her impervious might. She had all the power, and Kayden craved it with a desperate hunger. He could never hope to stand against her though. Chaos fed the darkness, and as such her power would always dwarf his.

"Their bastille of ignorance weakens, Kayden." He nodded. She knew not whether he believed her, but it mattered little. "The trial of your brother shall commence in one week's time. Come, we must discuss the role you are to play."

"Of course, Mistress." He bowed his head in deference to her will. The prophet of the Faithful turned her back on her animus warrior, eyes glowing in anticipation of the trial. On that day, the world would finally see her vision for Terra, they would all finally see the extent of her faith and brilliance.

Look what I can do, Momma...

VI: BLACK AND WHITE

Kayden Burai cared little for the glares directed his way by the sycophants of the Faithful as they scurried past him within the cramped tunnels of the catacombs beneath Kackritta City. Their wild disapproval of his existence was made evident early on, though he found it more entertaining than disheartening. The mere notion that the opinions of these deluded humans could matter to one such as he was ridiculously laughable.

What had bothered him, however, were the doldrums he had endured in the week he had spent restricted within these dank tunnels. Such confinement was meant not for a creature of his unfathomable strength, whose domain was the very sky. How he longed to burst forth from these oppressive conditions and take his true form, traversing the heavens with mighty beats of his godly wings. He closed his eyes for a brief instant and tried to remember the freeing sensation that was his destined privilege.

For a week and a half now, he had been circumscribed not only to these long-forgotten subterranean tunnels that wound beneath Kackritta City, but to the small, weak, pathetic mortal form of his human body. Darkness swirled within him, begging to be released, pleading with him to shed this miniscule form, and take his true place atop the world. But Aleksandra had been specific in her command. He was to remain unseen unless summoned.

Sneaking up to the princess's chamber nearly one week ago was the first time he had felt the cool night air on his skin since returning to Kackritta. She had requested his presence to review strategy, to lay out precisely what was to occur when Valentean was brought to trial. What he had found there stirred the black depths of his soul. Aleksandra's power had faltered. Her temporary form had collapsed under the burden of her own weakness. This was good. It meant that the supreme sorceress was not invincible; there was a limit to her astounding power. This was a chink in her otherwise impenetrable armor that Kayden was saving in the back of his mind for later use.

He followed her out of necessity, the burden of servitude like a collar around his throat. He had no choice in the matter. She wasn't just powerful; she *was* power. He needed to learn from her until his strength rivaled hers. He knew he could defeat Seraphina. Valentean, while more of a challenge, would fall just the same. Aleksandra was the only problematic obstacle. He would bow down before her and genuflect in wonder—for now. His time would soon come, and then his darkness would cover the planet.

The Faithful who had begun to pour into Kackritta City from all corners of the globe had converged upon these hidden tunnels to meet en masse. Their sneers and sidelong remarks as he passed them could not be mistaken for anything other than naked contempt. Kayden cared nothing for their cause. The Faithful were as much a means to an end as Aleksandra. They threw all their belief behind the princess and her flames of chaos. When they saw the true force of Terra extinguish the savior of their ill-fated religion, they would find a new deity in Kayden, or they would be eliminated.

The catacombs lay half a kilometer beneath the surface of Terra, and thus Kayden was surrounded by the element he commanded. The stone called out to him; he could sense the planet's rotation and every minor shift in the landscape. It was as though he could feel the heartbeat of Terra itself. He chuckled and gave a wicked half smile to a group of Faithful clerics that he passed by. He knew that with no more than a thought he could bring the entirety of these twisting tubes of dirt and stone down around their heads.

He could also feel the shuffling and plodding of thousands of humans above as their every step sent waves of vibration through the rock. Though confined, he was still able to feel everything that was happening above. But it was far off, as though they existed in another world. The humans were so weak, so pathetic, and a swell of pride filled his chest at his obvious superiority over them. This sense of preeminence over those he used to consider his people was not born when the power of darkness made his dreams a reality. He had felt this prideful impression of his own destiny for years.

"Kayden," Vahn had said wearily, entering their chamber within Kackritta Castle and glowering down at his nine-year-old son with a mixture of annoyance and worry etched across his normally quiet, chestnut eyes. "The royal guard informs me that you were involved in yet another ... altercation this afternoon."

"If that's what they want to call it, Father," the young Kayden replied with a short laugh, setting down the book he had been reading.

"And you would classify it as something else?" Vahn asked, folding his arms over his chest and raising an eyebrow.

"Altercation implies that the outcome might have been in question," Kayden muttered. "This was not a fight; it was a beating..."

"And who received this beating?"

"Zoran," Kayden smiled, thinking happily back on the memory, "the stable boy."

"And what could this stable boy have done to deserve such a thrashing?"

"He disrespected me, Father."

"How?"

"He spoke to me as though I was his peer."

"And are you not?"

"Of course not!" Kayden exclaimed, ignited with offense from his father's implication.

"And what makes you so different from this stable boy?"

"I am strong and he is weak!" Kayden said, rising to his feet, and balling his tiny hands into tight fists. "I'm going to be a warrior. He is meant to muck out the leavings of animals."

Vahn pursed his lips in thought, his brow furrowing as he silently contemplated his son's words. "Are you?"

"Am I what?"

"Strong."

"Of course I am! You've trained me to be the strongest!"

"And did you ever for a moment doubt your ability to defeat this stable boy in single combat?"

"Ha," Kayden spat, "never!"

Vahn reached out with blinding speed and grabbed Kayden by the tunic with one thick hand, tossing him onto the floor, like trash. Vahn dropped into a combat stance and brought his leg up, sending it flying down toward Kayden's head.

It was all the boy could do to roll out of the way as his father's boot stomped the ground. As Kayden rose, Vahn pressed his attack. He rushed the boy with speed Kayden had never seen before, raising his fist. Kayden, overcome with shock and fear, threw his arms up over his head and fell backwards. The terrified youth landed in a seated position, wide-eyed with alarm. Vahn stopped, stood straight once more, and allowed the cold stoicism of a warrior to fade from his eyes as he stared kindly down at his son.

"Why did you retreat?" Vahn asked calmly.

"What?" Kayden spat in disbelief.

"Why did you retreat from my attack?" his father repeated slowly.

"I ... you ... I can't fight you, Father!"

"Why not?"

"Because you're bigger than me, stronger, more experienced."

"And this stable boy, did he flee from you? He had to know that you were bigger, stronger, and more experienced than he."

"No," Kayden said slowly, "he did not."

"So, who is stronger, the boy who faces down a larger opponent knowing full well that defeat is assured? Or is it the boy who will inflict a beating on a weak opponent but fall on his ass in the face of one who is his superior?"

Kayden's face flushed scarlet and he looked up at his father in dumbfounded fascination. The clouds parted from his mind's eye and he realized that his concept of strength had been wrong. He would gladly pummel a boy weaker than he, but when faced with the deadly challenge of his father, he had succumbed to fear. Had the stable boy felt that same sense of hopeless terror? And had that boy still managed to face him regardless?

"I had never thought of it that way..." Kayden said. "I had never thought about what it would be like to stand across from an opponent who was ... superior."

Vahn smiled at his son and sat beside him on the floor, laying a strong hand on the boy's shoulder. "Kayden, you'll find that, no matter how strong you are, there will always be someone out there who is stronger, or faster, or more gifted than you."

"Unless you're the best."

"Well, maybe you're the strongest boy in all of Kackritta, stronger than the stable boys, the noble boys, stronger than Valentean. But Valentean is faster, more agile. Who, then, is the best? One who attempts to be the very best at everything will find himself the master of nothing at all."

Kayden narrowed his eyes and nodded in understanding. Was his father correct about the nature of strength? Or could there truly be a person who could be the very best at everything?

"Do you want to be strong, Kayden?"

"Of course."

"Do you believe me to be strong?"

"Yes, Father, you're the mightiest warrior I know."

"Do you think I go around haphazardly picking fights with others over imagined slights just because I know I can beat them?"

"I suppose not," Kayden said, looking at the ground.

"Kayden, if you want to be strong, you have to stop holding yourself so far above everyone else. Remember that people are people, just like you and just like me, and every one of them deserves your respect. Every one of them is your peer. Prove to yourself that you are truly strong by fighting, not because you can or because you feel that someone is beneath you. Fight for something you believe in. And when you encounter an unmovable opponent, have the courage and the strength to stare that adversary in the face, and then make *them move!"*

Kayden nodded at his father's wisdom, but the lesson he took away from it was not the one Vahn had intended to teach. There were people out there who were stronger than him. This sobering thought brought Kayden's world to a halt. He knew that he was destined for greatness, and it was unacceptable to believe that anyone could be his superior. The only way to prove his true might was not to pick on the weak but to topple the strong. He had to rise to the challenge of his rivals and better himself over them. Only then could he truly be the best.

"Just remember," Vahn said, moving his arm around Kayden's shoulder and pulling him close, "that no matter how strong you will one day become, Kayden, you will always be my son, and I will always love you." Vahn kissed his young son on top of the head and despite his silent, prideful stirring, Kayden smiled.

"I love you too, Father," Kayden said, laying his head against Vahn's chest.

Kayden snapped out of his daydream as he stormed into the large clearing that served as his temporary chambers. He was astounded to feel the foreign yet familiar sting of tears forming in the corners of his eyes. What was happening to him? Since the moment he had unlocked the power of darkness, he thought such human feelings were expunged from his blackened heart.

Why, then, was this simple, tender memory stirring such powerful emotion within him? *What is wrong with me?* He tried to focus on the true meaning behind that memory, that being his epiphany about the nature of power and strength. Aleksandra was the only opponent remaining that could exceed him. She would one day fall like all the rest, and he would finally be the strongest being in existence.

"No matter how strong you will one day become, Kayden, you will always be my son, and I will always love you."

He gritted his teeth trying to force the unwelcomed quote from replaying its echoing performance through his mind. He needed to get out of these ridiculous tunnels. Aleksandra's rules and consequences be damned. He had to clear his head of the unwanted memories and emotions of Kayden the human being.

He was Kayden the Rosinanti now, Kayden the sovereign of the land, Kayden the spirit of darkness. There was one person in all of Terra that he knew could help him push through this momentary weakness, and it was time to pay him a visit.

Anxiety pressed upon Valentean's addled mind with far greater force than the multitude of chains that kept him pinned down. What manner of horrors were Kayden and Aleksandra inflicting upon the planet while he rotted in here, rooted in one spot, cut off from the empowering warmth of the light inside of him?

And where was Seraphina? What had become of his princess? He knew she was in grave danger. Despite the device upon his face sapping his strength and power, he could still feel the echo of Seraphina's agony in the back of his mind. Each time he heard her cry out for him, he thrashed with the infinitesimal shreds of strength left in his wracked body. But it was useless, he was overcome with exhaustion and weakness.

Everything dies, Valentean, came the mocking ceaseless voice of his fear that repeated its silent mantra incessantly throughout the duration of his incarceration. *No flame can burn forever.* Was Aleksandra truly killing her? Was her life in serious danger while he rotted within this tiny chamber? He could not even take solace in the strength of the dragon that had always lain coiled around his heart. Its power did not exist within the crushing torment of this bleak prison.

It had been days since he had eaten or felt even a sip of water. Occasionally, a Kackrittan guard would enter his cell, flanked by an entourage of elite warriors, and pour a chunky a grey gruel and a few sips of dirty water through the grate covering his mouth. It was a vile, odious paste, but he devoured it greedily, his body desperate for nourishment.

Light exploded around him, and he recoiled as if struck. The sudden illuminant change nearly blinded his weakened eyes. As the heavy vaulted door of his cell slowly swung open, a lone figure stalked inside with only a small hand torch to light the way. It was irony seeped in sorrow that he, the paragon of light, cowered from the dull burn of a lone torch.

"You look pathetic," a voice, as familiar as his own, spoke. Valentean snarled behind the grating that covered his lips and slowly swung his face forward to glare into the eyes of his twin brother. "Thin, too, from what I can see beneath all of this … well, I suppose I don't have to tell you."

As Kayden drew closer Valentean lunged at him, chains clanking in protest and holding him steadily in place. "Do you even know how long you've been down here, brother?" Kayden asked, crouching in front of Valentean so that they were at eye level with one another.

Valentean tried to answer but the only sound that pushed through his dried cracked lips was a gurgled hiss that could not have been mistaken for actual words.

"It's been a week and a half," Kayden said. "You know, when they told me about this … thing," he said, pointing to the metallic whirling muzzle, "I thought that there was no way something made by *humans* could have any kind of effect on you. But I suppose I overestimated you, didn't I, Valentean?" Kayden stood and began to pace. Valentean's eyes narrowed as he followed his brother's course throughout the room.

"Tomorrow, they're taking you to trial," he stated matter-of-factly. "They're going to parade you out before the entire kingdom as a monster to be feared. Then, the king and queen will pass judgment upon you, and you'll be executed."

Valentean's heart was beating fast now, there had to be some way out of this mess. Were he to die, then it was all over. The dimensional barriers would break down and chaos would once again rule Terra. There had to be some way he could speak to the king or queen. And what of their father? Where did he stand in this mess?

"Don't fear, brother," Kayden said, outstretching his arm as he mockingly rubbed the back of Valentean's greasy hair, "I will not stand by and allow them to murder my own flesh and blood."

Valentean's eyes widened with realization. There was a larger game at play here. But what was it?

"Ah, I can see that silent question in your eyes," Kayden laughed, smacking the back of Valentean's head lightly. "Don't worry about what's going to befall the humans. Just know that your big brother will be at your side on that day to protect and save you. This day will be an event long remembered, not just in Kackritta, but by the entire world."

Valentean thrashed against his bonds with renewed intensity, the whirling gears of the confining muzzle spinning in his ears in response to his desperate plea for energy.

Kayden chuckled lightly. "You know," he began, "she doesn't know I'm here. If Aleksandra knew I had disobeyed her, to risk all of this so close to the end game, she'd probably rip the heart from my chest. But I had to see you, and I have to thank you. Seeing you like this, so weak and pathetic has reminded me of the one constant truth of my existence. *I am better than you.* And that means I am better than *everyone*." He turned to leave and Valentean let out a last desperate hiss and grunt, tears now spilling onto his grimy cheeks. Kayden turned in response, inclining his head in interest.

Valentean pushed his split lips apart and with desperate willpower managed to move his cracked tongue enough to utter one word. "S … Sera…" he managed to spit out through his teeth.

Kayden's brow furrowed. Rage flashed across his eyes as he lunged, grabbing Valentean by the mesh of his muzzle and bringing his face close as he spoke in an intense whisper. "Spend less time worrying about that useless woman and worry more about the entire population of humans in this city! You're going to watch tomorrow as the kingdom they've spent one thousand years building upon the blood and bones of our people comes crashing down! And as far as your whelp princess is concerned, she's the only life I can assure you will not end tomorrow. She's safe at the moment … but she's not having a fun homecoming."

Valentean glared at his brother with the most intense dark hatred he could muster. It seemed as though Kayden was truly lost. There appeared to be nothing left of his quiet, stoic sibling who, despite their rivalry, was a loving and dedicated member of his family. The darkness had consumed him, and all that was left in its wake was a black dragon driven by pride in his own power, as well as a mission of vengeance for a people he had never even known.

"Your princess is screaming in agony," Kayden spat, "it echoes through the halls outside her chambers every day, all day, and her animus warrior just sits here, helplessly violating his sacred oath. But don't worry, brother. Her screams will soon be drowned out by the fear and agony of an entire kingdom!"

They stared at one another for a brief moment, and hatred gave Valentean the strength to utter one more sentence through the dried-out plane of his parched throat. "Father ... would be ... ashamed," he spat with great difficulty, as hot, red blood flushed his face in anger. He expected Kayden to laugh or fire back in some infuriatingly arrogant manner. Instead his brother took a large step back, bringing a hand to his face to cover his nose and mouth. He took a deep intake of breath and turned his head. Valentean was shocked to see a tiny glistening drop of moisture forming at the corner of Kayden's left eye. He stared in silent wonder as a familiar expression darkened his brother's face.

Kayden regained his composure with alarming suddenness, his eyes flashing purple as he gathered the darkness unto himself. He seemed to draw strength from the brief burst of power, his posture straightening as he turned on his heel and rushed from the room. The vaulted door slammed shut behind him.

In the silent aftermath of Kayden's exit, Valentean sat still as the silent realization of what he had just witnessed continued to blossom in his mind. In the crackling light of Kayden's fallen torch, the corner of Valentean's mouth twitched into what could almost have been a half-smile.

Kay, you're still in there...

VII: THE TRIAL OF VALENTEAN BURAI

They came for Valentean the next day, just as Kayden had promised. It was an entourage of thirty warriors. Standard issue soldiers surrounded him, pulling levers and turning various bits of machinery on the platform he was chained to. Golden armored elite warriors leveled cocked crossbows at his head, ready to fire at a moment's notice. Valentean heard the unmistakable sound of turning gears around him as the platform began to rise. After a click, the soldiers attached long steel pipes to the base.

"Forward!" one of the elites commanded. The soldiers gripped the steel rods and pushed. Wheels turned and Valentean crept forward through the massive vault door of his cell. His eyes darted back and forth, taking in the unfamiliar surroundings of the dungeon corridor. It was composed of dark stone and lit by a series of torches. There were no other cells around him; this corridor seemed to have been reserved specifically for a prisoner of his prowess. He was pushed along slowly onto a large lift that rose into the air at the flip of a lever. Valentean had no idea how deep underground he had been kept, but surmised that it must have been quite far due to the amount of time the lift continued to climb.

The corridors of Kackritta Castle were void of life, it seemed as though his transfer had been carefully planned out and the busy traffic of the bustling palace was nowhere to be found. He looked out upon the night sky, the dull glare from the light of a full moon hurt his weakened eyes. Valentean recoiled and closed them, only to open his eyelids again very slowly to adapt to the unfamiliar brightness.

Now removed from the suffocating tight confines of his underground cell, Valentean could sense Seraphina's pained cries with far greater intensity. Heat prickled against his skin and bursts of crippling pain exploding along his arms and torso. The soft echo of her screams reverberated through his mind, and he began to thrash against his bonds. She needed him. He could feel not only panicked flashes of agony but also a deep wallowing despair. Was she giving up hope? Giving up on her belief in him? He ground his teeth together, turning his gaze up toward the source of the wailing agony of the woman he loved. Valentean silently vowed to find some way out of this awful mess in order to return to her side.

And what of Maura? He had heard nothing of her. Was she still alive somewhere within the confines of the castle dungeon? Valentean would never forgive himself if something awful had befallen her. How much more could that poor girl endure? Thoughts of Maura's father brought another deep issue bubbling to the forefront of his mind. Where was *his* father in all of this? Had he stood by and allowed the imprisonment of his son? Did he hate him now that the truth of his origin had become common knowledge? The thought broke Valentean's heart to pieces.

You're going to watch tomorrow as the kingdom they've spent one thousand years building upon the blood and bones of our people comes crashing down around them! Kayden's promise of assured destruction ate him alive from the inside, and his arms and legs shook at the thought of this dark promise coming to fruition.

The platform came to a stop before the massive double doors that led into the castle's throne room. They swung open with agonizing slowness and Valentean took a deep breath.

Aleksandra stirred proudly as her moment approached. She stood to the side of her mother's throne, eagerly awaiting the arrival of Valentean. Various officials and nearly the entire hierarchy of the Kackrittan military lined the interior of the vast chamber to witness the sentencing of the first Rosinanti in a millennium. He would, of course, receive a death sentence, but Aleksandra would not follow through with her holy mission of ending his sacrilegious life just yet. Her failure in the Northern Magic had forced her to reevaluate her plans. There was much she could accomplish throughout Terra before releasing the goddess. She wanted to present a united world to her holy mother, a world banded together in worship of her flames. Today would be the first step in that glorious movement toward harmony.

"The caravan should be arriving momentarily," Christina said from her seated position upon a red and gold throne.

"Indeed," Aleksandra replied, glancing sidelong at her mother. "It shan't be long now, Mother."

"How fares your sister?" King Roan asked, his voice a hushed whisper in the tension of the moment.

Aleksandra silently sighed and turned to face her father, his knuckles white as he gripped the armrests of his throne. "I am told her rehabilitation advances at a steady yet reluctant pace."

"I still wish you had allowed us to at least…"

Aleksandra held up a small hand to silence him. "The demon's power remains deeply entrenched within her, Father. I understand your desire to converse with her, but the being that lies in that chamber is not Seraphina."

"Aleksandra, this entire ordeal is ridiculous," the king said, rising to his feet.

"Be silent, husband," Christina said, laying a hand upon his forearm, commanding the room with the strength of her authority. "Save your anger not for our daughter, but for the monster that perverted Seraphina with its dark powers."

Roan's face fell, and he silently sank back down into the supple cushion of his throne.

Aleksandra smirked at this small victory. The concern and love her parents showed for her sister was pathetic. Had they ever shown such devotion to either princess as they grew to adulthood, Aleksandra might have regretted what was about to transpire.

Her attention was drawn to a side door as a pair of guards ushered Maura into the room, disheveled and shackled at the wrist. Maura's gaze instantly found the princess, and she glared at her in violent venomous hatred. Aleksandra's lip curled in disgust for the wretched whelp. Before Maura could say anything, the room came alight with nervous energy as the main doors slowly swung open.

Come to me, Valentean, she mused silently. *Come forward and give meaning to my movement!*

A gasp could be heard and a collective shudder felt throughout the room as Valentean was wheeled within. He saw heartbreaking terror along the faces of the various nobles of Kackritta who had packed into the throne room, along with seemingly every military official of significance. It was as though every important person in the kingdom had turned out for this trial, and that thought terrified him. Kayden was going to strike, and when he did, he could take out the entire infrastructure of Kackritta in one blow.

Looking at the base of the royal family's throne platform he saw Maura, looking haggard and shackled. She locked the blue pools of her eyes with his, a look of helpless desperation greeting him. He tried to keep his gaze strong and gave her a slight nod of his head, to communicate with her that all would be well and to trust in him. She nodded back and swallowed hard. At least she was unhurt, which was more than Valentean could say for Seraphina, whose pained sorrow could be felt with even greater intensity this deep within the palace interior. He struggled against his chains once more in the wake of yet another agonized wave that reverberated through him and felt the steel links groan in response.

He had purposely avoided looking directly ahead at the royal family, as he was unsure how he would react upon seeing his tormentor in Aleksandra's steely gaze. Now, he slowly and painfully raised his muzzled face. The imprisoned animus warrior glared ahead at the princess in blazing hatred. Aleksandra's expression softened, and she gave him a fleeting smirk before mocking him with a brief almost imperceptible red flash across her eyes. The gaze of the woman who had so easily beaten him to within a centimeter of death stirred dueling feelings of rage and terror within his heart.

As the moving platform came to a stop before the royal family, the various soldiers who had accompanied him began pulling levers and tinkering with bits of machinery. The platform settled and locked back into place. The hulking form of General Zouka came into view as the black-armored Gorram stalked forward and mimed the process of checking the strength of his restraints.

"Don't disappoint me," he whispered to Valentean as he brought his face down toward the captive animus warrior's ear.

Valentean groaned in annoyance and disgust at the general's single-minded obsession with meeting him in combat. Seemingly content with the strength of his prisoner's bonds, the general straightened to his full commanding height, turned, and nodded at the queen.

Valentean's eyes met those of the king and queen and he silently pleaded with them to see reason. The irony of the moment was not lost on him. This was the exact spot he had stood upon nearly a decade earlier when he avowed his intentions to serve as Seraphina's animus warrior. On that day, their eyes had met his with kindness, pride, and gratitude. Now, the queen glared at him with the icy resolve of a ruler, and the king looked off to the side, intentionally avoiding his stare.

"The prisoner, Your Majesty," Zouka said in way of introduction to the queen. "Lord Valentean Burai, animus warrior of Kackritta." There was a collective murmur of hushed, terrified whispers throughout the room which died as Christina rose.

"Valentean Burai," the queen said slowly, "you stand accused on this day of the crimes of wanton destruction of a sovereign land, murder, and attempted regicide of Princess Aleksandra Kackritta. Furthermore, you stand accused of violation of the Oath of Animus by infecting Princess Seraphina Kackritta, your avowed charge, with the spirit of a demon that has bonded to her soul. Most damning of all, you are accused of being a member of the tainted Rosinanti race, an unforgivable abomination with no human right to defense under the law of Kackritta."

Valentean's spirits were crushed by the queen's words. She would not even allow him to defend himself based solely on what he was. This was not a trial; it was a sentencing.

"Maura Lorne of the former Village of Lazman, come forward," she continued, turning toward Maura as the guards pushed her forward to stand beside Valentean's platform. "You stand accused of aiding and abetting a member of the Rosinanti race. As such, you have betrayed your entire species and have also forfeited your right to a defense."

"That's garbage," Maura spat back at the queen as the entire congregation gasped. "Your disgusting daughter and her animus warrior destroyed my home and..." she was cut off by a hard fist from one of the guards who flanked her which sent the boisterous young woman to her knees.

"You will remain silent!" the queen roared in response, clenching her fist in the air and conjuring a spell that slammed Maura's jaw closed. She flailed on the ground, chains clanking in her panic as she grasped at the invisible grip that silenced her.

"In the face of these grievous charges, the likes of which have not been seen since ancient times, this royal body sentences the pair of you to death, to be carried out immediately without pause or mercy."

A triumphant cheer abounded throughout the room and a dark sorrow struck Valentean's heart. This was it. He would die here along with Maura, leaving Seraphina to her agonizing torture and the world to the reign of a fire goddess who would plunge the planet into chaotic upheaval.

"Stop this at once!" came a booming, commanding voice that rose above the enthusiastic rabble. The gathered masses fell silent and Valentean felt a thrilling rush of happiness and relief flood through him. This was a voice he knew well. His eyes doubled in size as his father, Vahn Burai, strode forcefully before him, locking eyes with his son. In that one look, Vahn confirmed Valentean's greatest hope. The mysteries of his origin mattered nothing. He was still his father. Vahn turned his gaze up toward the royal family, standing between them and Valentean as if trying to shield his son from this bleak sentencing. King Roan stirred in his throne at the sight of his old friend, and Christina wore a look of incredulous shock.

"Vahn Burai, you will stand aside at once by order of your queen!"

"I will not," Vahn spat defiantly at the enraged monarch. "You would sentence my son here in this place without so much as a chance at defending himself against these mad accusations?"

"Your son is not a human being, and thus it receives no right to human defense."

"My son is a citizen of this country and has been, by your command, since the day I carried him into this very chamber!"

"Your son is a Rosinanti dragon, avowed enemy of this august body."

"And he is also the Champion Animus of Terra! He is also the kind-hearted boy who swore his life to that of your daughter! He is the child who gave you a crown of flowers to commemorate the anniversary of your rule when he was six years old! If he is, in fact, a Rosinanti dragon, are we to forget that he is also the good man who has lived and breathed with us for over two decades? A warrior who fought for the glory of his princess and kingdom? All because your daughter offers a testimony with no discernible proof?"

"You will fall silent, old man," Aleksandra said, stepping forward with a dangerous edge in her voice.

Valentean's heart pounded as he strained against the protesting chains that bound him helplessly.

"Your daughter seeks to unleash a horde of demons into this world, and my son is the only thing that stands between us and annihilation! Lazman was destroyed upon her command. It was only through my son's actions that your daughter Seraphina managed to survive!"

"Seize him!" Aleksandra bellowed as the king and queen looked at her in disbelief. Elite warriors rushed toward Vahn at the princess's command.

"Roan, you know my words to be the truth!" Vahn yelled to the king. Roan's ruddy face contorted with conflict, and he rose sharply from his throne, despite Christina's disapproving stare.

"Is this true, Aleksandra?" he roared at his eldest daughter. "Is any of that true?"

As the elites moved in to encircle Vahn, Aleksandra stepped forward and looked meaningfully at both of her parents. "Yes," she said simply as a gasp tore through the room. "Execute him!"

In the confusion of the moment, Vahn struck, disarming and disabling the four elite's that surrounded him. Aleksandra turned to her astounded parents and gripped each one by the throat, easily lifting them helplessly into the air.

Maura sprung into action as the distracted queen's spell dissipated and rose to her feet, striking the pair of guards beside her with quick and precise elbows to the face. As Vahn attempted to run toward the royal family, he was intercepted by the impossibly fast Zouka. The general punched the old man hard in the stomach, following through with such force that the former elite warrior was flung back, slamming hard into the ground with a sickening smack five meters away.

The sight of his beloved father so callously brutalized stirred something primal in Valentean's heart. In his fury, the empowered resolve of the dragon rose up within him, overriding the restricting magic of the muzzle. He felt the familiar rush of light flooding through him and the distinctive shift in vision which indicated the return of the white glow upon his eyes. He grunted for a moment as the energy burst from him, erupting to his feet as the chains and muzzle exploded in a blast of wind that swept throughout the throne room.

Valentean vaulted to the ground, his legs feeling no fatigue or weakness, as he glared through alabaster radiance at the general. Zouka smiled excitedly at the empowered Rosinanti, beckoning him forward with one gargantuan hand. The dragon uncoiled from around his heart, hardening his resolve in the wake of his father's thrashing. Valentean snarled at the foreboding mountain of muscle and dashed forward, fists crackling with mana, ready to beat vengeance into the Gorram's face.

Aleksandra savored the moment. It was replete with delicious irony. Her foolish parents, so concerned with the re-emergence of the Rosinanti yet their undoing would be at the hands of their own blood. She loved the way they squirmed in her clutches. As a child, her parents, and in particular her mother, had looked so massive, so terrifyingly authoritative. Now, she saw them in the same way she saw all humans of Terra: weak, tiny, and drowning in a flood of their own ignorance. Her mother gasped helplessly, trying to speak.

"What's that, Mother?" Aleksandra asked, her eyes alight in fiery crimson hues. "Now you wish to speak to me? Now you *fear* me?" Christina gasped for what little air Aleksandra was allowing her to breathe. "Do not fret, Mother. I have taken all of your lessons to heart, and I shall go on to become the true monarch this world has so desperately sought since your feeble rule began." Smoke began to pour out from around her hands, causing both of her parents to thrash wildly against the strength of her grip. Her palms became super-heated and scorched the flesh along their throats. Aleksandra looked deeply into her mother's eyes one last time.

"Look what I can do, Momma," she whispered as the heads of both of her parents exploded out in a flame-soaked burst of super-heated energy, splattering the princess with gore.

She took a moment to savor this long-awaited victory, feeling the chaos churn within her as the blood of her parents trickled down her face and neck. She released the bodies and watched with twisted pleasure as they crumpled to the floor. Then, the sorceress turned contently back to the center of the room to watch the rest of her grand stratagem play out.

As Valentean broke free of his bindings, Aleksandra watched the gathered assemblage of dignitaries, officials and military leaders attempt to flee the throne room. Before they could reach the exit, the space between them and the door filled with a hazy, red glare, out of which stalked two dozen Skirlack soldiers. Her creatures wasted no time diving into the fray, tearing through the flesh of any human within the reach of their claws.

Screams built to an incredible crescendo around her as the stain of her parents' legacy was washed away in a river of blood.

Valentean vaulted into the air with a cry of rage and drove his knee into the general's chest. Zouka momentarily faltered and charged at him. The spry young animus warrior was already moving, connecting with a hooking right handed punch soaked in the green glow of mana energy. The resulting explosion along the side of Zouka's head threw the Gorram to the ground.

The dragon within his heart roared in approval and urged Valentean onward. In his anger, he obliged the silent order. The general sprang back to his feet as Valentean advanced and reached out with impressive speed to grab the Rosinanti by the throat and heave him backward. Valentean crashed onto the prison platform he had been wheeled in on and grabbed one of the discarded chains.

As Zouka ran in, Valentean wrapped the chain around his closed fist and smashed it into the face of the man-mountain. Zouka was once more taken off his feet and slammed hard into the polished floor. He gazed up at Valentean, who slowly stalked off the platform, throwing the chain off to the side. In Zouka's smile there burned a wonderment born of the challenge.

Their eyes met and Valentean felt an obsessive desire to tear the neck from this monster who dared to strike his father. Zouka chuckled lightly, wiped a trickle of blood from his lip and stared at it in wonderment. He reached behind his broad back and gripped the thick handle of his black sword, brandishing the massive weapon as though it weighed nothing at all. Zouka twirled the blade through the air in an impressive flourish that Valentean took to be a challenge.

Zouka moved the blade with speed Valentean had not thought possible. Despite this, the nimble Rosinanti managed to duck out of the carving path of two powerful swipes and leapt over a third, allowing the ebony stone instrument of violent destruction to pass harmlessly beneath him. As Valentean landed, Zouka raised the weapon over his head to cleave his smaller opponent in two. Valentean took this opportunity to summon the wind, feeling the light bunch together in his chest before releasing it in a powerful gust that sent the general flying back, smashing hard into the wall behind the royal family's thrones.

It was as Zouka crashed to the floor that Valentean noticed the two smoldering headless corpses that lay before the empty seats of power. They were unmistakably the bodies of King Roan and Queen Christina. He gasped as the world re-materialized around him, now free of the all-consuming thrill of the dragon's desire.

He turned at the sound of violence to see Skirlack soldiers engaging in a blood-soaked massacre of the gathered warriors, nobles, and officials of Kackritta. Scanning the room, he found no trace of Aleksandra or, to his mounting horror, his father. Now removed from the energy brought about by his momentary rage, he felt a crushing fatigue and weakness born of his extended captivity. His vision blurred in and out as he tried to focus on individual sounds. Everything slammed together in his mind in a jumbled mess of noise. He needed to focus. His father was missing, and Kayden could not be far off. He had to stay strong.

"Valentean!" Maura called out from across the long throne room. He spotted her, still shackled at the wrists as she attempted to fend off two Skirlack demons with the discarded sword of a Kackrittan soldier. The sight of his friend aided his focus and Valentean dashed to her, driving his forearm into the back of a Skirlack that approached Maura from behind. The monster bent with his thunderous blow and Valentean drew his arm again, charged it with mana energy, and slammed it down into the creature's face. It fell, unmoving. Maura let out a cry of exertion as she pierced the heart of her other opponent with the borrowed blade, kicking it back as it slid to the floor, leaving a trail of thick black blood upon the weapon.

"Are you all right?" Valentean asked, clasping his companion by the forearms.

"I'm fine," Maura replied, pulling away and flicking some of the demon's remains to the ground. "I'd fight better without these, though," she said, holding up her wrists. Valentean nodded and grasped the steel bindings, one in each hand, and crushed them with his Rosinanti strength. Maura nodded to him in way of thanks and whirled the sword around her body a few times.

"We need to get these people out!" Valentean yelled over the screams.

"Right. Let's make sure we can carve a path through to…"

Before Maura could finish her sentence, Valentean saw a small projectile careening toward her face. He reached out with speed born of the wind itself and managed to catch a small dagger, centimeters from Maura's left eye. She gasped in shock and Valentean turned, hurling the blade back toward its point of origin.

General Zouka smiled with maniacal glee as he smacked the tiny knife from the air. Valentean's eyes blazed to life with white light once more.

"I'll handle him and then join you," he said to Maura. "Help as many of these people as you can, but be careful!" She nodded and took off into the fray. The dragon stirred within Valentean's heart, but this time he bit back its energetic bloodlust. There was too much at stake, and he had to remain sharp.

Both Zouka and Valentean ran toward one another. Valentean called for an added burst of speed from the wind and reached the Gorram in seconds, aiming a tightly squeezed fist at his opponent's broad chest. Zouka blocked Valentean's blow easily and flung his armored fist forward. The broad knuckles of the general's hand slammed into Valentean's face three times, driving the animus warrior back with each strike. He then grabbed Valentean by the tunic and lifted him into the air, pressing him over his head with a cry of battle before slamming him down into the floor with enough force to crack the polished surface.

Valentean felt the air fly from his lungs upon impact. He tried to roll to a standing position, but Zouka reached him before that was possible. The Gorram reared back and kicked him, hard, in the torso. Valentean soared back, skidding to a stop four meters away, where he managed to regain his vertical base and charge back toward the burly general, who was already on the move toward him.

Just as the two warriors were about to collide, the ground between them exploded in a haze of purple light that threw both combatants in opposite directions. Between Valentean and Zouka, Kayden stood with arms extended out amidst a circle of destruction. He glanced down at Valentean with gentle amusement.

"I told you I wouldn't miss your big day, brother," he said, his eyes alight with dark purple energy.

"Kayden, no!" Valentean screamed, rising to his feet and running at his twin with a desperate burst of speed. Kayden's entire body erupted in a burst of purple light, so bright that Valentean had to cover his eyes with one arm. A powerful pulse of energy erupted through the room, tossing the young animus aside. When the glow subsided, Valentean gasped in terror. Kayden nearly filled the entire room with his bulk, as the black dragon loomed massive and horrid above the scene of destruction. Purple energy began gathering around him, building to an intensity Valentean felt throughout his body. The dragon within him also felt the growing power, and urged Valentean to take cover.

Kayden folded his wings inward as the energy continued to gather and strengthen. Realizing he had only seconds to spare, Valentean ran with all the speed his mana and the wind would allow, grabbed Maura as she sliced the head off another Skirlack demon, and dove with her to the ground, covering her with his body. The instant they touched the floor, the energy gathered in Kayden's titanic scales erupted outward in a massive explosion that tore the throne room apart. Valentean shielded his eyes as the blazing inferno threw both he and Maura across the room.

The sound of the blast was deafening and, in its aftermath, Valentean heard only a gentle ringing in his ears. Weakness and pain wracked his back and legs. His flesh had been burned and torn, and steady trickles of oozing blood seeped onto the floor. His head ached, joints alight with agony, and his ribs felt as though they were on fire. He groaned in pain and rolled off Maura, who moved slowly and seemed relatively unharmed save for a few burns and scrapes.

The floor felt cool beneath his scorched back, which radiated biting pain throughout his extremities at the unwelcomed contact. He winced at the momentary avalanche of agony, but a frenzied gasp from Maura forced him to open his eyes.

The throne room, along with everyone and everything within it, had been completely obliterated. What had once stood as the shining beacon of

Kackritta's royal authority now laid in blackened fiery ruin. Every human and Skirlack that had occupied the space moments prior laid in charred pulpy pieces. There was no sign of Zouka, and Valentean wondered if the Gorram had somehow managed to avoid the wanton destruction.

The entire roof and most of the east wall had been completely blown apart. Valentean stared upwards at the night sky as it filled with wispy clouds of smoke and embers from the flames that ate at the throne room's remains with a greedy hunger.

Kayden still towered over the scene, narrowing his blazing purple eyes at Valentean, gloating over this nightmare of dark chaos and daring him to try and stop it. Valentean continued to push himself up with both arms, reaching a seated position, a mixture of sweat and blood falling into his eyes at the exertion.

As if seeing no challenge in his brother, Kayden turned and began to plod toward the rubble-strewn mess that had once been the throne room's east wall. The newly opened space looked out over the whole of Kackritta city, and Kayden sat perched there, gazing out over the land, massive black lips curling to expose fangs that could bite through stone.

"Oh no," Maura said, now on her hands and knees, "he's going to…"

She was cut off as Kayden released a bestial roar that shook the entirety of Kackritta Castle. Valentean imagined the citizens of Kackritta City shaken violently awake by the thunderous sound only to look out their windows or doors to be greeted with their harshest nightmare given form. A Rosinanti had laid waste to Kackritta Castle, and now it was coming for them. Valentean's momentary dark musings were interrupted by Maura as she grabbed him by one arm and attempted to pull the animus warrior to his feet. Valentean felt sensation return to his numb legs and struggled to regain his footing, leaning on Maura for support.

Kayden spread his wings and leapt through the open wall, falling out of view for a brief second. Valentean and Maura stumbled across the rubble and unrecognizable remains of cooked human and demon flesh to gape at the once unfathomable sight of a dragon flying slowly over Kackritta City. The exclamations of terror from thousands of Kackritta's citizens could be heard even this far up. Panic filled the streets as men, women, and children stumbled over one another in blind panic.

The world seemed to move in comically slow motion as Kayden opened his jaws, bathing the people below him in the violet radiance of destructive energy which had already gathered in the back of his throat. Maura screamed in Valentean's ear as death poured from Kayden's mouth in a blazing beam of light. The destruction carved into the city and moved forward with a slight tilt of the dragon's horned head, obliterating buildings, roads, and human lives. A long, devastating gash was left across the cityscape in its wake, smoldering like a fresh scar upon the once pristine face of humanity's greatest civilization.

Tears spilled from Valentean's eyes as the dragon within him stirred, filling him with enough energy to stand under his own power. He took several steps away from Maura, agonizing as he tried to come up with something, anything, he could do to stop his brother's destructive rampage.

"Can't you turn into a dragon and stop him?" Maura yelled.

Valentean took a deep breath and tried to let the dragon out. His eyes burst to life with azure power, and a faded white light sparked around his body several times before fizzling out. "I … I can't!" he exclaimed helplessly, clenching and unclenching his fists in frustration as Kayden began to gather energy for a second strike.

Since his ordeal in the Northern Magic, the ability to transform into the white dragon had somehow fallen out of his reach. Until now, he had taken solace in this hindrance. He had no desire to return to the murderous bloodlust of a beast, which had almost caused him to end Seraphina's life. But now, the dragon was the only means to protect his home. His inability to call upon its strength filled him with a frustrating sense of dread and uselessness.

"What do you mean, you can't?" Maura cried out over the sounds of panic. Kayden released another mighty wave of power which carved through the city like a knife into a fresh loaf of bread, violently extinguishing lives in its wake.

"I can't do it anymore!" Valentean exclaimed in an agonized admission of weakness and failure. "It just doesn't work!"

"Well, we have to do something! He's going to destroy the entire city, just like he did to Lazman!"

Valentean tried over and over again to connect to the transformation but found only an emptiness where that once empowering, all-encompassing energy had been. He looked at the twin gashes that smoldered below him, each nearly a kilometer long. Kayden seemed to be drawing this out for some reason. Had he so desired, Valentean knew the entirety of the city could have been obliterated by now. So, what was he doing? Was he purposely savoring the cruelty of this moment? Or was there some deeper and darker plan? He desperately sought some way to combat this terrifying reality when a thought erupted into his mind.

"Sera!" he exclaimed.

"What?"

"We need Sera! In the Northern Magic, we worked together to stop Aleksandra's dragon, and that was much stronger than Kayden! We need to get Sera and together maybe she and I can stop him!"

"All right, but where is she?" Maura asked.

"Her bedchamber. That's where they're keeping her. Kayden let that slip yesterday when he came to visit me in the dungeon."

"All right, let's go!"

"I don't think you're going anywhere just yet, dragon." Valentean whirled around to see General Zouka, relatively unscathed, advancing on him with a platoon of a dozen Skirlack soldiers flanking him. "You still have a battle to fight right here!"

Valentean cursed at his luck. Zouka was a formidable opponent, and while the Skirlack did not pose a terrible threat to him, they were many, and Maura would be in danger should a fight erupt. Valentean still felt weakened from his prolonged captivity, coupled with the aftermath of Kayden's initial attack. He doubted that he could be a match for the mighty general at this point. Both he and Maura began to step back, nearing the edge of the east wall, only centimeters left now between them and a drop stretching hundreds of meters.

"He's killing people down there!" Valentean exclaimed to the general. "I can stop it!"

"I do not care," Zouka spat, drawing his sword as he continued to advance. Valentean saw only one conceivable course of action that would allow them to survive and escape. He turned to Maura.

"Do you trust me?" he yelled.

"What?"

"Do you trust me?"

"Yes..."

"Good." Valentean shoved Maura out into the open air, hearing her scream as she plummeted toward her death. He took a deep, calming breath and leaped headfirst after her.

***

Zouka was shocked as the Rosintai jumped out into the night. He dashed toward the ledge and stared out into the still blackness. There was no sign of either of them. Had the dragon truly given up all hope and opted to end his own life rather than give Zouka the satisfaction of claiming his head? Such tactics did not seem to fit with what he knew of this creature, but Zouka understood that terror and despair could have unexpected effects upon the weak-willed.

Leaning over the edge, Zouka was suddenly accosted by a bright white glare which erupted from the darkness below. He leaped backwards, falling to the ground as the Rosintai, fully empowered with eyes aglow, rose into the air with the girl in his arms, *flying*! There were no wings, no transformation into a dragon-god, just a man moving through the air, free of the crushing embrace of gravity as he rode the wind up into the sky above Kackritta Castle.

Amazing, Zouka thought as he followed the rising form of his greatest opponent into the night. His excitement continued to build toward their inevitable confrontation. This would be a challenge worthy of the wait.

Maura screamed in his ears as they rocketed into the air. Valentean tried to block it out. He tried to ignore Kayden and the cacophony of screams he elicited from the innocents who suffered below. The sheer act of staying aloft was taking extreme amounts of concentration, and should he lose focus now, there was no River of Freedom to catch him this time.

"You're actually flying!" Maura exclaimed, her voice alight with shock and wonderment.

This should have been a freeing, joyous moment. Throughout his life, Valentean had often watched birds in the sky, moving unhindered through the air and wondered what that freedom must feel like. Now, here he was, experiencing the miracle of flight for the first time, and all he felt was the biting smack of dread.

He could still sense Seraphina's agony coming from her chambers in the east wing. He directed the wind to alter their course, and dove toward the castle ramparts. As a renewed twinge of Seraphina's agony exploded within his mind, the air faltered around him.

"Valentean, slow down!" Maura exclaimed, as the stony ledge of the rampart rushed upwards at them. Valentean cursed as the light died from his eyes and the wind vanished. Maura screamed as Valentean turned, making sure he would take the brunt of the impact as he slammed into the unforgiving stone.

Maura climbed off him, unharmed. Valentean groaned in pain, spitting a small pool of blood onto the ground as he rose to his hands and knees.

"Graceful landing, dragon-boy," Maura said sarcastically, as she draped his arm over her shoulders and pulled Valentean to his feet. "Are you all right?"

"I'll be fine," he replied through clenched teeth. Now, so close to Seraphina, her tortured pain reverberated within him along with a prickling, all-consuming heat that seemed to seep beneath his skin. "Come on, she's close!"

VIII: TOGETHER

You can do this, Seraphina, the princess thought as another round of pain wracked her body. *Ten seconds, just get through ten seconds...*

She counted backward, telling herself that she could withstand the agony for that short burst. When the scorching heat subsided after the number four, she took those added seconds of relief as a reward for her strength.

In the last week, she had taken to these mental rituals to preserve her mind from giving in to the never-ending torture inflicted by the mad, old crone Finstra. When she felt the putrid humidity of the sadistic old woman's breath on her cheek, she slowly opened her eyes to glare in hatred at the weathered, pockmarked face of her tormentor.

"Such resolve in you, princess," she remarked, not for the first time. A familiar, gleeful, evil smile played out over her ancient features. Seraphina had realized early on that the infliction of such intense pain on a non-believer like herself brought Finstra untold spurts of cruel joy. "You continue to resist the purifying flame of the goddess, and in doing so, only prolong your torment. Let go of the Harbinger's power, dear. Let go and be carried away by the gifts born of the blaze."

Seraphina clamped her jaw tightly closed. She had learned long ago that engaging in conversation with the old hag only weakened her resolve when the pain returned. And the pain *always* returned.

The vile crone's grin showed a mouth filled with a collection of thin rotting teeth. She looked like some undead monster, but Seraphina continuously reminded herself that she was but a mortal woman. She would not empower her torturer by imagining her as anything more than what she was: a weak, feeble, old woman.

Finstra reached toward the floor and pulled a long, curved blade into view, the tip of which pulsated with an orange super-heated glow. She moved about the bed toward Seraphina's legs and leaned over, smiling that same infuriating rotten grin, nearly bursting with glee in anticipation of inflicting pain yet again on her victim. Seraphina braced herself as the crone touched the scalding point of the blade into her ankle. The sharpened weapon sliced a deep gash down the side of her bare foot and into her sole. Finstra pushed it deep into a nerve cluster found there and Seraphina shrieked in agony.

Ten seconds, Seraphina ... just ten more seconds!

"*Seraphina,*" she heard the distant weak voice of Aqua rising from the shadow of her mind once more. Had it been a hallucination all along? Over the week and a half since being subjected to this grizzly torment, she had heard the voice of her predecessor on more than one occasion, often reaching out with words of comfort that she could scarcely hear.

"*Be strong, Seraphina, help approaches!*"

As Finstra roughly pulled the blade from Seraphina's flesh and moved toward her other leg, the chamber door burst open. Seraphina's head snapped to the left and her heart leaped at the sight of Valentean. His arm was still outstretched, eyes glowing, while Maura stood behind him, sword in hand. It had felt like ages since she had laid eyes on the man she loved, and the hope he inspired within her dulled the ache that still throbbed through her leg. Finstra moved between Seraphina and the door, the flames of Aleksandra's inferno separating her and Valentean.

"Be gone from this place, Shogai," the hag commanded, her weathered voice rising above the sound of crackling fire. "You are powerless in the face of the prophet's magic." Valentean attempted to step forward, but the flames leaped into the air, barring his entrance and Seraphina's salvation. The glow subsided from his eyes and he looked distraught for a moment. Was he giving up on her? Was there actually a challenge her mighty animus warrior could not meet?

"I'm not coming in," Valentean relented.

"You finally see that your heretical rebellions are as nothing before the might of the prophet and the most holy goddess!"

"No," Valentean simply replied, "I don't have to come in there because my princess is going to stop you herself."

Seraphina inclined her head as Valentean reached out of sight and held aloft a large wooden bucket nearly overflowing with water. Finstra gasped as Valentean threw the bucket into the room. The liquid sang to Seraphina, calling out to her like a welcomed friend, begging to be utilized.

Blue light exploded along her eyes as she reached out with her left hand. Seraphina pulled the water from the bucket, froze it into a jagged, pointed icicle and yanked it into the room with blinding speed until it impaled the withered old woman through the chest. Seraphina exhaled forcefully through her nose as Finstra gurgled unintelligibly before falling forward into the blaze.

Seraphina panted as she allowed the power to dissipate from her eyes. She stared wordlessly at the crumbling, frail husk that was Finstra's body. This had been the first human life she had ever taken, and a rush of horror and revulsion accompanied the moment. Had there been any food in her body she might have vomited but, instead, she simply gagged. A single tear fell from the corner of her eye and instantly evaporated upon the plane of her cheek. She took another long, deep breath and reminded herself to be strong as she looked at Valentean, still so far from her, still separated by what felt like miles of red hot flame.

"Sera," he called out to her over the raging fire, "hold your breath!" She did not question it, she simply complied, taking a long intake of super-heated air and holding it in her lungs. White light exploded along Valentean's eyes as he raised both arms. Seraphina felt the wind around her rushing from the room towards him. He was removing the air from the chamber, and without the gift of oxygen to feed it, the inferno died out. The last tiny ember flickered from existence as her lungs ached. Valentean lowered his arms and rushed into the room.

Seraphina exhaled as she rolled from the bed, limping into the strong arms of the man she loved, burying her face in his chest.

Valentean held his princess tight against him, very nearly forgetting the awful slaughter taking place just outside the castle walls in his selfish desire to lose himself in her touch.

"Are you all right?" he asked, pulling back to look into her deep chestnut eyes. There was something off about the look in them, something not entirely Seraphina. He could not fathom the depths of agony she had undergone while he sat rooted in that horrible dungeon.

"I'll be fine," she said, suddenly gripping his hands with surprising strength. "Whoa, Val what is happening outside?"

"You can sense it?"

"Yes, removed from the pain it's like … I can feel the panic … the terror … the chaos…"

Valentean took a long intake of breath. "Kayden is laying waste to the city as a dragon…" He could see panic forming in her eyes. "There's more," he continued slowly. "The entire line of Kackrittan military command, except for Zouka, is dead. And Aleksandra … she murdered your parents." This news seemed to strike his princess like a fist. There was shock in her eyes before tears began to well up and she collapsed against him. Valentean sunk with her to the floor.

"No, Val … no … she can't have … she … Val … no…" She buried her face into his chest once more and sobbed. He could feel the wet streaks of her tears through the various rips in his white tunic and gave her time to let it out.

"Sera, we need to try and…"

"We have to stop them." Venom dripped dangerously from her voice. She pulled away and the blue light of order had returned to her eyes, blazing there, violently illuminant. "We have to put them down!"

Valentean was momentarily taken aback by the princess's rage. Her lips flattened together as her jaw clenched tight with anger. The room around them shook in the wake of her gathering power.

"Together then?" Valentean said to her. She gave a curt nod of agreement.

"Always."

Kayden allowed the thermal draft wafting up from the rising flames beneath him to fill his wings and project him further into the night sky. The scene below was one of carnage and terror. The screams from the survivors of his smoldering wrath arced up to his hypersensitive ears like a sweet song from afar. He circled the city several times, drinking in the panic of frenzied humans. How many had he slain thus far? Hundreds, easily. Had it breached a thousand yet? He hoped so.

His ego stirred as he examined his handiwork. Kackritta City was in flames. Stretching gashes of devastation lined the districts like scars, deep and black and smoldering on the edges. Despite the turbulent chaos unfolding beneath him, Kayden felt truly complete and at peace for the first time in his life. It felt as though he was finally engaged in his true purpose; destruction. He was a perfect engine of death.

The anticipation of this day had been building to an undeniable crescendo within his heart. There had been a small part of him that anxiously wondered if, when the time came, he would feel an unnerving tug of conscience. Destroying Lazman had been easy. Those people and that place meant nothing to him. This, however, was the land he had called home. This place held so many memories for him, both pleasant and dismal alike. But once the thrill of murder and destruction was upon him, Kayden felt nothing but a contented pride in fulfilling his ultimate calling.

Here, searing below him in radiant crimson beauty, was the very concept of human superiority. Kackritta had always been the world's shining beacon of hope against the Rosinanti threat. Kackritta City was the centerpiece of the undeserved smug sense of accomplishment the humans reveled in. This city's very existence was a monument to genocide. He took pride in upending every bit of it.

As he circled above like a great bird of prey, he sensed a tingling burn erupt from the back of his mind. He had come to realize, over the past several weeks, that this odd sensation meant that one or more of his counterparts were near. Aleksandra's magical double did not generate the energy necessary to trigger this internal warning system, so that left Valentean and Seraphina. The strength of this sensation showed him that it was not one, but both, out on the furthest edge of Kackritta's ramparts.

He knew the time was fast approaching to enact the final stage of Aleksandra's plan. But he wanted one delicious moment, when he could look his puny brother in the eyes, drink in his fear along with that of the doomed masses below and show him that there was nothing he could do to halt the darkness.

Valentean sprinted up the stairs of the city ramparts and skidded to a halt as the true extent of the destruction came into view. He stood on the rocky path atop the city wall, the lush plains of Kackritta and the River of Freedom stretched out behind him, while in front, Kackritta City burned.

"No..." Seraphina whispered beside him as the full scope of Kayden's unleashed fury settled around them. To his left, Valentean sensed Maura shaking in the familiar face of a community toppled by Kayden's power. "Val, we need to do this now."

"Agreed," Valentean said, glaring up at the massive, circling form of his twin. Kayden's glowing purple gaze shifted to their location, and he altered his course to veer directly at them.

"Whatever the two of you are going to do, you might want to start," Maura said, panic rising in her voice at the Rosinanti's approach.

Valentean looked beside him to Seraphina. He found no fear or hesitation in her icy gaze, only the steadfast determination of a warrior staring back at him, unwavering.

Kayden's massive bulk grew closer. Valentean clenched his jaw and locked his knees to keep his legs from shaking. Just as the dragon seemed as though it were about to smash into the wall upon which they stood, Kayden's wings unfurled, slowing his momentum until he hovered before them.

Valentean's eyes met those of his reptilian brother, and Kayden uttered a low growl while spreading his wings further out to open his belly to attack. It was a dare, a goad, a challenge laid out between the two. Kayden did not fear Valentean or Seraphina, so content was he to bask in his superiority. Individually, neither princess nor animus warrior posed a threat to the mighty Rosinanti, but together, Valentean vowed they would teach Kayden the meaning of humility and fear.

He spoke not a word as the white glow of light erupted from his eyes. He glanced sidelong at his princess whose azure energy filled her round pupils. Valentean held his right arm out, palm upturned toward Seraphina who reached out to take it. He braced for the rush of energy he remembered from the Northern Magic, that empowering might which had filled them, made them one, and allowed them to topple Aleksandra herself. Valentean took a sharp intake of breath in anticipation of the explosion of power but found only the faintest echo of its might pass between them.

Valentean's head snapped toward Seraphina, who returned his gaze with panic dawning upon her face. Why wasn't it working? What were they doing wrong? There was power passing between them, but it was nothing like what they had experienced in the Northern Magic. It was not nearly enough to combat Kayden. At that time, there had been perfect symmetry between the two. They moved and spoke as if they were one. All sense of individual identity had vanished in the face of what they had become. Valentean still felt like himself, still shuddered inwardly at the death-bringing demon that filled the night sky.

Everything dies, Valentean…

"What are you waiting for?" Maura yelled. Valentean looked at her helplessly and thrust an arm out toward the dragon's exposed belly. Seraphina followed suit a fraction of a second later as a jagged shard of ice the size of three grown men formed and hurtled upwards at Kayden. The black dragon made not one move to defend itself as their attack shattered like glass against the scales that covered his torso.

It seemed even the power of gods could not last forever. The energy they had once unknowingly tapped into remained locked beyond a veil of their own useless ignorance. The light died in Valentean's eyes as he gripped Seraphina's hand tightly, looking at his two companions with a look of panicked apology. There was nothing that could be done to save them.

Kayden, seemingly bored with their attempt at upending him roared down at his foes, nearly bursting their eardrums with the cacophonous volume of his bellow. He thrust his wings once, creating a forceful gust that sent all three of them falling back onto the hard stone. As Valentean braced for the finality of Kayden's attack, he was shocked as the behemoth turned from them, flying higher into the air, back toward the city.

"He didn't attack," Seraphina said between frenzied gasps of breath.

"He didn't have to…" Valentean replied quietly, watching his brother soar back into the night. "He wants me to watch…"

"Is there nothing we can do?" Maura cried out, tears of frustration falling in streaks down her cheeks. As Valentean was about to answer, he was met with a burst of heat from the direction of Kackritta Castle, and a glare so bright, it lit the entire area as though it were noon.

A massive fusillade of red flame flew out of the gaping hole in Kackritta Castle, engulfing Kayden, who recoiled, shrieking, through the air. A collective gasp rose out from the displaced and panicked populace as Aleksandra floated out of the wreckage of her home, twin fireballs dancing along her palms, her eyes aglow with crimson energy.

"What!" Seraphina exclaimed in disbelief as her sister flew into the fray, sending a shower of hungry fire soaring through the air to strike at the black dragon. Kayden cried out in a reptilian shrill as he was propelled through the sky, a tumbling mass of bulk, scales, and wings as he dropped, smoking, to the ground. The colossal impact of his landing upended an entire neighborhood of Kackritta's lower income housing district.

"What on Terra is happening?" Maura screamed, now on her feet and clutching at the rampart wall in front of her. Kayden leapt back into the sky, but Aleksandra was instantly on him, firing off a steady blaze which drove Kayden back over the city wall. Then, with a gesture, every flame burning around Kackritta City leapt upwards and formed around Aleksandra, creating a massive ball of crackling inferno which she held above her head like a miniature sun. With a cry of exertion, the princess heaved the gargantuan orb of fire toward the black dragon, where it collided with his beastly form, creating a deafening explosion that bathed the entire countryside in harsh light.

"A dragon has attacked Kackritta City," Valentean said, as realization dawned in his frazzled mind, "murdering the royal family."

Kayden took off into the sky, his scales smoking and scorched in the aftermath of the princess's attack. Seraphina gasped as she followed her animus warrior's train of thought. "A sorceress with the power to control fire has come before the people of Kackritta and driven the dragon away…"

"No…" Maura said, "she's…"

"She's recreating the Great Rosinanti War…" Valentean said, as the sounds of a jubilant kingdom erupted into a joyous mixture of exaltation below him.

"She's uniting the kingdom behind her…" Seraphina said in mounting horror.

"No," Valentean said, "she's going to unite the entire planet."

"So smart," Valentean heard a voice say, rising up behind him. He turned to come face to face with General Zouka, who in the commotion had managed to sneak up on the trio undetected. Before Valentean could make a move, the prepared Gorram stabbed a short dagger into the animus warrior's gut. The universe dimmed around him until the only sound his darkening mind could discern was Seraphina's horrified shriek.

No flame can burn forever…

IX: SERAPHINA'S STRUGGLE

Seraphina forgot how to breathe as Zouka roughly pulled the blood-stained blade from Valentean's stomach and jabbed it back through the animus warrior's torso three more times. The Gorram's brutish, swift strikes seemed to lash out in slow motion, carving deep into the flesh of the man she loved without a hint of mercy or compassion.

The princess heard a scream, as though it came from far off, only to realize the shriek of horror had involuntarily leapt from her own throat. In her rising panic, the power of order roared like a river through her body, empowering her in this unthinkable moment. Small electric sparks erupted around her legs, arms, and head, given off by the swell of magic gathering within, begging to be unleashed.

Zouka's face shone with bloodthirsty fervor as he stared into Valentean's darkening eyes. He paid no mind to Seraphina or Maura, and that mistake was going to cost him. Seraphina's horror subtly shifted to all-consuming fury. Her left arm rose, her index and middle fingers pointed at the general. With a scream of unquenchable rage, she released her power in the form of a thick bolt of blue lightning which erupted from her outstretched fingertips and clawed through the air. The sizzling spell struck Zouka in the center of the chest as he was about to plunge the knife down once more.

The Gorram let out a gasp that sounded more surprised than pained and released his hold on Valentean's limp body as Seraphina's soaring fury threw him from the rampart. He smashed roughly into the roof of a nearby general store before rolling off its edge, vanishing into the darkness of Kackritta City's streets. Valentean crumpled to the ground, his legs folded beneath him, arms flopping like wet noodles. Both Seraphina and Maura rushed forward to catch him.

Maura had been closer and hooked her arms beneath the sinking animus warrior's shoulders, slowly guiding him to the ground as she fell beneath his weight. Seraphina knelt beside them, hands pressed against the gaping wounds in Valentean's stomach, trying to stop the spouting fountain of blood which erupted out of him.

"Val, no," she whimpered, looking into his eyes, which began to slowly close. "Val, look at me!" she cried out, feeling helpless as the life seeped from her love, staining the white robes of his oath to her and pattering onto the stony floor.

"Valentean, you're okay," Maura said, tapping the side of the fallen warrior's cheek with her palm. "Come on, you can do this. You're the white dragon. Come on, Valentean, don't give in!"

Seraphina wanted to chide the girl. Valentean would never give up. He had never given up on her; he didn't have the weakness of a quitter in him. If there was a way to beat this horrifying reality, Valentean would find it.

"Val, listen to me," she implored, bringing her blood-stained hand up to caress his pale cheek. His skin already felt cold. "Val, you can't leave me. Please, Val." He stared at her face through half open slits of emerald between his caving eyelids. She did not know if he could comprehend anything she was saying, or if he could see her at all. "I love you, Val!"

"He has to be able to heal from this!" Maura stated, breaking through their tender moment. "There's no way a dragon-god dies from a knife wound!"

"I have no idea!" Seraphina nearly shouted. "For all I know, he's dying right here!" Her anxiety and grief outweighed her ability to contemplate Maura's question. She knew not whether her protector would be able to heal from such a grisly assault. Tears streamed down her cheeks as her desperate mind imagined a life without her constant companion, her unquestioning protector, the only love she could ever know.

"Seraphina!" Maura cried out, her voice tensed with fear. The princess managed to tear her eyes away from Valentean for a solitary second to follow Maura's focus and gasped as two dozen brutish Skirlack soldiers advanced down the rampart toward them. She turned around and noticed a group of similar size approaching from behind them as well. They were surrounded.

The princess gritted her teeth in frustration and gazed through a mist of tears at her animus warrior. She took a deep, calming breath, leaned in, kissed Valentean on his cold lips and stood. Both hands curled into shaking fists at her side. Valentean would never back away from a challenge. He would meet these monsters head on, determined to protect her no matter the cost to his own life. Seraphina's eyes narrowed at the approaching demon horde, each one identical to the nightmare beast that had nearly ended her as a child. It was an army of her worst fears brought to life. She was afraid, but she knew Valentean had never let fear stay his hand, and neither would it stop her from protecting the one person she valued above all else.

The demons were no more than three meters away when Seraphina leapt into the sky, hovering above the ground as radiant blue energy ripped across her eyes. She swept her arms up as she reached out with her consciousness, pulling a large swell of water from the River of Freedom, hundreds of meters below. The massive globule rocketed toward her and surrounded Seraphina, Maura, and Valentean in a tight liquid barrier which separated them from the Skirlack on three sides. The open end of her fluid shield looked out over the countryside and the River of Freedom from which it was born. With a grunt of exertion, Seraphina urged the shard of light within her to freeze her temporary haven solid, forming a magically impenetrable fortress within.

The Skirlack soldiers arrived a fraction of a second after the spell had solidified. Seraphina could hear them slamming their powerful fists and bulky bodies into the ice, and continued to hold her arms out, giving it added strength through the power of her will.

Maura looked up at her, still cradling Valentean on her lap as he bled. "Will it hold?" she called out over the thumping noise of the Skirlack's attempts to penetrate their defense.

"Not forever," Seraphina answered, struggling as every pounding blow weakened the magic which safeguarded their lives. "We have to get him out of here!"

"How? We're surrounded!"

Seraphina's gaze shifted to the open section of the ice dome, reaching out again to the flowing liquid of the river. A stream of crystalline water rose into the air, and latched onto the rampart. Another thought from Seraphina's frazzled mind froze it into a curved chute that led down into the flowing river's surging stream.

"Get him out, Maura," Seraphina yelled as small cracks began to form along the ice.

"What about you?" Maura cried out.

"I need to hold them off," Seraphina said, the words difficult to force out as such continued pounding against her magic began to take a physical toll.

"I'm not going anywhere without you! I'm not going to let another person sacrifice themselves!"

"Get him out!" Seraphina shrieked in both annoyance and desperation. "He might still have a chance! We don't know the extent of his healing power! But if those things get through, they *will* kill him, and you know what will happen if he dies!" She watched realization blossom behind Maura's eyes. Valentean's death would be the endgame for Aleksandra and The Faithful, their ultimate goal achieved. Ignis would cross into this dimension, and all would be lost. "You're not just protecting a friend, Maura; you're saving the entire planet!"

Maura nodded and began to drag Valentean over toward the chute that would deliver them to safety, leaving a trail of bright red blood. "You'll follow once it's all clear?"

"I will," Seraphina said as Maura grunted and lifted Valentean just enough to place him back first on the icy slide. "Maura," the princess called out, causing the young woman to lock eyes with her once more, "Please protect him…"

"I will," Maura replied with a nod, a tear falling off her cheek, "I promise."

"And tell him that I love him!"

"He knows."

"Just tell him!"

"All right…" Maura pushed Valentean further onto the curved ice and laid down behind him, hooking both of her arms beneath his armpits. "You had better hurry and join us, you spoiled twit!"

"I will be right behind, you infuriating fool!" Maura smiled at Seraphina lightly, a new respect for the princess seeming to shine through her stare. With one more nod, she pushed both herself and Valentean onto the chute and slid with him down the steep, winding slope into the water below. As they impacted the flowing liquid, Seraphina could sense them. Maura resurfaced, keeping Valentean's head aloft. A silent order from the princess urged the river to flow faster, sweeping both Valentean and Maura in its wake and propelling them away from Kackritta City with unnatural speed.

Seraphina breathed a sigh of relief as they disappeared from sight. The cracks in her protective ice dome deepened. The Skirlack demons would break through at any moment, and she had wanted to give Valentean and Maura more time and distance to aid in their flight.

She decided not to give the Skirlack the satisfaction of shattering her barrier. If they wanted a fight, then she would take it to them. The princess slowly brought both of her hands against her chest and focused on the power of order within, gathering it and feeling the calming serenity pulsating and beating like a second heart. Her entire body, and subsequently, the protective ice fortification began to glow a pale blue. Seraphina threw her arms outward with a scream of exertion and the dome shattered, throwing the Skirlack back. Some plummeted from the ramparts to their deaths, while the bulk of the attacking horde remained on the stony path, now rising to their feet.

Seraphina attacked, liquefying the broken shards of the former dome and summoning the water to her, where it flowed around her body in two circular arcs that crossed one another diagonally. She lashed out with her magic, sending powerful streams of liquid rage at her foes, striking as though they were whips and driving the Skirlack back. As she continued to exert herself, blue sparks began to shine around her arms and head. She called upon the lightning within her, creating a cage of electricity around her body. She lashed out with dazzling bright bolts of azure lightning, shocking the remaining demons as fast as they would advance.

This lightning was so different from the electric spells she had dabbled in prior to her ascension as the spirit of order. This was so much stronger and far wilder. The lightning erupted from her fingers with such force that it threw her aim off course. While some of the scorching static managed to land fatal blows on her red-skinned opponents, many of them veered off, striking glancing blows that threw the Skirlack away from her—wounding but not killing.

Seraphina's world was a crackling storm of lightning. She struck with no mercy, turning in a circle, sending scorching, clawing bolts of electricity in every direction. The princess was determined to show these monsters that she was no longer the helpless child whom they had once wounded so easily. The fact that they all shared the face of her childhood tormentor only fueled the fury behind her attacks. It was so easy to lose herself in the thrill of the fight, to feel mighty for once and revel in the vengeance she enacted upon the Skirlack. However, she held her will with iron determination, holding a vision of Valentean in her mind's eye, remembering what she was fighting for.

As she continued to lash out, Seraphina sensed a powerful presence rocketing toward her. She jumped to the side, narrowly missing the blade of General Zouka's black broadsword as the Gorram landed upon the rampart. One hulking red-skinned brute ran at her, arms raised. Seraphina held out a hand and summoned a translucent hex which slammed into the demon, sending it soaring away from her.

Zouka pressed his attack, running at the princess, screaming, sword held over his head. As the massive man swung a powerful cleaving strike at Seraphina, the princess called upon the same invisible spell to veer his slash to the side, narrowly missing and cutting a blue shard of fabric from her dress. Seraphina attempted to strike out with a concentrated bolt of lightning once more, aiming at the center of Zouka's armored chest. The attack exploded from her fingertips with shocking strength and flew off course, landing a glancing blow on the general's right shoulder, causing him to drop his sword and spin, landing on his knees.

The Skirlack rushed at her. Seraphina knew that it was only a matter of time before she was overwhelmed, now that Zouka had returned to the fray. She took a deep breath and leaped from the rampart down into the shattered remains of Kackritta City, gliding onto a nearby roof. Looking back, she saw Zouka bound from the high wall after her, landing with a thud on the same roof, the shingles cracking under his girth.

"You cannot run from me, Princess," he said slowly, the dueling scorch marks of her lightning having dented and discolored his armor on the chest and shoulder.

"I wasn't trying to," Seraphina replied, lashing out with blue lightning once more. Her spell veered uncontrollably to the left, giving Zouka the opportunity to spin to the right and advance upon her. The speed in which the big man moved was unreal, and Seraphina weaved a protective blue shield around her body to brace for impact. Zouka slammed a gauntlet-covered fist into the princess's stomach, pushing Seraphina into the air before she fell to her hands and knees. Despite the shield's protection, the air had been pushed from her lungs by the force of the general's assault and she gasped for breath.

Zouka roughly grabbed the princess by the hair and flung her from the roof. Seraphina's arms and legs flailed as she soared through the air, her lower back slamming into the top of an adjacent building, forcing her to roll onto the shingled structure. Pain exploded throughout her lower back as she scrambled to her feet. Zouka easily leapt after her, smiling as he stalked his prey. Seraphina pulled water from the air and attempted to heave it at the general, but in her mind's addled state, the liquid quivered and splashed uselessly to the roof.

"So weak," Zouka remarked, advancing on her. "You are an insult to your family's name. Even with the power of order at your command, you are still the same weak girl you've always been, Your Highness."

A tear of frustration squeezed out of the corner of Seraphina's eyes. The general was correct. The power of order was failing her. Desperately, she turned and leapt into the air, trying to take off in a magically controlled glide to create some distance.

Zouka was far too fast and caught Seraphina by the ankle, slamming her face first into the roof, shattering several shingles in her rough landing. The general tightened his grip on the princess and spun, taking her into the air and gaining momentum before flinging the young woman, with all of his might, further into the city. Seraphina smashed into one roof and ricocheted off, soaring over several blocks before crashing into the hard street at the mouth of the bridge leading into Kackritta Castle.

She gazed up at her smoldering home, and the scorched hole that had been torn into its face. Plumes of black smoke still rose into the air, and Seraphina knew that somewhere in that mess laid the bodies of her mother and father, along with countless other men and women who had sworn a vow to keep Kackritta safe. She heard a deep thud behind her which told the princess that the general had caught up.

Seraphina rose to her hands and knees and coughed a small trickle of blood onto the pavement. She had to rise, had to defend the honor of her home, the death of her parents, and the slaughter of her people, but she just didn't have the strength.

"Pathetic," Zouka said, she could hear his slow intentional footsteps as he advanced. "My people abhor weakness such as yours. It was a punishable offense. Weak women such as you were dropped into the fighting pits with hungry dogs and given a short sword to defend themselves. Do you know how many of them emerged? Not a single one, because weakness cannot be overcome. It is who you are. No matter what kind of power you surround yourself with, at the end of the day, you are still a meek little flower who needs the protection of her animus warrior to survive. If not for your sister's orders, I would disembowel you right here and right now, girl."

Her arms shook as she tried to push herself to a standing position. She was taxed beyond her limits, both physically and emotionally. She felt the echo of rage on the edge of her mystical exhaustion. She wanted so badly to rise to her feet, to hurl lightning, water, ice, fists, feet, anything she could at this horrible man. Not only had he batted her about the city streets like trash, but he had wounded Valentean, possibly killed him.

No, she thought, *don't even think that, Seraphina!*

The general unsheathed the sword from his back, holding it aloft with both hands. "Exactly as I thought. You cannot even rise to defend yourself. Your sister's orders be damned; you are not fit for this world." He raised the titanic blade above his head and savored the moment of stillness before the inevitable slash that would cleave the life from Seraphina's body. The ebony edge fell toward her. As Seraphina began to close her eyes and accept that her life had come to an end, they snapped back open, pulsating and glowing as she felt her body rise on its own. Her left hand shot out, independent of her wishes, and a wave of energy slammed into the general. He fell back several meters, until he managed to gain control of his momentum and rolled back to his feet.

What was happening? Her body had suddenly come alive, reinvigorated and pulsating with magical might. Seraphina felt relief awash with disbelief and fear. She was like a passenger in her own flesh. The magic continued to gather within her as Zouka stormed forth. Seraphina threw her arms out to the side. An explosion ripped its way out from her and hung in the air around her body. She felt cold and confined, and the world looked strange, as though it were crystallizing.

Ice, she realized, *forming around my body?* The numbing frost continued to grow in the face of the general's approach, engulfing Seraphina and freezing her in place. She took a terrified gasp as her own power solidified around her face. The princess's field of vision was engulfed in a bright blue hue and she moved no more.

Zouka skidded to a stop as the massive globe of ice finished forming. It hung there, floating a meter off the ground, bobbing up and down. He could just vaguely make out the silhouette of Seraphina's body: dark, blurred and unmoving. Even the strands of her hair hung frozen out to the sides. The only feature still fully visible through the haze of frost was that of her eyes, pulsating and glowing with the light blue shine of order.

Coward, Zouka thought in disgust. *She cannot hide in there forever!* The general gathered up his sword and leapt into the air, bringing it down upon the hovering sphere. An instantaneous shock of blue lightning erupted out from the cold smooth surface and struck him, sending the Gorram spinning and crashing onto his side.

He shook his head free of the momentary haze as blue sparks still tingled around his extremities. This defense had lashed out with far greater strength than any of the princess's previous attacks. What had happened? Where had this come from? And if Seraphina had this energy within her, why was she hiding now?

"You can't stay in there indefinitely, Princess," he spat at the icy orb. "Rest while you can because when you step foot out of this paltry prison you've fashioned for yourself, I'll be waiting to end you! And just remember that, somewhere out there, your Rosinanti protector's blood stains the ground by *my* doing!"

He knew not whether she could hear him within her self-imposed confinement, and did not care. Zouka had not been felled by an opponent since the days in which he stood beside his own people. Now, in one night, it had happened twice. The Rosintai he accepted as an equal and felt a swell of excitement burn within him as the mighty dragon prince had knocked him about. But to be flung aside by this weak-willed human woman was humiliating.

There would be no more mercy. He would face these foes once more; it was inevitable given what he knew of Princess Aleksandra's plans. Until then, he would prepare. He would wait for the boy to heal and for the girl to emerge from her conspicuous hiding place. He would wait, and then, for the first time, he would demonstrate the fullest extent of his long-buried power with the whole of humanity as witness.

X: A NEW WORLD

Maura had struggled to hold Valentean's head above the flowing force of the river as the churning water battered them. Seraphina had all but sacrificed herself to cover their escape, and she had asked only one thing of Maura before diving into the fray.

Maura, please protect him.

Maura owed the princess that much. She had seen strength in Seraphina's eyes that had nothing to do with the unnatural blue glow of Aqua's power. This girl, who at one time Maura had written off as a stuffy, spoiled brat, had grown so much in the time since the destruction of Lazman. A particularly choppy burst of water forced Maura's head under the river's surface, she pushed Valentean up, ensuring that he did not join her.

Maura managed to breach the water once more, and gasped in a much-needed breath of sweet oxygen, as the current suddenly died around them. The river ceased its rapid streaming and returned to a state of peaceful meandering. Maura gripped Valentean with renewed force and kicked her legs to move them up onto the riverbank, where she set the animus warrior down. She coughed river water up out of her lungs and laid back against the soft silt, glad to be, once again, on dry land.

The current had stopped, but what did that mean? Had something happened to Seraphina? Had they simply traveled far enough? Or had they passed outside of Seraphina's sphere of influence? Either way, Maura looked back with trepidation, hoping to see the princess trailing behind them, safely in one peace, ready to regroup. She stared for nearly five minutes, but there was no movement, save for the river's gentle flow.

Wincing through her disappointment, Maura turned to Valentean, who lay on his stomach beside her. She slowly and carefully turned him over onto his back. He did not grunt or move in any way and she feared the worst. She was relieved when she laid him down and saw the slow, ragged rise and fall of his chest.

Maura gingerly lifted the bloodstained fabric over the animus warrior's abdomen to ascertain the extent of the damage done by the general's blade. She gasped when she saw it. There were no wounds, just small spots of discoloration where there should have been gore soaked gashes. Maura let out a small laugh of disbelief that nearly turned into a sob. She brought her knees up to her chest and buried her face atop them.

"He's all right, Seraphina," she said aloud, as though the princess could somehow hear her from wherever she was.

"Sera..." she heard Valentean grunt beside her in response. She turned her weary head toward her fallen comrade and saw that he lay with his eyes still closed, his head moving back and forth with eerie slowness. He tried to raise a shaking hand, but weakness quickly overtook him and it dropped into the dirt. Maura reached over and took Valentean's hand from the ground and laid it neatly across his chest. She looked upon him now in a far different manner than she ever had previously. At one time, she found him attractive, an interest in him forming almost instantly upon laying eyes on his chiseled face and lush green eyes. Then she had, to her fault, imprinted the tragedy of Lazman upon him and viewed him as an enemy.

It had taken Aqua's death to snap her away from such misplaced anger. But even afterwards, she had been hesitant around both Valentean and Seraphina. Their proximity had caused her to replay those traumatizing moments in her mind over and over again: the sound as her father was violently decapitated, the intense heat of the flames that ate at places once so familiar. She would recall the sight of that black-scaled behemoth hovering above them, waiting to exhale death and destruction down upon her, wiping everything she had ever known off the face of Terra in one haunting final moment.

She worried that these memories and emotions would never leave her, that she was doomed to replay them repeatedly. Even as she rotted in a prison cell for weeks, she thought of nothing else. As Sophie returned day after day to spout the spiritual nonsense of that ridiculous chaos-worshipping religion, Maura had retreated to a dark corner of her mind recalling those visions of destruction and loss. Each time those memories performed their terrible dance, she wallowed deeper and deeper within her own internal prison of despair.

When she had been summoned to the throne room of Kackritta Castle, she was almost hoping that she would be executed. She had wanted to rejoin her father, rejoin the entire village of Lazman in death. Maura had fallen so far that the carefree, brash young woman she had once been was but a hollow memory of someone else's life. But then she had found her purpose once more. Valentean and Seraphina's heroic actions had shown her the value of her continued existence. Maura realized that she owed it to both of them to carry on.

"You're all right," she said to Valentean, softly patting his muscular chest, "you're going to be all right, you crazy, wonderful man."

"You shouldn't get ahead of yourself, dear," a female voice called out from behind her. Maura turned slowly and saw a large horse-drawn cart filled with supplies, and four figures clad in heavy animal furs smiling at her. There were three men, all large and wielding a variety of weaponry from swords, to knives, axes, and flails. In front of them was the woman who had interrupted her, seconds earlier. She was tall and lean, ginger-haired and mousy, with a scrunched-up nose dotted by far too many freckles.

"If I'm not mistaken, those are animus robes your sleepy friend there is wearing. You're traveling with a fancy lord, girl. No doubt he's carrying something of value."

"Piss off and nobody has to get hurt," Maura said.

"I don't think that's really up to you, dear," the ugly girl said with a laugh which Maura likened to that of a braying ass. The thief drew from her belt a pair of short daggers, clearly trying to intimidate a water-logged young woman out of her possessions.

Maura sighed and slowly rose to her feet, grunting and stretching her aching joints. She looked at the daggers in the ugly girl's hands. She held them like an amateur. Her grip was laughably poor, and Maura felt it was a shame for such beautiful weapons to be in the possession of someone who hadn't even bothered to learn their proper use. She raised her gaze up to meet that of the ginger and felt a smile tugging at the corner of her mouth. She was amused and excited, and for the first time since that fateful night in the Lazman town square, Maura felt like herself again. She audibly cracked her knuckles.

"Let's see what you can do then, gorgeous."

Echoes of dull pain reverberated through Vahn's body as he slowly regained consciousness. He opened his eyes and found himself in a dimly lit wooden room which smelled of mold and smoke. His midsection still throbbed from that one all mighty slam of the general's fist, and he grimaced, holding his torso as he sat up.

As the elite warrior moved his legs, he heard a clanking sound, as though metal were dragging along the wooden floor. Looking down, he saw that a metal cuff was attached to his ankle, over his boot. The thick heavy links of chain wound from the circle of iron across the floor where they were connected to the opposite wall by a heavily bolted metal base.

Vahn realized he was leaning against a circular window composed of wooden blinds. He forced them open and peeked out into the night. What he saw made him gasp in shock and grief. Kackritta City was decimated. Huge swaths of destruction had been carved throughout, leaving nothing but charred devastation in their wake. Kackritta Castle still smoldered, and a massive hole had been torn in its side. He realized that he was on the very top floor of a run-down old house in the city's slum, located far from the decimation.

He stared through glistening unshed tears at the home he loved so well, now a burnt-out husk of its former self. He tore his eyes away from the senseless destruction and slammed his palm down on the blinds, closing many of them, while smoke and the acrid stench of scorched flesh wafted in through those he had missed. He took a deep, calming breath, trying to push these awful feelings of grief and dread from his mind.

He looked around the room with confusion. Why was he here? Shouldn't he have been in the dungeon of Kackritta Castle? Why, then, was he so far from the kingdom's official prison cells? The room was barren and lit only by the thin beams of moonlight that filtered in through the closed blinds of the room's three windows. A heavy layer of dust covered nearly every bit of what, now, Vahn could clearly make out as an attic, save for a trail leading from the center of the room to where he now lay. Squinting through the darkness, Vahn could scarcely make out a trapdoor in the floor that led down into the dilapidated house.

Movement from a shadowy corner caught his attention and Vahn's head snapped to the side, his eyes focusing through the darkness as the black-robed figure of Kayden slowly walked into a thin shaft of moonlight that illuminated half of his face.

"Kayden," Vahn said slowly, "what's happened?"

"She wanted you dead, Father," he said slowly. "She had a list of military personnel and officials of the kingdom, and you were on it."

"Aleksandra?"

Kayden nodded, his eyes moving to the floor as he swept a bit of dust aside with his left boot. "You were supposed to die in the throne room, and I was supposed to carry it out…"

"Why didn't you?"

"I don't know…"

"You're lying to me, Kayden," Vahn said, using the same tone of voice he always had while scolding his larger son as a child.

"I just…" Kayden looked pained as he tore his gaze away from Vahn and slowly tromped over to one of the attic's windows, moving the blinds and looking out. "I accomplished so much today, took so many lives. They deserved to die for their arrogance, and for the crimes humanity has inflicted upon the Rosinanti race. But you didn't deserve to die, Father."

Vahn's worst fears were proven true in that horrifying instant. Kayden was responsible for this brutal scene of death. How many had died? Hundreds? Thousands? "Kayden, this is not you…" he started, causing Kayden to slam his gloved palm against the window, blotting out the light as he rounded angrily on the old man.

"How would you know who I am? Who I *truly* am?"

"Because I'm your father!" Vahn insisted with authority, despite his precarious position.

"You are *not* my father!" Kayden's voice shrieked, and Vahn thought he could vaguely make out the wet streak of tears against his cheek. "My father is some Rosinanti who I never met, who died one thousand years ago! You're just some old man who found me in a cave!"

Kayden's words cut Vahn to the core. For over two decades, he had feared the day when this conversation would occur. "I have loved you as my son since the day you entered my life."

"Because you didn't know what I really was!"

"I've known long before you found out, Kayden."

"That's a lie!"

"I always knew that there was something supernatural surrounding the two of you. I tried to hide it away from the world. I attempted to guide you down a peaceful path."

"But you didn't know that we were Rosinanti! Had you known that, you would have killed us because that is what humans do!"

"I had my suspicions," Vahn said slowly. "For years, I've wondered. Now, I know for certain, and I don't care, Kayden."

"You … you're lying!" Kayden said, slowly advancing toward his father.

Vahn chose his next words carefully. "No matter who you are, Kayden, no matter what you've done, it changes nothing." Kayden reached Vahn and dropped to one knee, looking into the old man's eyes with curiosity, skepticism, and Vahn believed he could see a bit of hope in there, as well. "I will always love both you and Valentean, equally."

With alarming swiftness, Kayden's eyes darkened, and he sprang forward, grabbing his father by the throat with an impossibly strong grip, slamming the old man's head back into the wooden window.

"I think we both know that's a lie, Father," Kayden hissed in Vahn's ear. "Tell me something, when that ignorant fool defeated me in the tournament, did you clap? Did you cheer in the face of my humiliation?" Vahn gasped for breath as Kayden's grip tightened around his windpipe. "You say you love us equally, but who did you choose to bless with your training when *both* of your sons entered into the Oath of Animus? It wasn't me, Father, it was *him*! It's always been him! You've always showered him with your attention and your praise, making me feel like a stranger, a freeloader in my own home!"

Vahn's eyes bulged as his skin began to take on a pale blue color. He clutched at Kayden's arm, unable to so much as budge one of his mighty son's fingers. How could he make Kayden understand? How could he properly convey the reasons he had for his seemingly preferential treatment of Valentean?

"He … needed …it … more," Vahn managed to choke out. Confusion clouded Kayden's face and he released his grip. Vahn coughed air back into his aching lungs, reaching up to wipe tears from his eyes. "You were always … stronger, Kayden. You were always so confident, whereas your brother needed the extra push. I never doubted for a second that you would make a fine and strong animus warrior. One that Kackritta could be proud of. Your brother needed me more. I wasn't ignoring you, Kayden. I wasn't casting you out. I *trusted* you. I had more faith in your abilities than I did for Valentean."

Kayden stared at Vahn wide-eyed for what felt like an eternity. Vahn returned Kayden's manic gaze with the caring, compassionate, eyes of a father who spoke nothing but the truth. Kayden did not speak at first. He stood slowly to his full commanding height, his eyes never leaving Vahn's until he turned around and stalked slowly toward the trapdoor in the center of the room's floor. He bent down and pulled it open before standing straight once again, looking back over his shoulder.

"I may not have needed your attention, Father," he said slowly, softly, "but I wanted it." He stepped into the open air over the trapdoor and dropped out of sight, the heavy wooden passage slamming shut behind him.

Aleksandra walked amidst the charred blood-stained interior of what was once her parents' throne room. At her feet laid the headless, burnt corpses of the humans who had once controlled her life. Aleksandra found it oddly fitting that they had given her the gift of life, and she had taken it from them. She chuckled at the irony. Her mother often spoke of her own duty and destiny as the leader of Kackritta. She believed herself to be a person of importance, and in a way, she had been right. It had been her destiny to give birth to the savior of the world, and she had fulfilled that purpose long ago.

Aleksandra enjoyed the stillness of the destruction's aftermath. She could practically taste the fear that bubbled up from the people of Kackritta. The chaos that fueled their paranoia churned within her. The feeling made her flush with happiness and caused her heart to flutter. She wondered if this was what love felt like.

"Your Highness," a deep voice said, cutting through the delicious silence. She turned and saw General Zouka, his armor dented and scorched.

"General," she replied in way of greeting. "It appears as though the Rosinanti presented a challenge to you."

"Indeed," Zouka replied, looking haggard and annoyed. She knew that he above all others understood the power she possessed. The Gorram respected strength, and Aleksandra was the strongest being on the planet by incredible leaps and bounds. That, above all else, commanded the general's unquestioning loyalty. "However, your sister…"

"I am cognizant of the situation, thank you, General," she said sharply, turning from him.

"But Your Majesty…"

"If that will be all, General, I shall thank you to take your leave." Aleksandra could imagine the dumbfounded expression on his face. There was silence for nearly a full minute before the sound of the general's receding steps reached her ears.

She had been watching her sister. She sighed in annoyance as Seraphina utilized the Harbinger's sacrilegious power to upend Zouka several times before sealing herself within an impenetrable fortress of ice which still floated just below Kackritta Castle. There would be time for that later. Seraphina's rebellion was an annoyance, but she would see reason in time. Until then, Aleksandra had to show her sister the tough love that would harden and strengthen her. Just as chaos had to unfold around the whole of humanity to strengthen and unite them, so, too, must Seraphina endure equal amounts of strife until she arose from the flames, better for the experience.

Aleksandra slowly approached the open wall and gazed down at her kingdom. It was beaten, nearly decimated by her animus warrior. But still, as she looked out, she saw her people picking one another up, cooperating as they rooted through the wreckage seeking out survivors and holding one another in shows of solidarity. They had survived chaos. The weak had been burned away and those who walked from the blaze unharmed were now rebounding, regrouping, and her heightened senses could feel the hardening of the kingdom's resolve.

"This stratagem of yours worked splendidly, Mistress," Aurax said from beside her. His presence had not surprised the mighty sorceress. Nothing ever surprised or frightened once such as her.

"Indeed," Aleksandra said softly, closing her eyes and breathing in the smoke carried up to this great height from smoldering swaths of chaos. "The gift of the goddess has befallen Kackritta, as it had one thousand years ago. Now, once again, they shall ascend from weakness and become mighty."

"Though even now the Shogai flees across the countryside, and The Harbinger sleeps in our midst."

Aleksandra's head snapped toward her trusted servant, her eyes narrowing as they glowed with crimson rage.

"My sister is *not* The Harbinger," she said slowly with more than the edge of a threat straining her words.

"Of course, Excellency," Aurax replied with a polite genuflection. "However, The Harbinger's power still rests within her, and she continues to use it against the true believers of the Faithful. I need not remind you that, together, she and the Shogai managed to defeat you."

"You do not have to caution me in this regard," the princess replied as the crimson death stare upon her face softened. "Valentean can run wherever he pleases. Once I am free and my power fully unleashed upon the world, there will be no barren corner of Terra in which he can hide from me."

"He could become stronger as we wait."

"What would you suggest, Aurax?" she asked, annoyance beginning to bleed into her words. "He is formidable, and should I face him in this limited form, I am not certain I could defeat him."

"Of course, Mistress, please forgive my inquisitive musings on the night of your greatest victory." The Skirlack Cleric took a step away from the ledge, allowing Aleksandra to stand there undeterred, gazing out over the land she was now to rule. The totality of her new station stirred mixed feelings of excitement and pride. For her entire life, she had been told that one day she would rule Kackritta, and now, here she stood atop the crown jewel of what would become an empire that spanned all of Terra.

"Have you walked amongst the rabble, my loyal one?"

"Indeed, I have, Most Holy One."

"And what of their temperament?"

"They are humans, Excellency. They cower, they wail, they mourn. But beneath that, there lies a sense of awe at your display. There are whispers amongst them that you are … a deity … mostly from those who mistakenly believe your holy ancestor to be divine, herself."

"Well, the time has come to educate them. Is the gift you bestowed up me prepared?"

"Of course." Aurax bowed once more and backed away, vanishing in a haze of red, leaving Aleksandra alone.

The world was at her feet, she need only take one step forward and claim it. She savored the moment, pushing all thoughts of her deceased parents and their ill-fated regime from her mind. Raising one foot, Aleksandra stepped off the ledge and continued walking along the open air as though it were solid ground.

She took several steps, naught more than a tiny red spot amongst the night sky. Many of Kackritta's survivors had poured into the central hub of the city, out before the giant bridge which led to Kackritta Castle. Many of them gazed in wonder at the shining frigid sphere which housed Seraphina, but none dared approach it. What few Kackrittan soldiers were left alive surrounded it on all sides, keeping onlookers away. Many more still ushered into the center of the hub until a sea of moving humanity scurried below her. Aleksandra curled her lip in disgust; they resembled an insect hive, scurrying about beneath her boots.

As the first of them noticed the skyward disturbance that was their princess, cries of shock and pointed fingers rose up toward her. The commotion built until an indiscernible rabble of noise erupted. Aleksandra decided a demonstration was needed to awe them to silence. She stretched both arms out to the side, from which dueling streams of flame erupted, flowing out of her, illuminating the thousands of shocked onlookers.

Aleksandra quenched the flames, straightening her spine. Her arms remained outstretched, all the while silently casting a spell over her vocal chords which would amplify her voice, ensuring that all would hear the most important speech in one thousand years.

"My people," the princess began, "you huddle before me, burnt, beaten, and bruised but, I am pleased to see, not broken." There was a murmur of agreement from below, but it was quiet. Their attention was fixated upon her, desperate for answers, for hope. "I look down upon you, and I sense the dread any sane man, woman, or child would feel in such a time of tragedy. There is no abashment to be found in fear. It is natural, and it keeps us human. Just know that your friends, your neighbors, your families were taken, and nothing can be done to reclaim them from such ruination. But rest easy knowing that they shall soon be *avenged*."

She felt the pride of a people united spread beneath her and knew that she was prodding them in exactly the direction she sought. *Just a bit more,* she thought, pressing on with her speech.

"On this night, the darkest we've faced in over one thousand years, our ancient enemy returned from their rightful place in obsolescence. The Rosinanti have risen, more powerful than before, and they have openly and drastically engaged us." Their cries of terror fed her delight. Fear would keep them in line. "Just as they had once before, these monsters fell upon the peaceful humans of Terra and obliterated the queen and king of our fair home."

News of her parents' death sent a wave of panic coursing throughout the crowd as shocked exclamations of grief exploded from all corners of the gathering. Aleksandra held up one delicate hand, and they instantly fell silent under her command. *Perfect.*

"Yes, on this night, I mourn for my mother and father, your queen and king who, through a rule defined by tolerance and understanding, unwittingly fostered the environment in which these creatures were able to return, unnoticed. But fear not, good people of Kackritta, because as before a leader comes before you, blessed with the gift of the blaze." Twin fireballs erupted upon her palms as the people cried out. Many genuflected in reverence.

"I know that many among you seek to deify me for this unique gift. But, please, save your adoration for the true savior of Terra, the goddess through whose love and kindness I was granted these amazing abilities, as was my legendary ancestor before me." There was confusion emanating from the gathered mass of humanity but not outrage, not any form of resistance. Their desperation made them hers. She took a deep breath, preparing to share with them her ultimate truth, in the exact words that had captured her faith as a child, the exact words she had spoken to Valentean and her sister in Lazman. The truth behind their eternal struggle against the ancient evil.

"It has been said that Terra was once a paradise, ruled over by an ancient goddess known as Skirlack..."

Vahn stared through slits of the wooden window as knots of dread pulled at his insides. The princess wound a spirited tale of loss and betrayal. She spoke of a fallen goddess and the besieged faithful true believers who kept her flame burning for thousands upon thousands of years.

Her words were spoken with such sincerity, such passion and love, that Vahn knew the princess was not simply deceiving the masses. She actually believed what she was saying. A swell of pity clenched his heart for this young woman whom he had known since the day of her birth.

Vahn pulled on the chain that anchored him to the wall. He could not simply sit here and allow his city, his homeland, to fall like this. The weathered old attic wall gave in just a bit, and he knew that it was only a matter of time before he would be able to free himself. He braced his feet against the wall on either side of the chain's anchor point and tugged with all his might.

"The goddess loves you all," Aleksandra said upon completion of her tale. "She protects you, though you know nothing of her. She suffers, imprisoned in a torturous reality, but we have the power to free her. We have the power to bring divinity, grace, and peace back to Terra!" She had them, their awe-struck faces desperate for more information. "The Rosinanti now hide in plain sight, gaining our trust and lashing out viciously from the shadows. I am saddened to report that the black dragon which descended upon our home this evening was none other than my own animus warrior, Kayden Burai." There was a collective gasp of shock and several screams. "He and his brother, Valentean Burai, Champion Animus of Terra, are the leaders of this dragon insurrection! We as a kingdom took them in, sheltered them, fostered them with love and kindness. We cheered with national pride as they engaged one another in the Tournament of Animus, never knowing the truth behind their seemingly human faces."

Paranoia spread amongst them, exactly as she had planned. Let them look to their friends, their neighbors with a sense of dread. Let them trust no one save for her.

"It weighs heavily on my heart to admit my suspicions that there may be more Rosinanti hiding in our midst, behind the smiles of those we believe to know. That is why I implore all of you good people of Kackritta to be vigilant. We are all a part of this battle now, and we shall never suffer the tragedy of this night again!"

She took a deep breath; the people were solidly behind her. The truth of her passionate speech on the plight of the goddess had reached them. Now would come a true test of the faith she had instilled.

"This tragedy was an inexcusable act of war, but we as the kingdom of Kackritta did nothing to prevent it. Sadly, the leadership of my late parents led us into an era of complacency and weakness. As such, Kackritta became a shell of its former glory, and through our own inaction, we have tarnished the very name of our kingdom. Make no mistake, my people; to combat such a foe, we will need to unite the world as we once had! We cannot do it alone! We must become a conjoined empire of humanity, together under one leadership, one vision for the safety and security of our children, and our children's children!" A triumphant cry of support rose up, and Aleksandra fought the smile that wanted to erupt upon her face.

"We may defeat this foe once more on the field of battle, but I desire so much more than that! What we must do is create a global society which will eradicate not only this enemy but every potential threat that shall ever arise! We will create a society of human dominance, united under one vision, one destiny, and one faith! Those who reject the gifts of the goddess are the tool of the enemy and must be stamped out in the name of justice and security!" Another resounding roar flew up from the crowd.

"To that effect, we must cast off old traditions. We must be reborn in the fires of Skirlack's love! Kackritta has stood for one thousand years and now it lies in ruination! As such, on this night, the kingdom of Kackritta has died!" She raised one hand which glowed with the red power of chaos. Behind her, magical flames of her creation spread amongst what remained of Kackritta Castle, burning hotter and hotter until the stone towers began to melt and explode. The people gasped below her but not in fear. Flames erupted from the ground around the ruined palace, and the massive structure began to slowly sink. Squinting in concentration, Aleksandra threw her arms out to the side, and a fiery explosion obliterated what remained of her childhood home.

Maura piloted her newly acquired horse-drawn carriage across the countryside, trying to create some distance from Kackritta City, so Valentean could heal in peace. She kept a loose, one-handed grip on the reigns of the lone brown horse who led their cart along the dirt path. She wore the heavy animal skins of the ugly bandit girl who had foolishly attempted to attack them. Her other hand rested on the handle of one of the girl's twin daggers, both of which hung from her belt.

She had not killed the brigands, opting instead to incapacitate and strip them of their belongings, leaving them tied to a tree in naught but their underclothes. She vowed to put their ill-begotten supplies to good use in the inevitable journey to retrieve Seraphina and topple Aleksandra.

She glanced back to see Valentean still lying prone in the cart, the shaking of the wooden structure doing nothing to rouse him from his deep slumber. She sighed. At least he was still alive. Though Maura had to admit that the silence had become deafening between them. She was very much looking forward to his inevitable waking, if only to fill the long periods of quiet.

She shivered in the chilled evening air, thankful for the thick warmth of her pilfered attire. Her horse suddenly stopped and began to look back and forth in a panic, rearing up on its hind legs and whining against its restraints.

"Easy girl … um … boy?" She had not checked earlier to see which was accurate. The horse continued to thrash and rocked the cart to and fro. Maura pulled back on the reigns with both hands, attempting to control and calm the frightened steed. An instant later, she saw the cause of the animal's anxiety. It appeared floating above the mountain range that ran along the left side of the path. It was an immense, hovering piece of jagged, blackened ground that flew through the air with the swiftness of an airship.

Atop the soaring landscape sat the largest, most foreboding structure Maura had ever seen. It was black beyond black, a fortress of dread with six thin, jagged curved towers that rose into the air behind a tall spiked wall. In the center sat a thick pointed tower, nearly as wide as the structure itself, looming high above the rest. She gasped in wonder and terror alike.

How could anything so massive fly like that? It would be impressive had it not been so unnerving. Maura was not shocked to note that the floating fortress was heading in the direction of Kackritta. As it passed overhead, eclipsing the moonlight, Maura held her breath, hoping that whatever dark presence might be steering the castle would not notice them. She exhaled as the shard of land passed harmlessly over their heads and continued on its course. Whatever was happening back in the city, there were sure to be serious ramifications felt throughout the whole of Terra in its aftermath.

Seraphina, I hope you're safe!

Aleksandra stared with pride as the centerpiece of her new empire came into view, hovering over her city. Many of her subjects cried out in fear at first, clutching at one another as the massive shadow fell over them. Aleksandra simply raised her hands, as if quieting a noisy puppy, and they instantly complied.

"Behold, the long-forgotten Fortress of Skirlack, the mobile command center of Sorceress Bakamaya, hidden away in the years subsequent to the Great Rosinanti War. From this blessed sanctum, I shall rule over our new world. From this perch, I shall extend Skirlack's love to all corners of Terra, and from this seat of power, I shall crush the Rosinanti into obliteration *once and for all*!" Another score of cheers sounded, though she could feel their fear as they gazed at the foreboding palace of power. This was good; more fear would continue to keep them in line once initial paranoia over the Rosinanti's reappearance had subsided. "Our goddess has sent us one final gift."

She heard screams emanating from the outskirts of the gathered mass. As she looked down upon them, she could see the hulking brutish forms of Skirlack soldiers appearing throughout every street. They moved in from all sides and encircled the crowd, one thousand strong. There was mass terror as her people recoiled from the horde that would safeguard their home.

"Fear not. These are the children of Skirlack, sent by the goddess herself in the thousands to replace our decimated military force." The beasts bared their fangs at the gathering of humans and batted the air with their claws. She could sense their desire, their overwhelming need to descend into the throng of meat and begin tearing flesh from bone. But they dared not take a single step without her approval. "Those who follow the path of the righteous shall have nothing to fear from these noble protectors. But those who betray us, those who resist us, those who shun the love of the goddess, shall feed their bellies." The fear-fed chaos in the air was palpable and exhilarating. The Skirlack soldiers represented yet another form of control through fear that she would use to keep the foundation of her new empire intact.

"On this night, we shed weakness, we shed the complacency of the fools who led us in the past. We shall look forward as a family of humanity, united against the power of our ancient enemy. Kackritta is no more, and I shall not be the queen of a dead kingdom. I am empress of the most powerful nation to ever exist upon the face of Terra." She rose higher into the air, holding her arms out once more, allowing red flames to form upon her palms and travel up to her shoulders, burning like wings of fire. "Tonight, we create a new world, and we move forward not as the Kingdom of Kackritta, but as the glorious and never-ending *Empire of Aleksandrya*!"

The new empress threw her flaming arms into the sky and a giant red ball of light appeared overhead. It spread over the entirety of the newly named Aleksandrya. The glow extended beyond the city's walls. It dug into the ground and continued onward into the planet, forming an impenetrable dome of energy which surrounded the once proud capital city of the now dead Kingdom of Kackritta.

XI: TEACHERS

Grass and ground lay beneath Valentean's back as he shifted uncomfortably. His eyes fluttered open, and he gazed up at the swirling incandescent sky. He watched silently as the wisps of magical energy which traversed the heavens entangled with one another in an endless loop of color. How had he gotten here? The last thing he remembered was failing to stop Kayden and watching Aleksandra enact a farcical fight with her animus warrior over the skies of Kackritta City. Then, General Zouka had appeared and…

Valentean's hands shot to his abdomen, and he was relieved to feel nothing but torn fabric and skin beneath his fingers. Hadn't he been stabbed? Did the power of his Rosinanti blood truly allow him to come back from such a grievous injury? He sat up and noticed that he lay alone on a patch of lush green grass at the lip of a sparkling blue lake.

"Sera?" he called out into the emptiness, "Maura?" There was no response to his cries. Valentean stood to take in his surroundings. He felt neither pain nor discomfort as he rose back to his full height. The area he found himself in was a circular oasis surrounded by tall mountains. How had he gotten down here? And where were Seraphina and Maura? He had been in Kackritta before losing consciousness; what had happened there?

The renewed animus attempted to summon the wind to lift him up into the air so he could gain a better understanding of where he was and what had happened. The familiar feel of the light flooding through his body was absent. Try as he might, it seemed as though the air had abandoned him. Without the power of the Rosintai, how could he hope to stand against Kayden and Aleksandra? Valentean wiped a stray bead of sweat from his brow and stalked over toward the lake to splash some cold water onto his face and regroup.

As he kneeled on the grass and bent over toward the clear cool water, Valentean caught sight of his reflection and leaped back in fear. It was not the ebony-haired, emerald-eyed face of a human that greeted him there. It was the half-human, half-dragon, white-scaled, glowing-eyed snarl of the Rosintai. Valentean fell back onto the ground and gazed at the now churning water as the tall, powerful, winged, white dragon hybrid rose from its surface. He hovered there, moving the lake in ripples from the wind which emanated from his muscular form.

The Rosintai glowered down at the young animus warrior, glowing eyes narrowing in disapproval. His face was identical to Valentean's own, only covered with alabaster scales. Long white locks cascaded past his shoulders, and two twisted horns ran out from his temples. He was adorned in torn and tattered green robes, out of which stretched two leathery wings and a long tail. Every bit of his exposed skin was scaled, alabaster, and aglow with the energy of light.

"Y … you're … The Rosintai…" he stammered, attempting to rise once more and only making it to his knees. The Rosintai said nothing, and merely nodded his head while continuing to study his successor. "How did I … get here? I was in Kackritta with Sera and Maura! Where are they?" The Rosintai remained silent and pointed with one long, clawed finger over Valentean's left shoulder. He turned to follow the spirit of light's gaze and saw that the mountain range behind him had opened. There he saw Kackritta, off in the distance but still visible. Only something was wrong. In place of the grand spectacle of Kackritta Castle, there hovered a fat floating black fortress, which radiated a foreboding sense of doom. Then, as he turned to question this, a red dome of energy came down, covering the city and blotting it from sight.

"What is this? Some kind of dream?' Valentean asked, jumping to his feet and spinning to face The Rosintai, who shook his head slowly. "You mean this actually happened?" The dragon hybrid nodded once more. "So, what I'm seeing actually happened, but I'm not really looking at it, am I?" The Rosintai shook his head. "That means we're … in my mind…" The Rosintai nodded again.

"Aleksandra destroyed Kackritta Castle and surrounded the city with a magical barrier?" This time Valentean did not wait for the Rosintai to respond. He spun around and glared at the crimson arched shield which contained his home and blocked it from view. He sensed something else from behind that thick red wall of magic. "Sera is in there!"

His horror mounted as he whirled to face the Rosintai once more, coming right to the lake's edge, closer to the dragon-god than he had previously dared to venture.

"I have to break down that barrier," he insisted. "What can I do?" The Rosintai continued to stare at him, unblinking in his glowing glare. "Tell me what I can do!" the young animus warrior cried out once more. The thought of Seraphina separated from him by such an obstacle was unthinkable. Valentean would not shrink back from the gaze of this paragon of light, and he stared back with equal intensity, trying to gauge any kind of emotional reaction from this curious creature.

The Rosintai seemed to find what it had been seeking and gave one short, curt nod. "Seek out the vanishing city of the magic makers," he said, his voice sounding like a distorted electrically charged version of Valentean's own. "And remember that you shall find in the unknown a true brother in arms."

"What does that mean?"

But the Rosintai spoke no more and raised one muscular arm. A blaze of white erupted throughout the landscape and Valentean awoke once more in the real world.

Maura jerked around at the sudden rustling commotion coming from the rear of the wagon. Looking back with hopeful eyes, she breathed a sigh of relief when she saw Valentean slowly moving. Pulling back on the reigns, Maura directed their steed to pull off to the side of the dirt road. She leapt out of the wagon and ran around, looking in at the struggling animus warrior as he attempted to crawl out.

"Shhh, Valentean it's all right," she said, grabbing him by the shoulders, trying to keep him inside the wagon.

"Sera," he grunted through the pain that obviously still ate him alive from the inside.

"Just stop for a second."

"We left her … there, didn't … we?"

Maura sighed and draped one of Valentean's arms around her shoulders, helping to guide him out of the wagon and onto the ground, where he lay on his back gazing up at the sky. "She covered our escape, but I thought she was right behind us."

"Where?

"Back in Kackritta City…"

Valentean hissed a curse and fought his way to his hands and knees. "V … vanishing city…"

"What?"

"Magic … makers…"

"Start making sense, Valentean," she said, walking around him, and then crouching to look into her companion's eyes.

"Have to … try…" White light flickered across his eyes and died out several times.

She watched him take an abnormally deep breath as the light reformed along his pupils. "What are you doing?"

"Need to … get to … Sera."

"Not until you're fully healed, you're not!" She felt the wind swirl around their location. Valentean pushed off with both hands and the air carried up into a slow shaking hover. As he attempted to glide away at the pace of a snail, Maura simply stood, reached out, and grabbed him by the ankle, stopping the animus warrior in mid-air.

Valentean looked back at her in dumbfounded confusion, as though he were shocked at his weakness. Maura held onto him for several seconds before the light in his eyes flickered and died. Valentean crashed down onto the grass.

"Come on, tough guy," she said, gripping him beneath the arms and dragging him back against the wagon. "Just stay there for a minute so I can fill you in on everything that's happened, all right?"

Valentean's focus continued to fade in and out, and Maura waited until his eyes locked on hers to continue. The spirit of light nodded to her once, and she sighed in relief. She moved to take the reins of their horse and unhitch it from the wagon. This would be a good enough place to make camp for the night.

"I have a lot to tell you…"

"Seraphina…"

There it was again, that haunting familiar voice, like that of a ghost echoing through the darkness to find her. Was it Aqua? Was it some trick of the Faithful? Or was it her own mind finally succumbing to madness, unable to function under the burden of this power she now commanded? Seraphina hovered in the dark, unable to move or speak, fighting the nagging questions that grated on her, but grateful to be alive and whole.

"Seraphina…"

There it was again. This time it was stronger, as though whatever was calling out was coming closer and closer to her through the infinite void in which she floated. How long had she been here? Time seemed to have no meaning, and the seconds folded in upon one another. She felt as though she had just arrived in this confining murkiness while, at the same time, feeling as though she had been there for months, or even years.

"Let me … in … Sera … phina."

Let you in? she thought. *Who are you?* After her ordeal at the hands of Finstra, suspicion overrode any sense of hope. Her sister was devious, more underhanded and ruthless than she had ever dared to imagine. Her mind raced with possibilities. Was this some new form of torture? Was her own power rebelling against her? Where *was* she?

"Quiet … your mind … and let me … in…"

Who are you? Seraphina asked silently.

"You … know … me … but your mind is … clouded…"

Aqua?

"Yes … dear … girl … Open your mind … to … me."

Seraphina's anxiety roared with hundreds of unanswerable questions. It certainly sounded like Aqua, but how could she be sure? She realized there was no way to escape her current predicament, so she forced these angst-ridden musings from her thoughts, and tried to focus on the sound of her breathing. It was then that she discovered she was not breathing at all. She continued to exist, but there was no intake of oxygen. Her numb limbs were not numb at all. They were nonexistent. She was nothing, just a disembodied consciousness floating through some calignosity where there was no up, no down, left, or right. Sensing her rising emotional frenzy, the voice reached out once more.

"You are in ... no ... danger ... Just let me ... in..."

The princess decided that she had nothing left to lose. Even if this voice was some insanely cruel deception orchestrated by Aleksandra, it could not lead to a fate much worse than that of a formless spirit. She accepted the voice and opened her mind, feeling a familiar warmth bonding with her, calming her, and suddenly she could feel her arms and legs.

Dim surroundings faded into her field of vision, and soon she felt the ground beneath her feet. She saw a blurry mass of pulsating blue light which inevitably solidified into the familiar and welcomed sight of Aqua's luminescent fountain chamber. She whirled around upon recognizing the calming blue glow of the radiant stone wall. There, in the center of the room, was exactly what she had been hoping to see: the raised polished fountain of water, upon which Aqua stood atop as though it were solid ground. A kind and warm smile creased into the dimples upon her cherubic face.

"Aqua!" Seraphina exclaimed, sprinting toward the base of the fountain and running up the steps. She stopped just before the pool of glowing blue water. "You're alive!"

Aqua's smile turned sad, and she slowly shook her head. "No, Seraphina, I am not ... well, not in the manner in which you mean."

"I don't understand."

"Seraphina, when I bestowed upon you the power of order, I gave you much more than a burst of magical energy. I gave you everything I am, everything I ever was and ever could hope to be. I fused my essence to yours, and though my body may have died, I continue to live on, within your soul."

"So, you're saying that we're..."

"Within your mind, conversing upon an astral environment known as the dreamscape."

It all made sense. She did not have to breathe nor could she feel her body, because in this place, there were no bodies. There was no need for oxygen. This was a plane of existence solely of the mind. "But it's been weeks!"

"Yes, dear girl," Aqua said sadly. "The joining was taxing on me. More so than I had believed it would be. In the time since our souls fused into one, my consciousness has been floating through the void of your psyche. I was lost until just recently, when I began to piece the fragmented shards of my essence back together so that I could serve as a proper guide."

"You were … lost inside my mind?" Seraphina said in disgusted awe. Someone as good and pure as Aqua had undergone such an ordeal just to provide her aid.

"Do not fret, sweet dear," Aqua replied, instantly understanding Seraphina's train of thought. "I entered into this partnership of my free will, and I would do so again an infinite number of times if given the choice."

"So, that was you who pulled me out of the battle?"

"Indeed," Aqua said. "It is not a feat I would be able to duplicate any time in the near future, but I was able to temporarily take control of your body and seal you within protective shielding. This shall allow me the time to properly train you in relative peace and safety."

"Train me?" Seraphina asked, her voice alight with hope.

"Yes, I shall teach you to control the power of order. I will instill upon you the mental state necessary to harness the full extent of your new power."

"I lost control…" Seraphina said, trailing off. "I … the water failed me against Zouka."

"And why do you think that is?" Aqua asked, folding her hands neatly in front of her blue gown.

"I'm not strong enough…" she replied, looking down in shame.

"No," Aqua said with such fierce insistence that Seraphina's eyes rose instinctively to look up at her. "Seraphina, your power failed you not because you are weak, but because you *believe* yourself to be weak!"

The princess spoke not a word but stared at Aqua in curious wonderment.

"Seraphina, for so many years, you have believed yourself to be inconsequential, and unimportant. But I need you to see the truly amazing, intelligent, powerful woman within. You have to learn to accept who you truly are. You must learn to calm your mind and keep order in your thoughts. How can you hope to call upon the power of order when your mind is wracked in a state of constant chaos?"

Seraphina nodded in understanding. It was comforting to know that Aqua believed in her with such passion, but Seraphina could not help but feel as though her faith was ill-placed. She had failed in the Northern Magic against Aleksandra, she had failed against Zouka, she had been nearly ended as a child by that Skirlack soldier. Had it not been for Valentean, she would have died long ago.

"I can feel the turmoil churning your mind, Seraphina," Aqua said. "Please do not give in to defeat before we have even begun. You are destined for great things, and I will show you the true strength that I feel in you, unhindered by the prison of doubt you entrap it within. Simply trust me."

Seraphina sighed. She so badly wanted to believe in Aqua's ascertains regarding her potential and destiny, but it was difficult to even imagine. The only time she ever truly felt safe and strong and confident was when she stood beside Valentean. Apart from him, she felt the crushing hopelessness of the mediocre second-born princess who stared dully back at her from every mirror she had ever gazed into.

"I can try," she replied, looking down and away.

"You shall do far more than that, my dear," Aqua said, reaching one hand out, touching Seraphina's chin with her forefinger and lifting her face to coerce the princess to lock eyes with her. "You shall *be* far more than you ever thought you could."

Aqua snapped backward, causing Seraphina to tense with alarm. The deceased spirit threw both of her arms into the air and Seraphina saw an intense blue glare ignite around her, pulling her consciousness from this construct of Aqua's fountain chamber, back into the disembodying void of her mind.

Valentean allowed the heavy words of Maura's tale to settle, choosing not to speak for several moments as he slumped uselessly at the base of a large tree, close to a small campfire. He stared at the dancing flames contained within the small clearing of dirt and stones. One tiny spark of red-orange could ignite this entire forest.

This was what he faced; a blaze that began so small, one that he thought had been readily contained. Aleksandra's flames, however, had spread outwards, engulfing his home, his family, his … Sera. How much longer would it be before the fire his weakness had allowed to grow became an inferno that would scorch the world?

"Valentean, are you all right?" Maura asked from across the fire's glow, her face a dancing merge of shadow and light as the crackling flames danced along her strong feminine features.

"I don't really have an answer to that question," Valentean said, trying to straighten his back and grimacing as sharp pain exploded along his abdomen. With each tiny movement, it felt as though Zouka's blade were carving into him once more. He could actually feel the power of the Rosintai within him, healing him, rejuvenating him. But it was clearly a lengthy process and there was much damage to repair.

"I'm sure Seraphina is safe," Maura said, clearly trying to say what Valentean wanted to hear.

The animus warrior knew his ally was right. Their connection was still active, and Valentean could sense Seraphina's life even from this distance. However, it felt … different. Seraphina's mind felt clouded, as though it were being forcibly hidden. He knew she was alive but could not discern anything more regarding her mental, emotional, or physical state. All he could feel as he reached out silently was … cold. A chilling all-consuming cold coursed throughout his body whenever he attempted to apply his senses to the well-being of his princess.

"She is definitely alive," he said, trying to ease Maura's worry. He could see the question forming on her lips and gave her a small half-smile, pointing to his head before she had a chance to ask. "I can sense it."

"Ah," she said, nodding her head, "that's weird." Everything was quiet for another moment before she spoke again. "You would have been so proud of her, Valentean. The way she protected us both … I never would have expected her to do something like that. No offense meant, but she didn't seem the type."

"That's because you don't know her like I do," Valentean said, a sad smile on his lips. "I'd say if you'd asked just about anyone that knows Sera whether an act like that was in her character, they'd all say no. Sera herself would probably have said no. There's a deeper strength within her, one that has nothing to do with being the Spirit of Order."

"She loves you," Maura said. Valentean, unsure of how to respond, blushed in response. "She told me to tell you that, right before we escaped the city."

Valentean nodded, his heart tearing to pieces at the mention of Seraphina's parting words. "I owe you more than I could ever repay, Maura. You saved my life."

"You don't owe me," she said, tossing another log onto the dying fire. "You're still up two against one in the great game of saving each other's lives. If anything, I owe *you* one still."

Valentean chuckled lightly. "I didn't realize you were keeping score."

"I'm a competitive girl."

"Well, let's hope this is a game we don't need to keep playing."

"I think we both know that's not the case."

"Sadly, yes … But I feel safe knowing that you're watching my back, Maura." She smiled at him, a slight curvature of the mouth Valentean had once believed her incapable of ever forming again. "According to that vision I told you about, we're supposed to seek the vanishing city of the magic makers."

"Well, it's a good thing that's not vague and completely unhelpful," Maura scoffed, pulling an apple from her discarded supply bag and biting into it. Valentean laughed. "I mean, would it be so hard for a spooky vision man to be like, 'this is exactly where you need to go, and this is exactly what you need to do?'"

"I guess it doesn't work that way," Valentean said, still laughing lightly, trying not to rattle his insides more than necessary. It felt good to be able to smile and laugh. It was proof that Aleksandra and Kayden had not taken everything from them. He was thankful to have Maura and her unique personality beside him.

"I have a theory," he said slowly.

"Oh?"

"I think the Rosintai wants us to go to Grassan."

"Gra-what?" Maura said, grimacing at the unfamiliar name.

"Grassan, the mysterious magical metropolis, they call it."

"Ugh, *who* calls it that?"

"One of my tutors in Kackritta Castle."

"That's the worst alliteration I've ever heard."

"Nevertheless," he said, chuckling, "Grassan is the home of the mage smiths. They construct machines that run on magic. That muzzle you saw me wearing in the throne room … that was definitely a creation of Grassan."

"That thing was pretty intense…"

"Yes, but Grassan doesn't part with its creations easily. They never export or trade any of the machinery they construct."

"So how did Aleksandra have that thing?"

"I don't know … Maybe it was stolen, or maybe Kackritta forged some kind of deal with the king of Grassan. The two kingdoms have always been allies. My father knows the King of Grassan very well."

"So, you've been there?"

"No," Valentean replied quickly. "No one goes to Grassan. Ever. The only people that I've ever heard of going there are King Roan, Queen Christina, and my father."

"Why?"

"I asked that once. My father just smiled at me and said that they're a proud and secretive people. But he always told me that Grassan and Kackritta were ancient allies, and if one fell into peril, the other was bound by treaty to provide aid."

Maura processed this information for a moment and sighed. "Well, then going there is definitely not going to happen. If they're allies of Aleksandra, we would not receive a very warm welcome, and I don't feel like being thrown into another dungeon."

"Aleksandra surrounded the city with an impenetrable magic bubble; I saw it in my vision. She's hunkering down, protecting the city from attack. Yet she knows I'm not going to fly in there and start blowing things up. She spoke to me in the Northern Magic about how Kackritta should be a global powerhouse, covering every bit of Terra. She's going to move on Grassan. There's no doubt in my mind. The king *has* to see that. The Rosintai clearly knows a lot that we don't, so we have to trust in what he said. *The vanishing city of the magic makers*. It makes sense, doesn't it?"

"Yes," Maura said nodding, pulling a map from her travel pouch and unfolding it. "I don't see it on this map, though; or any map I've ever seen, for that matter."

"I told you they're secretive," Valentean said, motioning for Maura to come closer. She rose to her feet and moved to sit beside him as they studied the map together. "Right here." He pointed to a large open space on the east side of the mountain range which ran down the Eastern Continent. "The map just ends here, once you pass to the other side of the mountains from Kackritta. That's where we will find Grassan, I'm sure of it."

"That's going to be a long trip, and it's going to involve crossing right by Kackritta City again … How sure are you about this?"

"Seventy percent … Sixty at the least!"

"Well, then, I'm sixty percent in," Maura muttered, flashing him a small amused smile. "We should turn in for the night. I assume I'll be driving in the morning as you still aren't looking so good."

"I'm feeling stronger by the hour. But you might need to carry the brunt of the travel for a little while longer…"

"That's fine, I don't mind it. You just get back into fighting shape so you can kick that red-eyed bitch in the throat next time you see her." They both laughed and Valentean nodded in agreement. "And Terra help you if there's no city there…"

"I know, I know. Just trust me…"

"I do…" Maura said, and Valentean knew that she meant it. She stood and walked back to her side of the campfire and laid down as Valentean gingerly moved into a horizontal position.

"Valentean," Maura said, "one more thing I wanted to ask of you."

"Name it, Maura. I told you I owe you."

"Teach me how to fight like you do…" There was silence for a moment as Valentean let her request hang in the air. Maura was already a skilled combatant. There was little he could teach her in terms of fighting style or weaponry. That only left one thing.

"You want to learn how to use mana…"

"Can you teach me?"

Valentean contemplated this for a long moment. He had never imagined teaching someone else, being a trainer; a master. But then he remembered what Maura had said about Seraphina. *I never would have expected her to do something like that*. Coupled with his response to her, *Sera herself would have probably said no*.

"We begin at dawn," Valentean replied, turning over slowly and closing his eyes, letting his weariness carry him off into a deep sleep.

XII: MONSTER

Kayden despised the Fortress of Ignis. Everything about it just felt *wrong* to him. He tromped through the sleek black stone hallways, shuddering at the unnatural palace that Aleksandra had made the centerpiece of her new empire.

He ran his gloved fingers along the uneven wall. It felt as though the stone that made up the floating fortification had been slammed together roughly with magic as shards of shattered rock still jutted out at odd angles within the castle walls. What felt even stranger to the black dragon's unique senses was his inability to mentally connect with the strange glistening mineral.

Every time he mentally reached out, trying to establish contact, he felt a wave of cold, prickling dread spread throughout his entire body. It was powerful magic. Old magic. Kayden loathed it. He was, by right of his birth, sovereign over the land. The fact that the magic of a long-dead sorceress could shield his element from him was both infuriating and troublesome.

He walked through a long, curved walkway in the central tower of the fortress. Despite Aleksandra's insistence that he remain hidden from the eyes of the humans who dwelled within Aleksandrya's walls, the only beings granted admittance to the fortress were Skirlack demons and initiates of the Faithful. Aleksandra had deemed her ordinary citizens unfit to enter, and thus the castle's interior was a safe space for him to wander freely.

While Kayden enjoyed his freedom from the filth of the catacombs beneath the former Kackritta City, the Fortress of Ignis was still a confining prison meant to contain him and his great power.

Taking his true form amidst the skies of Kackritta, raining death soaked vengeance down upon those who had oppressed and obliterated his people … the memory of it tingled his spine. The experience had been freeing, empowering, and all-consuming.

He felt liked winged death as he hovered over their pathetic, tiny, cowering forms: hearing their terror, their cries for mercy, and then passing judgment upon the whole of humanity. The experience had been all too brief, though. He had only just begun when Aleksandra had leapt into the fray, bringing their farcical encounter to a quick close.

Later, he had stood upon one of the many balconies found upon the palace's towers and gazed out at what he had done. He viewed the desolation and destruction carved into the face of the city to be a dark signature, his promise to not only the people of Kackritta but for the whole of humanity. Darkness had descended upon Kackritta, raw and unhindered for the first time in a millennium. This had only been the overture to his symphony of death.

As he rounded a corner, drawing ever closer to his destination within the massive, looming central tower, Kayden thought back to that delicious moment upon the castle rampart, when Valentean had made a laughably pathetic attempt to thwart his efforts. He had done nothing but try to hold the hand of his princess and count on her power joining with his. He could have transformed, taken his own true form and battled Kayden amongst the skies. Instead, he had done nothing. His tiny eyes had surrendered in that moment. He had believed Kayden would end him, and he knew that there was nothing to be done to stave off that fate.

Kayden savored that delightful memory as he finally arrived at his destination; a pair of gargantuan crimson doors which rose overhead, coming to a point nearly eight meters high. Standing between Kayden and entry way were five hulking Skirlack soldiers, all adorned in bulky black and red armor. He had to stifle a laugh at the sight of these simple brutes forced into the confining armaments.

He also found it amusing how Aleksandra bothered to play these boring power games. Why did she need sentries posted outside her door? There was no foe in the entirety of Terra that could storm past these doors and threaten her life. So, why the theatrics? Why the posturing, when no one save he, Zouka, and several high-ranking clerics of the Faithful would ever see it?

She does these things because she can, Kayden reminded himself, realizing Aleksandra was still prone to displays of vanity, still susceptible to the corruption of absolute power. It curled Kayden's lip in disgust. It was so … *human*.

While he now considered himself above such rabble, it was clear Aleksandra still identified as one of them. She wanted to rule and unite them, strengthen them in the name of her goddess and forge a new path for humanity. Aleksandra wanted to see humanity rise from the flames, stronger and better than they had ever been.

Kayden just wanted to watch them burn.

The sentries shifted together at his approach, barring his entrance. Kayden sighed in annoyance and rubbed the bridge of his nose with two fingers. Why were they making this difficult?

"Stand aside, beasts," he commanded. Still, the Skirlack demons did not budge. "I said, move." A dangerous edge tinted Kayden's voice, as the faintest hint of darkness started to shine upon his eyes. Still, the demons held fast to their positions, not relenting in the least. Kayden focused on the anger welling up within him and soon the purple glow which shone brightly from his face illuminated the doomed creatures and cast their massive shadows against the doorway.

"Truly?" Kayden heard an irritatingly familiar voice speak from behind him. He whirled around, the dark shine dissipating from his gaze as he glared in unabashed hatred at Aurax. The Skirlack cleric stood with his hands clasped in front of his brown robes, shaking his head at Kayden's outburst in disgust. "It must be so burdensome being you, so ill-suited to control that brutish power of yours."

"Be quiet," Kayden said, snarling into the sickly yellow eyes of his hated rival.

"You forget your place yet again, creature," Aurax replied, beginning to walk around Kayden in a bored circle, stopping between the disgruntled animus warrior and the Skirlack sentries. "Is it your wish to anger our empress just as you are about to be summoned into her holy presence?" Kayden cursed under his breath but remained silent. Aurax had been correct. Were he to pound these mindless beasts into pulpy gore-soaked remains, Aleksandra would inflict harsh penalties upon him. Though their lives were meaningless, these creatures represented her power, and to openly attack them would be an attack on her authority.

Kayden scoffed at Aurax's logic but internally he felt relieved. He could not afford such emotional outbursts, yet they seemed to define him of late. The darkness was strong, its well of power ran deep. With it, though, came these sudden bursts of anger that often urged him toward potentially disastrous consequences. He had to retain some semblance of mental clarity in the face of these damning urges.

Kayden found his mind to be a troublesome place as of late, causing him to partake in actions so unbecoming of a spirit of darkness. *Why did I rescue Father?* It was a question that had been racing through his thoughts since the moment he pulled the old man from the throne room.

He was a human, small and weak like the rest of them. He had lied to Kayden, denied his true heritage while doting favoritism upon Valentean. So why then was the concept of eliminating him so troublesome? Vahn shared no blood with the black dragon and served the former kingdom that had facilitated the downfall of the Rosinanti.

Furthermore, he had been ordered by Aleksandra to end the elite warrior. By choosing to keep Vahn in the relative safety of that abandoned old shack, Kayden was placing his own life in jeopardy. Was that why she had summoned him? Had she discovered this betrayal? Was she inviting him into the throne chamber to easily cleave him in two? Or rip the head from his shoulders? He shuddered at the ease in which the princess could enact such atrocities.

The great double doors slowly swung open, and Kayden winced. The fortress's throne room might have been his least favorite location on the planet. Aurax nodded to the armored Skirlack demons, and they stepped aside, granting Kayden passage. He hurried forward, trying to ignore the unsettling reality of the room's unnatural features.

Magic cast a haze throughout the chamber, which was so vast it filled the entirety of the central tower. It looked like an open field. Lush green grass spread out before him, with one red paved walkway leading through the landscape which would take him to Aleksandra.

He took in the surroundings, never ceasing to be both impressed and unnerved simultaneously by the unique locale. One could easily forget they were indoors while looking at the lush green hills, flowering plants, and even a large lake filled with sparkling blue water, which made up the throne chamber's interior.

Gazing up, Kayden scoffed at the spell which transformed the black stone ceiling into a vision of the clear blue sky, dotted with wispy white clouds and colored strands of magical energy. He thought with a sting of irony that this illusion was now the only place within Aleksandrya where one could look up and see the sky above their heads.

He followed the path down to the far wall, upon which a massive circular glass window could just barely be seen. On either side of him, far off in the distance, ran twin balconies that stretched around the entirety of the circular area, from which one could look down upon the people of Aleksandrya from its highest point.

Several armored Skirlack soldiers flanked him as he made his way down the wide walkway, making him once again feel as though he were being marched toward some inescapable fate. His rising anxiety caught in his throat like a lump, causing a small cough to nearly choke him. Kayden hated fear. Fear was weakness. He was meant to inspire fear in others, yet here he was, barely managing to keep his knees from rattling together in abject terror as he marched toward his mistress.

As Aleksandra became visible amidst the vastness which surrounded him, Kayden could not help but find relief in the change the room underwent. As one approached the far end of the chamber, the magic which created the artificial field of green and blue slowly started to unravel. The clear sky darkened, giving way to the cold back stone which truly ran overhead. The grass became yellow and dead until it stopped suddenly, transitioning with abruptness to a series of hexagonal crimson tiles pulsating with blood-colored energy.

As Kayden stepped onto the first tile, an orange and red discoloration surrounded his boot. Explosions of color erupted around him with every step as he continued through the room's magic. The circular red and black stained glass window loomed above, and Kayden stared at it, gathering enough strength to look down at the truly disturbing feature of the room.

Aleksandra referred to her seat of power as the skeletal throne. It was immense and black, the princess a barely conceivable dot of movement at its base. The entirety of the great chair was composed of the charred bones of Rosinanti dragons, salvaged from the end of the war. Behind Aleksandra the curved enormity of a dragon's head and upper jaw ran overhead, rows of still sharp, pointed teeth stretching over the empress.

From behind the giant skull on either side, stretching up into the air and curving back down, ran the bones normally found within a Rosinanti's wings. They framed the perverse seat, casting a span of scale to the already impressive object.

On the floor, in a looped semi-circle, ran the burned, fused bones of a Rosinanti's tail, three on each side, creating a pathway which corralled one into the space before Aleksandra. Her seat was composed of a variety of bones, all large in scale, some filed down to jut out in sharp dagger-like points.

She sat upon the great cathedra, adorned in a red regal gown, eyes aglow with crimson power which lit with greater ferocity than Kayden had ever seen. He nearly had to avert his eyes from her flaming gaze but fought the urge, even as the light scorched his retinas. The ancient bones of his brethren seemed to act as some form of conduit for the mountain of magical energy which coursed through the room, funneling it into Aleksandra, strengthening her temporary body.

At the base of this sickening seat stood General Zouka and Sophie. Aurax appeared beside Sophie's red-robed form and all three of them gazed at his approach. Aurax looked upon him with the usual disdain he seemed to reserve solely for Kayden, while Sophie always gazed at him with an unreadable desire or hunger. Was it lust? Kayden scoffed at the notion of copulating with a human. No, it couldn't be something so base.

What, then, did the Faithful priestess see when she locked her eyes upon him? He realized that the answer to such a question mattered not to him, and he pushed it from his consideration. Zouka was as unreadable as ever. Though they had stood within the same vicinity several times, the general had never uttered a single word to Kayden nor acknowledged him in any way.

The black dragon stood between Aurax and Zouka and raised his shaking gaze up to his mistress. The power coursing through her from the skeletal throne spread a chilling dread through the air. Looking closely, Kayden could see red energy flowing through tiny cracks found within the bones of the unfortunate long dead members of his race. He finally forced himself to lock eyes with Aleksandra and instantly bowed at the waist before her.

"Empress," he said, his tone quiet and respectful while keeping the shaking fear from impacting his words. "It is an honor as always to be summoned into your presence."

The sorceress nodded at him, studying him fiercely with her cardinal stare. There was silence for several seconds, and Kayden inwardly tensed, waiting to see if Aleksandra was going to attack or command the general to engage him. He knew the room's layout well and began to quietly discern the speed in which he could flee, should a dangerous situation arise.

Finally, as he straightened himself back to his full height, Aleksandra spoke.

"Kayden, my animus warrior, welcome. Now that you have arrived, we can commence deliberation concerning our subsequent actions."

Kayden exhaled. This was a war council meeting, not an execution. Vahn's presence within the city seemed to have escaped the mighty empress's notice, as he had hoped from the beginning.

Aleksandra turned to Zouka. "General, how fares my new army?"

"They continue to inspire loyalty and dread amongst your subjects, Empress," Zouka said, motioning toward the armored Skirlack. "We have bolstered our ranks with the Champions of the Faithful, as requested, and they have proven to be most proficient in addressing matters too delicate for the Skirlack."

Kayden closed his eyes to hide his disgust. The Champions of the Faithful were a militant brigade of warriors, honed in ancient combat styles. They were skilled, but they were human.

"Interrogations proceed then?"

"Indeed, Mistress. As predicted, the terrified populace has begun to turn upon itself, offering information on those disloyal to your rule. The champions have begun interrogating all prisoners within the dungeon of this fortress. They are bled for information and then publicly put to death as per your command."

"Excellent," she turned her gaze from the general, past Kayden and towards her former handmaiden. "Sophie, have the citizens of Aleksandrya been taking to the teachings of the true faith?"

"Indeed, they have Your Holiness," Sophie said, stepping forward, arms folded into the deep sleeves of her crimson robes. Aleksandra had recently named her Pontifex of The Faithful, and she had taken to the role with the righteous zeal of fanaticism. "We initiate hundreds per day. The temples to our Holy Mother are being constructed amongst the devastation caused in the creation of your empire. We continue to take the offerings of our new members, and welcome them to the truth of the blaze."

Kayden suppressed a gag, imagining the forced removal of hundreds of fingers from the populace. Was such mutilation truly necessary? It was quicker to just incinerate them and be done with it.

"Have you encountered much resistance?"

"There have been some who flee before the truth of our mission, but they are quickly being rounded up and dealt with, as the general has described previously."

"It is imperative that they not be allowed to organize," Aleksandra added.

"Indeed, Mistress," Sophie responded, "several of the former Elite Warriors of Kackritta who managed to escape the devastation have engaged in the beginnings of an organized rebellion, but they are small in number."

"This cannot suffice," Aleksandra said, turning back to Zouka. "I require haste and utmost brutality when disposing of these heretical insurgents."

"It shall be done, Majesty," he replied.

"Aurax," she said, inclining her gaze toward the Skirlack Cleric. Kayden gritted his teeth in annoyance. Did everyone have some essential duty to perform while he hid away in this dark monolith? "What of my sister?"

"The Harbinger's magic holds strong, Oh Most High and Holy Mistress," he replied with a deep bow, causing Kayden to once more internally scoff at the cleric's sycophantic nature. "It is strong magic, similar to that which holds prisoner your true divine form. However, much the same as that wretched hex, this cannot hold forever. We shall retrieve the princess soon, but for now, she remains out of play and separated from the Shogai as you had always intended."

"Double the guard surrounding her at all times. No one is to approach."

"There … have been whispers reported to me through my informants," Sophie said slowly.

"What whispers?" Aleksandra asked.

"There are rumors throughout the kingdom that your sister rebelled against you during the Rosinanti attack. Many Aleksandryan subjects who oppose your holy truth are rallying around this tale."

"And what do they say?"

"Well … there were many who witnessed the princess's struggle with your soldiers and our esteemed general. They saw The Harbinger's unnatural power coupled with the Shogai's borrowed magic … they…"

"Speak freely, Sophie."

The Pontifex cleared her throat and straightened, taking a deep breath. "The insurgents pledge loyalty to your sister and her imagined cause. They refer to her as … the Ice Queen."

Red light exploded from Aleksandra's glare, as the room began to quake and the Skeletal throne shone with her crimson fury. The empress's face contorted in rage, and Kayden felt the magical energy within the fortress converge upon her.

"*Triple* the guard around my sister, General, and let it be known through all corners of Aleksandrya that any mention of this *Ice Queen* is punishable by death!"

"It will be done, Mistress!" the general shouted over the cataclysmic quaking.

As suddenly as the onslaught of movement had come, it dissipated. The glow upon Aleksandra's eyes shrank back to its normal pulsation and a sense of calm normalcy settled around the room. "Aurax, what of the airship?"

"It is nearly complete, my Queen."

Kayden's eyebrow raised at the mention of an airship. This was the first he had heard of such a thing. "The inventor's plans proved quite beneficial. The prototype engine has been installed and should be ready for testing within the week."

"Excellent…" she purred, softly stroking the polished black bones that served as her arm rests. "Will it truly allow wide-range travel throughout the planet?"

"Indeed, Your Holiness," Aurax replied.

Kayden was now truly interested. A long-range airship? One which could transcend the boundaries that currently restricted such travel? While he had no need for such a cumbersome device, it would be a true boon to the fledgling empire's military might.

"Once testing proves fruitful, move to mass scale production. I want my combat fleet ready to take to the skies within the month."

Aurax nodded and bowed.

Kayden was shocked and impressed at this stratagem. No kingdom on Terra would have a chance of resisting an attack from the sky. It was technology that simply did not exist anywhere else.

"If that is all there is to report, then let this council meeting be finished," Aleksandra said.

Was that truly it? Why had he even been summoned here to this vile room if he were not to be acknowledged?

"Go forth, strengthen Aleksandrya, and enforce my will." Aurax vanished in a haze of red as Sophie and Zouka turned to take their leave. Kayden stood in place, looking at the empress incredulously. She met his gaze with her unblinking, flaming stare and he turned to leave. "Kayden," she called out after him, causing the animus warrior to turn back around, "remain for a moment."

He stood at attention, his eyes fixed upon her slight red-clad figure as it slowly rose from the skeletal throne. As she stepped away, there seemed to be a disconnect as the magic in the room ceased its vortex-like rush toward her seat of power. The red glow which had pulsated beneath the throne's surface died and Aleksandra slowly advanced upon her animus warrior. Kayden's heart raced once more. *Did* she know after all? Was she approaching him to attack? Were these to be his final moments? The untimely end to his glorious destiny? Aleksandra stopped before him and offered him a cold smile, laying a hand upon his bicep.

"Walk with me, Kayden," she stated, making it almost sound like a request.

Kayden knew better. She never issued requests, every utterance from her was a command. Kayden quickly fell in step behind her as they walked across the crimson tiles, spreading magical discoloration in their wake. He swallowed hard as they continued onto the thick grass, moving with agonizing slowness until they came to the edge of the lake.

"I can scarcely allow myself to believe we have finally arrived," Aleksandra remarked quietly, gazing down at their reflections in the water's clear surface. "We have, together, expunged weakness from our home, Kayden."

"It was your perfect planning, Mistress."

"Kayden, you are being modest," she said, as though chastising him. "I know that not to be your true self. You were instrumental to this endeavor. It was our cooperative accord that led us to this end."

"You honor me, My Lady."

"I can sense your growing unease, Kayden. You see this fortress not as your home but as a prison."

"I…" He decided to be truthful. "I feel as though my true place is in the skies, Mistress."

"Of course, you do," she replied, nodding. "To that end, I bring you welcomed tidings."

Kayden held his breath as she moved away from him, he followed in step once again. She spoke not a word until she reached the black balcony overlooking the entirety of Aleksandrya City. The red gloom of the barrier she had erected blocked out all natural light, tinting the entire city in a blood-colored glare. She pointed one slender finger toward the barely conceivable blue dot that represented the ice sphere which contained Princess Seraphina.

"My sister remains ensconced in that blasphemous magic, unreachable to me. Now, there are those who rally behind her. They see my own flesh and blood as a means to usurp my throne and my empire." Kayden nodded in understanding, not daring to speak until he was certain it was what she wanted. "She remains beyond my reach, but until she emerges, she is of little threat to us. Your brother, however, remains at large. He escaped the city and despite grievous wounds, no doubt continues to plot against us."

Kayden's dark power began to churn with excitement. Was she about to say what he hoped she would say? What he had dreamed of from the day he entered into the service of her holy war? Would he now, finally, be given the freedom to hunt his brother down and kill him?

"I want you to find Valentean," she said, her words igniting the darkness within him. He could scarcely contain the flicker of purple light which shone briefly across his eyes. "Take note of his location, track his movements, and report back to me. Remain unseen and undetected at all times."

His heart sank. She was sending him to *spy* on Valentean? To hide from him in the shadows like a thief in the night and silently report his progress? To watch him embark on his own adventures while he, himself, remained doing the work of an errand boy? His lip curled in disgust involuntarily, which did not go unnoticed.

"Do you take issue with your assignment, Kayden?" She inclined her head at him, almost *daring* him to put up a fight.

He wanted so badly to spit in her face, to tell her that this assignment was trash, more deserved for one of her so-called Champions of The Faithful. But then he remembered exactly who it was he stood face to face with, and swallowed his pride and rage with a quivering gulp. "Of course not, Mistress," he replied humbly. "You honor me with this important task."

Aleksandra smiled once more and turned her attention back out toward the city, her encased prize. Kayden took her distraction as his queue to leave. He quickly moved from her and began his long trek back to the throne chamber's exit.

"Oh, and Kayden?" she called from over her shoulder, causing the animus warrior to stop and look back. "I've allowed you to keep your … *pet* chained within that ramshackle hovel. But betray me again and I shall melt the flesh from your bones."

He gaped open-mouthed as she turned her back. His breath exploded out from his lungs in a panicked cough as he turned and rushed from the throne chamber into the hallway. The armored Skirlack soldiers paid him no mind as he breezed past them.

Aurax, though, waited for him just beyond the wall of armored demonic bulk, saying nothing, but silently smirking at the troubled Rosinanti. He continued onward, past the cleric into the dark corridors of the Fortress of Ignis.

Kayden burst up into the tiny attic where his father remained chained and alone, desperately needing a sympathetic soul to speak to. But as he entered the dust infested space, he gasped.

The anchor point which had kept Vahn safely chained to the wall had been torn away, and a gaping hole had been smashed into the circular window.

Kayden screamed in rage, empowering both of his arms with green sparking mana energy. He smashed them down into the wooden floor, as the entire shack exploded in an emerald burst. He landed crouched in the decimation. The only light a harsh purple glow pulsating in the night from his ignited eyes.

Everyone had always fled from him. Other children kept their distance throughout his childhood, his own brother would rather befriend a princess than stand beside his own kin. And now, the one person in all of Terra who was supposed to never waver, eternally by his side, fled also.

He had no friends, no family, no humanity left. He was what the world believed him to be; a monster. So, let them all be agreed, and let them all fear him. He would carry out Aleksandra's orders and fumble through the menial task assigned to him because her orders were a means to an end.

At the end of this road, there was only one conceivable outcome. He would lay waste to the world of humanity. He would reclaim the dominance once denied the Rosinanti race. Humans would drown in their own blood, every last man, woman, and child. The darkness would flow, and the light would die amidst the shadows of his vengeance. Kayden stood tall amidst the wreckage, the inner turmoil that once besieged him but a distant memory.

He finally felt like a monster.

XIII: ELITE

Fearful faces lined the streets of Aleksandrya, desperately trying to avert their gaze from that of another human being as they hurried along in panicked shuffles. It wounded Vahn's heart. He had always looked upon his home with pride, taking solace in the smiling faces of Kackritta City's citizens as they greeted him with respect and kindness.

Vahn held the floor length hooded robe he had been forced to don in the wake of his escape tightly against his body. His right arm pressed firmly against his side so as not to allow any sound to come from the metal chain which had once entrapped him within that tiny attic space. The confining metal cuff remained clamped around his ankle, and he had run the silver links of chain up through this robe and down into the baggy sleeve.

The raised hood was a serious risk. It screamed of suspicion. The conspicuous head covering was necessary, however, as the sight of Vahn Burai walking freely through the streets of Aleksandrya was guaranteed to attract unwanted attention.

It had been nearly three days since he had broken free of the crude prison Kayden had stowed him away in, and part of him felt guilty for his unannounced flight. He knew, deep down under the purple glow of Kayden's darkness, there still beat the heart of a good man. His son had many faults, and he had committed crimes from which there would be no redemption, but he was still his son, and Vahn loved him.

He had broken free out of necessity. He could only sit helplessly in that tiny room and listen to the sounds of beatings, screams, panic and execution for so long. Though his career as an elite warrior had ended some years prior, he still held steadfast to the duty which had once defined his existence. This land was still Kackritta, despite what Aleksandra wanted to call it, and as such Vahn had to uphold his oath to protect its people, no matter the cost. For several days, he had remained hidden in the shadows, watching the Champions of the Faithful and their Skirlack demon compatriots as they strutted through the streets, harassing the citizenry, taking what they pleased, and dragging several people away toward the floating palace which hovered threateningly above them all.

Vahn gazed up at the imposing structure and shivered involuntarily. This gentle quaking of his limbs was born in part from of a sense of dread at such an unsettling sight, and the frigid chill that permeated the city thanks to the red barrier which blotted out the warm light of the sun. While some might have bought into the idea that the clouded red dome was a protection against future attacks perpetuated by a risen Rosinanti, Vahn saw it for what it truly was: a way to keep Aleksandrya's citizens *in* as much as it was meant to keep others out.

As he wandered along the trenches of devastation left in the wake of Kayden's murderous assault, he had noticed large red stone temples being erected throughout the city. Citizens were being dragged into the half-completed structures, willing or otherwise, likely to be indoctrinated into The Faithful. Vahn noticed more and more frightened individuals on the streets with bloodied bandages covering their hands. He was aghast at the thought of these zealots mutilating his people.

So much death and devastation had occurred in what was once known as the safest kingdom in all of Terra. He swallowed a gasp of grief as his mind traveled to Roan, his beloved childhood friend, closer to him than any blood relative had ever been. The sad irony of his friend's violent demise was that it had been at the hands of one of his beloved daughters. Roan had always been a carefree soul, much the same as Valentean. As they had grown together as warriors, the future king had taken such pride and happiness from his duty to the home he so loved. That all changed the day Aleksandra had been born. From then on, Roan's pride and happiness were bundled in the lives and accomplishments of his children. Though Christina had often been harsh and cold toward the girls, Roan had done his best to fill their lives with smiles and love. And yet it had been one of his own children who had executed him with no shred of love or remorse.

You shall be avenged, my brother, Vahn thought to himself bitterly as he continued through the darkened streets, making his way ever closer toward the city's central hub. The large circular clearing, which stood just before the former entrance of Kackritta Castle had become a place of daily, brutal public executions. As he crept closer, Vahn could hear the frightened whispers of a populace in bondage and fear. The hub was positively packed with humanity, shaking together as they raised their eyes toward a large platform, upon which stood a mound of wood and a tall stake.

What poor soul shall it be this time? Vahn thought to himself. He had only heard tale of these savage demonstrations, having not ventured this far toward the city's center up to this point. As he shouldered his way into the crowd, Vahn could just make out the distant sight of a large bobbing orb of glowing blue ice that hovered a meter above the ground towards the northern most point of the hub. It was surrounded by a wall of Skirlack, and while he could just barely make out the shadowy figure which hung frozen at its center, he knew all too well who it was.

Whispers of the Ice Queen of Kackritta had reached the dingy corners of the taverns and alleyways he had been forced to seek refuge in. Seraphina, the princess without magic, had suddenly become a rallying point of hope for the downtrodden populace.

There were still a great many who swore Aleksandra to be a holy warrior of justice, delivered from on high to save them from the Rosinanti. But in the ensuing weeks subsequent to that initial assault, discontent had quickly begun to grow. One by one the rights that Kackritta had afforded its citizens were stripped away, in favor of this totalitarian violent empirical society. As Vahn studied the crowd, it was nearly impossible to tell the loyal Aleksandryans apart from those who carried the spark of rebellion within their hearts.

"Good people of Aleksandrya!" a familiar voice rang out. Vahn looked up to the pyre and saw the face of a man he had not so much as thought about in over a decade. He stood proud and tall, grey hair straight and down, stopping just below the shoulder and thinning at the top and front, giving the man a pronounced forehead. His face was hard and cold as steel, the face of an elite warrior. Or former, as the case would have it. Vahn's fists clenched at the resurgeance of this ghost from his past. "Today, our holy empress brings before you one who has sinned in the eyes of our benevolent goddess."

His name was Landon. He was a former elite warrior of Kackritta, one who had assisted Vahn on many of his early missions, whom in his youth he had once called friend. Vahn tried to blot out the memories of that dark, terrible day Landon had been excommunicated from their noble order. Try as he might, Vahn would never be able to forget the heat of the flames, the stench of stale blood, and the screaming … the horrid, ever-present screaming.

Vahn remembered standing alongside Roan before the late Queen Rose, mother to Christina, and testifying to Landon's outrageous crimes against humanity. He had never imagined that he would see this man standing, once more, in a position of power and authority within these city walls. But here he was, donned in the red robes of the Faithful, arms spread before them, showing off the stump where the middle finger of his right hand had been removed. It was an old wound, having healed over long ago. How long had Landon been in league with The Faithful?

"Traitors hide in our midst, blaspheming against both our sainted ruler and our forsaken goddess. But my Champions of the Faithful work tirelessly to weed them out and bring them before the divine justice of the blaze!"

His Champions of the Faithful? Was Landon leading the group of savages who had assaulted Vahn in the wilds, and now betrayed the whole of humanity in service to Aleksandra's chaotic agenda?

"As Empress Aleksandra has stated, the kingdom of Kackritta has ceased to exist. We are reborn, an empire of flame, and an empire of *faith.*" There was movement behind Landon as a pair of shrouded red-robed Champions of the Faithful dragged a tattered man onto the platform, donned in rags with a potato sack over his head. The figure's hands were tied together at the wrist in front of him.

"What we bring before you today is a relic of a failed regime. A sinner who speaks of false heroes, false leaders, false gods. He spreads his blasphemous filth to those of you who have allowed your souls to be bathed in the vivid glow of the eternal flames." Landon moved toward the captive man and laid a hand atop the sack which restricted his face. "I give you Tiberius Woltram, former elite warrior of the dead kingdom of Kackritta!"

Vahn gasped as Landon tore the bag from the head of a square-jawed, barrel-chested man who despite the bruises that splotched along his dark skin, glared in hate at the fallen elite with eyes so dark brown they were nearly black.

Vahn could see the skin tense along Tiberius's shorn scalp as he lunged toward Landon, before being forcibly pulled back by the shrouded figures who flanked him. Landon turned and slammed his thick fist into the elite warrior's head three times in response to this attempted rebellion.

Tiberius had once been Vahn's protégé, and when he had retired from active duty, Vahn had selected Tiberius to be his successor as Captain Elite. Landon composed himself and took a step back, away from his intended victim. The two champions moved him back toward the pyre, latching the ropes that bound his hands to the vertical stake aloft over his head.

Consequences be damned, Vahn had to do something. He could not very well let his friend and former student be put to death in the name of this madness. He made his way briskly through the crowd, not giving one damn if his progress was noted by the Skirlack stationed throughout the hub.

"Tiberius Woltram, you are given one final chance to repent for your sins with minimal punishment, and swear allegiance to The Faithful, the Empire of Aleksandrya, and the blessed mother of all, Skirlack."

Tiberius did Vahn proud when, before the name of the goddess had fully left Landon's mouth, he let loose a wad of blood-soaked spit from his mouth which flew through the air striking the former elite in the eye. This time, Landon's temper did not flare. He simply chuckled and held one hand out, not even moving to wipe the crimson wad of mucus from his face. "As it shall burn..."

A Champion of The Faithful rushed forward, crackling torch in hand, and placed it in Landon's waiting palm. The leader of the champions continued to laugh lightly, savoring the moment before he would touch the flame to kindling and incinerate the captive captain.

Vahn reached the front of the crowd. Now there were only Skirlack soldiers and champions between he and the life of a friend and ally. He ran, grabbing a dagger from the belt of a nearby champion, bringing it up swiftly to carve a deep swath into his jugular vein, and turning as the hot spray of dooming blood exploded outward.

Vahn continued to turn, driving the rigid fingers of his left hand into the throat of another champion, relieving him of his short sword and slashing him with it along the chest. Vahn spun and flung the dagger toward the pyre, its point cutting through the ropes that bound Tiberius's hands just as Landon dropped the torch.

The flames spread unnaturally fast, soon eclipsing Tiberius from view. As the chaos brought upon by Vahn's actions began to unfold, Skirlack and champions alike dashed to encircle him. Vahn could not pull his gaze from the growing inferno, hoping against hope that his old friend would somehow emerge from within. He nearly cried out with glee as the dark-skinned elite leapt out from a curtain of flame, hands prepped like the talons of a hungry bird as he rocketed toward Landon's throat.

Landon, seemingly having lost none of the skill which had once defined him upon the plane of battle, caught Tiberius by the wrists at the last second, falling back with the momentum, driving his boots into the larger man's solar plexus and vaulting him off the platform onto the street below.

Bedlam erupted and Vahn dropped into a flurry of defense, moving away from the now panicking mob of civilians, further into the hub's center. He slashed two oncoming champions before they had even a moment to mount an attack and ducked beneath the lurching bulky arm of a Skirlack soldier, silently dropping the chain still attached to his ankle down through his robe.

Vahn kicked out with his shackled leg, throwing the chain up and forward to smash into the face of an oncoming Skirlack and knock it to the ground. He kicked out once more, wrapping the long chain around the throat of an oncoming champion, flinging him violently face-first into the street. Another champion came at him, sword raised. Vahn met the incoming slash with a kick, feeling the sword strike the shackle, breaking the lock as the binding fell empty from his leg. The metal on metal contact forced the weapon to fly from the champion's grip and his flesh soon met Vahn's own blade, which carved through him in a spray of hot gore.

He tore the cloak from his body, now fully exposing his identity. Tiberius had risen to his feet and managed to wrestle a spiked mace from the grip of one of their assailants. He met Vahn's eyes with a look of incredulous shock and gave him one silent nod. Together, the two Kackrittan elites went back to back, seamlessly complimenting the other's style as they had so many times on the battlefield, pushing back the swath of demon and human alike.

"Burai!" Vahn heard Landon's unmistakable rasp bellow out in hatred born from decades upon decades of resentment.

Vahn looked up at his one-time friend who vaulted to the ground and began to advance. Vahn rushed forward, taking the head of another Skirlack demon as he plowed through the battle toward his foe.

Landon wrenched a sword from the grip of a dead champion and ran at the oncoming Vahn, a smile of long-awaited challenge roaring from his sharpened facial features. Just as the two warriors came within striking distance, a series of loud explosions and a blinding, thick haze of smoke spread between them.

Vahn ducked out of instinct and felt the displacement of air as Landon's sword just missed beheading him. Immediately thereafter, he felt several pairs of strong hands grip him along the arms and torso with surprising strength. Vahn struggled for a moment until a blunt force smacked the back of his head and he fell into unconsciousness.

XIV: THE VANISHING CITY

Empowering waves of mana energy coursed through Maura's body, warming her as she sat upon the frigid, snow-covered ground. The air was thin upon the high winding mountain path, but the higher they climbed, the more abundant the energy became.

It had not taken her long to master the ability to fill her body with its invigorating rush. She had first felt the tingling energy two days after the instruction began. She believed herself to be well on the way to harnessing this wild magic, however, she had hit a frustrating roadblock at the next stage of her training.

"Feel the energy flow within you," Valentean ordered. Though she sat with her eyes closed, she knew that he was across from her on the other side of the dormant fire pit they had dug out when stopping to camp for the night. She had been shocked at the strict taskmaster Valentean had become through the course of her instruction. Though the frigid cold bit into her flesh like a hungry animal, he had calmly explained that no fires would be lit within any campsite until her lessons had ended for the day.

"If you're cold, then call upon the energy to keep you warm," he had said on her first night under his tutelage. Maura had shed the heavy animal skins to fully expose herself to the harshness of the elements, sitting in only a small shirt and short pants, brow furrowed in concentration as she held on with iron-born determination. Should her concentration break, she risked freezing to death within the span of minutes.

Despite the danger, Maura knew that she could handle the task set out before her. What did gnaw at her was the sudden halt in her progress.

"You cannot force the energy through your body, it is not your slave," Valentean said slowly, calmly. "It is merely a passenger, and you serve not as its master but as its humble guide."

Maura had heard this particular line several times in recent days. She was beginning to feel the edge of irritation build in her throat, ready to snap out a strongly worded snippy response. But as her mind wandered, she felt the numbing paralyzing cold of the harsh environment strike her and redoubled her concentration.

Energizing her body was all well and good. But the true power Maura was seeking through these training sessions was the ability to use mana offensively. Valentean told her from the beginning that powerful emotion was the key to unlocking this dormant skill. He had described a scenario wherein his own personal self-doubt coupled with a moment of anger toward his brother and father pushed him beyond this barrier as a teenager.

Powerful emotions defined Maura. She focused on that moment of wrenching terror as Kayden had obliterated her home, the rage and grief which had torn her heart to pieces as that same monster tore the head off her father's shoulders, and the desperate depression she had experienced as a prisoner in the dungeon of Kackritta Castle. Maura pulled inspiration from every harsh memory she could muster, yet still, no spark or glow would form around her limbs.

Is my pain not enough for you? She silently raged at the mana energy within the private confines of her mind. *Do I need to lose even more to this horrible world before you'll deem me worthy?* She knew it was silly to blame the energy for her own deficiency.

"Trust the mana, allow it to feed off your emotions, fuel your fist with its power, and feel its energy strengthen and defend you," Valentean continued.

His words were meaningless at this point. There was nothing he could say that would suddenly part the clouds from her mind and grant her the ability to accomplish this task. She had been sitting like this for hours now, endlessly cycling through the most painful oppressive moments of her life, and getting nothing from it. It was a frustrating cluster of emotional strife, and a tear of angst spilled from the corner of her eye and traveled down her cheek. The sting of additional tears welled up within the shadow of her eyelids, and Maura gritted her teeth in anger, determined not to let this crippling defeat play out upon her face.

A soft warmth spread along her skin, and her eyes snapped open to see a large fire flaring to life in the center of their camp. Valentean stood just behind the snapping, crackling flames, looking down at her through the hazy heat streaked air between them.

"Why are we stopping?" Maura snapped, allowing the mana energy which had preserved her through the night to dissipate. "I can do this!"

"I'm sure you can," Valentean said sternly with no hint of sarcasm to be found within his soft baritone, "but you've exhausted your resolve for tonight."

"I have not! I can keep going!"

"That will not do anyone any good, Maura," he insisted. "You're mentally and emotionally exhausted. It's time to take a breather, get some sleep, and be ready to move at first light."

She wanted to argue but forced herself to see the wisdom in her teacher's words. This journey was not about her or these lessons in mana control. They had a mission to accomplish, and the rate at which they had been pushing themselves through the mountain range demanded both Valentean and Maura to be rested and at their best when they began anew.

"All right," she acquiesced, "I understand."

"Think on this tomorrow as we continue on," Valentean said, fully taking on the role of mentor. "Identify the blocks that prevent you from progressing further and try to find some way to break through."

"Understood … I will."

"Good." His stance softened as he smiled kindly upon her once more with the eyes of friendship. "Throw some clothes on, you look cold!"

She rolled her eyes at his subtle joke but could not muster even a fake chuckle. Maura gathered her discarded garments and began to stand, stretching her aching legs. Valentean, ever the gentleman, averted his gaze and allowed her privacy to redress.

"I don't know what's wrong with me," she said as she tied a brown sash around her waist. "I should be able to do this."

"There's absolutely nothing wrong with you," he replied. "This isn't easy. I should remind you that no human has managed to accomplish this in centuries. You're not going to pick it up right away."

She realized that he was correct. Valentean was a Rosinanti, and it had still taken him considerable time and effort to instruct his body to act as a conduit for the destructive power.

Maura knew that she could not allow such vexations to push her towards surrender. She nodded and gave Valentean as much of a half-smile as she could muster. He smiled back and sat down across from her, stretching his arms slowly, wincing in only slight discomfort while favoring his midsection. He had nearly healed, but there was clearly still some damage left to mend.

Maura mused on how kind he had been toward her throughout this journey. He was no doubt in a great deal of pain and, emotionally, he had to be dealing with such deep strife. His home had fallen, his father was missing, the love of his life was suffering some unknown fate. Yet he still managed to smile at her and take time from their journey to teach her to better herself as a warrior. She did not deserve a friend such as he, and Maura promised herself that she would be there for him and, perhaps, ease some of his burden.

"Valentean, how are you doing?" she asked softly, giving the white dragon a long, reassuring look.

"Oh, I'm holding together," he said. "I can feel my old strength coming back. I'm almost back in fighting shape."

"What about … emotionally?"

Valentean shifted uncomfortably and looked away. "I'm fine."

"I don't think that's true."

"Sorry, I'm a bit tired, Maura. We should get some sleep. I'll see you at dawn." He turned from her as he curled up beside the fire.

Maura nodded, her suspicions as to his mental state now confirmed by his deflection. She decided to let him sleep but promised herself that she would not let this conversation die. In the morning, she would press the issue again. She wanted Valentean to know that he was not alone and that he could trust and confide in her.

"At dawn, then..."

The morning's first light shone off the undisturbed white snow and cast a glare along Valentean's eyes. He shielded his vision with one arm and championed through it, his legs sinking into calf-high snow as he trudged onward. They had set their horse free some days ago and abandoned the carriage, opting to traverse the treacherous mountain path on foot for fear of the narrow winding snow covered passages. Both he and Maura carried a multitude of supplies salvaged from the cart upon their backs, and Valentean hoped that what they had managed to bring would last until they arrived in Grassan. His pack was feeling especially light that morning.

"You know..." Maura said, "if there's anything you'd like to discuss I'd be happy to listen."

Valentean sighed. Maura had been relentless in her desire to force him to air his thoughts. It had progressed to the point in which he was anxiously looking forward to making camp for the evening and beginning Maura's mana instruction. During those periods of reflective meditation, she was required to be silent.

"Oh, don't worry about me. I'm holding up well," he replied, lying through his teeth. His mind was heavy with what felt like a thousand dark thoughts, but he did not want to burden Maura.

"Valentean, Seraphina is..."

"I know, Maura," he snapped, wheeling around to face her, the dangerous edge of the dragon's rage tinting his tone at her constant badgering. He took a deep breath as Maura's eyes doubled in size, and he bit back on the dragon's empowering influence. "I'm sorry ... I know she's all right ... I can feel it. We just have to get to Grassan so that we can help the rest of Kackritta..."

Maura nodded as Valentean fixed her with an apologetic stare. Her glance back at him showed that there were no ill feelings. He turned and continued onward.

Since the unfortunate events in Kackritta City, Valentean had been free of the dangerous temptation of the dragon within his heart. It was as if the entirety of the Rosintai's spirit had been focused on healing his injuries, limiting his ability to call upon the wind or the strength of the light. But as his wounds had finished knitting themselves back together, the dragon's fury came roaring once more from the shadows of his subconscious.

He glanced back at Maura, who kept pace behind him, muttering to herself non-stop throughout their journey. "...had better be a damn city at the end of this or I'm going to kick you in a place where even a dragon will feel it..."

Valentean chuckled, realizing that vocalizing her discomfort was helping his friend commit herself further to their journey. He had been proud of her progress in mastering mana control and marveled at the rate in which she had learned to enrich her body with the natural energy.

He understood, all too well, Maura's frustration. He had been there himself, for many years, desperate and hungry for knowledge denied to him by Vahn's strict tutelage. The memory of his father's harsh training only served to make Valentean worry. Vahn had vanished from Kackritta Castle during the chaotic assault, after being handily defeated by the same monster which had nearly ended Valentean's life. Was he safe? Was he even alive? Valentean found the uncertainty to be a constant strain. At least he knew that Seraphina was still breathing.

His confusion as to her well-being only increased with each day. Every time he tried to sense her life force, he found the faint echo of her essence surrounded by that same deep, concealing cold, masking her location and freezing her in place. *Sera, please be all right,* he thought over and over again. While the cold masked her exact location, one thing was certain: she was within the confines of that magical shield which covered what was left of Kackritta City. The oath of animus demanded he return to her side.

The Rosintai's message, though convoluted and irritatingly vague, had been clear. Aid would be found in the "vanishing city of the magic makers." Each time he had drifted off to sleep since that initial vision, he had hoped that another nocturnal visit from his predecessor awaited. His hopes were for naught, and it seemed as though the Rosintai had said all he was willing to convey in that first message.

Valentean knew that they drew close to their quarry. The magical energy in the air all seemed fixated on one point just beyond the mountain. Excitement quickened his pace.

"I hate the snow ... I hate the cold ... I hate mountains ... I hate walking ... I hate dragons..."

"All dragons?" Valentean playfully called back.

"That answer is dependent on what we find once we get past this mountain!"

He smiled and soldiered on. Truth be told, he was worried this entire journey had been all for naught. What would their course of action be if Grassan was not there? Or what if it was present and they refused aid, or worse yet, attacked them?

"I want to soak for a week in a hot spring once this is all over … I want to have half-dressed servant men feed me grapes while I sip wine…"

"That's the spirit, just focus on goals."

"…I want to punch Valentean Burai in the head…"

"Not nice."

"Neither is freezing to death. Mana can only do so much while you're moving. I'm shivering non-stop and I'm bundled in layers. You're still just wearing those same robes!"

Maura had asked him if he wanted some heavier clothing which she had found in the commandeered wagon, but Valentean refused. He was an animus warrior of Kackritta, and these robes signified his devotion to Seraphina. The once radiant white garments were covered in black scorch marks, tears, grime, and splotches of old blood. Still, he wore them with pride for his lost home, his missing lady, and his oath. The cold hadn't bothered him much. His Rosinanti body adapted to the frigid temperatures and protected him from the harsh elemental might.

"Well, I…" Valentean stopped short as a gargantuan surge of magical energy reverberated through the air. It was as though every bit of magic in the area had converged upon one point further up the path. "Maura, do you feel that?"

"Feel what?"

"Reach out and sense the shift of magic and mana in the air. Concentrate."

Maura closed her eyes for several seconds before they shot back open in alarm. "Whoa!" she exclaimed, "That is … just … wow!"

"It's Grassan," Valentean said with a smile. "It has to be!"

"Oh, thank Terra," Maura said, throwing her head back and laughing with glee. "Come on. It can't be much further!"

They broke into a happy sprint through the snow, eager to see the spectacle of a city very few outsiders had ever laid eyes upon. With every step, the strength of the converging energy grew until Valentean's whole body trembled. They hopped and jumped through the deep snow, seeing an end to the path up ahead. The pair approached the edge of a cliff, from which they'd undoubtedly see the glory of Grassan spread out before them. They skidded to a stop as they came to the edge. Valentean took one shaking deep breath and gazed out at … nothing.

There was nothing there; no city, no people, no structures. Nothing but open barren land at the base of the mountain, a massive empty space stretching out toward the sea. For a moment, there was silence. Valentean gaped, open-mouthed, in disappointment as the vast emptiness seemed to mock his earlier excitement. Then, Maura filled the silence.

"Are you serious?" she exploded, following that up with a burst of expletives that would make a Kackrittan dock worker blush with embarrassment.

Valentean was dumbfounded. This should have been it. This was the other side of the mountain range, the end of the map, a large space which would accommodate a city, and the center of the magic convergence he had sensed. A burst of haze in the air drew his attention as Maura pounded on the snow with her fists, continuing to rage and spew curses in her frustration.

Just as quickly as the slight distortion of the air had appeared, it vanished once more. Valentean slowly walked to the edge of the cliff, studying the area carefully, one hesitant hand raised at waist height in trepidation. After a moment, the distortion returned, making the area appear wavy, like the air above a roaring fire.

Valentean lashed out with one hand, his arm a blur of speed. He touched the distortion, which felt stretchy and wrinkled beneath his palm. The instant he made contact with whatever magic this might be, an explosion of power ripped through him, causing the light spirit of the Rosintai to respond. His eyes and skin exploded in white energy, causing Maura to yelp in surprise and fall back into the snow.

The magic pushed inward through the channels of energy within Valentean's body and met the light which had been building within his chest. The entire area shone with the radiant, ivory glow of Valentean's power. Soon a sound like that of shattering glass could be heard echoing off the mountain. There was a small burst as Valentean stumbled back, and before his eyes, a marvelous sight began to appear.

Grassan materialized in the vast empty clearing, and it was more miraculous than Valentean had ever imagined. It easily dwarfed Kackritta City. The entirety of it was covered with buildings large and small, all with red pointed roofs that gave a city a prickly appearance. Dozens of large rectangular buildings with long cylindrical rods that rose out from them, spewed smoke in tufts of color, ranging from red to green to blue, black, white, and purple. At the center of it all stood the most magnificent and impressive structure Valentean had ever seen.

It was almost a small city in its own right with large buildings that towered above the rest of Grassan. They were of varying heights, arranged close together, seemingly at random. All of them were the same shade of light brown, and upon many of them giant gears slowly turned together. In the center of them all rose a tower which formed the highest point in the mage smith city. The tallest structures of Grassan did not so much as reach one-quarter of the way up the massive tower's height. There was a giant clock face on the front of it, surrounded by gears of various sizes, some of which continuously turned, and others that moved slowly at set intervals.

From the top of the tower ran six clear light blue jagged shards of what looked like crystal. They curved downward, forming a stationary half-globe around the center of Grassan. Hovering above, level with the top quarter of the tower, were a series of metallic airships which silently glided along the limits of the city. It was the single most impressive sight Valentean had ever seen.

"I can't believe it..." Maura said beside him, now back on her feet and gaping with wonderment at the grand sight below.

"The vanishing city of the magic makers..." Valentean said, repeating the Rosintai's words aloud as they suddenly made sense. The city had been cloaked in a monumental spell which he had shattered. He wondered if that was going to anger the city's leaders and make his mission here more difficult.

"Freeze where you are!" a loud booming voice sounded from above them. Looking up, Valentean saw four miniature airships, each no larger than a horse-drawn wagon. They were open, offering no shelter from the wind, and upon each stood four armored guards.

Each soldier of Grassan wore a simple brown jumpsuit, covered with light body armor on the chest, shoulders, forearms, pelvis, knees and shins. Their hands were covered in long, thick brown gloves that traveled halfway up the forearm. Atop each of their heads, they wore a simple white helmet and a pair of goggles over their eyes.

Maura and Valentean huddled back to back as a pair of soldiers descended from each airship in a magically controlled glide. They brandished weapons ranging from swords to daggers to long whips, all of which crackled with sparking bursts of electricity that seemed generated by the soldiers themselves, using magic. Valentean knew that the simple platoon couldn't possibly hope to defeat them, but he had already made enough of a ruckus by breaking their city-wide concealment spell, and he did not want to add a brawl with Grassan's soldiers to any list of grievances the king might levy at him.

"Maura, stand down," he instructed, standing up straight and raising his arms in surrender.

"What? I'm not going to another dungeon!"

"Just trust me, please. We don't want to cause a scene here before we've even set foot in the city."

"I ... ugh! Fine," she replied, lowering her daggers.

"We surrender," Valentean said. "I am Valentean Burai, animus warrior of the Kingdom of Kackritta, and we seek an audience with King Matias."

The soldiers stopped short at the mention of his name and glanced at one another. Though their eyes remained shrouded behind the black glass of their goggles, Valentean could sense fear.

"Looks like they've heard of you," Maura muttered back to him.

"Despite what you may have heard, I'm not your enemy!" he assured, showing his palms. "Please, allow me a chance to speak with the king!"

Shockingly, the soldiers all lowered their weapons.

"Lord Burai," one of them said, inclining his head toward Valentean in a bow of respect. He removed his helmet, showing a mop of long brown hair with unnatural streaks of purple spreading along his locks. "Please come with us, the king will surely see you."

Valentean exhaled in relief at the acceptance of these soldiers. Did they know he was of the Rosinanti? Or were they simply reacting to his title of Champion Animus of Terra? Either way, Valentean was happy to see that there would be no confrontation.

One of the small airships began to lower, and the soldier motioned for them to climb on board. Valentean stepped up onto the humming machinery, extending his hand to help Maura up beside him. As the airship rose into the air and tilted toward the sprawling metropolis of Grassan, Valentean felt hope burst to life within his heart for the first time since the fall of Kackritta.

Hang on, Sera, he thought, *I'm coming for you.*

XV: FEAR

Sights and sounds were distorted to Seraphina's perception, as though she were underwater. Yet she felt no touch of moisture upon her skin. She had been floating through this odd reality for some time now, enjoying the peace of the moment, reflecting on her mission to master the element of water and return to the physical world as a fully realized spirit of order.

The hazy murkiness faded as the world Aqua constructed within the astral plane of the dreamscape began to take shape. Seraphina recognized the lush green forest leading toward the outer wall of Kackritta City, which loomed in the distance. It was all so familiar to her, the sights, the smells, the sunlight that filtered down in dancing shafts of light through the leaves. She raised one hand to her eyes to block the morning glare when she noticed something odd. Her hand looked different, smaller, her fingers slightly pudgier than before.

Looking down, Seraphina found herself in an unfamiliar red dress, her body lacking the curves of womanhood. She ran her hands through her hair and found it to be far shorter than it should have been. What was this? Where was she? It was as though she were … a child again…

Whirling around, Seraphina noticed with a startled gasp where she stood. The ground beneath her was barren, brown, and crusted, and she stood at the base of a tall, grey, dead tree, upon which nothing grew. She once again stood at the leafless tree as a thirteen-year-old girl. That could only mean one thing … Aqua had brought her back to *that* day. The day she had fallen into a coma. The day she had been assaulted by the beast. It was the day which had spawned the series of events that led her to this reality.

She heard commotion coming from the forest behind her and turned in mounting horror to see the thirteen-year-old forms of Valentean and Kayden, racing one another at an even pace, rocketing toward her. Her breath came in ragged frenzied gasps of all consuming panic as events unfolded once more, exactly as she remembered them in her nightmares. Valentean pulled ahead of his larger brother, and Seraphina winced. She knew the all-consuming dark shadow of the beast would soon envelop her.

The light around her shifted as the darkness cast by the monster's girth fell. She watched Valentean's face fall into a look of shock and horror as he looked back at Kayden, determined to reach her in time. But this was the one time Seraphina knew that her future animus warrior would be too late. She did not want to turn around, hoping that, maybe this time, if she ignored the beast's presence it would simply cease to exist. These were the desperate desires of a child, and despite the form she occupied, Seraphina was a woman now and had to face her fears.

As she turned, a chilling cold spread out from her heart, numbing the rest of her body. Every centimeter of the monster was as large and imposing as she had always remembered. The rubbery red skin, the filthy loincloth, the individual thin black hairs that fell around its head: it was the truest definition of her greatest fear. She had faced off against many Skirlack soldiers since that fateful day, but this monster always seemed to be so much more than the simple grunt she now knew it to be.

As the beast brought its massive arm back to swipe down and plunge her into the dark sleep that would incapacitate her for weeks, the terrified princess raised her arms, attempting to call upon the power of order to defend herself and show the beast exactly what she had become. She felt the faintest echo of power spark to life within her heart, but it faded and died before she could unleash it. She was powerless once more, no longer a spirit of order, just a weak-willed, frightened thirteen-year-old girl.

The beast's arm shot out at her, and Seraphina jumped back, landing on the ground and letting the burly appendage pass harmlessly overhead. She gasped in shock. They were in uncharted territory. The beast grunted and raised a gargantuan foot into the air, attempting to bring it down on the princess's tiny frame. She scrambled out of the way of the titanic stomp and ran toward Valentean.

If they could reach one another then perhaps she would make it through this ordeal unscathed. He would never fail her. Even then, he could never fail her. She heard the beast lumbering after her, but her eyes were affixed on the younger version of the man she loved and adored. A renewed sense of hope and relief washed over her strained heart and mind. Just then, as her outstretched fingers were about to touch his, Kayden dashed with unnatural speed, wrapping a large, meaty arm around Valentean's throat and pulled him roughly back, away from Seraphina who skidded to a halt.

"Val!" she cried out in desperation. His eyes registered surprise and fear simultaneously as he reached for her, agonizing over his inability to get to her in time. Kayden smiled wickedly and leapt into the sky, dragging his brother along until they vanished into the bright light beyond the trees. Seraphina turned once more to gaze in horror at the beast, which had grown by an entire meter in the brief time that her attention had been diverted. She scrambled back, tripped over the uneven ground, and landed in a seated position as the red-skinned demon slowly advanced.

"*Fear is an instrument of darkness, and in turn fuels chaos,*" the voice of Aqua said, her words echoing through the forest. "*The tides fear nothing, the waves do not shrink before the shoreline. Order cannot flow unfettered in the face of such terror.*"

"Aqua, help!" Seraphina screamed, her thirteen-year-old voice shrill with panic as she scooted back away from this awful foe. As she continued to quake, the beast began to glow with red energy and grew another several meters. Its horns elongated as well, becoming jagged and sharp. It's pointed, yellow teeth now extended out through its lips, framing its terrifying face. Hungry saliva dripped from a mouth so large, Seraphina's entire head could have fit inside.

"*When we succumb to our fears, we empower them,*" Aqua continued. "*As we flee before painful memories, or allow panic to take hold of our hearts, our fears will only grow.*" The beast continued to inflate, looming larger until it towered over the trees themselves. It stepped beyond the tiny princess, upending the forest with every step. Seraphina watched in horror as the now gigantic monster thundered toward Kackritta City. Tears stung her eyes as she envisioned the panicked streets, people fleeing in every conceivable direction as this monster born of her own terror upended their lives.

"What am I supposed to do?"

"*Conquer your fear. Take its power. Show this manifestation of your darkest dread that it holds no sway over you.*"

"How am I supposed to do that?" she cried up into the air. This time, there was no response from her invisible mentor. "Aqua?" It was clear from her predecessor's silence that there would be no further aid given. She had to do this on her own, without Aqua, without Valentean; just herself.

She raised her shaking hands, pointing them at the beast's immense back as it kicked in the wall surrounding Kackritta City. Still, the power of order turned from her in this hour of need. She cursed herself silently and desperately tried to take control of her quaking limbs.

I'm calm. I'm not afraid, she silently assured herself, but deep down she knew this to be empty lies. How could she conquer something so imposing? When it was naught but a simple Skirlack soldier, it had nearly ended her life. Now it was a monster of immeasurable might and power, stomping out the homes of her people callously while roaring with rage and bloodlust.

Valentean would know what to do. He would be able to control his fear and face this beast. He was supposed to be here, standing with her. They weren't supposed to be apart. As the beast approached Kackritta Castle, Seraphina imagined her parents, now violently murdered in the real world but still alive here in her mind, and in her heart.

My mind... she thought, *my heart...*

Seraphina tried to focus, closing her eyes and pulling forth another memory, one from when she had been far younger, only five or six. She had so few memories that persevered from those early days of her life, experiences of the present eating away at the remnants of childhood experience. But there was one evening that still shone strong. One bright, shining, happy moment of love and support which she had often called on in dark times.

She had screamed for her father on that night, a terrible nightmare rousing the young princess from a fitful sleep. Her tutors had begun instructing her in the history of Terra, and instilled in her, even at such a young age, the severity and savagery of the Great Rosinanti War. Her subconscious that evening had dredged up awful images of mammoth, scaled dragons hunting her, destroying her home and family in a blood-soaked quest for vengeance.

An attendant had roused her father when it was clear the child would not cease her fussing without him. Roan entered Seraphina's bedchamber, his hair and beard a disheveled mess as a red evening robe emblazoned with the phoenix of the royal family fluttered with his quickened steps.

"What's wrong, peanut?" he asked, kneeling at her bedside and taking her chubby cheek in his strong warm hand.

"I saw the Rosinanti, Papa," she said through sobs, clutching at his thick wrist with both tiny hands in desperation, as though he could ward them off with nothing but his mere presence. "The dragons are coming to get me!"

Roan's expression softened as he realized these were nothing more than the panicked imaginings of a young girl and not some deep emergency. "Peanut," he said, always referring to his youngest daughter by that simple term of endearment until she had turned ten and demanded he stop. "There are no dragons. They cannot hurt you, ever. You're safe here, you're safe with me."

"But Papa, they could destroy cities with their magic and they killed kings and queens and ... and..."

"Seraphina, it is not a bad thing to be afraid."

"It isn't?" she had asked in wide-eyed fascination. "But you and momma are never afraid!"

The king laughed softly. "Peanut, I'm afraid all the time."

"You are?"

"Yes, of course, I am. No one, not even kings, queens, princes, or princesses are fearless. But when I get afraid, do you want to know what I do?" She nodded furiously, desperate and hungry for any such knowledge that would end her nightmares. "I think about whatever it is that I'm afraid of, I take a deep breath, and I say, 'you do not rule me; I rule you.'"

"And that works?" Seraphina had asked him, unconvinced.

"It works every time." He leaned in and kissed his young daughter on the forehead, touching the tip of her nose briefly with one finger. "So, the next time you see these scary dragons in your dreams, what are you going to tell them?"

"You do not rule me. I rule you."

"That's my girl."

Over the years, Seraphina had attempted many times to control her fear using this mantra. She had never found it to be particularly effective or helpful. As a child, she had uttered these words whenever she felt alone or afraid, and they did nothing but provide a repetitive exercise that helped to keep her mind occupied. But burying fear was not the same as conquering it.

She had not thought back on that day in quite some time. Now, with the experience of adulthood, she believed the wisdom of her late father might hold truer given recent events. She looked at the beast as it eyed the castle with a hungry lust for destruction. Despite the pounding of her heart, she narrowed her eyes.

"You do not rule me ... I rule you," she said quietly, reflecting on the words as they left her mouth. These experiences and memories that created such a terrifying visage were only that, memories of a dreadful moment. One that she had overcome by continuing to live on. Why should a specter of the past matter to her now? Why should the memories of an event nearly a decade removed continue to hold such undeniable power over her?

"You do not rule me ... I rule you," she repeated once more, raising her arms, palms up as the beast reared back one massive arm to punch through the protective walls of Kackritta Castle. She felt the pulse of order alight within her heart once more, and a shifting quake moved the ground beneath her feet. The beast's wind-up moved slowly, as though it were savoring the moment. But Seraphina would ensure that moment would never come.

"You do not rule me ... I rule you," she said, louder now and with more force. The spreading tingle of order churned inside her. It prickled beneath her skin, warm and powerful. Her father's calm smile shone in her mind's eye, that smile she would never see again. She owed it to him to use the lessons he had taught her to take Kackritta City back and avenge his death.

"You do not rule me; I rule you!" she screamed as an explosion of blue energy ripped out from her tiny body. As the glow subsided, Seraphina stood taller than before, her visage returning to that of an adult. Her body rose into the air as the folds of her blue dress billowed about in the wake of her power. Her eyes once more shone with the sapphire light of order.

From behind her, a monumental burst of water erupted from the ground. With a single motion of her arms, she sent the liquid tube hurtling across the decimated countryside, and it wrapped around the beast's arm like a rope. The creature grunted and attempted to wrestle out from the water's powerful grip, but Seraphina held on with fierce determination. She pulled her arms back, making her fluid projectile pull on the beast, wrenching it out through the large hole it had formed in the city's wall.

It glowered down at her with rage, its eyes now shining with the same red energy as Aleksandra's. One last surge of fear attempted to rise within Seraphina's throat but the princess bit it down, took a deep breath, and repeated the words of her father one last time.

"You do not rule me; I rule you!" she screamed as five equally huge bursts of water flew out of the surrounding ground. In response to her will and a flinging flail of her arms, they rocketed at the beast, joining together to form a single, thick, powerful column of glowing blue energy which tore into the nightmare's chest, exploding out of its back and soaring unfettered into the sky.

The beast released a great wet gurgle of shock and pain before it fell forward onto its face. As it impacted the ground, there was a massive explosion, ripping the remnants of the castle-sized creature's form to shreds and temporarily blinding Seraphina in the glare.

As her vision returned, Seraphina found herself once more in a representation of Aqua's fountain chamber. The former Spirit of Order was once more standing before her atop the waters of her fountain, smiling with genuine pride.

"You've learned to accept your fears, to turn them against your enemies," Aqua said.

"I just took some very old advice that finally paid off," Seraphina replied, panting with exertion.

"It takes greater strength to embrace one's fear and choose to ignore it than to be fearless and ignorant of the concept. Your sister knows no fear because she has grown to believe herself to be invincible. You've accepted your terror and made a willing choice to subdue it. That is the truest definition of bravery, dear Seraphina."

Seraphina felt a swell of pride as a heavy burden lifted from her shoulders. She finally learned to let go.

"Does this mean I'm a fully realized spirit of order now?" Seraphina asked with mounting excitement.

Aqua giggled in response. "Oh no, sweet girl," she said, shaking her head. "We've scarcely begun."

Aqua's eyes shone with blue energy once more, and Seraphina saw the now familiar murky glare of her surroundings melting away. Whatever Aqua's next lesson had in store for her, she would face it head on, proudly, and without fear.

XVI: THE COLLECTIVE OF LIGHT

Every corner of Grassan represented a burning, unasked question which flared to life in Valentean's mind. Though his mission was of utmost importance, he could not help but feel the excited, jubilant tug of wonder born of a mind that once sought travel and adventure.

He and Maura, along with four soldiers of Grassan, rode the tiny airship down the mountain, passing over the walls that marked the entrance to the magical city. Valentean's eyes bulged as he saw the factories and homes of Grassan up close.

The colored clouds of smoke that rose into the sky, high above him, cast a fascinating hue across the afternoon sunshine. All throughout the city, coupled carriages moved along preset tracks as the same multi-colored wisps billowed from a tiny smokestack at their front. It was unlike anything Valentean had ever dreamed possible, and he could sense the powerful forces that urged these advanced machinations onward.

"It's all run by magic, isn't it?" he asked over the roaring wind.

The soldier who first addressed him atop the mountain nodded once, a flash of kind, gentle amusement in his eyes. "Yes, Grassani society blends a mixture of machinery with magic. They come together to create the foundation of our great city. Magic is life in Grassan."

"Then, why are those people working with their hands?" Maura asked, pointing down at a group of burly workers, men and women alike, who toiled amidst a large-scale construction project, digging with shovels, pounding with sledgehammers, and working up a hard day's sweat. They were all marked by the same colorful splotches along their hair, as that of the soldier who was addressing them. The colors ranged from blue to red to purple and white. "Can't they just use magic to do all of that?"

"Oh, those are the Shormloch," he replied, as though this were a term anyone should know offhand. When he saw the blank stares of his charges he explained, "Citizens of Grassan born without magic. They lack the ability to power the machinery which is vital to most upper tier operations of the city. So, they help as they can, usually through manual labor."

"And how do they feel about that?" Maura asked, raising a skeptical eyebrow.

"They're paid a very fair wage, miss," the soldier replied.

One of his colleagues audibly cleared his throat and shot his peer a sidelong glare. "Keep your mouth shut or the captain will have your head," he scolded. "They're outsiders!"

The soldier looked down as he turned a bright scarlet. Valentean wanted to question them as to the identity of this mysterious "captain," but did not want to do anything to further implicate the man. He met the young man's goggled stare and gave him a reassuring smile, hoping to convey his thanks.

Asking about this captain of theirs could wait. Valentean had a feeling his identity would be revealed once they reached their destination.

The airship had come to a stop atop one of the large buildings outside the central tower in the center of Grassan. They were ushered down a series of brown stone hallways until they came to a pair of purple and gold double doors. They opened, seemingly on their own, to reveal a large circular office. Along the curved walls ran a series of grates, within which various gears and machines churned along. The room was decorated in an extravagance not seen since entering this structure. The desk was a dark, red wood and polished until it shone in the sunlight which filtered in through the large curved window that ran along a section of the wall directly behind it. Every bit of the floor was covered in purple and gold carpeting that matched the hues of the door in which they had entered. Several pieces of art decorated pedestals around the chamber, ranging from vases, to sculptures of abstract amorphous forms, to a scale model of Grassan itself.

"Captain!' one of the guards said, stepping forward with a crisp salute to a man Valentean had not noticed.

The Captain stood nearly a head taller than Valentean, long-legged and thin. He kept his back to the outsiders, adorned in an ornate flowing purple coat which hugged tightly against his slender frame and extended past his calves. His pair of black heeled boots trimmed in golden flourishes looked as though they had been made specifically to blend in with the posh carpet. Atop his head of dirty blonde purple streaked hair, rested a tall, black top hat with a purple and gold sash run around it at the base.

"Hello, captain," Valentean said, trying to initiate the conversation, "my name is…"

"Yes, so I've heard," came a crisp, rich voice which carried within it the unmistakable mark of aristocracy. The captain held up one hand, covered in a thick black glove similar in style but more lavishly produced than those of his soldiers. "My knights inform me of your claim. Champion Animus of Terra, indeed. And if the murmurings I'm hearing are true, that is the *least* interesting thing about you, Valentean Burai."

Something in the way he spoke ruffled Valentean. An accusatory edge stained every word, and the captain would not so much as turn to look the visiting animus warrior in the eye.

"You have me at a bit of a disadvantage, Mister…"

"Yes, as I do with most everyone who walks through that door." The captain turned around slowly, revealing a young man, maybe a few years older than he. His blue-eyed stare pierced through Valentean and Maura like that of a bird. His skin was olive, and his neat hair was meticulously combed back into the confines of his hat, save for a single blonde and purple lock that drew down onto his forehead and forced into a swirling pattern. His chin and sharp nose remained pointed up with pride, allowing him to glower down at his uninvited guests.

The purple coat that he wore was latched across his torso by a series of horizontal purple straps with golden buckles that ran parallel with one another from his chest to his waist. Along his belt, he carried two of those electrified whips that had been brandished by the soldiers who had come out to detain them. The captain raised one hand elegantly to the brim of his top hat, upon which Valentean could now make out a pair of dark goggles strapped to its center. He tipped his hat ever so slightly and inclined his head just a bit in way of greeting.

"I am Nahzarro, captain of the Knights Mystic of the Kingdom of Grassan. You will be taken before the king, as requested, once certain … measures have been taken to assure your compliance with the laws of our kingdom."

"What kind of measures?" Valentean asked, trying to remain calm.

"Disarmament," Nahzarro replied quickly, once more turning back to the window and gazing out over the landscape of Grassan. "I will not permit you to step into the presence of King Matias armed as you are."

"I'd be happy to hand over any weapons we have on us."

"Your shormy friend there will be relieved of those crude blades," he continued.

Valentean felt Maura stir beside him and turned to stare his now red-faced companion in the eye and offer a subtle shake of his head.

"But for you, *Lord* Burai, it is my understanding that you do not require a weapon to be considered dangerous, therefore we must take other measures in your case." Nahzarro whirled about once more with a flick of his coat, brandishing a large crude-looking device that he had pulled, seemingly, from thin air and placed with a hard, metallic clunk upon the desk. Valentean tensed upon seeing what it was: a smaller, sleeker version of the magic restricting muzzle which had kept him powerless while in the dungeons of Kackritta Castle.

"Absolutely not," Maura said, stepping forward in outrage.

"Tell your shorm friend to..." Nahzarro said to Valentean before Maura cut him off once more.

"I'm going to 'shorm' my fist into your mouth if you call me that one more time!"

"You *dare* threaten the captain of the Knights Mystic?"

"I'll do a lot more than threaten if you step anywhere near my friend with that barbaric torture device!" She began to advance upon the captain, whose hand fell to his belt, resting upon one of the whips he kept there. The knights around the room tensed, and Valentean stepped quickly between the two.

"Captain, please, excuse my friend." He turned and gave Maura a glare that could make a Potentias soil the ground. "If wearing this ... measure will aid in our audience with your king, I will, of course, comply."

Maura fidgeted behind him but remained quiet. Nahzarro, seemingly content with how the situation had resolved itself, dropped his arm once more and clasped it with his other behind his back. He nodded to one of the knights who moved to retrieve the device as the doors to the office burst open.

A hunched older woman limped her way inside, parting the wall of knights that lined the room's only exit as they genuflected with deference to her. She was withered and grey, adorned in long brown and green robes, upon which leather straps and copper buckles ran in seemingly random directions.

"Minister Khara," Nahzarro said respectfully, this time removing his hat and bending in a grandiose bow upon meeting the woman's grey-eyed gaze.

"Stand down, Captain," the old woman's voice shakily commanded. "The king knows of these visitors and has commanded they be brought before him with no restrictive measures put in place."

"What?" Nahzarro roughly placed the hat back upon his head. "But doesn't he know who this is?"

"He knows perfectly well, young one, and you must remember your place!" Khara snapped at the captain, who grimaced at her words like a scolded child. She turned from the distraught and disbelieving Nahzarro, smiling kindly at Valentean and Maura.

"Lord Burai, Miss Lorne, please accompany me," she said warmly. "King Matias requests the honor of your presence in the central tower throne room."

"The honor is all mine, Minister," Valentean replied, offering his arm to the old woman who gratefully took it, leading them out of the room. From the corner of his eye, Valentean saw Maura give a small, victorious smile and a tiny wave to the still fuming Captain Nahzarro.

"Have a lovely day, Captain," Maura said, intentionally fake sweetness staining every word.

After a short ride on another of those remarkable tiny airships, Valentean and Maura walked on either side of Minister Khara down a long hallway within the central tower. Two sentries stood guard on either side of a pair of steel bolted doors and, after a wave of dismissal from the old woman, moved aside and allowed the trio to pass within the throne room of King Matias.

Valentean's first thought upon entering the round chamber was that this must be what the inside of a clock looked like. The walls and ceiling were alive with turning and whirling gears and various mechanisms, all working simultaneously toward some unknown goal. Whereas the throne room of Kackritta Castle had been lavish and ornate, the bare chamber which housed the royal seat of Grassan's power was quite plain and unremarkable in comparison. The walls and floor were barren brown stone. The room was kept void of all accoutrements, save for the large metal throne at the far end which sat before the rear side of the enormous clock face Valentean had seen upon the tower at their approach.

An honor guard of twelve Knights Mystic stood on either side of the throne, in which sat the stocky King Matias. His bearded chubby face regarded the advancing strangers with cold indifference. Upon his round body sat tan and dark brown robes that fell toward his calves, adorned in the now familiar sight of various leather straps and golden buckles which fastened the garment. Atop his unruly brown and white splotched shoulder-length hair sat a bronze, pointed crown, around which hung a pair of dark goggles.

Khara motioned for Valentean and Maura to halt before the king, and she greeted him in a deep curtsy. Valentean and Maura followed suit with a bow of respect and rose back to attention along with the minister.

"Behold," Khara announced with precise and practiced poise, "you stand before King Gerald Matias, lord of the free kingdom of Grassan, sovereign of the mage smiths, commander of the Knights Mystic." The round-bellied monarch continued to regard both of these new guests with a deafening lack of visible emotion. The old woman turned and regarded her two charges. "Your Majesty, may I present Miss Maura Lorne of the village of Lazman, and Lord Valentean Burai of … of Kackritta."

Valentean found it odd that the minister would pause before speaking the name of his home. She had clearly not forgotten it, so why the pause? Was there something he did not know?

The king snorted in interest and leaned forward in his riveted bolted throne, emblazoned with the familiar design of silver gears which were actually turning along the backrest. "Lord Burai," he said, rising to his feet with a grunt of effort. The king stepped down onto the floor and causally approached. "I've heard a great deal about you, boy."

"Your highness honors me," Valentean replied.

"Do I?" he replied, raising an eyebrow. "You don't know what I've heard yet."

"I have nothing to hide, Your Majesty."

"Who would have thought it," the king mused to himself, pacing back and forth before them. "The bloody Rosintai, in my throne room."

Valentean's blood practically froze in his veins. The king was remarkably well-informed, not only at Valentean's origin as a Rosinanti dragon but at the term Rosintai, which was far from common knowledge.

"Tell me something, boy," the king motioned to his side and one of his guards brought forth a large goblet of wine. He drained the entire cup in one massive gulp as it spilled out along his long, scraggly beard. He wiped his mouth clean with a thick forearm, drawing a stain of red along the brown sleeve of his robe. "Are you a god?"

Valentean's knees weakened. To call this a loaded inquiry would be an understatement, and to be honest, Valentean had no real answer. He knew that the tingling power of light which dwelled within his soul was the power of an ancient god, but to actually call himself one... His thoughts fell upon Kayden, and how he might answer. Valentean imagined his larger brother throwing his head back and laughing with glee as he'd proudly pronounce himself a deity worthy of praise and worship. Valentean though felt his stomach turn at the thought.

"Well, boy?" Matias continued. "A king has asked you a question. Are you a bloody god, or not?"

"Well, Your Highness," Valentean said, his voice soft and withdrawn, "you seem to be rather well-informed about me and … what I can do. To answer your question … I'm just a man, same as any other. Same as my father, same as any of your guards here, and frankly, the same as you. Power, riches, even a crown never truly change who we are. We're all people. Whether one is a human or a Rosinanti, I don't think that matters. What does matter is what we choose to do with the opportunities and advantages we're given. How I choose to use my powers, how you choose to wield your authority, how any person might go home and choose to treat their family; those are the things that truly mark us as people. So, am I a god? No, I'm just a person who can do things no one else can. The fact that I choose to use those gifts to help others, and to stand up for the people I care about … I don't know if that makes me a god, but as sure as I'm standing here … it makes me a man."

There was silence throughout the room; an eerie deafening stillness as Valentean and King Matias locked eyes. After what felt like an eternity, the king's ruddy face came alight with a toothy smile that shone through the bushiness of his beard. Valentean did not know how to react so he smiled back, albeit shakily. The king brought his hands up before his chest, covered in the same thick, brown gloves Valentean had seen many others wearing throughout the city, and placed them together, fingertip to fingertip, forming the shape of a diamond before his heart. His smile faded, and King Matias of Grassan bent at the waist and bowed before Valentean Burai.

The animus warrior took a step back in shock. A king bowing before him was something he never believed he would see. He turned back toward minister Khara to find her, too, following suit with her king, engaging once more in a deep curtsy. The members of the Knights Mystic who stood on either side of the throne also genuflected down to one knee. Valentean turned his head to Maura, who was smiling at her friend. She gave him a quick wink and then bowed as well.

Matias stood back to his full height, followed by everyone else in the room, and clapped a strong meaty hand onto Valentean's shoulder.

"If you had any idea how long I've waited for this day … and to think it'd be the son of that damned fool Vahn Burai," he said with a barking laugh that told Valentean he had not been seriously trying to insult his honored father. "Come, boy, we have much to discuss!"

Valentean and Maura found themselves sitting in a sparse office adjacent to the larger throne room. They sat in small cushioned seats before a riveted steel desk and matching chair upon which King Matias rested, wine goblet still in hand.

Valentean had noted that the king's private office was kept very simple, a far cry from Nahzarro's lush accommodations. There were no decorative items or flair within the room, and the large desk was kept bare, save for a feathered quill pen, a roll of parchment, and a large model of a ship which sat in the desk's center.

Valentean had spent the better part of twenty minutes explaining everything that had transpired on their journey. Matias took it all in between sips from his comically large wine goblet and nodded as Valentean's tale caught up to the present.

"I bet you didn't expect me to know the word 'Rosintai', did you boy?" the king said with a hearty chuckle, leaning his bulk upon the large desk.

"I was a bit taken back by it, Your Majesty," he replied.

The king laughed once more. "So proper. You really are old sly Burai's boy, aren't you?"

"Sly?"

"Aye, your father was … well, I suppose we can reminisce about old times some other day. Right now, there's a lot I have to fill you in on." The king dug into the front of his shirt and pulled out a small, white pendant on a chain. It was perhaps made of marble, and carved into its surface was a large eye, though the pupil ran as a vertical slit, similar to that of a reptile. "Do you know what this is?"

"No, sir," Valentean replied, studying the bauble closely.

"Those Faithful, worshipping their fire god all these centuries, growing in secret, plotting their revenge, surely you had to suspect there were some who knew the truth?"

"You mean…?"

"Son, you've spent quite a few days waiting to meet me, but I've been waiting to meet you all my rudding life." Valentean stared, open-mouthed, at the king. Could there really be a group that rivaled the Faithful? "There are only a handful of these pendants in the world, worn in secret by those who have sworn loyalty to The Collective."

"Collective?"

"Aye, the Collective of Light, the truth-keepers. Those who have passed down the true story of the Rosintai's struggle and awaited his return to rid this world of Ignis and those Skirlack beasts."

"A … whole group of you?"

"Don't get too excited, boy," Matias said, holding up one hand as if to halt Valentean's train of thought. "We're not an army, just a few dozen people spread around the world, placed in positions of power and prestige to wait for the moment when we can aid the risen Rosintai in his hour of need."

"That's … remarkable!"

"It's a relief is what it is," Maura added, sitting back in her chair and crossing her legs.

"My father was a member of the Collective and his father before him and so on, going back to the time of the Great Rosinanti War, when there were those who knew the truth. One long forgotten fact about those times is that not all humans fought against the Rosinanti. The group that would one day become the Collective stood firm against The Faithful, and their damned sorceress burned most of us to ash."

"But … that means you'll help us?"

"Help you?" the king asked, draining his wine goblet and slamming it down upon the desk forcefully. "Why, if I refused you, my old man would crawl his way out of the grave and kick my arse up and down this tower!" Valentean smiled fully at the king for the first time since entering his presence. "The Collective is small, and spread throughout the world, but luckily Grassan is united behind me, and I'm united behind you."

"It's nice to see someone making sense around here," Maura said. "Maybe you can share some of that wine and we can toast to it!" The king roared with laughter and reached down under the desk, pulling out two glasses and a bottle.

"I like this girl, here!" Matias yelled. He filled one and handed it to Maura, then the other, which he offered to Valentean. The animus warrior held one hand up, turning down the offer. "Oh, you're sure Burai's son, you are!" Maura and the king toasted briefly and each gulped down their respective glasses. Maura immediately started coughing at the intense strength of the foreign alcohol. The king laughed with his entire body once more. "You'll develop a stomach for it, girl." He patted his large belly. "Though hopefully not one like mine!"

Both Maura and Valentean laughed along with the bearded monarch, enjoying a moment where there was no tension weighing down the air around them.

"So," the king continued, "our next step is to find a way into Aleksandrya."

Valentean's brow furrowed at the unfamiliar word. "Into where?" he asked, shifting uncomfortably in his seat, a gaping pit forming in his stomach. He was certain he already knew the answer to this question.

"Ah, you hadn't heard," Matias said sadly. "I'm sorry, boy. The princess took control of Kackritta, renamed it after herself, and declared it an empire. The crazy fire bitch clearly has her sights set on the rest of the world, and I'm sure we're first on her chopping block."

Valentean's mind reeled with this news. Kackritta had always been his home, and it had always been *Kackritta*. As sure as the sky was blue and the grass were green, so too had he always been sure that his home would remain unchanged and untouched long after his days in this world were over.

"That's vile," Maura spat, continuing to sip at her wine after that ill-fated first gulp. "I'd expect no less from the queen of vile herself."

"It's worrisome," Matias added, looking hard at Valentean. "But, unfortunately, with that damned barrier surrounding the city, we can't get anywhere near her."

"The barrier is definitely a problem," Valentean said. "We were hoping that there might be some kind of magic here that could help us bring it down." The king shook his head sadly.

"I've had some of the brightest magical minds of our time examining that thing since the day she blinked it into existence, and unfortunately, it's thick and strong. It's not a dome, it's actually a sphere, buried deep under the surface of Terra. So, tunneling in is also out."

"So, there's no way?" Valentean asked, his fingers gripping the armrests of his chair.

"Now, I didn't say that, boy," Matias replied with a wink. "I just said there's nothing *here*."

"Where then?"

The king sat back in his chair, filling his goblet once more with wine. "Tell me, son, have you ever heard of the Kingdom of Kahntran?"

Valentean's eyes widened in surprise and he nodded, unsure what the story of that long-abandoned locale could have to do with their conversation.

"What's Kahntran?" Maura asked.

"A dead city," Valentean said, "on the shores of the Northern Continent."

"Aye, your old man taught you well," Matias remarked. "Did he tell you anything else about it?"

"I know he was there the day the city fell, as was King Roan when he was still a warrior, before he had taken to Oath of Animus."

"As was I, lad. Though I was a wee prince at the time. The three of us fought together, Kackritta and Grassan, shoulder to shoulder, as it should always have been."

"What was so bad about Kahntran?" Maura asked.

"It was a mage smith city," Valentean said, "much the same as Grassan, but more … I don't know if ambitious is the right word."

"They were bastards, the lot of them," Matias roared. "Kahntran wasn't content to sit around and be friends with the rest of us. They wanted the world. And to get it, they built the single strongest magical weapon in the history of Terra!"

"The cannon?" Valentean asked.

"Aye, the cannon," the king replied, nodding. "What'd your old man tell you about it?"

"It could fire a burst of magic powerful enough to destroy an entire city, and it could reach anywhere in the entire world."

"Indeed, it could, and it was a scary time to be alive, let me tell you! That weapon was armed and ready to fire. Had we waited much longer, Kackritta and Grassan alike would have been wiped off the face of Terra."

"But you three went in undercover, if I remember the story correctly?"

"Aye, we got in there, your father, your king, and I. We disabled the damned thing which let the combined armies of both our cities launch an attack from the sea which destroyed Kahntran once and for all."

"My father said it's nothing but ruins now," Valentean added. "He didn't talk much about the day the city fell."

"It was a dark day; I'll tell you that. Forty-three years ago, last month, and I can still hear the screaming and the explosions as we cut our way through their soldiers like wheat in the field. Their refugees were relocated and welcomed into our cities, should they choose to come, but the city itself was decimated beyond repair. I can still remember how unsettling a sight it was. The city sat there in the mouth of that frozen hell of a continent, but the magic within was so strong that it kept the snow away, and it was more humid than the inside of a knight's crotch guard on a summer day."

"That's some pleasant imagery," Maura remarked dryly.

"Vulgar but true" the king replied.

"How does this help us against Aleksandra then?" Valentean asked.

"Patience boy," the king crooned. "Humor an old man and let me relive these old battle memories. Anyway, the city is in ruins, and we've heard tale it's been overtaken by a jungle, the growth of the plant life accelerated by the magic that's still there. But, while the city lies in pieces, the *cannon* is still intact!"

Valentean sat bolt upright. "Seriously?" he questioned, wide-eyed with fascination born of hope.

"Truly," Matias replied with a knowing smile. "It's disabled but mostly intact. A skilled mage smith could repair it and operate it, and we can use it to blow that barrier to pieces. Then, we can invade and take your home back!"

Valentean was suddenly alive with tingles of excitement. They could do this … it was possible.

"Much the same as when I invaded with your old man and your king, we send in a small strike team. The two of you and the finest magical mind Grassan has, the only person in this whole rudding city I'd trust to make those repairs: my son, the prince."

"We'd be thrilled to have the help of your son!" Valentean blurted out. "You truly honor us with this, Your Highness."

"Well, I'd love to go myself but I'm too rudding old, and I've got this kingdom to look after. My son knows exactly what I did to disable it so many years ago, and it won't take him long to fix it. He can then pump it full of magical energy and one of you can blow that red globe to bits. He's the brightest mage-smith in the entire kingdom and the most powerful mage of his generation."

"I look forward to meeting the prince," Valentean said, still overcome with emotion at this very doable plan. "It will take time to sail there, though."

"Ha!" the king laughed in response, "clearly you don't know anything about Grassani ships!"

"How could he when you people keep yourselves so hidden?" Maura chimed in, and the king laughed in response.

"I love this girl!" He picked up the model ship on his desk. "Our ships don't have engines the way your Kackrittan-made crap does. They run on magic, that being the power of one mage, controlling all aspects of the ship. It can be crewed by a small team, like yourselves. But the truest marvel of it all is that, if needed," he lifted the ship up into the air, "it can fly on the currents of the mage's energy, becoming a cross continent long-range airship!"

Valentean nearly fell over in shock. "A long-range airship?" he replied, completely aghast at the notion.

"Aye, our most guarded secret!"

"That's amazing!" Maura added.

"With something like that we could reach Kahntran in…" Valentean scrunched his face in thought.

"Less than a day," the king replied, finishing his thought.

"King Matias, there is nothing I could ever do to repay this great kindness you've shown me today," Valentean said, standing and offering his hand to the king. Matias smiled and stood behind his desk, grasping Valentean by the forearm in a sign of respect, trust, and friendship.

"Make my world safe again, boy, and we're even. I've waited my entire life to help the Rosintai complete his mission. I can go to my grave proud of what I've done if we manage to wipe that fiery witch off the face of the planet!"

"I promise you we will," Valentean replied, releasing the king's forearm. "When can we set off?"

"Once my son arrives. I had already sent word for him." Just then, there was a rap on the door. "Ah, there's my boy. Well, come in then!" The door to the king's office swung open and Valentean turned to face his new ally. Maura, too, stood with a smile on her face, eager to greet this powerful mage. They both stood, open-mouthed, when the purple-coated, top hat clad Captain Nahzarro stood in the entryway.

"You summoned me, father?" he said, removing his hat with a deep elegant bow. His eyes met those of Valentean and Maura and he instantly straightened back to his full height, nose pointed in the air, once more gazing down at them.

"Oh, you have got to be joking," Maura said.

XVII: REBELLION

"Captain Elite," a voice called out from the direction of the tiny room's entrance. Vahn heaved a heavy sigh and turned to face Tiberius Woltram, who looked expectedly at his former mentor.

"I've asked you not to call me that several times now," Vahn replied, rubbing the bridge of his nose in uncomfortable agitation. "That has been your title for several years now, my friend."

"It is not a title I need or deserve at this time," Tiberius answered. His face was drawn, with lines forming upon his forehead. "If not for you, I would be nothing more than ash and blackened bone right now. The cause needs you."

Vahn exhaled heavily once more. Since he had come to join his loyalty with the rebels, Vahn had tried to blend into their ranks, loaning naught more than his sword arm, and counsel. But there had immediately been a movement from within, spearheaded by Tiberius, to have him lead the rebel forces into battle. The very thought of assuming command of the rag-tag team of warriors, outlaws, and misfits left him with a feeling of dread.

"Surely you did not come to see me solely to engage in this argument once more."

"No, of course not," Tiberius said, with more than a hint of bitterness forced out with his words. "We are convening for a meeting, and I thought you might want to attend."

Vahn nodded thoughtfully. It would do him good to get out of this room for a bit, stretch his legs, and see where the minds of these rebels were at. In the week since he had come into their service, Vahn had attended only one such meeting. It had been one that he himself had been at the center of.

Vahn had regained consciousness amidst a swell of disorientation. He could see light filtering through some kind of patchwork netting that surrounded his face and completely eclipsed his line of sight. All around him came the sound of many voices speaking atop one another. The fever pitch of their clashing tones caused his already aching head to throb. Vahn attempted to move, only to find his arms bound at the wrist to the chair he sat in. Moving his legs proved even more fruitless as they too were restrained.

Where was he? Had he fallen back into the hands of the Faithful following his scuffle with Landon? Was he sitting now before Aleksandra herself, about to be executed for treason against her new empire? Vahn struggled against his bonds and suddenly there was a break in the argumentative chatter.

"He awakens!" a horrified voice called out. Whoever the person was, he viewed Vahn as dangerous. Hushed frenzied whispers still spread around him and the sound of movement shuffled from behind. Light exploded across his field of vision as what Vahn had discerned as a brown sack was pulled roughly from his head.

The glare subsided after but a moment and Vahn found himself in a very small, red stone, torch-lit room, surrounded by battered men and women of all ages, shapes, sizes, and countenances. Some were clearly highborn, still donned in the shredded remains of the finery they enjoyed when the kingdom was still Kackritta and life still made sense. Others wore tattered rags, many were shoeless, and all looked as though they had not bathed in weeks. Some were unmistakably warriors, several of which Vahn recognized, wearing robes and bits of armor with the insignia of the Kackrittan royal family still emblazoned upon them. At the head of the room, directly in front of him stood six elite warriors, donned in the golden robes of his former order. Though even the proud shrouds of the elites were torn, burnt and ragged. One of them had been Tiberius, whom Vahn stared at, brow furrowed in confusion.

"Captain Elite," Tiberius said, bowing his head toward Vahn in a show of respect.

"You'd bow to the father of monsters?" one woman from behind Vahn's seat called out in disgust, clearly discernible above the rabble.

"My son died in his son's attack!" another bellowed.

Vahn felt a twinge of horror. The devastation of Kayden's rage-soaked assault upon Kackritta City was so massive in scope that it was easy to focus only on the large-scale destruction and neglect the deeply personal tragedies that such an event creates.

Tiberius raised his hands into the air, as if halting an oncoming attacker, and the crowd's cries for blood died down. "Vahn Burai was Captain Elite of the Kackrittan army for many years," he said. "He protected our city time and time again, and the crimes of his son are not his to answer for." Tiberius turned a pleading glance in Vahn's direction. "Captain Elite, will you please address the gathering and answer as to their concerns?"

Vahn looked around at the assemblage, estimating there to be upwards of fifty people crammed into the room, all staring at him desperate for any answers he might offer as to the nightmare their lives had spiraled into. "My sons are indeed Rosinanti dragons..." Vahn said, steadying himself with a deliberate breath, "but there is much more to this situation than you are being led to believe. If you give me the opportunity, I shall tell you the tale."

Vahn had talked for nearly an hour, recounting everything he learned from Aurax, as well as the bits and pieces he had learned from Kayden. He told them of the Faithful's true purpose, the identity of their goddess, and the different roads his two adopted Rosinanti sons had taken in this conflict. He spoke of Seraphina, enraptured them with tales of the princess who rebelled against this insanity and combated the forces of chaos. The rebels had been calling her the ice queen and Vahn urged them to use the princess as a rallying point, a battle cry, a monarch they could believe in.

In the end, his impassioned plea had reached them, and he was accepted into the rebellion without a moment's fuss. It only took two days for Tiberius to approach Vahn with the offer to lead them into battle. The elite warriors had taken charge by default, but they needed a strong central figure to fall in behind. Someone who could inspire confidence, loyalty, and respect. Tiberius had confessed to his former mentor that he did not believe that person to be himself.

Vahn traipsed out the door alongside Tiberius, moving single file through the narrow, stone hallways. The structure the rebels had overtaken was a dilapidated guardhouse near the outskirts of Aleksandrya, unsettlingly close to the magic barrier which kept them ensconced within the city limits. As such, a small party of mages who had pledged allegiances to the rebel cause had been able to draw upon the power of the shield's magic to create a glamour over the ramshackle building, which gave it the appearance of being empty. This would not fool one gifted in the mystical arts, such as Aleksandra, but for the simple Champions of the Faithful and Skirlack soldiers who patrolled the area, it was more than sufficient to shield the rebels from prying eyes.

They wound through several equally thin corridors, passing by the men, women, and children who had been taken into the facility. The rebellion seemed to grow by the day, and Vahn knew not whether these headquarters could continue to house them should this trend of recruitment continue.

Finally, they arrived at the large room in which Vahn had first awoken. A circular wooden table sat in the center of the floor, and around it, the five other elite warriors who made up the rebellion's leadership council. They nodded in way of greeting as Tiberius and Vahn entered and took their seats. To Vahn's shame, he did not know the names or faces of these men and women upon first arriving. They were young, having achieved their rank long after he had begun Valentean's animus instruction and stepped down as Captain Elite. When he led, Vahn had prided himself on knowing the names and histories of each and every warrior under his watch. Now, though, these gathered elites looked more like school children to his eyes than grizzled warriors.

"We have to strike against the empress!" a raven-haired female warrior named Mera said, slamming her fist upon the table as Vahn and Tiberius settled in.

"That would be suicide," replied Jorah, a blonde man who sat immediately on Vahn's right. "She could incinerate the lot of us where we stand. She fought a dragon!"

"A farcical encounter which was meant to terrify a populace into believing in her," said Ninx, a bald male warrior with a stocky build.

Vahn allowed the discussion to play out, choosing not to intervene on any side just yet. To attack Aleksandra would be utter lunacy, and he hoped his fellow elites would arrive at the same conclusion in due time.

"Yes, but even so, that dragon bends to her will and obeys her," Tiberius interjected. "How powerful must she be then to tame such a creature?

Vahn winced internally at the mention of his son as a "creature." He hoped against hope that Kayden could be redeemed, that he might once more find the humanity within his heart. But the kingdom could never forgive him for the deaths of more than a thousand innocents.

"She has to be dealt with," came the voice of Herin, a dark-skinned, tall male warrior with a scoured head and a goatee.

"And what should happen when she eliminates us in the process?" asked Jesaya, a blonde-haired, blue-eyed female beauty who, according to Tiberius, was as fierce a hand-to-hand combatant as he had ever seen. "What happens to the rebellion if we are not here to lead it?"

The argument over the proposed assassination of Aleksandra continued on into the night, and all throughout the heated discussion, Vahn remained quiet. There were such differing ideologies at war within the chamber. How had they managed to get anything done when they seemed so split down the center?

Tiberius was right in his belief that they needed a strong leader, but for some reason, Vahn could not bring himself to accept their earlier proposal. For what felt like the millionth time, he silently contemplated his inability to take on this responsibility. He had led warriors into battle before, against seemingly insurmountable foes and emerged victorious on the other side. So why not these warriors? Why not this battle?

"We need to gut the bitch and choke her pet dragon with her remains!" Herin declared.

With a sharp gasp of clarity, Vahn realized what his issue was. To take on the mantle of captain elite once more would be to finally truly admit that Kayden was the enemy. He would be leading this group of elites, warriors, and civilians against his own son, and his heart ached at the thought. The only reasonable sentence one could receive in response to the heinous actions Kayden had undertaken would be death. But as the council argued and bickered in regards to the fundamental strategy of what this rebellion would be founded upon, it became impossible to ignore the call of responsibility.

For years, duty had always come first in his life. He had put honor and duty to queen and country before his own personal happiness and family on many occasions. When Valentean had undertaken the Oath of Animus, he had sworn that his duty would never again come first. But faced with such odds, and a mission of global importance, he realized that he had to step up. He did so not just for Kackritta's restoration, not just for the citizens being mutilated and forced into an oppressive regime, but for the entirety of the human race.

Vahn took a long, deep, calming breath. He took in the very essence of the loving and caring father he had always tried to be, held it within his heart for one last glorious second, and then forcefully exhaled it all. The solid resolve of the captain elite was all that was left behind in its place, hardening his heart into steel. Vahn rose sharply from his seat. The bickering stopped as his compatriots looked upon him with concern and curiosity.

"The empress is powerful; incredibly so. She is undoubtedly the single most powerful being on the entire planet. To launch a direct assault upon her person would be tantamount to suicide. However, we cannot stand idly by and do nothing. As a rebellion, we must be strong, we must fight, we must strike at the heart of our enemy. But we must do this in a way that does not lead to our assured eradication."

"What are you saying?" Jesaya asked.

Vahn felt the emotion drain from his eyes, the stoic calm of a true elite washing over his posture, gaze, and voice. "I am saying that, if you will still have me, I will agree to take the role of captain elite once more and lead this rebellion against our foes. I will see the Kingdom of Kackritta restored, with the Ice Queen seated upon the throne of our city. I will see to it that this random assortment of warriors and citizens who have gathered to our cause and believe in true justice, begin a movement that will free this world from the lash. If you will still accept my leadership, I promise you that we will achieve this goal, or at the very least, we will take a large piece of our enemy into oblivion with us!"

Tiberius stood, and placed his right fist into his left palm. He inclined his head in a show of respect. Jesaya followed suit less than a minute later, and, one by one, each elite warrior within the room found themselves on their feet, heads bowed, showing deference to their new captain.

Vahn stood at crisp attention, the beginnings of a plan already formulating in his mind. He stepped away from the table, arms proudly clasped behind his back, and marched to the far end of the room. "Now," he began, "I believe I know of a way to strike at the heart of the empress without directly engaging her."

"What would that be?" Tiberius asked, clearly burning with curiosity.

"Pontifex Sophie."

“Of course,” Herin replied, his eyes alight with determination and wonder.

“The empress values very little in this world,” Vahn continued, “but I have known her since she was a very small child. We know that she values her faith and the handmaiden who has stood beside her since the day she was born. I recall seeing the way the young princess would look up at Sophie, a gaze of fondness, perhaps even love for the mother figure whose mutilated hand rocked her cradle at night. By apprehending the Pontifex, we strike a blow both against the faith and familial bonds of the empress.”

“That is brilliant!” Herin shouted. “But should we take her, or kill her?”

“Bringing her alive allows us to parlay with an Aleksandra who is desperate to retake something of value. Murdering Sophie would set her rage and vengeance down upon us. I would sooner take her alive if possible.”

“Agreed, Captain Elite.” Tiberius nodded in agreement.

“Then it is decided,” Vahn continued. “We shall move to take the Pontifex as our prisoner. I need you all to spread the word amongst our numbers. We require information as to Sophie’s movements. We strike within the week!”

“Captain!” the Elites shouted in unison, all bowing their heads once more before the authoritarian might of their new captain elite.

XVIII: BATTLE IN THE SKY

It had been nearly an entire day since Valentean and Maura entered Grassan, and Kayden stirred impatiently. The winged dragon-god continued his never-ending hover over the sprawling magical metropolis. He made sure to stay high enough within Terra's atmosphere to avoid detection by both Valentean and the citizens of Grassan. Had his brother managed to sense him, this entire ridiculous mission would be at stake.

Despite the great height at which he soared, Kayden had no issues making out what was occurring within the city. While in his true dragon form, he could force his sharpened vision to zoom in on the world below, tracing even the tiniest bursts of movement. But since Valentean vanished within that silly tower at the center of Grassan, Kayden had grown restless and bored.

A low growl rumbled from the depths of his mighty throat as he stirred with annoyance. This assignment had been insulting and demeaning. He should be diving toward this miserable magic city, upending buildings, incinerating steel, and ending human lives. There would come a day in which Aleksandra would pay for such egregious misuse of his power and potential.

Finally, nearly a day after he first entered the structure, Valentean rode out on a small airship alongside Maura and an extravagantly dressed individual whom Kayden had never seen before. The tiny transport carried the three of them toward the docks on the far end of the city where they boarded a large brown and gold ship, adorned with steel and several of the preposterous turning gears that were so popular in this bizarre place.

What are you up to, brother? Kayden silently mused. The three of them had entered the watercraft alone, without a crew to pilot such a large vessel. Kayden was surprised then, nearly an hour later, when the ship suddenly roared to life, spitting out green colored steam from a large smokestack and taking off into the open water. He watched in glowing purple fascination for another hour or so, gauging that Valentean and his compatriots were moving northeast.

There's nothing out that way but the Northern Continent, he thought, now burning with curious wonder as to his brother's plan of action. Either way, this merited a trip back to Aleksandrya. His mistress would wish to be informed of this new development as quickly as possible. Kayden gave three hearty flaps of his enormous wings and put Valentean, Grassan, and the ship behind him as he hurried back to inform Aleksandra. He hoped his next assignment would be something more exciting and decidedly bloodier.

Valentean watched the churning ocean smack the side of the ship as it cut through the water, taking them ever closer to the former city of Kahntran and the weapon that would allow him to see Seraphina once more. He leaned upon the railing of the deck, awash in the cool ocean breeze, and remembered sailing upon the royal family's airship alongside Seraphina, Kayden, and Aleksandra. That had been the last moment when life seemed normal. Before his world had fallen apart.

He tried to recall the soft-hearted hope and awe that the pre-Lazman Valentean felt, journeying from his home for the first time, setting out for unknown sights. He had gazed down from the airship, watching the land pass below with bubbling excitement. Now, he stared blankly at an unremarkable sea, fidgeting with impatience.

Valentean wished they could be in Kahntran already, repairing the device to liberate Kackritta. Speed was of the essence. Every second he spent out here, traveling to a place that no one had been to in over four decades, Seraphina was alone within the imprisoning sphere of chaos that was Aleksandrya.

Despite the king's assurance that this vessel was capable of traveling at great speed through the air, Nahzarro seemed determined to keep them on the water's surface. Valentean's jaw clenched in frustration. The prince's reluctance to offer full support to their cause chewed at his patience. Even on the short ride to the dock, Nahzarro had remained distant and silent. What little words he had spoken were laced with condescension and open contempt. Maura's displeasure at being saddled with the arrogant captain had exceeded his own. Valentean found it easier to focus less on his own internal grumblings while trying to calm Maura's more boisterous reactions.

The seconds ticked by with agonizing slowness and Valentean tried to occupy his mind with other thoughts. The existence of the Collective of Light had come as a shock to him. He had felt so alone with the truth of the world, and of his supernatural origins. But now, he knew there had been an entire order of people who carried this tale throughout the generations, those that would stand by him in the oncoming struggle. He wished that he had questioned King Matias further, and learned the identities and locations of the other initiates of the Collective.

As Valentean stood straight to stretch his limbs and spine, he could still scarcely believe he was headed to Kahntran. The tale of what had transpired there decades earlier had been one of Vahn's most frequent stories. Valentean grew up hearing all about the noble mission to defeat this powerful enemy and, often in his days of childish whimsy, imagined storming the beaches of Kahntran himself. It was odd to think that he was about to do just that, though this mission would not be as glorious of an adventure as Vahn had undertaken so many years ago. Should all go as planned, this would be a simple matter. They only needed to arrive, make repairs, power the weapon, and fire it. No one lived in the ruins of Kahntran, as far as Valentean knew, and Aleksandra was ignorant of their plan.

How often do things go as planned? he thought, trying to swallow the lump of dread forming in his throat. *I'm just being paranoid.* Still, every precious second spent sailing through the foamy blue ocean waters felt like time wasted. Time in which something could go horribly wrong.

Valentean stepped away from the edge of the ship and set his eyes upon the helm, which stood just ahead up a small flight of stairs. Nahzarro stood there, tall and proud in the afternoon breeze. There was no wheel to be turned, only two cylindrical podiums, each topped with a handle. The prince held a tight grip on both, and where the flesh of his palms met the leather of the handholds, a light green glow emanated. It was fascinating. Valentean found himself staring at the interesting machination as he traipsed up the stairs, almost forgetting why he was approaching the helm in the first place.

"May I help you, Lord Burai?" Nahzarro asked dryly, as though he were using Valentean's honorific sarcastically.

The animus warrior snapped back to reality and cleared his throat before speaking. "I just had some questions," he said, coming to stand beside the prince.

"Yes, I'd imagine you do," Nahzarro replied with a sigh. "Seeing Grassani technology firsthand must be quite the departure from the primitive barbarism of the shormy hovel you call home."

Valentean bit back the defensive barb that was dying to explode from his lips. In the name of their mission, he had to maintain a level of decorum when speaking to his newest companion. "Kackritta has always managed."

"Miraculously..."

Valentean's face grew hot and the dragon within his heart stirred, but he maintained his composure. "As you know, time is definitely a factor here. The more time we take in reaching our destination, the longer Aleksandra and the Faithful have to–"

"Lord Burai," Nahzarro interrupted, "did you have any idea when you came to our city that such technology existed?"

"No, of course not."

"And are you aware of how we keep such wondrous things a secret?"

"I'm sure you'll enlighten me."

"We don't send our ships into the sky outside of our borders!"

"I think this is a situation that calls for–"

"Do you now?" the prince replied, rolling his eyes dramatically. "Of course, you do because it benefits you and your people. Meanwhile, my people would be showing our hand before the eyes of an enemy that sees all. How do you think your sorceress empress would respond if she knew that Grassan had an entire fleet of magically powered long range capable airships, ready to strike her at a moment's notice?"

"I'm not trying to put your people at risk!"

"But our future, our prosperity, the lives of our soldiers, they don't mean as much to you as the lives of *your* people, and they never will. So why should I risk mine for a populous of shormlochs I'll never meet."

Valentean was aghast. The mere thought that he might intentionally put an entire city at risk to achieve some selfish end was perhaps the most offensive statement anyone had ever uttered to him. "Your father was the one who told me of this ship's capabilities as a member of the Collective of–"

"Ah yes, my father's ridiculous devotion to this mysterious collective that hangs on your every word and action." Nahzarro shook his head and scoffed. "Do you know how often I had to hear the tales of the *almighty* Rosintai? For my entire life, I've been striving to live up to some impossible standard set by some dragon-god thousands of years before my home even existed! Then one day, that righteous role model walks right into my office. I looked into your eyes, Valentean Burai, and I realized then that I was a fool to–"

"Finally, you say something we can agree on," Maura said, stepping beside Valentean. "You are a fool." She was adorned in new clothing provided by King Matias to replace her heavy, damp animal skins. Tight, tan pants with a brown stripe running vertically up the side of each leg tucked themselves into dark brown, calf-high boots. Around her torso, Maura wore an uncomfortable looking brown and white corset, along which ran the leather straps and golden buckles that marked the typical fashion trend in Grassan. Over it all, she wore a long, thin, tan coat which extended down past her knees. She looked like any other citizen of the magical city, save for her hostile demeanor toward the prince.

"Oh excellent," Nahzarro said, "here comes an informed opinion to add to the conversation."

"What can I say? With all the hot air spewing from your mouth, I was afraid Aleksandra had found us and was tossing fireballs at the deck. I came ready for a fight. It'd be a shame to go back below deck without having hit something–"

"Maura," Valentean said.

"Come on, Valentean are you seriously going to let this swaggering peacock speak to you like that?"

Nahzarro's gaze darkened and the light around his hands began to build in intensity. "You insolent little…"

"Enough!" Valentean bellowed, so loud that his voice filled the vast empty space of their watery surroundings. Valentean's eyes narrowed and he stepped up, coming face-to-face with the prince and curling his lip in anger and disgust.

"I've tried to be nice out of respect for your father," he continued, "but you insult me, you insult my friends, and you insult my home with your bigoted, hateful rhetoric. Here's how the remainder of this trip is going to go Nahzarro: I am going to leave the ship's navigation and piloting in your hands, and trust your judgment. As you said, it is the technology of your home, and I won't dictate the way it is used and threaten your city's security. That being said, if I hear one more derogatory remark directed at either of us squeak its way past your teeth, then I am going to show you legends sometimes don't live up to the man." Valentean's eyes shone with white energy as he silently commanded the wind to blow harshly and rock the ship to and fro. "Are we clear, Captain?"

Nahzarro had gone wide-eyed, sensing the mountain of magical energy Valentean kept at bay. The Prince swallowed hard, appearing to use every ounce of royal poise to keep his lips from quivering. He nodded emphatically.

"And you," Valentean said, rounding on Maura who had been smiling in victory. Her grin vanished upon seeing her friend's authoritative glare directed at her. "Remember that we are guests aboard this vessel and, as such, we've been entrusted a great responsibility. At no time do I wish to hear the threat of violence come out of your mouth directed at one of our allies again, understood?"

"Understood," Maura replied softly, looking away in embarrassment.

"Good," Valentean stated, turning on his heel and walking away from his two dumbfounded companions.

Maura spun the new golden daggers, given to her by King Matias prior to their departure, in a complex flourish around her body. They differed greatly from any other weapon she had ever handled. Gold plating laid above and below a series of gears which sat silent and still. The added weight slightly threw off Maura's years of practiced balance.

As she continued to slash at imaginary foes, Maura attempted to adapt her polished style to account for the added bulk of these new weapons. Her mind drifted as the blades sang through the air to dark memories and the faces of those who had set in motion such horrific experiences. She imagined slashing through Aleksandra's pale, white flesh, hearing her cry out in fear as Maura cut her again and again. She pictured Aurax and his smug condescending sneer as she kicked out with one leg, imagining the feeling of smashing his face against the hard sole of her boot.

Then she saw Kayden, smiling wickedly at her through the hazy air born of the flames which chewed through her home. Maura screamed in rage and erupted into a frenzied flourish of quick cuts and stabs, all of which she imagined spraying Kayden's dragon blood in a fountain of gory vengeance. Finally, she gave one forceful stab with a grunt of anger, and she stopped to wipe a film of sweat from her brow.

"Shameful," she heard the annoying voice of Nahzarro call out from behind her. She turned slowly to glare at his purple coated back as he continued to steer the ship toward Kahntran.

"Something to say, your captain-ness?" she asked, annoyance and frustration tinting her voice.

"You use our elegant weapons, but in your hands, they are as unremarkable as a sharpened stick."

"What are you babbling about now?"

"Those daggers were forged by the mage smiths of Grassan, and as such, they are built to be a conduit for magical martial might. They're meant to channel the inner magical energy of a warrior and bring destructive beauty to the art of combat."

"Well, they still cut things pretty well."

"Spoken like a true shorm…"

"You know," Maura said, walking around the helm to look Nahzarro in the eye, "you say that word like it's some kind of insulting curse, but I spent time in your city and the only person I've seen look down on anyone without magic has been you."

"Don't presume to know me!"

"Oh, there's not much to know. You're just a bigoted, self-centered, spoiled, swaggering imbecile who places no value in anyone he deems below him, which seems to be just about everyone!"

Nahzarro let go of the helm podiums and stormed forth, now face-to-face with Maura. The girl immediately looked back in alarm, wondering if the ship were about to veer off course.

"You really know nothing," Nahzarro scoffed. "I don't need to stand there all day. I tell the ship where to go and it goes there. I just stay here to avoid pointless chattering conversations like this one!"

"You really are the rudest human being I've ever spoken to!"

"Tell someone who cares," Nahzarro replied dismissively, turning his back to return to the helm.

"And for your information, there is a little magic in me," Maura retorted, her wounded pride trying in vain to build itself back up. "I'm learning to control mana."

Nahzarro laughed once more, wheeling around and stepping toward her again. "The fact that you liken that base wild energy to the grace and gift of magic just shows how painfully ignorant you are!"

"How about you show me a thing or two about magic then," Maura shouted, stepping towards the prince. Blood ran hot in her veins, and she completely forgot about Valentean's edict to avoid confrontation.

"My pleasure, you wretched little..." Nahzarro stopped steps from Maura, his eyes wide with alarm.

He threw a hand up and Maura felt an invisible force throw her back several meters as she crashed to the deck on her side. Nahzarro moved simultaneously, leaping back toward the helm, landing between the twin podiums as the wooden deck where they had just been standing exploded in a shower of splinters. As Maura covered her head to avoid the spraying wooden shrapnel, she heard the unmistakable sound of cannon fire. A split second later, the ship bucked and pitched as dozens of hard fast projectiles slammed into it.

Rolling to her feet, Maura drew her daggers, ready for a fight, and could not believe what she saw as she looked up at the sky.

Valentean sat in silent meditation below the deck of the ship, resting on a small cot in the communal quarters found within. He was still huffing about his earlier exchange with Maura and Nahzarro, but also found it a bit odd in retrospect. The authoritative tone he had used was more reminiscent of his father than himself. Vahn was a born leader, and Valentean always assumed he had been made to command other warriors into battle. He had never imagined himself in such a role. Leadership was not something he had sought out, but rather, it seemed to fall to him out of necessity.

He sighed as he drew in mana energy from the air, filled his body with its invigorating rush and stored it away for later use. Suddenly, his body flooded with the emerald energy, though he had not called it forth. It was as if the power within him was tensing, bracing for something he himself could not yet see. As he silently questioned this turn of events, the walls and ceiling exploded in a loud, crashing cacophony of decimation. Valentean leapt to his feet and dove to the side as an incoming projectile whistled past his head.

Amidst the sounds of carnage erupting around him, Valentean leaped up through one of the holes in the ceiling onto the upper deck. He looked toward the source of the incoming canon fire and gasped. There, hovering several hundred meters in the sky sat an immense flying warship; a long-range, steel airship. It was a technological marvel. Valentean would have stood in awe had it not been raining death around him. It was the color of blood and fire. Red and orange flourishes spread out along its shining surface. A massive propeller sat underneath its bulk, and two wings, thick and jagged like the blades of a saw, spread to its sides with propellers whirling along them. Dozens of cannons lined the broad side of the vessel, and they fired.

Valentean ran toward the helm to find Maura on the ground, curled into a defensive crouch, while Nahzarro stood with his arms in the air, conjuring a blue shield which protected the two of them. He turned his head and glanced sidelong at Valentean in alarm.

"Nahzarro, get us into the air," Valentean screamed over the loud cannon blasts boring down around them. The prince did not respond verbally, he simply nodded once and dropped his arms, quenching the shield as he took hold of the twin podiums. Valentean ran to Maura's side and pulled her back to a standing position.

The ship lurched in response to Nahzarro's silent commands, and despite the falling death which pounded through its hull, the vessel launched into the air at an incredible speed, leaving a trail of debris falling behind. Valentean grabbed the banister that led down the steps onto the battered deck, and kept a tight grip on Maura, to ensure her safety in the take-off.

He was shocked at the speed in which the Grassani-built ship soared through the sky. He glanced over at Nahzarro, who was deep into concentration, his hands aglow with the power of magical energy. Standing tall once more, Valentean looked back at the steel wonder that had attacked them. It began to give chase, closing the gap with every second.

"It's fast!" Valentean called out over the whipping wind to Nahzarro, who grunted in response. The ship shuddered as he poured more power into it.

"So are we," he called back. The airship opened fire on them once more from a series of eight cannons built into its forward armaments. The projectiles slammed hard into the rear of the Grassani vessel, causing the deck to buck beneath them once more. Valentean silently urged Maura to hold onto the banister as he was needed to help subdue this assault.

"Can you do anything about those cannons?' Nahzarro screamed.

Valentean nodded and dashed to the rear of the ship. Another round of projectiles poured forth from the cannons accompanied by a chorus of explosions. Valentean's eyes came alive with energy, and he silently commanded the wind to veer the cannonballs off course. The gust which responded to the white dragon's order altered the destination of the iron balls of destruction. Several of them missed entirely, while two or three scored glancing blows off the ships' side. He met the subsequent two volleys that roared out of the oncoming vessel with equal amounts of success, but the larger ship was still closing in fast.

As Valentean readied himself for another round of cannon fire, he noticed movement along the ship's bow as two large circular doors slowly swung open.

"They're readying something else," he called over his shoulder to Nahzarro and Maura. "Brace yourselves!"

Two enormous grappling hooks roared from the twin openings, flying with blinding speed on the ends of two long mooring chains. The first hook sank deep into the rear of their ship while the second tore through the deck and out the bottom. The chains instantly grew taut as the enemy airship ceased its movement.

The Grassani ship strained against the heavy chains but soon found its momentum halted by the larger vessel's brute strength.

"Nahzarro, what's happening?" Valentean shouted.

"It's too strong and we're barely holding together," he replied, straining as he poured more of his energy into the ship. "I'm giving it everything, but it has us easily!"

"So, we're stuck?" Maura cried out.

"Indeed, it would appear that way," Nahzarro hissed, the edge of panic rising into his voice. Just then, a groaning sound echoed around them as the chains began to retract back into the enemy airship, pulling them along as well.

"They're reeling us in!" Valentean shouted as he struggled to maintain his footing.

"Dammit!" Nahzarro bellowed, smoke now rising from around his hands as he pushed the ship further and further.

Valentean glared at the airship as it grew larger. Soon, he noticed movement along the chains. Dozens of quadrupeds moved with nimble grace along the heavy iron links, down toward their ship. The speed at which they ran was remarkable, and as they approached, Valentean was able to discern more clearly the shining, cracked, red skin and yellow eyes of the creatures. Several black, bony spikes ran along their spines and continued down a long pendulous tail which ended in two curved talons. They were some terrifying new breed of Skirlack demon, some missing link in their evolutionary heritage.

"Get ready!" Valentean called to his companions.

Nahzarro released his hold on the helm and Maura stood, drawing her new daggers as the Skirlack hounds drew nearer. As the first of them arrived, Valentean saw their wide mouths open hungrily, showing off sharp pointed fangs made for the purpose of cleaving flesh from bone. The animus warrior ran forward, eyes aglow as he lashed out with the wind. Several of the advancing animals were blown over the side of the ship where they would plummet to their deaths. Another leapt over the gust of air that had evicted its fellows. Valentean reached out, grabbed it by the throat and spun, heaving the hound off the ship as he turned to face the oncoming swarm.

Several hounds made it past his first line of defense, and Valentean had to trust that his allies were capable of handling them. He heard Maura give a cry of battle as she leapt into the fray. The unmistakable snap-hiss of electricity reached his ears, likely coursing along the strands of Nahzarro's magic channeling whips.

As the Kackrittan animus warrior hammered the intruders with fists, feet, and bursts of wind, the ship edged ever closer to the larger steel monstrosity. As they drew nearer, Valentean saw armored Skirlack soldiers leaping from the top of the warship, barreling down at them. In his momentary distraction, a hound leapt on Valentean's back and sank its fangs into his shoulder. He howled in pain and the dragon within his heart thrashed in rage. Valentean reached back, hand empowered with mana, and gripped the hound by the top of its head. The explosion of energy caved in the creature's cranium.

Bulky Skirlack soldiers plummeted toward them. Valentean attempted to blow as many as he could off course, but a large number of them landed and advanced. He ducked beneath a lumbering arm that reached for his head. Wrapping his own arm around the muscular appendage, Valentean flipped the demon over his hip, stomping down on its face as it impacted the deck. He turned, blocking and dodging the powerful strikes of three Skirlack soldiers and the spiked tail of one of their war hounds. He bit back on the dragon's power and tried to focus on one opponent at a time.

Dodge, strike, kill, and move onto the next. Dodge, strike, kill, and move onto the next.

Maura stabbed through the wrist of a Skirlack soldier who had reached for her head. She dragged her blade vertically along its arm before punching it roughly in the face and pulling her dagger free as it bled out. One of the four-legged demons leapt in her direction, claws and teeth bared with murderous intentions. Maura ducked inside its guard and jammed both daggers into its chest, continuing to use its momentum against it as she guided the creature past her.

Not taking even a second's hesitation, she hurled one of her weapons with deadly accuracy where it buried itself in the throat of an oncoming Skirlack. As the monster doubled over in alarm, she ran forward, rolling over its back while gripping the dagger lodged in its flesh and dragging it out through the opposite side of its neck.

As she landed, Maura met a crushing blow from a Skirlack's fist. The impact threw her to the ground and she gasped for air. A hound charged toward her, sensing an easy kill. Maura was too slow, and for a brief instant, felt the panic born of doom blossom within her chest. But before it could strike, a sparking flash of light lashed over Maura's body and struck the slobbering monster in the face. It flew to the side with a cauterized slash running deep down the length of its head.

Turning to the source of this saving strike, Maura saw Nahzarro. His twin whips sparked with lightning magic as he continued to snap them about, creating a cage of electricity around himself. Maura drew breath back into her lungs and attempted to stand. She watched, awestruck, as Nahzarro moved so blindly fast. He flung both electric-crackling strands up in a diagonal slash that left two smoldering black scorch wounds going up the broad chest of a Skirlack soldier who spun with the force of the blow. Nahzarro then snapped both whips back down across its back as the creature fell, dead.

Maura was so stunned at the prince's display of skill and magical ability that she momentarily forgot her surroundings.

"Down!" Nahzarro cried out.

Maura instantly complied with the order, letting her knees buckle as she dove toward the deck. As soon as she began her descent, Maura felt the prickling heat of one of Nahzarro's whips sail past the top of her head followed by the unmistakable sizzle of lightning magic impacting flesh. She turned and saw the energized strand wrap tightly around the throat of a Skirlack soldier who had attempted to catch her off-guard. Smoke poured from the demon's neck as jolting arcs carved their way through its body. Nahzarro gave one strong pull and the lash bore through flesh and bone, decapitating the Skirlack, leaving only a cauterized stump where its head had been.

Maura gave Nahzarro a nod in thanks, which he returned with a barely perceivable inclination of his head as he turned to engage a group of Skirlack hounds that were closing in on him. Maura squeezed the handles of her daggers, pulled back a corner of her lip, bared her teeth, and leapt back into action.

Valentean continued to pummel any Skirlack who came within striking distance. He glanced back towards Maura and Nahzarro. They were holding their own against these demonic attackers, but the real threat continued to drag them ever closer. What was aboard that airship? Was Kayden up there, just waiting for Valentean to be pulled in like a fish? Was it Aleksandra herself? His knees weakened at the thought.

Valentean decided that he did not want to find out. He had to do something to eliminate those heavy chains and allow their ship to enact a hasty retreat. But they were massively thick and, even with his strength, he knew that he could not break them. That only left one option.

Valentean ran at a Skirlack soldier and leaped up, bringing both of his feet into its sternum. The demon was sent flying back over the side of the ship. Valentean rolled to a standing position, driving a mana-powered kick through the skull of a hound. He needed to reach Maura and Nahzarro to regroup with them.

A Skirlack soldier attempted to intercept him. Valentean dropped to his side and slid through the demon's legs. He slammed his fists into its kneecaps as he skidded by, feeling the sadly familiar crunch of splintering bones beneath his knuckles. He rose to his feet and used a mana powered jump to place himself between his two companions.

"Nahzarro, can you give us some breathing room?"

The Grassani prince, panted in exhaustion and nodded, conjuring a blue shield that threw their foes back and gave them a brief respite from the battle. The demons fell with the force of the spell but quickly rallied back to their feet and charged. They pounded on the translucent blue light with fists, claws, horns, and tails.

"This buys us maybe three minutes," Nahzarro yelled over the commotion. Beads of sweat coursed down his temples as he grimaced in extreme exertion.

"What are we going to do?" Maura asked as she wiped a splotch of blood from her nose with a sleeve, panting, and stretching her back.

"Those chains need to go before they reel us in fully," Valentean replied.

"Oh good. Well, if that's all…" Maura spat sarcastically.

"Now is not a good time for the quips," Nahzarro insisted. "Time is very much of the essence here!" Maura fell silent and nodded.

"I can do it," Valentean insisted. "I just have to get on their ship and take them apart from the inside."

"That's insane, you don't even know what you're looking for in there," Maura cried back.

"If it's big, looks important, and is attached to a giant chain, I'm going to break it!" Valentean replied, exasperated. "Nahzarro, the second those chains come down you take the helm and get what's left of this ship to Kahntran!"

"What about you?" Maura objected, interrupting him again.

"I will be right behind you!"

"That's what Seraphina said right before Kackritta fell! I'm not losing another one of you!"

"Maura, this mission is more important than all that! If I can't make it out of there in time, the two of you can still finish it!"

"If you die, there is no mission!"

"It's either stay here and die or go up there and *maybe* die! I'm going with the option wherein there's a chance that we live through this!"

Maura opened her mouth to object once more but stopped, pursed her lips in anger, and shook her head in frustration.

"Nahzarro?" Valentean asked, looking to his top hat clad comrade for some affirmation that he understood his role in all of this. The prince nodded, the strain of the Skirlack's continued assault on his shield taking a heavy toll on his stamina. "Ok, drop the shield and let's do this!"

"Valentean!" Maura said, reaching out and taking the animus warrior by the forearm. He looked back, expecting there to be further objections from his friend. Her steely gaze softened, however, and she brushed a strand of blonde hair off her grime and blood-soaked face. "Take that thing apart, and get back here quickly or I'll kill you myself!"

"I will," he said with a smile and a wink that was intended to be comforting. "Ready, Nahzarro?"

The prince nodded again. "Burai…" he said, his voice straining with effort. "Just … good luck up there, mate!"

Valentean nodded back and took a ready position, prepared to dash forward the instant the shield dropped. Nahzarro grunted once as his body glowed with a pale blue light. He slowly brought his hands down in front of his chest and gathered the energy of the shield unto himself. Screaming in exertion, he threw his arms out wide, sending the remaining energy flying out like a battering ram, which heaved the Skirlack demons back.

Valentean ran, a white and blue blur, as the combined forces of the wind and mana shot him on as though he were fired from a cannon. As he approached the aft end of the ship, a Skirlack tried to intercept him. All it met was a powerful, crackling fist, with the whole of Valentean's momentum behind it. As the demon fell, Valentean dragged as much mana in through his nose as he could hold and pushed it all out through his feet. He leaped with all his might, rocketing into the sky.

His eyes came aglow as he summoned the wind to carry him upwards in flight toward the opening at the base of the starboard chain. Valentean extended his arms over his head, fists forward as he crossed the threshold of the Aleksandryan airship. He instantly killed the wind and landed gingerly upon the floor of a large steel chamber.

All around him, important-looking machines hummed and churned and moved together, producing a powerful, burning aroma. Skirlack soldiers and hounds surrounded him.

Valentean lashed out with the wind, throwing them all back, and began pounding through flesh and bone with green sparking limbs. Within minutes, he had cleared the room of hostiles. The animus warrior looked around, trying to find the origin of the twin chains which continued to pull his friends in toward certain death.

He saw a large contraption near the opening he had entered through. It was big and green and the chain was wrapped tightly around it. It slowly turned in unison with a twin on the port side of the chamber, pulling the chains in. Valentean energized both arms with mana and began pounding on the strange device, caving its green surface in further with every blow until a large explosion threw him back into a seated position. He smiled in triumph as the chain broke away from the now smoldering apparatus and fell through the large circular opening.

One down, he thought, climbing back to his feet. As he turned toward his second target, a large hand clamped on his shoulder and spun him around. Valentean swallowed his surprise and crossed his arms over his midsection, just blocking a small knife from stabbing into his abdomen.

"Good," General Zouka hissed through clenched teeth, pushing against Valentean's defenses, "you're learning."

Maura smiled as the first chain fell from the Aleksandryan airship. The consistent flow of Skirlack pouring in to murder them seemed to have also halted. It took her and Nahzarro only a few more minutes to finish off the stragglers that remained onboard. Maura embedded her blade into the base of the final soldier's skull while Nahzarro split the last two hounds in half with his whips.

The two of them stood on the deck, panting through their exhaustion, watching expectantly, waiting for the final chain to fall. Much to Maura's confusion, nothing happened. Valentean must have encountered some resistance. The remaining chain was still pulling them closer to the giant steel airship.

"I wish I knew what was happening up there," Maura said, wringing her hands.

"He clearly needs some help," Nahzarro replied, deactivating his whips and returning them to his belt. The prince walked toward the side of the decimated deck.

"What are you doing?"

"Helping," he said, furrowing his brow with concentration and extending both of his hands toward the enemy airship. Crying out with strain, Nahzarro's fingers spat blue lightning which careened through the empty opening in the airship that had once contained the first chain.

"Valentean is in there!" Maura shouted.

"He will be fine!" Nahzarro insisted, ramping up the intensity of his assault until explosions could be heard from within.

"Are you out of your mind?"

"No, I just have more faith in your friend than you do, apparently," he said, storming back to the helm.

Valentean felt the general's thick, powerful fist slam into his throat, followed by a kick that sent him rolling across the hard metal floor.

"You struggle, you fall, but then you rise, stronger than ever," Zouka said, as he waited for Valentean to stand. "You are truly the ultimate foe. My respect for your skill is only eclipsed by my desire to defeat you, dragon."

"You insane monster," Valentean spat, coughing the feeling back into his vocal chords, "there is more going on here than you and me!"

"That's where you're wrong, boy," Zouka replied, crouching back into a combat stance. "There is nothing more to this world than this, right now, you and I locked in the dance of combat. Two warriors entangled together toward one inevitable ending." Zouka charged at him.

Valentean leaped over his head, gracefully, with a slow flip while summoning the wind to smash Zouka into one of the many machines that worked to keep this goliath of a ship in the air.

Zouka hit the unfamiliar device with such force that he dented the metallic covering which protected it and caused sparks to shoot out around his point of impact. As Valentean braced for the general to rise again, a burst of lightning erupted into the chamber, striking machinery and the bodies of the dead or dying Skirlack. Valentean leapt to the side, out of the powerful spell's path of destruction, and watched in awe as the brunt of it struck the general and the mechanism he had smashed into. Zouka cried out in pain, but those shrieks of agony were soon drowned out by a series of fiery explosions as many of the engines that filled the chamber began to combust.

Nahzarro, Valentean thought. *Reckless but definitely helpful.*

He ran at the apparatus which continued to reel in the final chain, fists crackling as he prepared to dismantle it. Before he could reach his intended target, the floor beneath him bucked and threw him to the side. The ship was crashing. Valentean knew that if he did not disconnect that last chain, the airship would pull Nahzarro and Maura down with it. He struggled back to his feet and leapt forward as the world around him began to tilt.

He managed to reach the base of the contraption and raised his empowered fist to strike. Zouka tackled the young Rosinanti from behind. Valentean desperately wrestled with the heavy Gorram, lashing out with fists elbows and knees.

"If this ship goes down, so do your friends," Zouka said in his ear.

"The only thing going down is you," Valentean replied, managing to leap up with the general still clinging to his back and smashed his opponent's body into the hard steel ceiling. Zouka released his hold. As they landed, the animus warrior was ready with a front kick to the chest that threw Zouka back into the exploding engines that signaled the end of this technological marvel. Valentean smiled in triumph and pounded his fists into the target device again and again as the ship continued to combust around him. Then, as he gave one last mighty blow which tore the chain free, his world erupted into fiery chaos.

Maura fell over as they were forcibly dragged through the sky by the crashing airship. Despite her own predicament, she kept her gaze fixed upon the falling ship, looking for any sign of Valentean.

Nahzarro continued to clutch at the helm podiums, pumping magic into them, preparing for the moment the chain would drop, and they would be free again. But despite the prince's insistence that Valentean would be fine, Maura was beginning to have her doubts. The explosions grew louder from within the Alexandrian ship, and with every second, they tilted more and more off course.

"Any time now, Burai!" Nahzarro exclaimed through clenched teeth. Just as it seemed all might be lost, Maura gasped in relief as the chain which held them captive broke away. "See?" Nahzarro said with glee as their ship began to right itself. "I told you he was all right."

Maura gritted her teeth in response, still waiting to see Valentean emerge, riding the wind towards them, a triumphant smile on his face. But instead, a loud explosion resounded and the airship violently veered off toward a large land mass.

Maura ran toward the aft end of the ship and saw flaming detonation rip out through the Aleksandryan vessel's metal side. She screamed as their own ship began to pick up speed.

"Turn around!" she screamed to Nahzarro, who paid her no mind. She stormed up to him, hands on her hips, her reddening face contorted in rage. "Turn the ship around now!"

"You heard Burai," he replied, making no movement to obey Maura's edict. "We have a mission."

"I don't give a damn about the mission. We're going back for him!"

"We most certainly are not!"

"You despicable, cowardly, rotten piece of…"

"Think for a second!" Nahzarro screamed at her. "If he were here right now, what would he tell you to do? What were his exact instructions before running off to give us our only chance to complete this mission? Now, you want to ruin those chances, defy his wishes, and demolish the entire operation because of your own selfish desires?"

Maura grunted in aggravation and kicked the side of the ship so hard it hurt her toes. Nahzarro was infuriating, but he was correct. She watched the remains of the Aleksandryan airship crash, and tears spilled from her eyes. Seraphina had asked but one thing of her. To look out for him, to keep him safe, and she had failed her.

Valentean, she thought to herself, *meet me in Kahntran.*

Valentean awoke upon a soft surface, groaning through the pain born of various burns and scrapes he had suffered in the airship's explosion. The last thing he remembered was being flung out from the destruction by a series of blasts which had ripped out from the dying engines.

His pain seemed to be subsiding, as if some warm light had entered his body and spread a comforting soothing energy throughout his injuries.

He tried to move but found he was too weak. In response to his stirring, just beyond the veil of darkness cast by his heavy eyelids, he heard something react. It sounded like the movement of wheels upon a wooden floor. A soft, tiny hand pressed into his forehead. The warmth of that hand's skin contained the same tingling sensation that had been working its way through his body.

"Shh, it's all right," he heard a soft, soothing female voice whisper. "You're going to be fine. My name is Deana. Welcome to Casid … Or at least what's left of it…"

XIX: DOUBT

"The princess without magic."

Seraphina had heard the moniker before, though no one had ever been cruel enough to say it to her face. Still, she had often overheard her lack of magical ability brought up as the source of gossip within the walls of Kackritta Castle. The words repeated themselves in an endless, reverberating echo as the darkness of her mind swirled around the troubled princess.

Finally, a spot of dull light began to shine on the furthest reaches of her eyesight, growing steadily until another fabricated world of the past formed around her. This time, Seraphina stood within the walls of Kackritta Castle, a common hallway that she often traveled through en-route to her daily destinations. She caught sight of her reflection in one of the many windows that looked out over the night shaded landscape of the city. By her estimation, she must have been eleven years old. The hallway she walked through was void of activity, but still, a sinking feeling hit her stomach. Aqua would not have sent her to this time and this place were it not for some reason.

"...peeked my head into that room and it was shameful," Seraphina heard a voice say from far off. She crept down the hallway, hugging the wall so as to listen to the hushed conversation. Realization began to dawn within her mind and the princess suddenly remembered this day. She wanted desperately to cover her ears to block out what she knew was coming, but Aqua wanted her to face this uncomfortable memory, and so she would.

"Oh, I've heard the queen is positively humiliated," another whispery voice joined in.

"Well, wouldn't you be? Her family is known for the gift of their sainted ancestor, and then she has a child who is as useless as a cart mule."

"Oh, Belinda, that's a terrible thing to say."

"But it's the truth!" Seraphina peeked around the corner and saw the two women, scullery maids of the palace, giggling to one another about her various failures as an aspiring sorceress. "What good is a member of the Kackritta bloodline who can't use magic?"

"Well, the kingdom is at least spared her rule. Thank the sorceress for Aleksandra. She is a truly gifted girl."

"Oh yes, do you remember when Aleksandra was her sister's age? She could upend an entire room with naught but a thought!"

"Yes, the kingdom is lucky that Aleksandra was born first. Could you imagine the shame of having that little nothing sitting on the throne?"

Seraphina fought back a sob at hearing her worst inner fears brought to life from the mouths of complete strangers. She could never measure up to her sister, could never command the awe and respect of her people. She would never live up to the Kackritta name. She squeezed her eyes shut and turned to run back up the hallway, but as she moved, the environment shifted and she was outside the grand royal ballroom, standing upon a stone balcony overlooking the courtyard.

The cool evening air of springtime felt frigid against her perspiring flesh. Looking down, she saw herself adorned in a white sparkling ball gown. She remembered this dress and this evening all too well: the royal celebration of her recovery following the Skirlack's attack. She had been so happy to see such a large number of people coming together in celebration of her renewed health and safety. She had awoken from that nightmare feeling powerful and invigorated, thanks to the shard of Valentean's light essence which was unknowingly latched onto her soul.

The princess had come out onto the balcony to catch a much-needed breath of fresh air and leaned against the cool stone of the wall next to the entrance. This kept her out of sight of the two noblemen who stood sipping wine on the adjacent balcony.

"Well, fortune favors the unremarkable I suppose," one man said with a small chuckle.

"Why, whatever do you mean?" the second man said dryly. "We're all just delighted at the continued health and wellness of our precious princess." They both gave into laughter as Seraphina's eyes stung with tears.

"Honestly, the best thing that could have happened for this royal line would be for the magic-less whelp to simply fade away. A horrible tragedy to be sure, but at least it would have spared the kingdom further embarrassment at having a princess unworthy of the blessed power that saved humanity."

"My word, man, that is a rather insensitive thing to say!"

"Oh pish, everyone is thinking it. I'm just the only one brave enough to say it aloud."

"Yes, quite brave enough to say it out here where there is only you and I. Maybe a few more goblets of wine and you'll go share your feelings with the queen herself."

"Maybe I will!"

"Oh, come now…"

"I'm sure she agrees with me. If I were her, I would have just smothered the princess in her sleep to spare the royal line the humiliation."

Seraphina slunk to the ground, dirtying her white gown with the filth of the balcony floor. She buried her face in her hands, overcome with devastation. Was this all true? Would her family have been better off without her? Had she been an embarrassment all along? Was her mother truly happy when she awoke, or bitterly disappointed as these two terrible men seemed to believe? These were questions that had haunted her these nine long, agonizing years.

"Sera?" she heard a young Val's voice call out for her, trotting out onto the balcony in his brown animus trainee robes. He would find her sitting there and question her as to what was wrong. She remembered she had lied to him, telling him that she was simply overwhelmed with this situation and these were tears of joy. He had never known her to lie, so he simply nodded and led her back inside.

As he turned to fix his kind green eyes upon her, he vanished in a blue haze along with the balcony. Seraphina stood, back in her blue gown, once more at her present age. The world rematerialized, and she found herself back in Aqua's fountain chamber. Her predecessor and teacher stood atop the waters of the fountain's basin staring down upon her with compassion.

"People are cruel," Seraphina whispered softly, looking down at the floor.

"Indeed," Aqua replied, gazing down at her charge with sympathy and sadness. "But, Seraphina, you cannot allow the words of others to impact you in such a profound way."

"Yes, that is quite easy to say…"

"Seraphina, you know that your lack of magic as a child had nothing to do with any skill or worthiness … You were born without the stain of chaos."

"Yes, of course, Aqua. But it doesn't change years of whispers, of fingers pointed in my direction, of feeling … inferior."

"A spirit of order cannot be bogged down by self-doubt. Such things take the heart to dangerous places, Seraphina; chaotic places."

"I know…"

"Yet you continue to let the words of these nameless people cripple you with depression and despair."

"It is not as easy as all that."

"Yes, it is. You have to see yourself for the strong, confident woman you have become. As you did when you overcame your fears; as you were when you faced down your sister in the Northern Magic."

"This is … different."

"It is no different than the fear you held in your heart, and like that fear, it can be overcome with willpower and belief in yourself."

"But I…" the room faded away before Seraphina could finish her sentence. This doubt and depression had been a presence in her life for so many years. It couldn't be as simple as just putting it out like a candle.

As the world reformed around her, Seraphina stood in her parents' throne room, still her present age, looking up at her mother who paced before her. They were alone together, something which very rarely happened.

"Today is an important day for you, Seraphina," Christina said, as she stopped walking, clasped her hands in front of her gown, and gazed down at her youngest daughter sternly. "On this day, you finally take an animus warrior."

Seraphina remembered this particular conversation. It was the morning of Valentean's animus coronation, the day he would speak the oath of animus and bind his life to hers forever.

"I find myself ... relieved by this." Seraphina winced. She knew what was coming. "For years, you have proven to be ... well, a novice when it comes to magic. Your father and I have been endlessly concerned as to your well-being and ability to defend yourself from harm since that day you were nearly taken from us, nine years ago."

"Well, Mother," Seraphina heard her voice say, reciting the words she recalled from that morning, "since that incident, I have developed some control over magic."

"Seraphina, the parlor tricks you have managed to learn are no doubt impressive, but when put to test in the real world, they amount to very little." The words were blunt and direct, much as her mother had always been. The queen did not sugarcoat anything when it came to her daughters. "Your sister is a prodigy, there is no denying that. I have never had to concern myself with her safety. But you ... Well, I'm just glad to see that Valentean will be able to keep you safe."

It was a crushing statement. Seraphina remembered, all too well, the feeling of humiliation, and self-loathing that ate at her insides. Was she really such a worthless case? Something so weak and fragile that her entire continued existence rested upon the shoulders of her animus warrior?

Meanwhile, her sister remained high atop this grand pedestal, the icon that she was meant to try and live up to. Little did her mother know that her golden child and heir was the truest definition of a monster, using her "gifts" as a prodigy to undermine the entire kingdom and bring about the end of everything their family stood for. Seraphina's anger began to build, her face flushing with color.

"Mother, how can you be such a fool?" she cried out at the queen, who looked aghast that her daughter would speak in such a manner.

"Seraphina!"

"You stand there in your palace of ignorance, praising one daughter while putting down the other. Little do you know, your precious Aleksandra is a lying, manipulative, evil, demon-worshipping traitor! If that's what you intended to raise in a daughter, then you've doomed us all!" The world shook in the wake of Seraphina's rage. Christina looked at her daughter, eyes widening with shock and fear. “All my life, you’ve convinced me that I’m some fragile little flower who can’t defend herself. Well, Mother, I am a strong woman, capable of so much more than you’ve ever done!” The quaking became fiercer as Seraphina smiled in triumph, fully believing in herself and her power as rage continued to flare. “I will show you, Mother. I will show everyone!”

She threw her arms out, feeling the force of her power burst forth from her body. It was not the reassuring, calm serenity of order that responded to her calls, but the fierce animalistic flames of chaos which erupted violently around the throne room, engulfing Christina who screamed in agony as the red-hot blaze blackened her skin. Seraphina screamed in horror and attempted to run toward her burning mother, but as she neared the queen’s outstretched hand, it crumbled to ash.

The fire continued to spread, untamable, until the once-familiar throne room had been reduced to a blazing inferno. Seraphina looked down upon her dress to find it had changed as well from the calm blue of order to a deep, chaotic shade of blood red. She panicked and brought her hands before her face, gazing in horror at the crimson glow that danced along her palms, given off by her eyes. Desperate to escape this nightmare, Seraphina ran through the wall of fire only to find Aqua standing amongst the burning devastation, sadly shaking her head in disappointment.

“Rage is the truest path to chaos.”

XX: NAHZARRO'S SKILL

The Grassani airship wobbled through the sky, and Maura was forced to grab hold of the banister. She looked to Nahzarro with desperation, silently begging him to do something, anything, to get the collapsing vessel under control. She had never been susceptible to motion sickness, but this was her first ride upon an airship and to call it turbulent would be an understatement. Maura tried focusing on her hands as they gripped the worn wood in hopes of stopping her churning stomach from emptying its contents onto Nahzarro's expensive looking shoes.

"Do not vomit," he said, glancing down through a furrowed brow while concentrating on their course.

"Well, just try and hold this thing steady."

"Considering we are flying three-quarters of an airship at the moment, I'm going to count my ability to keep us in the air at all as a miracle and a testament to my skill."

"Ok, ok, I don't want to argue." Maura held up one hand to halt whatever sentence was about to ooze from Nahzarro's mouth next. "Any sign of Valentean?"

"None," he replied, sounding troubled. "I had thought he would have found some way to catch up to us by now. You said he can fly, right?"

"Not well…" Maura struggled not to succumb to the heavy mixture of dread and nausea. "Not for long distances."

"Dammit," Nahzarro cursed under his breath, so softly Maura was certain she was not meant to hear it.

"So, what now?"

"Now we make our way to Kahntran and we carry out the plan. Burai isn't necessary for this to work. I can repair and power the device while you watch my back."

"I know you didn't mean for that to sound anywhere near as obnoxious as it came out. But let me make one thing clear: Valentean is necessary. Whether or not you believe it, he's the only one that has even an outside chance at taking down that evil bitch. Sure, we can open the door into

Aleksandrya, but if we tried to stand up to Aleksandra herself … we wouldn't last ten seconds."

"Speak for yourself," the captain scoffed. "I've met Princess Aleksandra. I've sensed her magic. I'm sure I could be a match for her."

"I'm going to let you just … continue to believe that," Maura replied, shaking her head slowly in disbelief.

"Clearly, you've never seen what I can really do…"

"Clearly, you've never seen what *she* can do." As Nahzarro opened his mouth, whatever he might have said was drowned out by a loud, ear-splitting, bestial roar that instantly stirred horrific memories in Maura.

"No…" she whispered, her voice trembling with fear.

"What on Terra was that?"

"No … not good! How fast can this thing go? Can you give us more speed?"

"What? We're barely holding together as it is!"

"Then we're dead…" Maura replied, the dread palpable in her tone as she wrapped her arms around the bannister.

"What are you…" Nahzarro was cut off by another deafening roar, this one far closer than the previous one had been. For a brief moment, there was silence, then a mountain of black scales and wings erupted into the sky in front of their vessel. "Damnation!" Nahzarro screamed, pulling the ship hard to the right. The airship lurched as the massive dark creature shot up like an arrow and vanished within the haze of clouds that had gathered above them.

"What was that?" Nahzarro screamed.

"Rosinanti…"

An instant later, the ebony dragon dove through the clouds on a collision course with the shattered ship, glowing purple eyes locked upon them. Anger burst through Maura's fear and she glared up at the monster who had taken her father. "Kayden…"

Nahzarro pulled the ship into another sharp turn that narrowly avoided the dragon. Maura knew better, though, than to believe Kayden had missed his mark. He was toying with them, drinking in their panic, enacting a cruel game of cat and mouse with his helpless prey.

"Hang on," Nahzarro screamed, muttering some hardly intelligible words under his breath. Maura felt an odd sensation around her boots and realized that her feet were now firmly attached to the ship's deck. "I need to do some creative flying. This will make sure we don't take an unexpected trip." Nahzarro sent the ship into a nosedive, causing Maura to scream in alarm. Kayden burst up behind them, displaced wind billowing out from his beating wings.

Maura could clearly see the frozen landscape of the Northern Continent approaching fast … far too fast. Utterly convinced her life was about to end, smashed into the jagged peaks of a snow-capped mountain, Maura gasped in relief when Nahzarro abruptly pulled the ship back up. He was pumping even more speed into the shaking vessel as it rocketed away. The sound of Kayden's bulk slamming into the craggy surface echoed like a thunderclap as they climbed.

"That will wake him up," Nahzarro announced triumphantly.

"He was already awake, trust me!" It took only seconds for Kayden to reappear on their rear, mouth now aglow with purple energy. "He's going to fire on us!"

"Gah!" Nahzarro bellowed in frustration, sending the ship into a spin that it was clearly never intended to attempt. The amethyst beam of energy sliced through the air, narrowly missing the tiny vessel. The maneuver took its toll, though, snapping off the ship's smokestack, causing green smoke to billow out from its lower levels. The green cloud obscured the dragon from view.

"Did you mean to do that?" Maura screamed in shock.

"He can't catch what he can't see!" Nahzarro answered over the whipping wind. The ship shuddered beneath them, suffering the ill effects of that desperate maneuver.

"You're insane! How are we going to stay in the air?"

"We're not! We are definitely going down but, this way, maybe I can lose him and coast us into Kahntran."

"You realize that's insane, don't you?"

"It's only insanity if it doesn't work, and when it *does*, then it's called brilliance."

The green haze was now all encompassing, taking up the entirety of the sky and Maura's field of vision. Had it actually worked? Had they truly outwitted Kayden? Maura basked in an instant of relief, believing for just a second that they were safe. Then, in one shattering moment of realization, it ended.

Kayden's destructive purple power exploded into the air once more, fired perfectly at the escaping vessel. Nahzarro cursed loudly and tried to veer to the right, but it was not enough. Kayden's attack slammed into their left flank, obliterating nearly half of the ship and sending them into a chaotic, spinning freefall. Maura screamed and reached for her daggers, a gut reaction that was beyond useless in this situation.

"Damnation!" Nahzarro screamed, letting go of the helm and running forward, wrapping both arms around Maura's torso while muttering more unintelligible nonsense under his breath. Maura felt her feet detach from the floor and, instantly, the two of them were surrounded by a sparking, glowing ball of yellow energy. "Hang on," Nahzarro said in her ear as he resumed his ceaseless chanting.

The remains of the decimated ship fell away, and the ball containing Maura and Nahzarro entered a freefall. Maura shrieked as they careened from the doomed vessel, watching in horror as it smashed into the face of a nearby mountain and exploded in a green and yellow mess. The ball which encased them slammed into the cold harsh ice that capped one of the larger mountains in the chain. To Maura's shock, they did not splatter against its surface. Instead, the yellow protective sphere bounced back up into the air, rocketing into an adjacent mountain, before bouncing off it like a child's toy.

It was astonishing magic, and Maura could scarcely believe how fully it protected them. They floated weightlessly in the center of the pulsating ball as it rocketed down towards the snowy landscape. They hit once more and bounced back, ricocheting off the ground several more times. It rolled to a stop near a ridge which seemed to fall off into nothingness. Nahzarro dissolved the spell and the two of them fell, entangled with one another, into the cold wet snow.

Maura laughed in spite of herself, completely awed at her continued ability to breathe. She was suddenly very aware of Nahzarro's arms wrapped around her and pushed away, desperate to be free of his touch, color flooding into her cheeks.

"I believe the word you're seeking is 'thank you,'" Nahzarro said, removing his black top hat for a moment to dust it off.

"Thank you," Maura said, still not turning back to face her unlikely savior. "That's certainly a handy little trick."

"Not an easy one, though," Nahzarro said, wincing with exertion and stretching his back. "I feel like I've been run down by a horse now."

Maura shivered in the harsh cold as the wind intensified. She focused on the mana within her, calling it forth to warm her body.

"You're regulating your body temperature using mana," Nahzarro observed, cutting through her concentration. He sounded almost impressed.

"Valentean is a good teacher," she said, her teeth still chattering due to some residual chills. "We're never going to reach Kahntran now..."

"What makes you say that?"

"We're out in the middle of nowhere!"

"Are we?" Nahzarro moved through the snow toward the cliff's edge and gestured broadly. "Surely by now, you've learned that I always know what I'm doing." Maura walked toward him and gasped. "Welcome to Kahntran."

Below the frigid ridge sat what had once been an enormous city, now in ruination. Kahntran sat as a perfect circle at the base of the mountain range. The sprawling community opened at the other end into the sea. Clearly defined sectors stretched out vertically, each separated by what once must have been a series of canals which allowed ships to sail into the city. Against the mountain upon which the desolate metropolitan wasteland sat, the ruins of a large structure had been cut into the stone.

"The royal palace of Kahntran," Nahzarro said by way of explanation, following Maura's line of sight. "They burned it into the mountain with magic. It was heavily fortified, nearly impenetrable in its day."

The remainder of the city had been overtaken by green vegetation, a jungle of vines and trees which stretched up out of what had once been shops, inns, homes, and streets. Maura could feel heat and humidity rising to meet them, mixing with the cold air and forming an unnatural combination of polar opposites which she found very unsettling.

The center sector of the city held the prize they had been seeking. Maura could scarcely believe it truly existed. It sat several times higher than the dead community's tallest buildings, angled up and pointed out over the open sea; an immense cannon which ran the entire length of the community. At its base, there was a large steel scaffold raised up in the air.

Upon this mass of metal, a variety of tubes and old looking devices ran off into the depths of the ground, obscured from view at this vantage point. The greenery which had overtaken the city seemed to have no effect on cannon, or the area immediately surrounding it. The magic contained within must still have been so potent that it warded off any invasive presence.

"I can't believe it..." Maura breathed, scarcely daring to trust their luck. Though perhaps it had not been luck. Nahzarro had known precisely what he was doing, and had through skill alone gotten them this far. It was impressive, though she was not about to inflate his ego by telling him so. She gazed around, half expecting to see Valentean waiting for them, but she exhaled in disappointment when he was nowhere to be found.

"I had nearly expected Burai to be here," Nahzarro said, echoing her exact thoughts in a moment that Maura found oddly unsettling.

"But I am," came a voice from behind them.

Turning to face this unexpected baritone, Maura felt her heart sink as she saw Kayden, smirking at her through the snow, black robes billowing in the breeze. "Though I suppose I'm not the Burai you were expecting."

XXI: CASID'S PROTECTOR

Deana wheeled her way across the floor of her modest one-room home, turning her back on the interesting figure she had been tending to since he had arrived quite suddenly into her life. She gazed up with a sigh at the gaping hole left in the house's roof, a stark reminder of the mysterious animus warrior's dramatic entrance.

A crashing airship was not a typical sight in a village such as Casid. Deana sat alongside her betrothed, Nevick, as he loomed heavily above her. The stoic strongman, who had won her heart so many years ago, stared with emotionless stoicism at the wreckage as it fell from the sky. At one time, the entire village would have been agape in the streets, watching such a spectacular and dreadful sight. Now, the mere notion that there could be any kind of disturbance was enough to send the two dozen surviving villagers running for cover within the safety of the precious few houses and structures which still stood within the decimated community.

"Nevick..." she said as if the mere mention of his name would provide some impenetrable, protective shield around her. The big man said nothing and simply laid one brown-skinned hand upon her shoulder. This was the closest he was going to come to being comforting in this situation. He had his "warrior face" on, as Deana liked to call it. In recent weeks, the stern, emotionless mask of stone seemed to be his resting expression.

"My airship!" a voice cried out. Deana turned in her chair to see Mitchell and Michael Duzel sprinting to join them. Mitchell, the older of the two, pulled his golden spectacles from his face, wiped them on his red shirt, and placed them back along the bridge of his nose as though he could scarcely believe his eyes. "Nevick, that's my ship!"

Nevick turned sharply toward the inventor. "You're sure?" he asked, his voice deep with concern.

"Positive," Michael clutched at the waist of his grey jumpsuit. "Trust me, Mitchell had me study those plans for hours. That's ours all right!"

Nevick's jaw tightened at the engineer's words. His hand left Deana's shoulder and curled into a tight shaking fist.

"Whoever is up there must have some answers," he said slowly. A loud explosion ripped along the side of the ship, shaking the ground beneath Deana's wheelchair. A lone figure plummeted from the wreckage, careening toward them. Michael cursed loudly as he and Mitchell dove for the ground. Nevick moved like the wind, sweeping Deana up into his strong arms before falling into a crouch, shielding her body with his burly torso. Several large pieces of debris struck the dirt road and a loud crash sounded from the direction of Deana's house.

Nevick continued forming a protective cocoon out of his body to safeguard his love. Deana clutched at his green tunic, all the while watching the airship vanish beyond her field of vision. The sound of a smashing crash and upended trees erupted from the forest, and for a moment, no one moved. The harsh noise faded back into silence and Deana relaxed. Nevick did not.

"It's all right, my love," she said, rubbing her hands along his solid chest. "We're safe."

Nevick remained crouched for a moment longer until he finally stood, keeping Deana wrapped in his arms like a small child. "We're never safe," he growled, walking back to the discarded chair and placing her back into its seat.

"I think that's all of it," Mitchell said, dusting off his long white coat as he and Michael stood from behind a pile of rubble left from the village's initial destruction. There were some large chunks of wood and metal strewn around the remainder of Casid's village square, but other than that, there seemed to be no major damage.

"Dammit," Nevick said, looking in the direction of Deana's house. She wheeled around, fearing the worst and saw a hole sitting in the middle of her roof. "Something big crashed inside."

He moved up the small ramp to the wooden door and fearlessly entered. She had attempted to follow behind, but Nevick held one hand aloft as if to halt her train of thought.

"What in the name of Terra..." she heard him say.

"What is it?" she called back.

"It's ... a man," he replied in shock.

Deana gasped, imagining the pulpy gore-soaked remains of an exploded corpse to be decorating the inside of her home. Michael moved up beside Nevick and peaked inside.

"What the ... Nevick, is he alive?" the grease-stained mechanic exclaimed. Mitchell came up behind Deana and pushed her through the door, following the two men into the wrecked domicile. Nevick and Michael crouched around the body of a handsome young man with ebony hair and a slight build. The stranger was clad in the unmistakable robes of an animus warrior. The garments were filthy, blood-soaked, and even scorched in many

areas. Nevick pressed two fingers into the young man's throat and nearly jumped back in alarm.

"He's still breathing," Nevick looked at Michael, who squinted at their unexpected guest.

He adjusted his round grey spectacles before his eyes suddenly doubled in size and he jumped back. "Do you know who this is?" he exclaimed, looking at Nevick and turning to flash a look of surprised excitement toward his brother.

"No, should I?" Nevick replied.

Michael pulled a roll of parchment out from within his jumpsuit and unfolded it in a hurry. Deana had seen this particular piece of propaganda many times. It was a detailed report of the Tournament of Animus. Michael had become enamored with the tale of the two Kackrittan animus warriors who engaged one another in what many were calling the battle of the century.

"This is Valentean Burai," he exclaimed, pointing to a very accurate drawing upon the parchment's surface, "the champion animus of Terra!"

Nevick had placed the fallen animus warrior into Deana's empty bed, asking her to look after him while he took Mitchell and Michael into the forest to investigate the airship crash. Since then, Deana had been utilizing her unique magical abilities to help heal the young man. She had been astounded as to the rate his body reacted to her special talent. Cuts sealed before her eyes, bruises melted into pale flesh, and he had regained consciousness momentarily, even speaking to her once. After she had briefly introduced herself, he fell fast asleep once more.

Since then, Deana had taken a much-deserved break to gather her strength. The miraculous healing magic she commanded took a toll on her body. Given the crippled state she had been left in following the attack which had ended the happy home she had always known, calling upon her unique skill had become increasingly more difficult. She sighed and rubbed the bridge of her nose with a shaking hand. Her arms felt so heavy, her eyelids drooped as she took slow, deliberate breaths to steady her insides.

She had been attempting to keep a smile on her face in the wake of tragedy. She was crippled now, trapped within the smothering confines of a ruined body and nearly everyone she had ever known and grown up with laid dead. The home she loved so much was naught more than a collective of remaining houses surrounded by a graveyard of rubble.

Above it all, though, beyond the personal tragedy and the loss of her legs, her heart ached for Nevick. He had always placed the burden of Casid's protection squarely upon his broad shoulders. In the aftermath of such a monumental disaster, Deana had watched the gentle soul she loved retreat within a fortress of skin and scowl. He vanished every single day to journey out into the forest and train his body, never wandering far, but continuing to push himself to grow stronger. He blamed himself—Deana could see the extreme loss of life, and her condition, echoed in his sad stare each and every day. He could harden his face into a stone wall of emotionless fury, but his eyes told an entirely different story. Though Michael, Mitchell, or any of the other remaining villagers might never see beyond the dark glower he carefully kept, Deana knew him differently. She knew his eyes, and she knew when they were hurting.

The tremor in her hands ceased and Deana took one last deep breath, feeling the color return to her cheeks. She gripped the wheels on the side of her chair and turned to face her charge. Sudden movement startled her and she cried out in alarm, throwing back the wheels of her chair into a hasty backpedal. Valentean Burai was sitting up, fully awake and alert.

"How are you…?"

"I'm sorry!" he replied with such honest sincerity that it took Deana out of the moment. He held his hands, palms facing her, a look of genuine concern on his face. "I didn't mean to startle you … Deana, was it?"

She shook her head to clear any lingering tingles and chuckled nervously. "Yes, I'm surprised you remembered. You weren't especially coherent when I introduced myself."

"Yes, sorry about that…"

"You're sorry for being unconscious? That's entirely too polite even for an animus warrior."

He looked down at his soiled robes and nodded sadly. "I suppose these do give me away, don't they?"

"Indeed," she said. "I've heard a great deal about you actually, Valentean Burai."

He stiffened, his eyes suddenly heavy with worry and … could that have been fear? "What exactly have you heard?"

"Champion animus of Terra, master of magic unseen on the planet since the days when dragons soared the sky. Just the same bit everyone seems to know."

He relaxed, closed his eyes, and nodded. "Yes, well, I suppose its…" his gaze traveled up toward the ceiling, taking in the massive hole in her roof. "Oh no … please tell me that hole wasn't…"

"You?" She slowly nodded her head.

"I am so incredibly sorry!"

"It's fine, don't worry," she said, wheeling up to his bedside. "It fits in with the rest of the village now."

"Casid, you said it was called?"

"Yes…"

"Did … something happen here? Was it the airship crash?"

"No, we were relatively untouched by that. The village was attacked recently by … monsters. Like something out of a story book."

Valentean grew very quiet. "What did they look like?"

"They were huge, their skin was red, like blood."

He reacted almost violently, reeling back in his seated position as if struck by a fist. "How many people?" he asked sadly, his voice breaking.

"Over seventy…" she said, feeling almost guilty for breaking such bad news to this total stranger who had no emotional ties to her home. He sniffled and wiped at his eyes, swinging his legs over the side of the bed until his boots touched the floor.

"You know what they are, don't you?" she asked, wheeling up closer and looking into his emerald eyes. He nodded sadly. "Please tell me." Deana grasped the gauntlets that covered his forearms, her own sadness which had been so expertly buried now starting to well up. "Please, I need to know. I need to know the reason for … for all of … this!"

Valentean was silent for a moment, raising his chin to meet her gaze. "All right," he said slowly. "I'll tell you everything."

Nevick followed the trail of debris which had plummeted into the forest from the falling ship. Eventually, it would lead him to the wreckage. If it were truly Mitchell's design, then perhaps there would be some clue inside as to the person or persons who orchestrated the devastation of his home. Then it would be time for revenge.

In recent weeks, he thirsted for vengeance so often that rage had become his common mental state. Anytime he walked outside and saw the aftermath of the attack or watched the woman he loved struggle to move in a chair with wheels, the fires of fury exploded within his furnace heart.

Weak, he heard the voice of doubt whisper into his mind. *You let your guard down*. He had grown complacent, attempted to take a day in which he laid down the resolve of a warrior and played the role of a normal human being. But Nevick now knew better. He could not enjoy the simple pleasures the rest of humanity reveled in. There was evil in this world—dark, cold, raging evil. There were those who perpetuated it, those who were swept up by it, and those with the fortitude to fight against it.

He had been gifted with extraordinary strength and abilities. It became his responsibility to focus that power, increase it, and protect the people he loved, few as they may now be. He hadn't asked for the strength to stand against the dangers of this world, but he had been given it nonetheless, and he would use it to do some good.

"Are we … almost there…" Mitchell asked, panting as he jogged along after the big man.

Nevick turned and fixed his stare onto the inventor. "I can smell smoke," he replied. "I'm sure that means we're close."

Michael's portly grey clad form came into view through the trees; his eyes alight with gratitude when he noticed that his brother and friend had stopped. He leaned heavily on a tree to regain his breath.

"Can we … just … for a minute?" he asked, motioning toward the tree, begging for a reprieve.

"You two can rest if you'd like," Nevick said, "but I'm going on ahead." He turned without a word or second's hesitation, not knowing or caring if his comrades followed. It was not annoyance toward them that drove him on. They were true friends and had saved his life during the battle which consumed Casid. Rather, Nevick had been regretting his decision to leave Deana with the unconscious animus warrior. He knew nothing of this man, save for Michael's third-hand account of his combat prowess and mastery of ancient magic.

He had acted rashly in leaving Deana alone with this unknown, though the stranger's lack of consciousness may have had something to do with his momentary willingness. *You're letting your compassion blind you again,* doubt whispered to him. He had always been too nice, too trusting for his own good. It had, on more than one occasion, blown up in his face. He had let many prospective residents of Casid settle in, believing their sob stories of Karminian oppression only to discover some dark, secret, criminal past that he needed to address.

The presence of this airship and Mitchell's assurance that it was, indeed, his design had momentarily blinded Nevick to the potential danger.

He was in that airship, his doubt called out to him. *What if he sent the monsters that killed them? What if he is responsible for crippling her?* Nevick clenched his fists at the thought, causing a rippling tingle of power to bulge his already massive biceps. He couldn't think about that now. He had to focus. Reach the ship and then hurry back to the village; that was the only course of action available to him now.

He could hear the Duzel brothers moving through the foliage behind him and knew that they had decided to forego Michael's requested break. He felt guilty, for a moment, at pushing them so hard. They were not warriors, not accustomed to traveling through the wilderness, and certainly not in the physical shape he was in. But they were brave and mighty in their own way. Nevick respected them both for it.

A smoky, choking intake of breath forced him to cough. His quarry was very close. He waited for his companions to catch up and held a hand up to let them know silence was needed.

"The ship is close," he whispered and the brothers nodded. Nevick crept over a large hill, half-crouching to avoid being spotted by any sentries that might be looking out for intruders. As he reached the top, he saw the ship, laid out in all its size and grandeur, still mostly intact. It was a steel monstrosity that had flattened the land and upended trees in its catastrophic landing.

"My word," Mitchell said, tugging on his shirt nervously. "There it is … my life's work, a smoldering heap in front of me…"

"Our life's work," Michael said, coming to stand beside his brother, head pointed to the ground. "Wait, what's that on the wing?" He pointed at the red-emblazoned phoenix bird, talons stretched as though attacking within the silhouette of a flame.

"It looks like the royal insignia of Kackritta," Mitchell replied, "but it's different."

"Kackritta," Nevick echoed thoughtfully. "Like the animus…"

Seeing no immediate threat, he moved into the newly created clearing, coming up on the rear of the ship. There was a hole blown into the metal surface, and Nevick cautiously approached the darkness of the downed vessel's interior. He gazed inside, his eyes quickly scanning for movement. When nothing leapt out at him, he motioned for the brothers to follow.

The three men entered the unknown chamber together, moving carefully within what Nevick could make out as an engine room, though it had seen better days. Fires smoldered in several areas, and the various machines and engines sparked.

"Remarkable." Mitchell quickened his pace as he approached a large mechanism near the rear of the chamber. Several gears were still slowly turning and a high-pitched whine emanated from it.

"What's remarkable?" Nevick asked, desperate for some answers.

"It's in one piece," Michael answered in place of his brother, who was so busy inspecting every odd and end of the completed engine that he failed to hear Nevick's question.

"Really?"

"Yes," the mechanic replied, running a hand over the smooth surface of the device. "This thing was so well-armored that the crash didn't really damage the integrity of the machine. It's completely intact." Michael pointed at a long scorch mark that ran the length of the engine. "Something hit it, though, so there are some components that were burned out which would explain the crash."

"So, what are you saying?" Nevick asked.

"That we can fix it," Mitchell said, his voice filled with wonder and awe. "And quickly, too. Maybe a month and we could have this thing airborne again. That's just a guess. I would have to do a full analysis of the damage, but from an engineering standpoint, we could have it flying again."

"Why would we need to?" Nevick asked.

"Well, the possibilities could be…" Mitchell's voice suddenly died in his throat.

"What?" Nevick asked. He saw Michael walk up to his brother and then heard the mechanic gasp. Nevick was beside them instantly and looked down, following their gaze. Lying in a doorway leading into a corridor was the bulky body of one of the red-skinned creatures that had attacked Casid.

Nevick turned his attention to the dark interior of the chamber they stood in, focusing on the debris that lay on the ground around them. He could just make out the flame-illuminated forms of nearly ten of those monsters strewn about the engine room. They were broken, bleeding, all dead. There appeared to be some other mangled corpses strewn about as well. They were four-legged, fearsome-looking, and clearly crafted from the same ilk as these other more familiar creatures.

Careless, the voice of his doubt resounded through his head. *This was their ship*. Silence hung around the trio in such utter totality that Nevick could hear the sound of his jaw clenching tight. *And the animus was up here with them ... the animus that you left with her.* This thought cracked like a whip within his mind.

"Deana!" he exclaimed, bolting for the exit, running with all he was worth. Mitchell and Michael were following but he could not wait for them. Time was of the essence now. The woman he loved was in danger, and he had to reach her fast.

"And that's when I fell from the ship and … I suppose crashed into your home here," Valentean said, concluding his tale. Deana had sat in silence taking in every detail, from Lazman's destruction to the plot of The Faithful, even his origins as a Rosinanti, without so much as blinking in surprise.

"And these … Skudlacks are what attacked my village?" she asked.

"Skirlacks," he corrected her. "Yes, and your loss weighs so heavily on my heart, Deana. So many of us have lost so much to Aleksandra and those that follow her."

"Some princess a world away makes a decision and hundreds of people die…" she said, letting her train of thought hang in the air. "It makes you feel so … helpless … and small."

"Your legs," Valentean said, dreading the answer she might offer, "was that a result of…"

"The attack," she answered. "Yes, it was."

His heart broke at the horrible reality this kind woman and her people were forced to live through. "I am so sorry…"

"It isn't your fault," she said kindly.

"I feel responsible, though."

"Well, that's just silly," Deana replied. "It seems to me as though you're the only one working towards fixing this world."

"I have help," he said, "friends who need me. That's why I need to get to Kahntran."

Deana nodded slowly. “That is a tall order. It’s far from here.”

“I know. I’m worried about my friends. How long was I out?”

“About two hours.”

“What? How is that possible? I fell out of an airship! Even I don’t heal that fast.”

Deana smiled at him, blushing. “Well, you aren’t the only one with magic.”

“Even with healing magic, I should have been out for days.”

“My healing magic is … different.”

“Different how?” Valentean inclined his head in curiosity. Deana opened her mouth to answer but seemed to think better of it and wheeled her chair over to the tiny kitchen on the other side of the room. She took a large chopping knife from the table and held it next to her hand.

“Like this,” she said, slicing deep into her palm with the blade, sending a spray of blood cascading down her arm and staining her blue and white dress. Valentean leaped up in alarm, moving toward her. Deana clasped her hands together and a bright white light emanated between them. He skidded to a halt as the energy blazed. The light died out, and Deana separated her hands, showing him that her palm had completely healed, leaving not even the slightest hint of a scar.

He gasped. “You…” he said, walking to her, crouching down and holding her wrist with both hands, gazing in pure wonder at her perfectly healed hand. “You’re a miracle…”

The door of the small house burst open and Valentean leaped to his feet. He saw an enormous man standing there in a green tunic and matching cloak, glaring at him through dark eyes ablaze with hatred. As he was about to address this new arrival, he rushed forward, fist cocked back, and struck Valentean hard in the chest. Just as the punch connected, he heard Deana cry out.

“Nevick!” she screamed.

The force of the blow nearly caved in the Rosinanti’s chest cavity. Outside of Aleksandra, Valentean had never been hit so hard in his life. The force of the mighty blow sent him smashing through the wall out into to the clear afternoon breeze. Valentean’s body struck the ground and bounced three times before he gestured back, using the wind to brace his landing. He crouched low waiting for this mystery attacker’s follow up.

The man leaped through the new hole made in Deana’s wall and ran at him with speed that could only have been born of mana. Who was this? Some powerful skilled assassin sent by Aleksandra to retrieve him? Some bounty hunter? Whoever this was, he had caught Valentean completely off-guard, and now he was going to see exactly what the white dragon was capable of.

Valentean ran at the big man, ducking under a wild hooking right-handed punch meant for his head and connected with a strong left to the kidneys that forced his opponent to recoil. Valentean's eyes lit up with energy as he urged the wind to aid him, shooting a concentrated gust which threw his immense adversary back. The man struck the ground hard before rolling up to his feet and leaped at Valentean, mana propelling him up and forward at a shocking speed for one so large. He raised both fists into the air, attempting to smash Valentean into the dirt.

The animus warrior jumped into a backhand spring that shot him away from the epicenter of the strong man's blow. His fists had landed with enough force to upend the ground. Had Valentean been victimized by such a heavy assault, this battle might have been over. He spat a small trickle of blood down upon the ground that had been welling up in his chest since that first punch. It was time to get serious.

Deana wheeled herself out the front door of her house as quickly as she could. This was a disaster. She had tried to call out to Nevick, to let him know that the man he was attacking was not a threat. Her betrothed had seen red in that instant, though, and nothing she could say had gotten through to him. Deana's mind raced with hundreds of possibilities. What if Nevick managed to kill Valentean? He would unknowingly unleash this chaos goddess that the Kackrittan princess worshipped. He could destroy the entire world over a misunderstanding. Or what if Nevick was simply not strong enough to withstand a battle with a Rosinanti and Valentean struck him down in self-defense. *Her* world would be destroyed…

She had to do something, find some way to come between the two men and end this senseless battle. Thunder-like blows echoed beyond her home and Deana knew that the battle must have been raging. But how could she reach them? Her chair would be useless in the uneven terrain of the surrounding forest. She was helpless.

The surviving villagers peeked out of their homes, looking to see what had caused such a loud bang only moments earlier. Deana gripped the armrests of her chair, prepared to dive forward onto the ground and crawl if she had to.

"Deana!" she heard Michael yell as he sprinted into the village square. "Are you all right?" Mitchell trailed behind him, both brothers looked positively terrified.

"You two have to stop him!" she said, desperately seizing Michael by the arms.

"The animus?"

"No, Nevick! He's attacking Valentean!"

"He was on that ship with the same monsters that destroyed the village," Mitchell said. "The ship came from Kackritta. They must have sent those creatures here to destroy the village and steal my airship plans!"

"No! He was *fighting* them!" Deana exclaimed desperately.

"What?" Mitchell cried out in shock.

"I knew it," Michael replied, looking relieved.

"Kackritta was conquered from within. It's a long story, but what you need to know is that Valentean is trying to save the world and Nevick is trying to kill him!"

"Oh no." The color drained from Mitchell's face.

"We need to stop him!" Michael replied, already dashing off into the forest. Mitchell followed close behind and Deana breathed a tiny sigh of relief. She hoped that the two of them could talk some sense into Nevick and calm his fury. She wheeled her chair back several meters, trying to see if she could make anything out, when a large, metallic hand clamped onto the back of her neck.

Valentean nimbly dodged and bent his body out of the path of a flurry of hard swinging lunges from the big man's arms. He had managed to stay relatively unscathed after that first attack, but his opponent fought with such ferocity that it was nearly impossible to counter into his own offense. Valentean dropped into a crouch, feeling the whoosh of air pass overhead from a missed punched meant for his face and drove his fist into the rock-hard muscles of the man's abdomen.

The sound of wind being pushed from lungs was like music to Valentean's ears. He shot up and slammed a mana empowered kick into the back of the warrior's shaved head, sending him face forward into the dirt.

Nevick smacked hard onto the ground. This animus warrior was as skilled as Michael's stories had indicated. Nevick pumped energy into his right arm, feeling the muscles nearly double in size. As the animus ran at him, Nevick slammed his broad fist into the dirt, causing a quake that threw his advancing adversary off-balance just enough for Nevick to lunge forward and connect with a strong punch to the head.

The animus was launched off his feet. Nevick moved fast enough to grab him by the calf and flung the stranger into the ground, back first.

Valentean cried out in agony as he roughly impacted the forest floor. He felt the man's grip tighten around his leg as he was tossed through the air, coming down, hard, on his side. Valentean attempted to pull mana from the air but his breath was cut off by a powerful kick that rocked his torso as he attempted to rise.

The warrior charged at him again, and Valentean stuck one hand out, summoning the wind to send him soaring back. As his opponent fell, Valentean leaped onto him, raining a series of punches down upon his face and chest. It was all the larger fighter could do to block his furious assault.

Nevick had been careless and allowed this much smaller opponent to overwhelm him. His strange ability to control the wind had proven unexpected and problematic. Nevick covered his face with both hands to block the impossibly strong punches that the animus warrior rained down upon him.

Finally, he noticed an opening and threw his mit-like hand up, grasping Valentean by the throat. He pulled the animus roughly to the side, smashing his head and face into the dirt while rising to one knee. Nevick stood, lifting Valentean effortlessly into the air with one hand still firmly latched onto his throat. Screaming with rage born of battle, Nevick threw his smaller opponent down.

Valentean impacted hard and grunted in pain. Nevick reached down to continue his assault, but the spry animus raised his knees to his chest and kicked out with glowing green boots that struck Nevick in the stomach and chest. There was an instant explosion that tossed him back.

Weak, the voice of doubt taunted him.

That kick had been an act of desperation. Valentean needed to end this fight quickly. There was something holding him back. Some foreboding sense of doubt stayed his hand and caused him to bite back on the bulk of his Rosinanti power. He had taken damage, though, far too much of it. This needed to stop.

Valentean sprang to his feet, left fist cocked and glowing. The big man also exploded up to a standing position and they ran at one another.

Nevick's legs pumped furiously beneath him, determined to end the battle with this pass. The animus was feinting with the glowing left fist, clearly a distraction. The true attack would come from the right or from an unexpected kick. Nevick was prepared to meet such a strike and disable him with a blow to the head at full strength. This man had associated with the monsters that had crippled his love and destroyed all that he dedicated himself to. For that, he deserved to be treated like a monster.

The muscles in Nevick's arms and chest bulged and grew with the power of his gathered energy. This was it, he would do or die. He owed it to Deana and the remaining villagers of Casid to remain upright and breathing. As the two warriors neared one another, a third figure leaped into the fray. It was Michael, waving his arms, each hand gripping the handle of one of the mallets he kept upon his belt. Was he insane, interfering in such a battle? Nevick jumped back and watched as Valentean skidded to a halt as well.

"Stop, both of you!" he cried out, turning to Nevick. "He wasn't with them!"

"What are you talking about?" Nevick replied, panting. The exhaustion of battle was beginning to set in as his adrenaline began to dissipate.

"He was fighting them! Deana said he was fighting *against* those things!"

Nevick's head snapped up, eyes meeting those of Valentean. The animus warrior could have easily charged through the helpless mechanic and ended this battle. However, he had stopped, choosing not to attack an innocent.

"The Skirlack?" Valentean asked Michael. "You're talking about the Skirlack demons?"

The word echoed through Nevick's mind. *Skirlack*, it was a hard and harsh word, befitting those nightmarish monsters. *Skirlack*. His enemy had a name. "Those red-skinned monsters," he said, meeting the eyes of his foe, speaking to him for the first time. "That's what they're called?"

"Yes," Valentean said, seemingly not at all fatigued from their encounter. "The Skirlack serve my enemy. They attacked my friends and me in the middle of an important mission to stop them."

Nevick's heart nearly stopped beating. He had attacked this man with the rage of his vengeance, blindly without any definitive proof of wrongdoing. But he was the enemy of his enemy. Did that make him a friend? "I almost killed you," he said, voice dripping with regret.

"If it makes you feel any better, no, you didn't," Valentean replied with a wink and a smile.

Nevick chuckled in spite of the situation, the first genuine laugh that escaped his throat since the dark day of his ill-fated wedding.

"Deana said he was trying to save the world," Mitchell added from further back in the forest. Nevick hadn't noticed the inventor's approach. "She said Kackritta has been conquered." Nevick's gaze turned to Valentean, head inclined in questioning.

"Kind of," Valentean offered by way of explanation. "It's a long story and I'm kind of sore after that. Can we head back to the village and I'll explain everything?"

Nevick looked this disheveled warrior up and down. His robes had certainly seen better days. Each imperfection carried a piece of this man's story upon it; a story he was eager to hear.

"Let's go," he said, nodding in affirmation.

"Great," Valentean replied in response, sounding ridiculously chipper for someone who had been in a battle to the death, not a minute prior. He stuck out his hand. "I'm Valentean by the way."

Nevick looked at his extended arm, flabbergasted that he had so quickly let go of any lingering anger or frustration at having been wrongfully assaulted. He reached out and shook the animus warrior's hand. "Nevick."

"Pleased to meet you, Nevick. You fight well!"

"As do you," Nevick replied, bringing a hand up to massage his aching jaw.

Michael edged up and stuck his hand out toward the new arrival. "Michael Duzel, it's an honor," he said, practically wrenching Valentean's hand away from Nevick to shake it. "I've been reading accounts of the Tournament of Animus and … well, it's just an honor."

"The honor is mine, my friend," Valentean said, smiling and returning the handshake.

Mitchell approached as well. "Mitchell Duzel." Valentean let go of Michael's hand and turned. "Your biggest fan here is my brother. We actually designed that airship you fell out of."

Valentean's eyes nearly leapt from his head in surprise. His face hardened in the wake of such an important revelation. "I need to hear everything."

"Of course," Mitchell said.

A large bang and the unmistakable sound of screaming reached the four men from the direction of Casid. Nevick's blood froze in his veins and the world seemed to slow down. The scream … what had happened while he was out here engaging in a pointless battle? Had someone else survived the crash? He could scarcely breathe.

"Deana!" he cried out, sprinting toward his home.

XXII: MAURA ALONE

Maura's worst nightmare was unfolding before her eyes. Kayden was here, and Valentean was nowhere to be found. The white dragon was the only person on the planet who might protect them from his brother's vicious, brutal nature. She swallowed a shuddering lump of fear that nearly closed off her throat and took a step back.

"What's wrong, Maura," Kayden remarked cruelly at her momentary retreat, "no warm greeting for an old friend?"

His taunting smile fanned the flames of her hate and Maura's lips pulled away from her teeth. "The only greeting I'll give you is a knife through the neck, you disgusting monster."

He feigned offense, mouth comically agape as he laid a hand against his heart for effect. "You'd say that after all we've been through? I mean, I was with you for the death of your father, the destruction of your home, that time you were tortured for a few days, the massacre in Kackritta. If you think about it, in all the hardest moments of your life, I've been there for you!"

"You were the cause of every single one of them," she spat, the power of her hate now overcoming any fear.

"Well, yes, there's that," he said dryly. "Why don't you come here and we can make some new memories?"

Maura drew her daggers and took a step, but Nahzarro moved out in front, holding his arm out to halt her momentum.

"Stay back," he commanded, adjusting his black top hat. "I'll handle this."

"Will you?" Kayden scoffed, looking this unfamiliar foe up and down. "I don't believe I've had the pleasure."

"Nahzarro Matias, crowned prince of Grassan and captain of the Knights Mystic," he replied. "And I assure you, this will not be a pleasure."

Kayden laughed. "Well, Nahzarro Matias, crowned prince of Grassan and captain of whatever that ridiculous thing you just named is, let's see what you can do."

Nahzarro quickly drew one of his whips and electrified it with magic as it snapped for Kayden's face. The Rosinanti was faster, though, bending his body back to avoid the sparking strand of energy. Nahzarro drew his second whip as he moved, activating it, and sending it on an intercept course for Kayden's legs.

The dark warrior leapt over the weapon, avoiding both the whip itself and the electrical discharge that crackled around it. He landed in a crouch, a smile on his face.

"Impressive!" he said as Nahzarro lashed forward with both whips, creating a sizzling cage of lightning that lashed out at Kayden from every angle.

The prince moved with far greater speed than Maura had seen upon the airship, his twin instruments whistling and cracking through the air as they lurched forward with a hunger to burn through flesh and bone. Kayden, though, was mind-blowingly fast, and managed to bob, dart and bend his body away from the electrified energy.

He did not counterattack, opting instead to continue this strategy of avoidance. Nahzarro's whips were melting the snow around them as the super-heated strands missed their intended target, often striking the ground before being recalled for another attack. After a particularly dazzling exchange, the captain managed to score a glancing blow to Kayden's right shoulder. The black dragon leapt back out of range and stared at the smoldering rip along the sleeve of his robe. Nahzarro pulled his weapons back, leaving them lying in the melting snow.

"Not bad," Kayden remarked, poking a finger through this new tear in the black fabric of his garment. "You're bordering on impressive."

"I don't need compliments from monsters."

"You say that word as though it's an insult," Kayden's expression darkened dangerously.

Nahzarro raced forward and lashed out with both whips, but this time Kayden was through playing around. A gesture from one hand sent a skull-sized rock tearing from the ground that smashed into Nahzarro's left hand, forcing him to drop one of his weapons. He turned back to his opponent and struck out with his one remaining whip, cracking it in an attempt to drive Kayden back.

The black dragon gestured once more and another rock flew out toward Nahzarro's arm, but the prince pulled back at the last second, the stony projectile just missing him. As he tried to strike downward, hoping his whip would score a blow to the top of Kayden's head, another rock flew at him from behind, slamming into his wrist and sending his remaining whip soaring out of reach. Maura winced as Kayden advanced, but Nahzarro was ready for him.

He held one hand out and a green beam of destructive energy flew from his palm, striking Kayden in the chest and sending him flying back. Maura heard the Rosinanti grunt in pain, and she was glad for it. As he rose, Kayden flung a large stone at Nahzarro who met it with another dazzling burst of emerald energy which blew the rock to bits. He continued firing at Kayden hoping to score another blow, but to no avail.

Kayden leapt over Nahzarro's next attack and advanced, fist crackling with mana. As he reached out to punch Nahzarro's exposed head, his hand passed harmlessly through the captain, who vanished in a haze of smoke. Nahzarro reappeared behind Kayden, shooting him in the back with another burst of light that sent him pitching forward into the snow. Kayden rose again and Nahzarro was starting to look frustrated. His usual opponents likely never had the stamina and stony resilience of the dark-hearted Rosinanti.

The prince struck out with another bolt, and then another, and then another. Kayden held his arms up against his face to block them, but Nahzarro was not finished. He continued to toss green bursts from his hands in every direction, and they filled the air like an emerald meteor shower. Then as one, they all switched direction and hurtled down at Kayden. As the rain of magic pummeled the black dragon, Nahzarro kept on firing. Maura could hear him, now deep into the energetic thrill, screaming as he hammered the Rosinanti. The energy kept falling for another minute, and there seemed to be no movement from Kayden within the epicenter of destruction.

Finally, Nahzarro succumbed to exhaustion, and the unrelenting assault ceased as he fell to his knees in the snow. The area in which Kayden had fallen was still obscured from view by a haze of smoke. For a moment, there was stillness, and it was agonizing to Maura. She wanted to see Kayden's burned and smoldering corpse laying there, the victim of the world's ultimate justice. She held her breath as Nahzarro looked on with a proud smile covering the heavy fatigued breaths which pushed through his lips.

The smoke cleared and Maura gasped in deflating agonizing despair. Kayden stood, unscathed, within a circle of blackened rock, staring expressionless at Nahzarro. He had not been so much as bruised by the onslaught. The prince's face fell, and for the first time, Maura saw fear in Nahzarro's eyes.

"Nice try," Kayden scoffed.

Nahzarro reached out with a desperate hand, summoning one of his discarded whips. He ignited it with bright bolts of white lightning and flung it out at the unburnt dragon. Kayden held an arm out, allowing the damaging, burning electric heat to wrap around his forearm, burning through his sleeve and pumping offensive energy into his body. The black dragon stared at the sparking weapon, no pain or discomfort registering on his stoic face. Nahzarro attempted to pull back, likely hoping the strand would sever Kayden's arm as it had the limbs and heads of many Skirlack aboard the airship. But to Maura's mounting horror, Kayden did not budge.

Nahzarro was aghast and, in his unbelieving eyes, Maura could see a desperate despair. It was as though everything the magical prince had ever believed about his own superiority had vanished in a horrifying, deflating instant.

"My turn now," Kayden said, pulling back on the whip which pitched Nahzarro off balance. Kayden shrugged the weapon to the ground along with half of his burned off sleeve as he met Nahzarro with a gloved fist to the face. The prince flew back several meters, his hat flying off his head as he crashed onto his stomach. "I've watched you throughout the course of your journey here, Prince Nahzarro Matias." Kayden kicked the rising captain in the ribs before smashing down along his spine with both fists. Nahzarro groaned as his body slammed back into the ground.

"Would you like to know what I saw?" He gripped Nahzarro's limp body by the collar of his jacket and pulled him up to his knees. His head drooped as though he had not the strength to lift it. A large purple bruise was forming along his jawline and blood leaked from his nose. "I saw the pompous arrogance of a man who holds himself above the human race." Kayden buried his knee into Nahzarro's chest three times, causing a gurgled howl of pain to push from his mouth. A trickle of blood spilled from his lips, mixing with a strand of saliva to pour slowly into the white snow. "It's a trait I know well. One that I share. But do you want to know the difference between you and me?" He threw Nahzarro roughly back. The prince soared through the air until a slab of stone erupted from the ground and his body smashed into it. He did not even have the energy to cry out. He simply sat there, slumped and defeated, trying with increasing difficulty to look up at his attacker.

"Mine is justified," Kayden said, vanishing in a blur of speed as he rocketed toward Nahzarro and struck him hard in the face with a knee, smashing the prince's head back into the rock. Nahzarro slumped to the side, unmoving save for a quaking twitch. His face was a lacerated mess of blood. The gooey red rivulets poured from his nose, cheeks, eyes, and mouth out onto the snow, staining it in a mess of crimson. "All those humans you've held yourself above all these years, all those that you felt superior over; and yet you will die right here, right now, in the middle of nowhere, cowering before one who is *actually* superior."

Kayden raised a glowing fist above his head, preparing to strike down and end the battle. Maura's grip tightened on her dagger handles. If she did not act, foolish as it might be, she would watch another die before this monster. She ran through the snow and attempted to drive her blades into Kayden's back. The Rosinanti turned at the last possible moment and drove a knee into her midsection. Maura gasped as the incredible force hit her, shooting her back amidst an explosion of pain along her ribs.

"Oh, Maura," Kayden said, now advancing on her with glowing purple eyes, momentarily forgetting Nahzarro. "Was that bravery? Desperation? Stupidity? It might just be all three."

She rose through the pain and tried to slash him along the chest, but he caught her wrist, the blade centimeters from his heart. She slashed out with her other hand, but Kayden casually blocked her, smacking the weapon from her grip. “Stupidity it is then.” He threw her off her feet, and Maura fell onto her side.

He advanced on her slowly, the snow crunching under his deliberate footsteps. She had to do this, she had to stop him and get Nahzarro to Kahntran. Seraphina was counting on her. Seraphina, who had risked everything to give Maura and Valentean a chance at survival, relied on the completion of this mission. With that in mind, she leapt up once again and tried to slash Kayden across the chest. He easily bent out of the way.

She righted her stance, reversed her grip on the blade and attempted to rebound by stabbing through his face. He caught her forearm once more and smirked before rearing back and smashing his forehead into hers. Maura fell back into the snow again, feeling a slow but steady stream of blood leaking from the space between her eyes. The oozing flow billowed around her nose and into the corners of her mouth until she could taste the copper bitterness along her tongue. Her vision blurred as the world spun around her. She was seeing four Kayden’s glaring down at her, eight bright purple eyes regarding her with icy finality.

Kayden shook his head and turned, once more, to finish off Nahzarro, but again, Maura struggled to her feet. This time, he turned before she had the chance to attack and laughed at her pathetically slow rise.

“Poor little Maura, all alone,” he snickered. “You know I could have ended you in my true body, just snuff you out like an ant scurrying on the ground. But for you, I wanted to get close. I wanted this to be personal.” His hateful, horrible words brought a snarl to Maura’s blood splotched lips. “I find this resolve of yours entertaining. What’s bringing you back up to your feet? It is him?” he asked, pointing back at Nahzarro’s prone body, face down in the snow. “Is this your lover? Do you love him? Please, tell me you love him. I enjoy killing the people you love in front of you.”

His mocking condescension lit her rage once more, and she jumped up on shaking legs, stabbing at his heart with a scream of sorrow, frustration, and rage. Kayden rolled his eyes and smacked the dagger from her grip. He punched her solidly in the stomach. The world dimmed around Maura. The horrific pain reverberated through her body like the echo of a voice. She dropped to her knees, wordless, as she desperately tried to suck air back in through her open mouth.

“Fine,” he said, now irritated. “I was going to save you for dessert but if you want to be the appetizer, that is fine with me. You die first.” Tears poured from Maura’s eyes, thinning the blood on her cheeks. This was it. This was her end, but she would not let this creature take her without a fight. She weakly tried to rise and punch at him. Kayden simply moved and Maura fell face first into the snow.

"I'm sorry. That was especially cruel of me," Kayden said with a laugh. "Not nearly as cruel as decapitating your father and obliterating everything you've ever known and loved, but cruel nonetheless. I'm going to give you once chance to save yourself. You get one shot. Go ahead, human. Take me down. Make me pay. Make me suffer for all of the lives I've taken." He laughed hysterically at his own premise, an eager mania alight in his eyes. He clearly couldn't wait to mock her last desperate attempt to end him.

If this was to be her final moment on the planet, Maura wanted to make it count. Though her strength was rapidly dissipating, she so desperately wanted to do something, anything, to leave a lasting impression on the smug evil twisted face of this monster. The fingers of her left hand slowly curled into a tight fist.

Her father's face flashed through her mind's eye. His kind, toe-headed, bearded smile and cooling stare. His stern lectures about responsibility and the role of a lady, which she had abhorred her entire life. Now, she would have given anything just to hear him scold her once more. She saw Seraphina, so gallant and brave as she selflessly threw herself into the fray to cover their escape. Valentean smiled at her from the shadow of her memory. He had never given up on her, never succumbed to his own inner doubts and demons. She was letting them down. Her father was dead, Seraphina was in danger, and Valentean was lost somewhere in the world. Frustration born of weakness and hatred sparked the inferno of her anger once more.

She imagined the screaming horror of the people of Lazman. Their lives had been obliterated as purple destruction rained down upon them. That same violet-colored death had burned and decimated so many along the streets of Kackritta. Now, it would finally claim her. And when he had snuffed out her life, Kayden would kill Nahzarro, and then bring his darkness to the rest of Terra. The good people of Grassan, the foreigners of the Western Continent—they would all suffer at his hand.

It was in the name of her father, her friends, and the rest of her species that she screamed, one long, drawn-out syllable which carried her undying hate and frustration. She stood and swung the hardest punch of her life at Kayden's smiling face. As her fist hurtled at this twisted abomination, from some deep, hidden, unseen shadow of her body, an involuntary explosion of power and strength shot through her arm. When her fist was mere centimeters from impacting this vile demon's chin, a green sparking light ignited along her entire arm.

Kayden saw the eruption of mana at the last possible instant, and his eyes went wide with surprise and fear. Maura's knuckles smashed into the Rosinanti's jaw. A mountain of magical energy poured out upon contact, creating a blinding green eruption that exploded against Kayden's face. He cried out as the detonation threw him with such violent force that he was tossed like garbage from the site of their battle. His body flew limp through the air, disappearing within the miasma of snow that fell around them as he plummeted off the mountain's edge.

Maura fell forward, mouth agape with awe and disbelief. She cried out in the joy and exhilaration of the moment and looked over toward Nahzarro who was holding himself up with one hand, completely flabbergasted as blood continued to ooze down his face.

"Yes!" Maura cried out, pumping her fist into the air in victory.

"Quick!" Nahzarro cried out. "That's not putting him down! We have seconds!" Maura realized the prince was correct and she half-walked, half-crawled toward him as fast as she could. He held his hands out, summoning his whips back to him. A follow-up spell pulled Maura's daggers close. She grabbed them, and then draped one of Nahzarro's arms around her shoulders. Kayden's screech of rage could be heard reverberating through the air from somewhere far off, and a bright purple light could be seen on the horizon. Spikes of rock erupted from the ground.

"Hold onto me!" Nahzarro said, gagging on blood.

She gripped him tightly as he held his hand out one more time, summoning his hat back to him, which he pushed down over his wet hair. Maura heard the familiar muttering of nonsense magical words coming from deep within his throat. The familiar mystical orb of yellow energy which had aided in their escape from the airship surrounded them once more. With another hushed slew of gibberish spoken around a mouth full of blood, the ball rocketed into the sky, careening toward Kahntran.

XXIII: A BROTHER IN ARMS

There was smoke in the air. Not a good sign. Valentean's legs pumped beneath him, outrunning his new companions as the forest moved past him in a blur of motion. He arrived to find what had been left of Casid in further ruination. Every building was in shambles. Many of them, Deana's house included, were engulfed in flames. The street was strewn with the bodies of the few villagers who had managed to survive the Skirlack's initial attack.

Nevick arrived a fraction of a second behind Valentean and, upon seeing the devastation, let out an anguished cry.

"Deana!" he screamed, his voice echoing through the empty streets.

"Is that the cripple?" Valentean heard a familiar voice say. From behind a flaming building came the black-armored bulk of General Zouka, Deana slung over his shoulder, alive and unharmed.

"Zouka!" Valentean shouted, ready to burst forward. A spark of anxiety stayed his hand. Deana could be hurt if he just ran in and assaulted the Gorram.

"There you are." He chuckled amidst the heavy devastation and threw Deana to the ground. Nevick nearly charged, but Valentan held an arm out to stop him.

"Don't," he warned the enraged goliath. "He will kill her."

"This is someone you know?" Nevick asked gruffly, almost accusatory.

"Unfortunately."

"Now that I have your attention," Zouka said, placing his mammoth boot onto the back of Deana's neck, pressing the crippled girl into the dirt, "we can finish where we left off."

"Did you seriously cause all of this just to draw me in to fight you?"

"Stop acting surprised! You want this battle just as badly!"

"You're an insane fool!"

"You know, after you ran from Kackritta, Seraphina and I had a grand time."

Valentean froze in place. "What?"

"You heard me. I knocked her around the rooftops a bit before smashing her into the street. She was weak and powerless, much as these people were."

Valentean's hands clenched into fists. The white haze of light flashed across his eyes. The dragon within his heart screamed and roared in rage, begging Valentean to open up and let it out. The vengeful beast whispered promises of the general's brutal demise for daring to lay hands on the woman Valentean loved. The animus warrior took a step forward when Nevick's large hand clamped down on his shoulder.

"No," he said as Valentean turned to face him.

"What?" he asked, looking the big man in the eye.

"This fight is mine." Nevick stepped in front of Valentean, completely eclipsing the general from view.

"What is this?" Zouka spat. "Stand aside, fool!"

"My name is Nevick, and this was my home. These people you've killed today were my family. And the woman you have there is my betrothed. Your battle here is with me, not Valentean."

"Nevick," Valentean said, but the big man shot him a serious glare. Valentean nodded and stepped back. "You heard the man, Zouka. You want me? Let the girl go, and then go through him."

"You think this is a game?" Zouka roared as Valentean leapt into the air over Nevick's head, white light aglow on his face as he called forth the wind to forcibly shove the general back. Zouka crumpled to the ground several meters from Deana, giving Valentean time to grab her up in his arms and move her to safety behind Nevick.

"You filthy wretch!" the Gorram screamed, running at Valentean.

Once more, Nevick stepped between them, scorching hate alight in his eyes. Zouka looked beyond him toward his Rosinanti target and drew his fist back, letting a powerful punch fly with the intent to disable the human standing in his way. Nevick reached out one thick arm and stopped Zouka's blow before it crashed into him. The general's eyes snapped toward Nevick as he continued to push upon the big man's arm.

Nevick remained silent, glaring at the man who had completely wiped his home from the face of Terra. Zouka wore a look of aghast disbelief.

"What in the…" he said, grunting in exertion. "What … are you?"

"Your consequence," Nevick said, driving a fist into the general's armored stomach. Zouka cried out and doubled over, a stream of slobber leaking from his mouth. Nevick clasped his hands together and smashed them into Zouka's face. The Gorram fell to the ground.

Valentean crouched next to Deana, who cried softly in the dirt. He gathered her up in his arms and stood.

"Oh no, not again!" Valentean heard Mitchell exclaim in frenzied anguish as he and Michael arrived on the scene

"Valentean," she sobbed into his chest, "the village … the people … he…"

"I know," he replied bitterly. "Your soon-to-be-husband is about to make him pay for it."

Nevick glowered down at the large armored general. Zouka, Valentean had called him. He had seemed shocked by Nevick's strength, but little did this monster know that Casid's protector was only just getting started. He folded his thick arms across his broad chest and glared as his cloak billowed behind him in the breeze.

"How did you…" Zouka exclaimed, rising to one knee. "No human has ever survived more than thirty seconds of battle against me!"

"Well, consider that record broken."

"The only thing that shall break here is you!" Zouka leapt to his feet and lunged at Nevick.

He managed to deflect the general's first two punches before letting through a chop to the throat. This staggered the protector and opened him up for a punch to the side of the head, a knee to the stomach and an uppercut which sent him down to the ground.

As Nevick attempted to rise, Zouka rushed him from behind, grabbing him under each arm and interlocking his fingers behind Nevick's head. He swept one leg out in front of his massive opponent and pushed forward with his arms, taking Nevick down to the dirt. He maintained his grip, controlling the big man's head.

"You're strong, fool," the general hissed into Nevick's ear, smashing his face into the dirt street, "but I am mighty!" He bashed his face down again, then once more, this time seeking to humiliate Nevick as he ground his head into the road.

Nevick's blood boiled in his veins as the voice of his doubts silently mocked him. *He's right. You're a fool. You let this happen by attacking the wrong man.* Nevick screamed in anguish and utter hatred, both for this horrible monster of a man and for himself, the protector who let his people down.

He pulled his arms down violently, breaking Zouka's grip and elbowed the general in the side of the head. As the armored warrior stumbled back, Nevick jumped to a vertical base and began to pummel Zouka with a series of well-aimed punches to the face, throat, solar plexus, and kidneys.

Zouka's only defense was to lock Nevick's arms down with his own, entangling their limbs and trapping them against his own torso. He slammed his head into Nevick's face three times, driving the larger man back with each strike.

The plane of Nevick's vision blurred and he locked his hands around the general's back, lifting him into the air, belly to belly, and threw him up over his head with such force that Zouka lost his grip. The general soared overhead and smashed down onto his face. Nevick stood once more and charged at Zouka, who sprang back up at him. The two men locked arms, grappling for position. The general stepped inside Nevick's guard and wrapped a strong arm around his head, holding it tight against his side and smashed his fist into his opponent's captive face. Each pound of fist against flesh rattled Nevick's brain, and he countered by wrapping his arms around Zouka's waist and lifting him off his feet, falling backward and dumping the black-armored general onto the back of his head.

Zouka screamed in frustration, unsheathing the massive black sword from his back. Nevick stood and jumped back as the blade sought to carve through his abdomen, but sliced only through the empty air. Zouka maneuvered the heavy blade as if it weighed nothing at all, stabbing and slashing from all angles. Finally, he attempted to bring the blade down at his opponent's head and cleave the big man in two; but Nevick caught the sword between his palms and struggled to hold it at bay.

Zouka pushed down, Nevick pushed up. The two men jockeyed for position, finding the other's strength equal to their own. Nevick cried out and wrenched his arms forcefully to the side, snapping the blade in two like a tree branch, and then kicked Zouka in the chest, sending him shuffling back several paces.

Zouka stared in awe at the shattered remains of his signature weapon. "How did you…? This is … impossible!"

"Clearly not," Nevick heard Valentean say as the animus warrior purposely strode onto the battlefield. Zouka glared in hatred at both of them as Valentean dropped into a ready stance. "I think it's time we end this together," he said. Nevick nodded in agreement.

Zouka grunted in frustration tossing the handle and shattered base of his sword to the ground. "Come on then!" he shouted, strands of spit flying from his lips. "I'll take you both on! I'll fight you on your own level!" he crouched low, holding his arms off to his sides, prepping for an attack from either direction. He did not stand a chance against both, and he had to know that. Nevick shook his head at this insane warrior's pride and resolve.

The sky above them darkened as a swirling black cloud gathered overhead with unnatural speed. Zouka looked up at it in alarm.

"What's happening?" Nevick called over to Valentean.

"I'm assuming Aleksandra," he replied.

"Who?"

Valentean held up a hand, making it known that he would inform Nevick at a later time.

"No!" Zouka called out into the sky. "Not yet! I can beat them! I *will* beat them! I am Zouka of the Gorram tribe, and I will not be defea…" a bolt of red lightning descended from the blackness, striking Zouka. When the crimson flash faded, both the general and the mysterious cloud were gone.

Nevick looked around in utter despair at the final and full decimation of the home he loved. He fell to his knees in the center of the lifeless hovel, a small house behind him crumbled as he descended. He had failed. He had finally and fully failed his people.

Valentean approached and laid a consoling hand upon his shoulder, but Nevick shrugged him off, in no mood to be pitied. Michael approached from the side, carrying Deana to him. He set her down in a seated position beside Nevick, and she leaned over, hugging one of his large arms to her. He wrapped both arms around her frail body and pulled her into a tight, almost desperate, embrace while a lone thick tear tumbled from his eye into her hair.

That night, Valentean stood off to the side, solemnly watching the last four survivors of the village of Casid gather together on the beach to pay homage to their dead. Valentean had wanted to show his respects and honor their loss, but he had not wished to intrude on the moment. So, he remained at attention, breathing deeply through the sadness in the air as the last flicker of sunlight died beneath the horizon.

They had placed the bodies within makeshift caskets and set them adrift upon the sea. Then, they huddled together, watching the tide drag them further and further away until they were naught more than tiny dots in the distance. Tears fell down Valentean's cheeks as he watched the four of them, all unmoving, all steadfast in their patience and devotion. They stood in place until the last of their friends had gone. It was a hauntingly beautiful and tragically sad moment.

Nevick turned and stared at Valentean. The animus warrior swallowed hard, concerned that these new potential allies might blame him for this tragedy. In his darker moments, he certainly cast the blame upon himself. Zouka had come to Casid seeking him, desperate to engage in that final, climactic battle to the death. Had Valentean not fallen in their midst, these people might have lived on. Now a dying village had been dealt a final and decisive death blow.

Nevick's expression never broke, he simply motioned toward Valentean and urged him onto the beach. The animus warrior nodded and walked through the crunching sand, offering his new friends a look of sad condolences.

"So, what's next for you?" Nevick asked, his voice carrying none of the emotion Valentean had seen following the battle with Zouka. He had expected silence, perhaps a discussion of the dead or what their lives had amounted to in the end. This abrupt change of subject was jarring.

"Well…" He stared at the sand and watched as the wind moved several grains along the plane of beach land. "My friends are waiting for me in Kahntran."

"Maybe," Nevick said. "From what Deana told me, they weren't fairing so well when you were separated."

"I'm not sure, and I have no way of knowing if they're in Kahntran or even still alive. But if I know Maura, if there's a breath in her, she's scraping and clawing her way into that city as we speak."

"I wish there was more I could do, but the best I can offer you is good luck. You might be able to book passage on a Karminian excavation ship. They sometimes head to the Northern Continent to dig. You could always make your way there and then travel on foot."

"That seems like it would be the best option," Valentean said, nodding.

"You know, out here, in a place like this, the effect of these battles and wars are felt, but no one will ever know. I'm sure all the major cities know about what happened to your king and queen, and all those people who died in Kackritta. Out here, though? These people will never be remembered. They'll never be celebrated outside of this beach and in the memories of those of us standing here today. They died and the world keeps turning, as though it didn't even notice. We're in the unknown."

Valentean froze. Nevick's words played on a loop through his mind. The unknown … it sounded so familiar. With jolting clarity, Valentean's memory was carried back to the vision he had of the Rosintai, the one in which he had indirectly been told about Grassan. There had been a second piece to that message which had, up until this very moment, gone forgotten.

"*You shall find in the unknown a true brother in arms.*" Here he was, in the unknown, faced with the single most powerful human warrior he had ever seen. Nevick was meant to stand with him. They were meant to fight this battle together; Valentean was sure of it. Nevick's dour-hearted speech concerning the victims of Casid's destruction struck deeply within his heart and mind. He was wrong. The universe was screaming to him that the big man was wrong.

"No," Valentean said, shaking his head and drawing a raised eyebrow from Nevick. For a moment, it felt as though the two of them stood alone. "They won't be forgotten. These people, their fates, *must not* be forgotten. But they easily could. We know history is written by those who stand victorious. When Aleksandra claims her final victory, all of their struggles, all of their sacrifices will be erased, carried away as easily as those caskets on the tide until there's nothing left!" He advanced several paces, standing within striking distance of Nevick.

"All of that would happen if Aleksandra were to win this. But she isn't going to. She never will. She can't because standing in her way will be two warriors. As she pushes her army forward, there will be two men who defiantly push back. She isn't going to win because we are not going to let her, Nevick. You and me."

The big man shook his head. "I can't," he said sadly. "I'm not a hero. I'm not a warrior like you. I'm just a man, and I'm needed here now, with my friends and with my soon-to-be wife."

"Nevick," Deana said, and suddenly Valentean and Nevick were no longer alone. The two of them glanced at her, sitting upright, back pulled forward in her chair. There was an adventurous, determined fire in her eyes that Valentean had never seen before. "You are the protector of Casid. You are the man who has given his life to the people of this village. You can't abandon them now."

"What?" Nevick asked, confused at her statement. "Dea, everyone is dead!"

"Yes, they are. And now you are the protector of their memory. You are the living legacy of a dead village. You are the last hope our friends, *our family,* have of making their deaths mean something more than just being the victims of senseless violence. Nevick, you have to go with Valentean. You have to confront this witch, and you have to fight her with everything you have! And I have to go with you."

"Dea, you can't!"

"I absolutely can. My legs may not work but I am a healer. It is what I was born to do. I can perform magic that, as far as I know, is unshared by any other human being in this world. If Terra is about the be plunged into war, and I can help save the lives of the brave men and women who are going to defend it, then anything else I could choose to do would be selfish!"

Her words hung in the air between the two warriors, passing around them and sending chills up Valentean's spine. She had summed his words up and declared her intentions for all to hear. She was the strongest of them all, and Valentean respected her for it.

Nevick looked down at his betrothed, studying her with the hard, indomitable stare of a warrior. Silence seemed to swallow even the sound of the crashing waves, creating a vacuum of nothingness as Valentean held his breath, awaiting the response he knew in his heart was coming.

Slowly, Nevick nodded and the world began to turn around them once more. "Valentean," he said, "I'm going to come with you. I'm going to fight with you. It's time to leave this place behind, but I'm going to carry Casid in my heart," he looked at Deana, "*our* hearts for the rest of my life. These people, my people, deserve justice. That's exactly what I'm going to get for them. I'm going to beat justice into the face of Zouka. I'm going to punch justice into this sorceress princess of yours, and the last thing she will see before she dies will be the last warrior of Casid closing in to deliver the final blow."

Valentean smiled at both Nevick and Deana, nodding in approval at their decision. "I promise you we will make them pay," he said, "and we will make a difference in this fight!"

"We should leave as soon as possible," Nevick added. "Karminia is a day's march from here and getting over that wall of theirs is not going to be easy…"

"I don't think you'll need to do all that," Mitchell said. All three of them turned to look at Mitchell and Michael, who were both smiling. Michael even seemed to have fresh tears in his eyes.

"True," Michael added, pointing towards the forest. "Who needs to book passage on a boat when we have a perfectly good airship sitting right out there?"

Valentean nearly pitched forward in surprise. "You can fix it?" he exclaimed, the first tingles of elation beginning to quicken his heart.

"Of course, we can," Mitchell replied with a scoff. "It's mostly intact. There just seemed to be some damage to the engine. With the proper tools and materials, which I have under the rubble that used to be our house, we can have it up and running within the month."

Valentean's face fell. A month was too long. He needed to reach Kahntran as soon as possible. Maura was counting on him. Sera was counting on him…

"Do better," Valentean said, his eyes challenging the gifted brothers. "Get us in the air by mid-day tomorrow."

Michael nearly spit in surprise. "That's not possible!" he exclaimed.

Mitchell nodded in agreement. "My brother speaks truth, Valentean. Anything that would get us there that quickly would be a patch job at the very best, a crude bandage wrapped around a gushing wound that would eventually bleed the ship to death."

"We don't need it to get us back, we only need it to get us there," Nevick said, echoing Valentean's resolve.

"It's not possible," Mitchell insisted. "We'd never generate enough power. The propellers would never turn fast enough to hold the wind.

Valentean's face lit up with a smile, and then more so literally, as white light burned in his eyes. The wind howled at his silent command, creating a small tornado around them that kicked the sand into a chaotic frenzy. Mitchell and Michael looked astounded and realization blossomed in their eyes.

"The wind is on our side, gentlemen," Valentean said, grinning.

"I had them where I wanted them!" Zouka screamed, pointing an accusatory finger at the throne-shrouded, petite figure of Aleksandra. "I could have beaten them! You robbed me of my greatest victory!"

"General, perhaps your simple Gorram mind has abandoned all sense of logic, and you've forgotten to whom it is you speak," Aleksandra said dryly, her red, blazing eyes narrowing dangerously.

"To oblivion with you!" he screamed in rage, spitting on the floor before her throne. "To oblivion with your damnable plan!"

Aleksandra suddenly vanished from view, reappearing before the giant general who gasped at the sheer insanity of such speed. She floated into the air, coming eye to eye with the Gorram as her hand shot out, taking him by the throat.

Zouka was utterly immobilized by the mystical powerhouse as she closed off his windpipe and lifted him over her head without effort. The simmering blaze gathering upon her palm scorched his neck. Zouka panicked, believing for the first time ever that his life was about to end. He would not beg, though, would not wallow in pity and shatter his pride. Instead, he glared in defiant hatred at the empress, as if to urge her to continue.

"Mistress," Aurax said, appearing in the room unannounced.

Aleksandra's gaze snapped to him like a hawk catching sight of movement. "Speak, Aurax."

"Mistress, I have ascertained the trajectory in which your ill-equipped animus warrior chased your fleeing foes."

Something was off. Aurax sounded nervous. Zouka had never heard anything from the frail specter save oozing confidence and demonic bravado. Aleksandra clearly sensed it as well, and she roughly tossed Zouka to the ground. Not forgetting that a punishment was being doled out, she floated gently back to a standing position and stepped hard on his neck with one high-heeled boot, pressing him in an unmovable smother onto the floor.

"What of it?" she demanded of her most loyal servant.

"My queen, if it pleases your divine will … you may wish to send reinforcements."

"Wherever to?"

Aurax took a long nervous intake of breath. "To Kahntran."

XXIV: THE EVE OF BATTLE

Vahn gazed through a small window, taking a long, labored breath on the eve of battle. Many of his soldiers were now either asleep or lying awake, anxiety keeping them conscious. It was a restless feeling he recalled all too well. It was what still, after all these decades, kept him awake.

"Still?" he heard Tiberius say in disbelief. He turned to give his former student a small shrug. "How many battles have we faced together, old friend?"

"Far more than I care to remember," Vahn sighed.

"And before every single one, I remember looking over and seeing you, the immovable rock of bravery, kept wide awake in anticipation of what was going to come. In all of this time, you still can't bring yourself to get some rest before a fight?"

"It is something I cannot help," Vahn said, rubbing the bridge of his nose. The fatigue was present in his aging body, but his brain would not quiet down long enough to allow for rest. "I remember Roan and I the night before our first battle, wide-eyed as baby deer caught in a hunter's crosshairs." Vahn laughed at the memory. "This grizzled, old elite, whose name I cannot even recall, had laughed at us. He called us 'greenies' and said that if we should manage to survive we'd be sleeping like babies before the next battle. Well, the next mission came, and then the next, and the next, and the next and I've still never found that peace of mind he had promised."

"I've never had an issue sleeping," Tiberius admitted, coming to stand beside Vahn at the window. "I don't know what that says about me. I'm certainly not braver than you. Maybe you just have a larger heart than I."

"I'm sure that's not true, Tiberius."

"I've known you long enough to know what thoughts trouble you on nights like these, Vahn. You're thinking about the loss of life we will sustain. You're thinking about your boys. You're worried about the consequences of failure. These are things I never think about. On the field, my thoughts are straightforward. Hack, slash, repeat and move onto the next target. It just happens."

"That's the true mark of a great warrior. Combat comes naturally to you."

"No," Tiberius said sadly, "you have something more important than combat reflexes. You're compassionate. You worry. You keep the things that you're fighting for close to you during the heat of battle. It's what makes you such a force. Your heart and mind work together out there. It's why you're far more suited to lead us than I am."

Vahn did not know what to say to this. He simply sighed and shook his head. "We are going to lose people tomorrow night," he admitted sadly. "There is no way around that."

"They knew what they were signing on for."

"Did they? These aren't warriors, Tiberius. They are men and women, some of them teenagers who have never held a weapon before. In training, we were molded, taught to bite back on our fear. We were instructed to put queen and country before ourselves."

"And you don't think these people capable of such bravery? Vahn, we were boys trained to believe in Kackritta's glory, and we fought because we actually believed in it. Our warriors fight for Kackritta's very survival. They're fighting because they want their home back. They want their world back. Kackrittan warriors fought in the name of monarchs that might never learn *their* names. This rebellion fights for an ideal, for our way of life, for our collective right to life itself."

Vahn stared at Tiberius with a new respect. His former pupil possessed an honest optimistic insight which had never occurred to him. He reached out and patted his old friend on the arm, a kindly knowing smile on his face. "You've come a long way since the days when your main duty was saddling my horse."

"That damned beast hated me," Tiberius laughed. "I swear it wanted to kill me more than the enemy combatants did!" Vahn gave a short barking laugh.

"You know, were I to stay up all night before a battle like you, I'd likely fall asleep on the front lines. But you, Vahn Burai … I've never seen you miss a beat out there. Just imagine what you could do with a full night of rest under your belt."

The two men smiled at one another and Tiberius walked away, leaving Vahn to his thoughts. As he looked back out the tiny window he was served a grim reminder as to why it was he fought this battle.

On nights such as these, he found solace in the soothing sight of the stars, peeking like pinholes through the black curtain of night. Tonight, though, there was no gentle starlight, there was no calm coloration of magic beaming down at him. There was only red—a deep bloody crimson which loomed overhead as a constant, sobering all-consuming truth. Kackritta was gone, and the only way to bring it back was to make the streets run the same color as the sky.

Vahn shook his head sadly. He would find no rest on this night.

Maura dragged Nahzarro through the uneven streets of Kahntran, holding him up by his waist with one arm draped over her shoulder. He was dripping blood and needed a place to rest. While he was still coherent enough to speak, Nahzarro had instructed her to head for the cannon and began trying to cast a number of spells that were meant to aid his body in healing. These efforts did not last long as his reserves of energy quickly ran out. Since then, he had spoken only in unintelligible gurgles and murmurs, hardly able to put one foot in front of the other. He was in no condition to make repairs on the cannon, and the mission would have to wait until he was capable of rational thought.

Maura had been desperately seeking a sturdy structure to hunker down in for the night, but the corpse of this city was an absolute wreck. It was perhaps the most inconvenient terrain to drag a nearly lifeless body through, as the roadways were cracked and uneven, with green vegetation sprouting through constant breaks in the pavement. The buildings were crumbling messes. Large vines and trees grew through many of them, breaking through stone and steel as they wound through the cityscape. As a result, the structural integrity of these former homes and centers of commerce were questionable.

It had been hours since their brush with death at Kayden's hand and she was shocked that he had not pursued them. Maura felt a quaking dread, expecting at any second to see him as an immense dragon hovering over them, energy building within his massive maw as he prepared to reduce the entirety of yet another city to ash. But despite her fear's constant twinge, there was no sign of him.

On the one hand, she felt relieved. Despite her initial valiance and excitement at having successfully fended off the black dragon with a mana soaked explosion of her own inner power, she doubted her ability to duplicate such a feat on command. It had been a momentary reaction, more of a reflexive response to an emotional moment than an actual breakthrough. But when Kayden did eventually come for her, she doubted he would mince words. He would not underestimate her again. It would be quick, brutal, and above all else, final.

"Mrrrphrrrr .... diiiiiiiddddlrompofferakc..." Nahzarro mumbled in her ear.

"You don't say," she replied sarcastically, grunting as she adjusted her positioning beneath the beaten prince so as to relieve her aching shoulders. "Why is it every time I go on a fantastic adventure with a handsome man I end up having to carry his unconscious body?" she asked aloud bitterly. She sighed and continued to pull him along.

"There has to be at least one damned building still fully standing in this ridiculous ruin," she said, walking carefully over a crumbling bridge that passed over one of the city's many canals. The sun had gone down hours ago, and Maura was beginning to reach the limits of her stamina. She needed to find a place to camp for the night, fast.

They were rapidly drawing closer and closer to their ultimate destination, and she looked up in awe at the enormous cannon that was to be the salvation of Kackritta. She was so distracted by its scope and scale that she nearly walked past a perfectly suitable fully intact, if run-down, building. She cried out in happiness. An end to this long arduous journey finally in sight.

The door easily swung open and Maura deduced it to be a guardhouse, as there were old rusted weapons hung upon the wall and strewn upon the floor. A holding cell sat empty within the abandoned structure. The ground was littered with more than a few skeletons, which Maura roughly kicked aside as she found a large empty bit of floor and wall on the far end of the room. She placed Nahzarro down gently, his hat tumbling off onto the floor. After ensuring that he would not pitch off to the side, Maura sat down beside him. Her knees and hips nearly sang with joy as she finally entered into a state of rest.

"When this whole Aleksandra mess is done, I'm going to lay in a soft, comfy bed for a month straight," she grumbled, rubbing one of her aching calf muscles with both hands. Adding to her misery were the residual pains she had earned during the beating Kayden dealt upon her. "I swear by Terra if anything happens to keep me from sleep tonight, I'm going to explode…" She gave one final look around the room, half-expecting the long dead skeletons to rise up to their feet and attack. "Wouldn't that be my luck?" she mused aloud.

Beside her, Nahzarro stirred. "Mmmmauraaa," he slurred through swollen lips.

Her eyebrows went up in curiosity. "I'm here," she said, touching him on the shoulder.

"Maura … Yooou … s … sa … saved … my … saved my … l…"

"Shh, it's ok." She gave him a light pat on the arm. "Not bad for a 'shormie' I guess, eh?"

"Thaaaaa … Thaaaaaank … yoooou…" he said, so softly it hardly reached her ears.

Maura smiled, touched by this sincere moment of gratitude from the normally hostile captain. He was being genuine, removed from the walls and formalities of pride he erected around himself. She was seeing the real Nahzarro for the first time, and it was a welcomed change.

He groaned in pain once more and fell to the side, his head landing on her shoulder. For a moment, Maura's body stiffened, but after several uncomfortable seconds, she relaxed and let him stay against her.

She leaned her head up against his and closed her eyes. "You're welcome," she whispered as she fell into the deepest sleep of her life.

The first rays of sunlight spread across the horizon. Kayden seethed as the site of his most humiliating defeat was illuminated by the light of a new day. He breathed forcefully through his nose, wanting nothing more than to transform and pounce upon Kahntran. He would hunt the bitch down, drag her into the streets, beat her mercilessly and end her slowly. This was such an egregious affront to his station in life, and every molecule of his divine being was deeply offended by it.

He had been ready to pounce immediately upon landing with a powerful, shuddering impact upon the snow-covered ground. He crashed nearly a kilometer from the point where the human's fist had met his face. He had risen to his feet, screaming in abject rage, upending stone and rock in a tantrum of unbridled fury. His jaw ached and throbbed with every tiny movement of his mouth, and he realized she had nearly broken it. A human female had nearly broken his jaw with one punch. What was happening? How was this possible? Even with the power of mana, even with his guard completely dropped, this still should never have happened.

As he had prepared to pursue his prey, he was interrupted by a distraught looking Aurax, who informed him that Aleksandra commanded he wait until dawn to chase after the duo of weaklings. As if that were not humiliating and deflating enough, she had also placed a platoon of fifty Skirlack soldiers under his direct command to provide back-up support in his mission. Fifty demon soldiers to aid the black dragon of the Rosinanti in hunting down two wounded humans. It reached a level beyond insulting into some previously unknown depth of degradation.

"It's dawn," he announced to the restless armored demons who stood at his words, looking to him for a command. They were pathetic, mindless things and Kayden abhorred them. "Prepare to move out."

"You have your orders, then?" Kayden heard the voice of Aurax speak from behind him. He turned to find the arch demon smirking at him in the fresh morning air. Gone was the desperate panic he had sensed within his normally stoic rival when last they had met. Kayden had enjoyed that moment. He had often imagined what fear looked like etched onto Aurax's hideous red face while envisioning his own hands wrapped around the demon's corporeal throat. Seeing it in reality, hands and throat not included, had been far more satisfying than Kayden imagined. He wished he could have enjoyed it more, but his anger outweighed all.

"I still don't understand why I can't just transform and blow the entire city to bits."

"Of course, you don't."

"And I don't suppose you feel inclined to share the empress's thought process?"

"I am flattered that you believe the thoughts of one such as her are understandable by one such as me. I am not sure if you are unintentionally complimenting me, or degrading the empress."

"Spare me," Kayden grumbled, wanting no further interaction with the demonic annoyance.

"Were *that* decision mine, you would find my course of action oddly predictable."

"I understand my orders! Take the soldiers down, find the girl and the prince, and take them out."

"Do not kill them."

"What?"

"The empress does not want them to die just yet."

"That's ridiculous! The girl dies for what she did to me!"

Aurax chuckled softly, which in turn grew into uproarious, cruel, humorless laughter. Kayden had never heard the demon laugh before, and everything about it unsettled him. The fact that his taunting, braying lark was directed at his expense made his temper flare all the more. He shook with the unconditional burden of rage until Aurax composed himself.

"That is a vile bruise she left you," he said, pointing to a black and yellowed splotch of skin along Kayden's jawline. An actual growl rumbled from his throat. "Regardless of your desires, the empress commands your *compliance*, not your approval." Kayden turned from Aurax and stomped toward the mindless brutes who would carry out his commands.

"I need to hear your verbal acknowledgement," Aurax said, basking in this moment of amusement.

Kayden fought the urge to scream. While Aurax had annoyed him countless times since his awakening in Lazman, he felt as though the demon had finally crossed a line. Still, though, Aleksandra's word was law on Terra and, even had he wanted to disobey her, there was nothing he could do to silence Aurax. "Acknowledged," he growled, purple energy flaring to life upon his eyes.

"Fantastic," Aurax said sarcastically, vanishing in a haze of red fog.

Once he was sure that the arch-demon had truly gone, Kayden screamed and slammed a glowing green fist into the ground. The force of the explosion threw the Skirlack soldiers back, startling them but not causing any harm. As the smoke cleared, Kayden Burai stood in the center of a small crater, gaze pointed down at the ground as he breathed in harshly through clenched teeth.

"Move out," he hissed, not even looking up to confirm their compliance. The steady march of enormous armored boots signaled the beginning of yet another Aleksandra-ordered mission meant to humble and abuse him. "Show no mercy," he added, "because I won't."

The mid-day sun shone brightly down upon Casid as Valentean Burai paced impatiently amidst the devastation of a dead community. The Duzel brothers had been tinkering for hours with the remains of the Aleksandryan airship but success was far from guaranteed. Still, though, Valentean had to believe in his new allies. He placed his trust in their abilities, and he was confident that he would not be disappointed. Nevick stood off to the side, lost in thought as he gazed out over the gentle waves that crashed against Casid's shoreline.

He's likely taking it all in one more time, Valentean realized. According to Deana, she and Nevick had called Casid home since the days of their teenage years, and the big man had never once sought to leave. Valentean realized how different he and the stoic protector were. As a child, he dreamed of journeying away from Kackritta, seeing great sights and having grand adventures. Nevick had sought to protect his people, but the home he so valued and the people he loved were gone now. He had to find a new purpose.

"Come quickly!" the voice of Michael exploded from the trees. "Valentean! Nevick! Come to the airship now!"

Valentean could just make out the form of the portly mechanic turning and running through the forest. What had happened? Was something wrong? Had the worksite come under attack? Any multitude of horrific happenings sprang to life within his battered mind, and Valentean ran off into the forest, Nevick trailing just behind.

They both overtook Michael easily, racing ahead of him toward whatever untold catastrophe waited in the darkness of the forest. It did not take long to come across the clearing where the airship sat, slunk on its side. To Valentean's genuine surprise, he found no attackers, no monsters, no enemy combatants attempting to murder their friends and abscond with the vessel that was to be their salvation.

The only person they saw was Mitchell, standing before them, fists firmly planted on his hips. Valentean locked eyes with the inventor, trying to read emotion and intent in his stare.

"What happened?" Nevick asked. "Is Deana all right?"

"I'm fine!" Valentean heard Deana call out. He turned to spot her off to the side, leaning forward in her wheelchair, perusing rolls of parchment. She gave both warriors a smile and a wave.

"My friends," Mitchell said. "In my life, I've accomplished many feats the world had deemed impossible. I always valued my imagination and know-how above their small-minded concepts regarding what is and is not doable in this world, and I took pride in proving them wrong. Well, today for the first time ever, I've proven *myself* wrong!"

Valentean inhaled sharply. "Do you mean…?" he asked the inventor, hope bunching around his heart.

Mitchell smiled and nodded back at him. "She's ready to soar."

Valentean cried out in happiness and had to overcome the desire to wrap Mitchell in a hug.

"So," Nevick said, "that means we can go…"

"As soon as you give the word," Mitchell replied.

"And it will fly?" Valentean asked, needing further reassurance.

"You may have to give us a windy boost here and there but she will hold together, at least for the trip to Kahntran."

"That's amazing, I…" he turned to meet Nevick's eye but stopped mid-sentence when he noticed the big man was missing.

Nevick sat alone on Casid's beach, gripping large handfuls of sand and feeling it slip through his fingers as it fell away. He believed this to be an apropos metaphor for his life and the course of action he was about to undertake. Nevick had never seen himself leaving Casid. While the option always existed for him to take off in the middle of the night and abscond to some exciting life, the desire had never struck him—not even once.

He remembered the days leading up to his wedding when the thought of binding himself to someone else had seemed scary. At the time, he had asked whether he truly could commit to this one place, to this one woman, for the rest of his life. He had looked deep within his own heart and found the answer to be an enthusiastic yes. For the first time, he fully embraced his destiny: to stand guard over this place and over the love of his life forever more. Then, just as he had come to accept his lot in this world, it was all violently snatched from him in a gore-soaked display of Terra's cruelty.

So now here he sat, alone on a beach that once teemed with life. Solely sitting on sand that once bore witness to smiles and laughter and the joys of a community united. He remembered how children laughed and played on the shore. The adults would congregate where he now sat to tell stories, share drinks and food, and be merry together. The silence that had descended upon this once happy place made it feel foreign.

But could he truly leave? Could he run off and play the hero alongside Valentean, fighting against a mighty sorceress to save the world and avenge his fallen friends?

"Deana said you'd be here," Valentean said from behind him.

Nevick did not turn to meet his gaze. "Just needed some time alone," he replied, hoping the Rosinanti would take the hint and leave him be.

"Anything you want to talk about?" Valentean asked, not yet making a move toward him, but also not leaving.

"No."

"You're lying."

"Because you know me so well?" Nevick said, rising dramatically up to his feet and turning with a purpose, shooting smoldering annoyance at Valentean through the fiery gates of his eyes.

The Rosinanti returned his glower with a look of compassionate sympathy that Nevick's pride could not bear. "You're doing the right thing, Nevick."

"Am I? You say that I am, Deana says that I am, but what about what I say? What about what I think? What I *want*?"

"What is it you want?" he asked simply.

Nevick stared at the ground and turned his back, taking in the sound of the waves, undisturbed by the once familiar chorus of laughter and frivolity. "I want my life back…"

Valentean was silent for a moment and soon Nevick felt the animus warrior standing beside him. It was unnerving how silently he moved, as though he were a ghost. "My father used to say that the cruelest casualty of war is normalcy. After being faced with the reality of the battlefield, you're forever changed on the other side of it. When we go to war, we leave the person and the life we used to have at the starting line, and no matter what we do … that person is just gone."

"I didn't go to war."

"No, war came to you. It's not fair, but there's also no changing it. Nevick, I've seen some of the truest, miraculous marvels of this world. But we can't change the past and we can't raise the dead."

"All things I'm aware of."

"Yes, you seem to know it all, don't you?"

"What are you talking about?"

"You know what it was like to live here. You know what happened in this place. You know how you are feeling now. But what about the unknown?"

"Now you're just talking nonsense."

"You know that if you stay here, you're going to continue to wallow in misery on this beach and play with sand. And you know that by coming with me and helping me stop this horrible woman who wants to burn our world, you can put your mind to work at something worthwhile. You still have a lot to give, Nevick. I truly believe you're meant to do this with me."

"So you keep saying."

"Look, there are three living residents of Casid other than you, and all of them are coming with me aboard that airship in an hour. If you're truly the protector of Casid, you'll be on that ship with us, defending your friends, defending the woman you love, who can't even walk but is still coming because she has a gift that she knows can help people."

Valentean's words burned hotter than the flames which had eaten through the village. He was not wrong, not about any of it, but Nevick still had his doubts. His fear. He remained silent and continued staring out at the blue water, trying to decide if he could truly say goodbye to it all forever.

"Mitchell and Michael are prepping the ship for launch. Honestly, if you're not there, Deana will likely remain here in this graveyard with you. You'll be denying the men and women fighting for this cause the gift of her miracle. It's up to you, but I hope you'll stand with me, Nevick. I hope you'll be the friend and partner that I need through this."

Valentean Burai turned and walked away, leaving Nevick alone with the echo of his powerful words reverberating through his mind.

"I hope you'll be the friend and partner I need through this."

The command bridge of the airship was oval in shape, looking out through a large, cracked, curved window that moved along the exterior bend of the ship's bow. While the airship was composed mostly of metal, the flooring of the bridge was covered entirely by dark red wood.

There were two levels to the high-ceilinged chamber, the lowest of which stretched out closest to the window. At its furthest point was a console which hugged the curvature of the ship. Above, sat a smaller, circular platform, surrounded by a black steel railing that ran at waist height and was reachable by a pair of staircases that wrapped around it on either side. Atop the raised area sat a tall, wide command chair. It was red steel bolted to the floor with a black cushion along the back and seat. Valentean imagined Zouka or Aleksandra occupying this throne of power and his eyes narrowed at it, as though it carried a piece of them within.

Mitchell and Michael sat at the long console, each taking a side and pulling a variety of switches and levers. There were also two large wheels which Valentean assumed could steer the ship. Deana's chair sat off to the side where the healer nervously wrung her hands, looking back with trepidation at the doors on either side of the chamber. She was waiting for Nevick to burst in and declare his undying support for their cause. Frankly, Valentean was as well.

"If he doesn't show up … I can't leave him," Deana said, meeting Valentean's gaze and answering his silent questioning stare.

"I understand." He looked back over his shoulder at the Duzel brothers. "Mitchell, how much longer until we're ready to take off?"

"Likely five or so minutes," the inventor shouted back over a series of beeps emanating from the console. Valentean had a sinking suspicion the brothers were working slowly in order to give their friend the chance he needed to come to his senses. Valentean didn't mind it one bit.

Several minutes passed, and a small sputtering vibration could be felt within the floor under their feet. The ship was coming to life.

As the seconds ticked by, the groaning rumbling of the ship's awakening intensified. Nevick was still nowhere to be found and it seemed as though Casid's protector was not going to be making this journey after all. Valentean's stomach fell in disappointment as he accepted the sobering reality that not everyone had the fortitude to face down the evils of the world. He bore no ill will toward his new friend for that.

A collective, head-hanging depression seemed to pass between the four occupants of the cockpit, until Deana broke the uncomfortable silence.

"I'm sorry," she said to Valentean, unshed tears making her eyes glisten, "I can't go with you. I really truly wanted to."

Valentean was about to assure her that the decision was her own and there was honor to be found in following one's heart but before the words could leave his mouth, he was cut off.

"That's a shame," a deep voice said behind them. "You're going to be awfully lonely here by yourself, Dea."

Her face erupted into a grin as she whirled the chair around. Nevick stood in the open doorway on the ship's starboard side, fists on his hips as he stoically nodded in greeting to Valentean. Deana squealed with happiness and threw the wheels of her chair forward, rocketing towards her lover who swooped the young healer up out of the seat and kissed her, fully and deeply, as they spun together in an energetic circle.

"I knew you'd be here," she said, those once unshed tears now spilling down her cheeks as she smiled and buried her face in his broad chest.

Valentean grinned watching them and his heart burned to hold Seraphina in his arms once more. It was a sensation he needed to feel again with the woman he loved, and the animus warrior made a silent vow that he would see her soon.

"I couldn't let our new friend here save the world by himself," Nevick said with a hint of gentle humor in his voice.

"Welcome aboard my ship," Michael yelled from his seat, waving at his friend happily.

"Your ship?" Nevick said. "It crashed in my village!"

"Whoa," Mitchell said with a smile and short laugh, "this ship is my baby. I thought it up!"

"Let's all just be thankful if it can actually lift off!" Deana joked.

"Speaking of which, what are we going to call this boat?" Nevick asked.

"The Duzel, clearly," Michael said, eliciting a snort from Deana.

She looked over at Valentean. "How about the Rosinanti's Revenge?"

Valentean scoffed. "No … no, no, no," he insisted, holding up his hands to halt Deana's train of thought. Everyone laughed at his embarrassment. "I do have an idea."

"What's that?" Mitchell asked.

"*The Heart of Casid*, because that's what the four of you are. You're the heart of a small but proud community based on acceptance, love, and protection. If this ship is going to take us into battle, that's the image I want it to inspire!"

There was a sad yet joyous silence throughout the bridge, the only noise coming from the ship's engine as it began to gather speed and power. Deana sniffled, Mitchell and Michael smiled, and Nevick nodded his head.

"You're an all right guy, Valentean," Nevick said, and the Rosinanti smiled back at him.

The Heart of Casid gave a mighty lurch, and Valentean heard the propellers built into the ship's wings roar to life.

"It's time!" Mitchell called out, excitement evident in his words. "Everyone hang on!"

Deana wrapped her arms around Nevick's head and Valentean braced one hand on the base of the raised platform.

"You're not going to take your seat?" Nevick asked, pointing with his chin at the command chair atop the platform. Valentean glanced back at it once more, visions of Zouka and Aleksandra running through his head. That was the seat of a military commander. He literally gagged at the idea of it.

"I'd rather stand," he shouted back over the ever-increasing noise. "You can take it, though." Nevick's eyebrows went up as he carried Deana up the wrapped staircase, sitting with her upon the large seat. Valentean heaved a heavy sigh of relief.

The ship shook as it rose off the ground, and Michael gave a hoot of excitement. The engine sputtered, causing Valentean's heart to clench, but it soon righted itself as they continued to slowly ascend.

"Valentean, we're going to need a little help here," Mitchell said, eyes glued to a variety of gauges and needles upon the console. Valentean let the white light take-over his eyes and urged the sweeping wind to rush around the damaged ship, creating a powerful, twirling tornado below which blew the ship upwards. "Now!" Mitchell yelled to Michael, who threw a large lever forward. The main propellers beneath the ship roared to life, slinging the airborne vessel forward as if it were shot from a cannon.

"Yes!" Michael screamed as the ship's engines held out against the strain. Deana applauded and cried out with excitement. Mitchell's face was alight with glee, but he kept his attention trained upon the console. A nearly invisible smile flashed upon Nevick's face, but Valentean could note the unease in his eyes as they shot across the sea, putting the former sight of Casid behind them.

Valentean, in spite of everything, felt a small tingle of excitement as the airship continued to build speed. He imagined how he might have reacted to this astounding sight had he experienced it just a few short months ago. He would have been agape with glee, climbing over the ship, bounding about with reckless abandon. Now, he simply smiled sadly. While this was a wild and exciting ride, it was still taking them into battle.

His attention drifted to Maura and Nahzarro and he hoped that they had managed to make it to Kahntran. Had anything happened to them in the wastes of the Northern Continent, he would never forgive himself. It was this sense of unease that brought an old, unwelcomed turn of phrase to his mind, taunting him in that same infuriating distortion of his father's voice from so many years ago.

Everything dies, Valentean, the voice of his fear silently mocked him from the shadowy edge of his subconscious. *No flame can burn forever.*

Within the crimson bubble that imprisoned Aleksandrya, no one could tell that night had fallen upon the outside world. There was no sense of time in such a place. The forced residents of Aleksandrya, many of them cradling mutilated bandaged hands, crowded as was the law into the large circular area that sat just below Aleksandra's floating fortress. There was to be another mass execution of heretics, and to miss such a spectacle was to fall under suspicion of the Champions. Citizens were dragged screaming from their beds every day, forced in the name of Rosinanti-inspired paranoia to face a farcical trial that had only one outcome. So many people had been burned to death that the entire area had become infused with a permanent stench of burning flesh that clung to every surface.

Perhaps the most unsettling aspect of this fledgling empire was the dichotomy found within its populace. While many opposed Aleksandra's rule, there were an alarming number of Aleksandryan citizens who had willingly pledged their fealty to the new empress and to the Faithful. Perhaps it was their desire to believe in something more than themselves and this mortal coil that urged them to sacrifice their flesh, even proudly displaying the mangled grotesque scarring left in the wake of their offering. Perhaps it was fear of the Rosinanti themselves who, despite the dark blood-soaked reality of life in Aleksandrya, still terrified the whole of humanity. Either way, there was a divide to be found within the entombed city.

But that was not to say that the people were without hope. Whispers had grown to frenzied excitement with every public execution, because just beyond the glow of the fire which ate at their compatriots, the citizens of Aleksandrya could see a blue pulsating sphere of ice, bobbing as it floated above the ground. Within that orb of magical frost there lay the final hope of Kackritta, the rallying cry of those who opposed the tyranny of Aleksandra.

Little did the populace know that within the freezing embrace of this self-imposed prison, Seraphina was burning.

XXV: THE POWER OF THE PONTIFEX

The dreamscape quickly turned into a crackling nightmare as Aqua's fountain chamber came ablaze with the flames of chaos Seraphina had unknowingly unleashed. She covered her face with both arms as the red-hot fire erupted but did not burn her. She was the grand architect of this inferno, and as such, could not be harmed by it.

Neither, though, had she any control over the raging blaze. The burning red glow of her eyes grew in volume, but try as she might, the fire was completely uncontrollable. Aqua stood atop the water of her fountain, looking around the once pristine chamber in a panic.

"Seraphina, you must regain control!"

"I can't!" she screamed, still lamenting that awful vision of her mother's melting body as it crumbled away from her.

"This is a real threat, not a vision! If you cannot douse these flames, then my consciousness could be destroyed and you will be trapped here forever!"

Seraphina cursed loudly. She had just found Aqua, had only recently come under into her tutelage, and now the former spirit might suffer a fate worse than death at Seraphina's unintentional hand.

She tried desperately to clear her mind, but the intense heat of the flames coupled with added stress made quieting her thoughts and purging negative emotion impossible. She held her arms out and closed her eyes, trying to drown out the red pulsing light which shone from her face like flaming beacons. She bit back her fears, breathed deeply, and tried to call upon the order that had to still exist within her mind. Before, when she had struggled to control her power, she could still feel the faint echo of order light up on the borders of her mind. Now, though, she felt nothing but the searing heat of chaos.

"Seraphina, listen to me," Aqua shouted, causing the princess to open her eyes and stare imploringly at her predecessor. "The power is within you. The blocks that hold you back are only in your mind. You can conquer them if you…"

Even through the haze of heat, Seraphina could clearly see a delicate hand with dagger-like nails erupt through Aqua's chest with a spray of blood that quickly evaporated as it touched the red kiss of the fire.

Seraphina screamed in horror, and Aqua looked terrified as she dissolved into a blue mist and floated away, leaving the red-eyed smirking form of Aleksandra standing in her place.

"Sister dear," she said, gazing in crimson glee at the inferno which surrounded them. "I am so proud of you."

Vahn crouched on a rooftop overlooking the central hub of the Kackrittan marketplace. The hovering bulk of Aleksandra's floating palace loomed overhead. Dressed entirely in black, his eyes, just visible over the lip of a dark mask, were locked onto the gathering crowd.

It was easy to discern those still loyal to Kackritta from those who embraced the teachings of the Faithful. It all came down to their eyes. Some looked upon the execution sight with hope and wonder, while others stared at it with dread. It wore heavy on Vahn's heart to see his people standing there, huddled and cold and forced to engage in this vile spectator-driven barbarism. Seeing the Kackrittan sympathizers cradling bandaged hands in the wake of their forced conversion replaced his sadness with rage. He stirred in a stew of emotional fury, but decades of training aided in his resolve to remain steadfast and still.

His warriors were taking point on rooftops around the perimeter of the circle. Elites and Kackrittan soldiers made up the bulk of these forces, as they were most likely to encounter resistance. The civilians, who comprised the majority of his nearly thirty warriors, were delegated to crowd control and maintaining the perimeter they would have to create to enact this lightning strike with the precision it required. They bravely wound their way through the crowd, dressed in plain clothes and blending in as they shouldered toward the front of the forced mob.

They were grossly outnumbered. Horrifically outmatched. Vahn counted thirty-five Skirlack soldiers surrounding the execution pyre, and the pontifex was jealously guarded at all times by a platoon of nearly twenty champions which would likely include Landon.

Following his absconding with the rebels, Vahn had noted the duties of carrying out public demonstrations had fallen to the Pontifex herself. Landon's diminished prestige had given the rebels an opportunity to strike at the head of The Faithful in a time and place they knew she would be present.

A loud resounding drumbeat signaled the approach of Sophie's entourage. Vahn braced himself, keeping his eyes trained to the northwest. The Faithful tribunal always approached from that direction, originating from the beginnings of what appeared to be a large black temple with red glass windows, created in the same sharp, jagged architectural style as Aleksandra's fortress. It was a half-completed skeleton now, but soon it would loom large as one of the tallest buildings in Aleksandrya.

As the entourage approached, Vahn heard the steady, synchronized footfalls of Sophie's honor guard, but there seemed to be a discrepancy. It sounded as though there were far too many! Vahn gasped as the company came into view, nearly one hundred strong. His gaze snapped further down the roof to make eye contact with Tiberius, similarly clad in black and crouched identically to Vahn.

His old friend's look said it all, a desperate frenzied terrified glance that seemed to scream *ABORT*, but Vahn shook his head. There was no way to signal his people on the ground. To leave now would be to send them into battle alone; a sure death sentence. Vahn would not abandon them. The mission would commence as planned.

Prisoners were led onto the stage first. There were eight of them: three males, four females, and a boy no older than eleven. Vahn's jaw clenched upon seeing the child's terrified glances, tears streaming down his chubby cheeks.

The Pontifex was visible a moment later, her red robes trimmed in black. Atop her head, she wore a large headpiece which looked like an upside-down triangle. It was a deep, bloody shade of crimson with swirling bursts of black and orange throughout. She carried a long staff which extended above her head. It was black, metallic, and emblazoned on the top with a red crystal flame.

Landon slunk behind her, relegated to simple guard duties in the wake of his epic failure. The champions fanned out around the platform, weapons ready to quell any insurgency. Sophie stepped up the stairs onto the stage with pronounced purpose. Those among the crowd who believed in the Faithful's cause cried up to the Pontifex, reveling in her presence.

Sophie held up her mutilated hand and the noise died immediately. She had them enthralled with the blind fervor of fanaticism. It turned Vahn's stomach.

"Brothers and sisters of The Faithful, it is once again my honor to come before you, the people of Skirlack, the children of the blaze, and offer up to our most holy mother the wretched souls of non-believers." A chorus of ugly boos rang out from the true believers as Sophie gestured to the prisoners being latched against wooden stakes upon the pyres. "We ask that our benevolent mother, gracious and loving is she, recreate their wretched lives among the ranks of her own Faithful, so they may repent for the sins of this life in their next."

Vahn's focus never left the boy—so confused, so terrified as he stood there, certain that his brief life was about to come to an end. Vahn braced himself against the roof and looked around the square. Thirteen warriors stood ready to pounce. His people had made their way closer, and they would be ready to strike upon his signal. He palmed a small satchel in one hand and stood at the ready.

"In her holy name, we sentence these blasphemers to death. We sentence them to be smothered by the red kiss of the goddess herself. We sentence them to purification, rebirth through fire." She closed her eyes, speaking a silent prayer before looking up once more. "As it shall burn!"

"As it shall burn!" came the echo of the entire crowd. Even those who despised the Faithful cried out its mantra for fear of being a victim on the next pyre. Right on cue, a man appeared out from the building directly adjacent to the one Vahn crouched upon. He held a large red and black torch, in the basin of which roared a crackling fire.

Now it was time to strike. Vahn had only one shot at this, and he had to make it count. As the man stepped further into the clearing, away from the crowd, Vahn threw the parcel with all of his strength and years of precision training.

As the bundle flew through the air, three of Vahn's people on the ground, who were gifted mages, held their arms up and began to chant. A light blue shield spread over the crowd as the package impacted the torch. An explosion ripped out from the basin, shredding through the bodies of several Skirlack and Champions, bouncing harmlessly off the magical shield.

Pandemonium overtook the street as people reacted to the deafening explosion, but Vahn and the warriors of Kackritta were already in motion before their enemy could regroup. They leapt from their hiding places, letting loose a series of freshly sharpened throwing knives which buried themselves into human and Skirlack flesh alike. The shield fell and his seventeen warriors on the ground sprang into action, hacking and slashing and stabbing at anyone or anything wearing Faithful robes.

Vahn landed in a tight forward roll and rose to his feet, drawing twin swords. He dove into the fray, lashing out in a swirling whirlwind of battle and blood. Vahn tore through his opponents in a mad dash filled with purpose. He sprinted onto the stage where the Pontifex was surrounded by Landon and ten Champions, though he made no move toward her. Instead, he turned and ran at the pyres, striking first at the bonds which held the boy by his arms, freeing him and the man next to him. He tossed one of his blades to the man, instructing him to free the others and keep the boy safe. The child looked at Vahn in wonder, astounded at his survival, determined not to waste this chance.

Vahn turned from him, hoping the boy would be all right, and attacked the champions who surrounded Sophie. They moved quickly, but Vahn was far faster, and within seconds, he had cut down or incapacitated four out of the ten. As one approached him, battleaxe at the ready, this new threat was halted by a spiked harpoon which exploded through his chest cavity. As the champion dropped, Tiberius joined Vahn on the stage and nodded as he pulled on the chain attached to the deadly projectile, freeing it to slash across the chest of his next opponent.

As Vahn faced off against two champions, Landon made his move. Vahn cut down one of his assailants and turned to face the next. He sensed Landon's approach at the last possible instant. Vahn leaped to the side as his former friend attempted to slash down across his back with gleaming fighting gloves. They were black with long curved red claws which arched out from the knuckles. A unique weapon, which Landon had been a master of for decades.

Landon glared at Vahn with hatred born of assumed betrayal and time as Tiberius moved in to intercept the remaining champions still surrounding Sophie. The leader of the Champions lashed forward at the Captain Elite, fast and deadly. Vahn jumped back, but the second strike scored a cut along his forearm. He dropped his sword. As it clattered along the wooden stage, Vahn used his arms to block Landon at the elbow and wrist as the fallen elite swung several well-aimed swipes at his unprotected midsection.

Vahn launched into a series of complex acrobatics, bending his body away from the creative angles of Landon's assault. He attempted to roll away from the chaotic onslaught. Landon anticipated this course of action and countered around him. As Vahn rose to his knees, his opponent was waiting there, looming over him from behind. Vahn knew he had no time to dodge, and he reached out with his right hand to grab Landon's forearm in a strong grip.

The Faithful warrior attempted to jam his other set of claws into Vahn's exposed left temple, but the aging warrior was still fast enough to catch his nemesis by the wrist. All Landon had succeeded in doing was slashing away Vahn's facemask, which fell to the wooden floor of the stage. They had entered into a stalemate of strength, both jockeying for an advantage as they pushed against one another. Landon's face came down near Vahn's ear and he hissed in a harsh whisper.

"Look at them, Burai," he said through clenched teeth.

Vahn turned his head away from Landon's voice and scanned the crowd with his eyes. Numbers began overwhelming his warriors, though they valiantly fought on, not one soldier fleeing the field.

"You've led these misfits so far only to meet their deaths. Did you think it coincidence that our numbers bolstered on the night of your ill-fated assault? We knew this was coming. The Pontifex is wise and cunning; as am I. Together, we have stamped out your rebels in one fell swoop."

Just as the desperate pangs of loss were about to impact his already battered heart, Vahn saw something that restored his faith and brought a triumphant snarl to his lips. One of the ordinary citizens who had not come as part of the rebel forces picked up a rock from the ground and smashed it into the head of a champion. As the enemy combatant dropped, there was stillness for a moment, and then a scream of battle from the crowd. The citizens, or at least those loyal to Kackritta, attacked the Faithful and the Skirlack with sticks and rocks and anything heavy they could get their hands on.

"I am looking, Landon," Vahn grunted in triumph, "and I see bravery and greatness!" Vahn jerked his head back, slamming it into the bridge of Landon's nose. The leader of the champions cursed as he recoiled. Vahn took him by the captive wrist and shoved Landon's own claws through his left eyeball. The old man shrieked in agony and fell back. Vahn erupted to his feet and kicked Landon hard in the chest, sending him soaring off the stage and crashing to the ground, grasping with desperation at the oozing, gory pulp that had once been his eye.

The Captain Elite turned to see Tiberius, blade and chain whirling around him like a sandstorm as he cut down the last of Sophie's guards. As the battle between the rebels and citizens against the Skirlack and champions raged on, two more elites jumped onto the stage and moved with Vahn and Tiberius toward Sophie, who proudly stood her ground.

"Pontifex Sophie," Vahn said, "in the name of the Kingdom of Kackritta and its rightful heir Seraphina Kackritta, I, Vahn Burai, hereby arrest you for crimes of treason, murder, and assisted regicide."

Sophie did not shrink back from them one iota. "Foolish heretics!" she cried out. "You dare to strike against the goddess's instrument on this world?"

"You are coming with us," Tiberius said, holding his harpoon by its base and brandishing it threateningly.

In response to their advance, Sophie slammed her staff down once against the stage. A huge shockwave blew the elites off the platform and they crashed to the ground. Vahn stared as Sophie rose into the air, hovering above them as her robes billowed in the wake of her power. The flame atop her staff began to pulsate with energy.

"Aleksandra?" Seraphina exclaimed as the final haze of Aqua's essence evaporated into the air. "You can't be here!"

"Why not?" her sister asked, one eyebrow rose as she hovered above the waters of Aqua's fountain. Seeing Aleksandra there atop that sacred altar, empowered by the might of chaos, churned a deep seething anger within Seraphina's heart. In response to her fury, the flames throughout the chamber doubled in size and strength.

"Ah, excellently done, sister," Aleksandra said, surveying the blazing results of Seraphina's rage. "Your anger makes you mighty. Chaos is power unhindered by conscience."

"No..." Seraphina said, taking a step back, "I'm nothing like you."

Aleksandra laughed with genuine-sounding amusement. "Clearly, that is not true." She gestured broadly around them. Seraphina's flames spread throughout the room, chewing every available bit of wall space until the mystical blue sheen found within the unnatural rock died out. Aleksandra reached out with the same hand that had just moments before exploded through Aqua's chest, and Seraphina recoiled.

"Stay away from me..."

"Dear sister, there is no place where you can abscond from my love. I am bound to you, as you are to me, by our familial bonds." Her eyelids narrowed around the crimson glow of her stare. "Now stop acting like a child and I shall teach you how to control your new abilities."

"No!" Seraphina shrieked in anger, and once more the flames erupted at her outburst.

"Oh sister, your potential is truly magnificent. Give in to it. Embrace your hate. Take control of the blaze. Let the blessed mother in and revel in her power!"

Seraphina gazed in horror at what she had become. This inferno of destruction and death had been called forth by her own fear and hatred. She was acting like Aleksandra, allowing emotions to guide her, to ignite the spark that now raged throughout her mind.

She looked at her sister's face, alight with awe and pride at this horror show, and realized Aqua had been correct. True power came not through emotional outbursts that fed on base feelings. It came from having control over one's emotions and not allowing them to fall out of control. It was good to feel, but she could not allow those feelings to overcome her. She stared at the fiery ground, at the folds of her crimson dress as they moved through the clouded heat. She took a long deep breath and slowly blew it back out, looking up at her sister as she exhaled.

For the first time since the Northern Magic, Seraphina did not feel that overwhelming sense of fear or rage upon seeing the face of her treacherous sibling. Rather, she felt something else. A swell of pity. Aleksandra was so far gone, her mind a cataclysm of fanaticism coupled with ego and insanity.

"You do not rule me, Aleksandra," Seraphina said, so softly it was little more than a whisper. "I rule you..."

"What was that?" Aleksandra cried out.

Seraphina's face softened and a tear fell from her blazing eyes, traveling slowly down her cheek. "You do not rule me, I rule you."

"Speak up, sister!"

The tear cascaded to the tip of her chin. "You do not rule me!" she said, loud and firm, but without the stain of rage. The tear fell from her face, splashing to the ground at her feet. "I rule you!" The point of the tear's impact caused an explosion of blue light that was echoed upon Seraphina's eyes as she shot up into the air. The power of order rushed about the room, sweeping the flames away as though they had never been there to begin with. As the last of the blaze died out, Seraphina hovered over the polished azure floor of the fountain chamber, her blue dress billowing with the frenzy of her power as a deep cobalt sheen glowed along her eyes.

"No!" Aleksandra screamed in putrid rage, raising her arms, fingers outstretched like claws.

"No," Seraphina echoed, with an air of superior stoicism that contrasted Aleksandra's fury. The water within Aqua's fountain leapt up like the jaws of a hungry beast and slammed around Aleksandra on all sides with an explosion of light.

As the glow subsided, Aqua hovered there once more, a look of gleeful triumph etched along her dimples. "You've done it," she said.

"That was you?" Seraphina asked, one eyebrow raised in confusion. "This was a test?"

"Yes."

For one moment, Seraphina felt betrayed. She had felt such fear and rage and guilt throughout that ordeal, fully convinced that she was dooming both Aqua and herself to a fate worse than death. But as she felt the silent strength of the power which now coursed through her body, she was thankful for her predecessor's deceptive tactic.

"Thank you," she said, inclining her head in a bow of respect toward her teacher, now at the end of their lesson.

"Anger and fear are natural byproducts of life, Seraphina. I felt them much the same as any mortal would. But a spirit of order must never lash out in anger. We must never call upon the water in response to rage or terror because such thoughts fly in the very face of our power."

"I understand," she said. "I'm ready to leave and find Val again."

Aqua shook her head. "Valentean is on his own journey, much the same as you are."

Seraphina felt a swell of selfish desire rise in her chest. "But…"

Aqua raised a hand to silence her. "Your people need you now more than your animus warrior."

Aqua waved a hand and Seraphina could see her once proud city imprisoned within a monstrous red dome that filled the sky. She saw people dying, burned alive, hands mutilated in forced worship of chaos, and she gasped.

"No…"

"As we have worked to prepare you, your sister has taken your home and perverted it into a city of chaos. But all of those people who once knew you as a princess without magic will soon know you as a conquering savior, the true heir who will wrest the throne of Kackritta out of the hateful hands of one blinded by chaos."

Grim realization settled over Seraphina. Her people needed her. "I understand, Aqua," she said sadly, but with determination and conviction.

"There is one way that you can help your people and Valentean at the same time."

"What? How?"

Aqua held up a hand once more. Seraphina saw Valentean's father, Vahn Burai, and a group of warriors attempting to move on Aleksandra's former handmaiden, Sophie. She slammed an ornate staff down upon the wooden surface they all stood upon and, using some very powerful magic, tossed the warriors back onto the ground.

"Val's father…"

"He is a great warrior, but he is outmatched."

"I can help him," she said.

"Yes, but there is one more task we must accomplish before you can go back."

"What's that?"

"We must meet with our allies."

Valentean had remained mostly quiet as *The Heart of Casid* shot over the calm waters of the northern sea. His new friends had talked loudly, enjoying the frivolity that accompanied old kinship. Valentean, though, still felt like a stranger to their group, an outsider who was being let in. That, coupled with his anxiety over what he was to find in Kahntran, kept his mouth closed in anxious thought.

He could hear a soft but very present ringing in his ear, and it grew until it exploded through his head like an invasive parasite. Valentean cried out and dropped to his hands and knees. Just as he blacked out, he could hear panicked cries coming from Nevick, Deana, and the Duzels, but he could not respond.

His eyes closed and the ringing stopped. The ground felt as though it had morphed into something soft, spongy, and covered by a film of liquid. The white dragon opened his eyes and found himself in a never-ending plane of hazy, gray fog.

As he stood, the ground beneath his feet felt like soft moss, and there was, indeed, a layer of water covering everything. He was completely alone, and panic swelled within his chest. What was this? Some trick of Aleksandra's? Some new dark torment his fear addled mind had cooked up?

"Hello?" he called out, hearing the gentle echo of his voice. "Hello?" His baritone bounced back from all directions. There was no response save for an eerie stillness. Then, he heard it.

"Val?"

It couldn't be … but somehow, miraculously, it was. He whirled in the direction of the voice, hope and the tentative birth of a joyous smile blossoming upon his face. "Sera?"

And suddenly, exploding out of the fog, sprinting to him was the blue-clad form of the woman he loved, smiling radiantly at him as she pushed herself faster and faster with every step. He dashed for her, his skin perspiring in anticipation of feeling the smooth impact of her flesh against his. They were centimeters away now, and as Valentean reached for her, the two phased silently through one another, as though they were ghosts.

Valentean turned in horror, and Seraphina spun back to him as well. They grabbed for each other again and again but were met each time with frustration and failure.

"This isn't fair," she said, her voice frantic.

"I know," Valentean said, desperately. "All I want is to hold you."

"That's all I've wanted for weeks," she replied, sniffling.

This was torture. Here was the woman he loved beyond the definition of love, whom he had sworn his life to, envisioned a future with—the only future he could ever know. And yet they could not touch. They could not reach one another. And their future together seemed a far off, distant dream rather than the assured reality he had always assumed it was.

"I am sorry," a familiar voice said. Valentean looked up to see Aqua, hands folded in front of her blue dress.

"Aqua?" he asked, dumbstruck at the appearance of the dead spirit.

"She's been helping me," Seraphina replied, "training me to control my new powers."

Valentean looked up at Aqua in thankful wonder.

"And now we call you here to the dreamscape, Valentean," Aqua said, motioning around. "You are not truly here, only your mind, and thus you have no corporeal form to touch one another. I apologize. It seems cruel."

Valentean nodded and held his hands out toward Seraphina. She responded in kind and their palms melted together in a hazy amalgam. It felt like nothing, with no texture to grasp onto. He gazed longingly into the eyes of his princess.

"It's all right, Aqua," he whispered past the lump in his throat. "I'm thankful for this moment."

"Do not thank me," Aqua said. "I did not summon you."

Valentean turned to stare at her with a furrowed brow. "What?" he asked, perplexed by the statement. "Then who di…"

The air beside Aqua shimmered and the fog parted to deposit the humanoid dragon form of the Rosintai, who continued to stare at Valentean, unblinking with glowing white eyes.

"You!" he exclaimed at the specter. "I figured out the answers to your riddles." He spat the words bitterly.

"Riddles?" Seraphina laughed, remembering Valentean's abhorrence for such games as a child.

"You have no idea, Sera," he said, his gaze once more shifting to her and only her. "I have so much to tell you."

"That will have to wait," the Rosintai's voice interrupted, sounding so eerily like his own.

"So, you speak now?" Valentean asked, reminding the Rosintai that their last conversation had been very one-sided.

"I speak when I have something to say, young one." Valentean's nose curled at the long-dead light spirit's tone.

"Please," Aqua said, passing her words between the two men, "now is not the time. Everyone's frustrations have been taxed."

Valentean nodded and the Rosintai stared at him, his gaze fierce and unblinking. "A battle awaits you in Kahntran, Valentean."

His heart leaped. "How bad? Are Maura and Nahzarro alive?"

"Nahzarro?" Seraphina asked, bewildered at the odd sounding name. "Where is Maura?"

Valentean was going to answer her but Aqua interjected. "They are both alive at the moment, but their continued survival depends upon you, Valentean."

"Are they in trouble?"

"Kayden hunts them," she said slowly, "along with fifty Skirlack soldiers."

Valentean's fist clenched through Seraphina's hand.

"I can sense your fear," the Rosintai hissed. "That is exactly the problem."

"What?"

"You fear me," he continued. "You fear yourself, you fear your power. That is why the spawn of Terros appears more powerful than you."

Valentean took a sharp intake of breath and looked at Seraphina. He wasn't just afraid, he was terrified. Here was his love, so close yet, in reality, a world away. His friends were walking into certain death, faced with Kayden and his horde of demons. Fear rose from Valentean's heart once more. Here in the dreamscape, it was able to speak aloud for all to hear.

"Everything dies, Valentean!" said the dark perversion of his father's voice. *"No flame can burn forever."*

Seraphina looked around wide-eyed. "What is that?" she asked him.

"It is his fear," the Rosintai said. "It is what keeps his power locked away. He is afraid."

Valentean said nothing at first. He looked down in shame, gathering his thoughts. "You know what would happen if I lost control … If I turn into you…"

"So, do not lose control."

"It's not that easy."

"It would be, had you the strength of character to keep yourself in check!"

"Hey, that's not fair!" Seraphina exclaimed. Aqua held up a hand to silence her, but Seraphina ignored it. "Val has beaten Kayden before; he can do it again! He's the light I hold onto in my heart. He has the strength to control that power and to not give in. I will never give up on him. I believe in him. He's … He's the love of my life." She looked him in the eye, unshed tears glistening beyond her eyelids.

Valentean had no breath. Her faith in him, her unquestioning love made him feel alive and content, and strong once more. Once he heard her declaration of love and confidence, something within his soul unlocked.

It was as if the dragon who laid coiled around his heart had heard this as well, and for a moment, there was no conflict between man and beast. There was simplified harmony, as though there was no beast at all. There was only Valentean Burai, one man, one warrior, the love of Seraphina's life.

"I love you," he breathed softly to her and leaned in to kiss her. Where their lips should have met, their faces entangled together in an incorporeal mesh. He could not feel the skin of her mouth against his, but he felt something else. A tingling rush spread between them, coursing between their mouths, electrifying their bodies. They each took a step back in surprise. Valentean looked to the Rosintai and Aqua, who had clearly felt something as well.

"Remarkable," Aqua said. The Rosintai simply nodded.

"What?" Seraphina asked. "What was that?"

"It was the power of your connection," Aqua replied. "Your love transcends realms. You managed to connect your spirits together for that brief instant. I've never seen anything like it."

Valentean was amazed. He felt a rush of energy swirling within his body. He felt invigorated. He felt stronger than he had ever before. But more so than that, he felt the dragon's power working for him and not against him, for the first time ever.

"You see now, boy," the Rosintai said. "There is no dragon. There never was. There is only you. The dragon is a part of you. It is not some invasive presence. Its power belongs to you. The dragon *is* you. Use it, control it, and don't give into your fears. Draw your power not from malice, not from the dark. Empower yourself with love. For it is love that is the source of light. Everything dies, Valentean. But love can burn forever."

There it was. A sweet crystalizing epiphany. The fist of ice around his spine melted in the warm light of Seraphina's love. Death was inevitable for all, but some fundamental forces of nature, like the love they shared, were immortal. He finally understood.

"I'm ready," he said, a stark, almost gently shocked admission of this long journey's end. He looked into Seraphina's eyes and drew strength from the love he saw shining through there.

"So am I," she said, sounding stronger and more confident than he had ever heard her before. Aqua and the Rosintai said no more and vanished into the fog, leaving princess and animus warrior alone as the dreamscape began to dim and unravel before them.

"This is it," Valentean said.

"No," she said, shaking her head back and forth. "No, this wasn't enough."

"Shhh," Valentean said, hovering his finger in front of her mouth. "I can wait a little longer, Sera. We have forever ahead of us."

She smiled, showing off her teeth in a grin that made his heart skip.

"I love you," she said, as the world around them faded.

"I love you," he replied, biting back on a sob at the prospect of leaving her once more.

"Val?"

"Yes?"

"Pound him into the ground for me."

Valentean smiled at her. "You really are perfect."

"*You're* perfect, my love," she replied as she faded from sight.

Valentean awoke once more on the floor of *The Heart of Casid's* command bridge. Nevick crouched over him as the ship continued to hum and sputter. When his eyes opened, he felt the big man breathe a deep sigh of relief.

"He's awake," he called out over his shoulder.

"Thank goodness," Valentean heard Deana say from the direction of the command chair. He sat up slowly shaking his head as he wiped fresh tears from his cheeks.

"Are you all right?" Michael shouted from his seat at the curved helm.

"I'm perfect," he said softly. "Full speed to Kahntran, boys!"

Vahn flew through the air like a child's discarded toy before slamming into the ground. The Pontifex gently floated down to the street and gazed at the gathering of warriors she had been systematically pummeling for several minutes, with no discernable effort. The square was filled with battered and bruised bodies, but the Pontifex had yet to take a life. Vahn knew this wasn't for lack of skill. Aleksandra had not simply appointed her out of affection. Sophie was a force to be reckoned with.

Vahn shot to his feet, sword raised, but a slight flick of Sophie's wrist sent him hurling to the ground once more. Each shot from this invisible energy hit like a heavy mallet. It was exhausting and debilitating. Even Vahn's reserves of stamina seemed to be drying up.

"Heathenous wretches," she proclaimed, "you have defiled the will of your goddess and struck out against her chosen servant. For that, you shall suffer a painful price." The crystal flame atop her staff sparked and pulsed with energy. She raised the ebony rod above her head, ready to lash out with whichever spell she had chosen to end their lives.

Before the staff could fall, there was an explosion of blue light and a loud resounding crack, reminiscent of an egg hatching that came from the far end of the hub. A bolt of blue energy shot into the air and rocketed toward them, landing with a pavement-cracking crash between The Pontifex and Vahn.

Seraphina Kackritta, crowned princess of the Kingdom of Kackritta, The Ice Queen, stood tall as blue sparks of crackling lightning erupted around her body. She glared at Sophie with eyes that glowed and pulsed with azure power.

"Back away from my people," she said, calm stoicism hardly masking the presence of a threat.

XXVI: THE BATTLE BEGINS

Maura woke with a start, sitting up with such sudden swiftness that Nahzarro, who still slept leaning on her shoulder, fell to the side. The prince's head smacked with a dull thud onto the wooden floor of the guardhouse.

"Agh!" he cried out in frustration as he slowly lifted his sore body off the ground. Maura crept toward a window, where she crouched and peered out. "What in Terra are you doing?" She ignored the cranky prince, focusing her attention on the dark night air which eclipsed most of the decrepit city's remains.

"I heard something. Someone is out there..." Maura said softly, listening intently.

"That's insane." Nahzarro braced himself against the wall and stood. The curative spells he had cast on himself prior to falling into unconsciousness seemed to have sped his recovery along. Then, from the haze of night, Maura noticed an armored Skirlack soldier, massive and hulking as it prowled the empty street. Nahzarro quickly ducked down alongside her. "They found us!"

"Really?" Maura snapped back. "If they knew we were here, they would have beaten the door in already."

"This is a fine mess you've gotten us into, girl!"

"*I* got us into?"

"Yes! I should have known better than to trust a shormloch with something this important!"

Maura's cheeks flushed with rage. "What happened to last night? You thanked me for saving your life!"

"I ... I did no such thing!"

"You arrogant, pathetic, little..." Maura began, before a voice from outside cut her off.

"Maura!" Kayden's vengeful tone echoed through the city. "Face me, you cowardly bitch!"

He was here, and he was looking for her. Nahzarro shifted. "You certainly seemed to have ... left an impression."

"You might have missed it. You were drooling into the snow at the time."

Before Nahzarro could respond, the wooden door to the guardhouse creaked under the pressure of a Skirlack hand.

"They're coming in," Maura observed, gripping her daggers.

"Once they spot us, it's over," Nahzarro said, "that Rosinanti will come and we won't be as lucky this time. He doesn't sound like he's in the mood to play games again."

"How much time do you need to repair the cannon?"

"It's a relatively simple fix," Nahzarro said, running through calculations in his head. "It shouldn't take more than ten minutes or so…"

"They're coming in, so we take these Skirlack by surprise, and then make a run for it."

"He will catch us long before we make the cannon."

"He wants me. I humiliated him. He's obsessed with things like this. So, we split up. You head to the cannon while I draw him away…" Maura's face was grim. She knew the very likely outcome of this tactic.

"Are you insane?" Nahzarro whispered in shock. "If you do that, he will catch you and kill you."

"Well, hopefully, I can get ten minutes out of him while you fix that cannon."

Nahzarro stared at her in disbelief. "No…" he said slowly, shaking his head at the thought. "I'm not letting you do this!"

"Well, then, it's a good thing I don't take orders from you, your highness." She moved to stand but Nahzarro clasped her forearm. Maura looked down at the prince as he gazed at her with a wide-eyed, pleading stare. She saw him for that instant, naked and awash in unguarded emotion, begging her not to give up her life. It was an odd moment that passed between them, where the hostility and annoyance they felt for one another vanished. They were no longer the prince-captain and the magicless country girl. They were just Nahzarro and Maura, and it was … nice.

Maura gave him a sad smile and slowly pulled her arm from his grip. Her hardened, determined stare illustrated her decision. She weighed the importance of the mission against her life, and it was not even close.

"I'll stay with you until we make it to the cannon," she said slowly, painfully, "but then you're on your own." Nahzarro's eyes protested for a moment longer, until finally he acquiesced and nodded in understanding. "Just promise me you're going to take that barrier down so Valentean can put a glowing green fist down that evil fire witch's throat."

"I promise," Nahzarro said with a long slow swallow. His voice sounded so odd, so tiny. Gone was the bravado of royal authority, and what was left was just a man.

Maura nodded and hesitantly held the side of his face in her hand. "You can do this," she insisted, "it will be okay." A tear spilled from Nahzarro's eye and Maura watched it fall with fascination. She had barely thought of the

Grassani prince as human up to this point, but in this light, he looked so … different. Their faces tilted toward one another with agonizing slowness. Maura felt it happen as though she were a stranger watching from afar. Her mouth moved independent of her mind, tilting closer and closer. Just as they were centimeters apart, as she could feel his warm breath wash into her mouth, the door to the guardhouse broke open and three Skirlack soldiers stormed into the room.

Maura's face instantly hardened as she leapt back, rolling over her head to her feet while drawing her daggers. She slashed one of the gargantuan fiends across the throat. Instinct told her to jump to the side as the remaining two advanced. Both were instantly cut down by the sparking strikes of Nahzarro's whips. She turned to look back at him, standing tall. His bruised and still swollen face was awash once more in the fierce pride she had come to know so well. He placed his hat gingerly atop his head and glanced at her with a raised eyebrow.

"To the cannon then," he said, motioning toward the open door with his chin. Maura nodded and together they sprinted out into the street. Grunts of surprise rose from the various Skirlack, as they immediately moved in to intercept their targets. There was still no sign of Kayden as they rounded a corner that brought the cannon into view. Every so often, a Skirlack would come straight at them or leap through a window or out of an alley. Each time, though, Maura or Nahzarro had handled it expertly. The cannon loomed closer and closer in its enormity. Soon the green vegetation which had taken over most of Kahntran stopped. The smoother streets, while still old, were easier to traverse.

The base of the scaffolding which led up to the cannon's main control platform was fast approaching. Maura held her breath, knowing that the moment was coming. All that mattered was that Nahzarro reached the top of that platform and had the time he needed to repair the massive weapon.

As they neared the stairs, a shadow fell from the sky with frightening speed and landed before the bottom step with a loud thud. Kayden crouched in the wake of his dramatic landing. He stood slowly and glared at Maura with smoldering purple hate.

"It's rude to keep a handsome man waiting, Maura," he said without a trace of humor. His tone was flat, emotionless, as if his rage had reached such an extreme level that it had evened out and reset.

"You may share the same face as Valentean, Kayden," she spat back, drawing her daggers. "But you're ugly and twisted."

Nahzarro's hand moved toward his whip, but Maura gave him a nearly invisible shake of her head. His place was atop that cannon, while hers was to buy time. Skirlack demons filed into the area, surrounding them on all sides. They must have been lying in wait while the others drove them here. It was a trap. Maura realized she had grossly underestimated Kayden's tactical prowess.

"No one is going anywhere," Kayden said, slowly, his voice alive with contempt.

Maura's mind settled on the edge of panic, but she managed to remain calm and attempted to formulate some way out of this inescapable mess. The wall of Skirlack demons would keep them penned in while Kayden would tear them to pieces. She held her blades up in a defensive position, goading the Rosinanti to attack. She heard the snap-hiss of Nahzarro's whips igniting beside her. This would be it, their final stand.

A shadow enveloped the battlefield. Maura, Nahzarro, and Kayden looked up to see the Aleksandryan airship which had chased them through the skies, hovering above Kahntran. Could it be? She held a breath in her chest, not daring to let it go as the bay doors on the ship's bottom slowly swung open. A lone figure leapt out, rocketing at them with such speed it seemed like a white comet as it smashed into the ground between Maura and Kayden.

Valentean Burai, animus warrior of Kackritta, white dragon of the Rosinanti, glared through alabaster slits at his brother. Confidence oozed from his posture in a manner Maura had never seen before as he glared at his twisted twin.

Kayden's furious stare softened into a smile.

"Finally," he breathed.

As the airship pulled away to find a safe landing zone, Valentean's eyes narrowed at his smug-looking sibling. Kayden was looking frazzled, perhaps a bit unbalanced. There was a deep black bruise upon his jawline, and he looked just a little off. This was good. Valentean would have to look for any advantage. There would be no last-minute rescues. It was time for them to finish this, once and for all.

"You look haggard, Kayden," Valentean said, keeping his voice flat.

The black dragon barked out a humorless laugh. "Yes, you'd like to believe that, wouldn't you, brother?" He spat upon the ground. "If I were facing my death as you are now, I, too, would try to grasp at anything to soothe my nerves."

"I'm not nervous."

Kayden laughed once more, holding the side of his head. "Well, then, you must have finally lost your senses!"

"No, I'm perfectly fine, Kayden. And you aren't going to hurt these two."

"It's adorable how you think you have a say in what I do, Valentean."

"I'm in control here, brother. Do not mistake that."

Kayden cackled in response, which Valentean assumed was mostly for show. "Clearly, you've forgotten your place, little brother. Do you remember how I bested you in Lazman? In the Northern Magic? In Kackritta City? Kahntran is no different."

"Everything is different now."

"Is that so?"

"I am different now."

"Oh please, Valentean. Do you think this is the Tournament again? You're going to suddenly pull out some great victory at the last second?"

"No, I don't."

"That's the first sensible thing you've said tonight."

"It's not going to be close. I'm going to beat you. Right here. Right now. Finally. Decisively. So that there is never again a question in your mind as to who is superior. You fall here, Kayden. This is where our story ends."

Kayden stopped laughing. He studied Valentean carefully, with trepidation in his eyes that he was working hard to conceal. He was confused. "You're not serious," he said, perhaps trying to convince himself. "If you had the stomach or the strength for anything like that, you would have done it in the Northern Magic."

"I'm deadly serious, brother."

Kayden looked long and hard at his smaller twin. Perhaps it was his ego refusing to accept Valentean's words, but his face broke into a smile once more and he laughed. He gripped his sides as he hunched over, hysterical in his amusement. His cackles filled the empty streets of Kahntran and did not stop.

This was it. This was the moment Valentean had been mentally preparing himself for. It was time to unleash the dragon. The dragon which had always laid coiled around his heart, whispering harsh desires for destruction and violence, was now his only hope. It made sense. The Rosintai had been right. There was no dragon, there was no darkness tempting him from afar. That darkness existed in him. That darkness was him as much as the light which he strived to embody. He closed his eyes and blocked out Kayden's laughter. Then Valentean Burai, for the first time in his life, just let go. He let go of the doubt, the fear, the anger. He let go of everything he was and let the power of the dragon fill him. The result was instantaneous and monumental.

He was startled for a moment because it felt as though his heart had exploded. So powerful was the blossoming energy that Valentean had to take a forceful step back. Tiny pebbles and bits of dirt levitated as the wind began to churn. Kayden abruptly stopped laughing as the street beneath his feet began to tremble. Valentean held the power within his chest, still under control. It was still his to swallow back down if he needed to. But that would not be necessary. The dragon was powerful, it was fierce, but Valentean Burai was its master.

"Now!" he heard the the Rosintai roar from within the shadow of his mind. Valentean threw his fists out to the side, flung his head back, opened his eyes, and screamed the loudest emotional exaltation of his life. A tidal wave of white energy exploded out of his eyes and mouth, igniting his skin in an alabaster glow which pulsated around his body.

Maura nearly screamed along with him. What was this? Where had it come from? Had this power rested within her friend all this time? She attempted to reach out with her mind, using her knowledge of mana to sense the energy rippling around Valentean's body as he shone before her, illuminating the entire city. What she sensed made her fall back onto the ground. The energy was so massive, so incredibly powerful that the being within its epicenter could not have possibly been Valentean.

Yet somehow it was, and as Nahzarro fell to a knee beside her, his eyes like saucers in wild wonderment, Maura laughed in glee. She lowered her arms and stared at the scorching hue until her eyes burned.

Lazman was about to be avenged.

Nevick hated letting Valentean go off alone, but someone had to ensure Mitchell, Michael, and Deana's safety. Sometime over the ocean, loud bangs and shudders had started to resound throughout the ship. It was touch and go for a while as to whether they were even going to make it to Kahntran, and had it not been for Valentean and his odd wind magic, they likely would have met their end beneath the ocean's waves.

Mitchell was in the process of landing amidst an area of dilapidated structures. Nevick heard him mumbling encouragement to the ship as though it were a living person who had some kind of decision to be made in their safe touchdown. Finally, Nevick felt the ship settle, and there was a loud collective sigh of relief throughout the command bridge.

"I told you she'd hold together!" Michael said, slapping his palm against the console in triumph. Deana cheered in Nevick's lap while Mitchell bowed his head and closed his eyes, seemingly overcome with the emotion of the moment.

"Excellently done, gentlemen!" Nevick said.

"I don't know if she'll take off again," Michael replied, shaking his head and grinning, "but we did it!" He clasped a hand on Mitchell's shoulder and the inventor removed his spectacles to wipe the mist from his eyes.

Nevick stood with Deana in his arms, and no sooner had he reached his full height did a shuddering quake start to shake the entire ship. "Mitchell, what's happening?" he roared, quickly settling Deana into the seat as he stumbled toward the railing to look down at the brothers.

"It's not the ship!" Mitchell exclaimed, looking at his console. "The engines are powered down! That's … something else!"

A bright white explosion that tinted the entire horizon caused all four of them to shield their eyes. Deana cried out in fear as Michael crouched beneath the console. Nevick peered over his arms and noted the direction of the powerful glare.

"Valentean…" he whispered with worry.

No…

That was Kayden's only thought as he sensed the magical energy pouring out of his brother. *No,* he thought as Valentean continued energizing his body and mind, making the very ground which answered to Kayden alone, quake. He hated that part most of all. It was as if even his element was acquiescing to Valentean's newfound power. This would not do … It would not do at all. Valentean continued to scream and the energy washed out over the area until he shone in an explosion of white amidst the devastation of a dead city.

This wasn't fair. Kayden was superior, Valentean was weak. This was the foundation upon which his belief system rested. Now, Valentean stood triumphantly in the face of everything Kayden understood. But all was not lost. The fool was stronger than before, but by Kayden's estimation, he could not have had much further to go until he reached his maximum level of power. This would bring him to within striking distance of Kayden's limit. This was bad, but it was not over.

Kayden wiped the look of shock from his face and snarled at his brother. He threw his head back and screamed, unleashing the bottled-up energy from the depths of his darkness. Purple light shot out around him, mixing with the white as the two energies intertwined, combatting one another in the space between them, foreshadowing the epic struggle that was about to unfold.

Let him come. Let him burn in his own power. Let the fool think he stood on the edge of victory. Kayden knew this was far from over. At least now, when Valentean fell before him, he would lose with the knowledge that even at his best, he was simply not as good as Kayden.

The purple energy explosion was unexpected but not entirely surprising for Valentean. He knew that his brother had yet to show him the fullest extent of his capabilities. Up until this point, he'd never had a reason to. Kayden caught up to him almost immediately, as he unleashed his energy all at once, not little by little, as Valentean had. While he knew that he needed to give into the dragon's energy, he could not allow himself to lose control. To do so would be to risk playing right into the Skirlack's hands. He had to hang onto his humanity and not become lost in the thrill of power. This had proved easy enough. He simply held onto one thought throughout every second of his powerful awakening.

"*He is the love of my life*." Seraphina's words echoed through his mind. This admission of love was all he needed to focus on, like a beacon in the night allowing him to find his way back home through any darkness. He could maintain his sense of self by remembering those seven words.

Finally, it seemed as though Valentean had reached the limits of his potential, and he threw his arms down, killing the outpouring of energy as it flowed through him. His body felt so different, as though it were both on fire and being electrocuted at the same time. The air around him rippled with white energy and his breath washed out in ragged gasps. His entire body shook with every inhalation. He was still bathed in the purple hue of Kayden's energy, which vanished as his brother reached his apex. As the glare died, purple eyes locked onto white within a circle of demons.

"So…" Kayden said, panting with exertion, "it looks like we're even, eh, brother?"

Valentean gave a stiff nod. "It appears so."

"Still, though, you're going to lose, Valentean."

"Am I?"

"Yes. You're going to blow some wind at me while I will move mountains to destroy you. You're defined by weakness, Valentean! You'll never be able to defeat me! I control the land itself! All you have as your weapon is the gentle tickle of a breeze!"

Valentean inclined his head, questioning Kayden's statement. A steady downpour pelted them with a thick, soaking rain. The kind that made it difficult to see through. Valentean smiled. "I've got something you'll never have, Kayden. It's why I'm going to beat you."

"And what is that?"

"Love!" Valentean shouted channeling the energy he had felt in the dreamscape when he and Seraphina had entangled in that incorporeal kiss. His white eyes shifted and the bright blue light of order erupted from them. Kayden took a step back. Valentean smirked and held his arms out, palms up. At his silent instruction, hundreds of raindrops halted in the air, froze into sharp, jagged ice fractals and turned to point directly at Kayden.

"Impossible!" the black dragon screeched. "No … how is this … No!"

"Come on then, brother," Valentean goaded. "Attack me!"

"This change nothing!" Kayden bellowed over the pouring rain. He reached back with both arms and mentally tore two large, jagged shards of rock out of the ground—twice as tall as he was—and pointed them at Valentean. "Do you hear me, you arrogant half-wit? It changes nothing!"

Kayden advanced on him, and the battle was on.

"Stand aside, Princess," Sophie said, eyeing Seraphina with deadly intent. She clearly did not share Aleksandra's affection.

"You will stand aside, Sophie," she answered, her blue eyes stare never wavering. Seraphina's mind and body were finally in perfect harmony, and the order within her shone with its force. "The people of Kackritta are under my protection."

"Stupid girl," Sophie spat, her entire body shaking with rage. "There are no people of Kackritta! Your entire kingdom has been laid to waste and transformed while you hid away in your blasphemous bubble. You stand upon the ground of Aleksandrya now, and you are a wanted fugitive within its borders!"

"This empire my sister has concocted is as false as the demon you worship."

Sophie's mouth hung open in aghast horror. "You dare to speak your blasphemy within the walls of our city of faith? Your sister has been blind to the truth of you for so long, Seraphina. You are weak. You are nothing, and you are not corrupted by the power of the Harbinger. You are the Harbinger!" She pointed her staff at the princess threateningly. "As Pontifex of the Faithful, is it my sworn duty to bring you to the holy justice of Skirlack!"

Seraphina glanced back at Vahn, their eyes meeting over a sea of wounded bodies left behind in the wake of Sophie's assault. His gaze questioned her. She gave one slow, confident nod to the father of the man she loved and turned to face Sophie.

"Do you really think you can?" Seraphina asked, floating off the ground.

Sophie's face contorted into an ugly mask of revulsion at the question. "Why don't you see for yourself?" she screamed, thrusting the staff forward.

The impressive translucent magic slammed into Seraphina. Sophie was clearly a mighty mage. But she was not the spirit of order, and her spell did naught more than blow Seraphina's hair back. She stood, completely unscathed, awash in the blue light that was her power.

Sophie gasped. "Wh … what?" she exclaimed, taking a hesitant step back. "You are…"

"The Harbinger," Seraphina finished for her. Raising one hand, she summoned a spell infinitely more powerful which flung the Pontifex back like an insect caught in a tornado. She slammed, back first, into the execution stage. The strength of her magical shield protected her as she burst through the wood, falling out the other end and rolling to a shuddering, stumbling stop.

Seraphina breathed in, readying herself, not allowing her emotions to rise, keeping order alive within her heart. The power pulsed through her in response. Sophie erupted into the sky. Lacerations bled along her face and arms. The ridiculous headpiece she'd worn had fallen off in Seraphina's attack. The Pontifex glared down at her, staff ablaze with red energy.

Seraphina took yet another calming breath. *You do not rule me*, she silently commanded her fears and doubts. *I rule you!* She leaped into the sky, a blue dot amidst the red backdrop of Aleksandra's energy shield. Her fingers crackled with sapphire bolts of electric order, and she flew forward into the fray.

Nevick ran down the ramp at the rear of the airship onto the cracked, rain-soaked streets of Kahntran. He knew he would find Valentean at the center of the conflict, likely near the base of that massive cannon he spotted on their approach.

"Nevick!" he heard Deana call to him. He turned and saw his beloved seated in her chair at the top of the ramp. He cursed under his breath at her reluctance to follow instructions. Before setting out, he had asked her to remain on the command bridge with the Duzels where it was safe. This place was new and dangerous, the first foreign land they had ever set foot upon. He knew that the monsters who laid waste to Casid were within the city, and he could not allow her to cross their path once more.

"Dea, get back inside!" he yelled, pointing back toward the ship.

"Please, just … be careful," she said, a look of longing desperation in her eyes. She knew he had to go, but her heart seemed to be fighting her brain.

"I will," he said, trying to press every last ounce of sincerity into those two words. He wanted to put her fears fully at ease, but he knew that to be impossible.

He tried to think of something to say, anything that might decrease her anxiety. With alarming suddenness, her stare grew wide and her mouth opened to scream for him, but she had not the chance to do so. A heavy armored fist slammed into the back of his head.

Nevick fell forward, smacking the side of his face into the stone street. His world became a dizzying haze of color and ambiguous sound. He forgot where he was and who he was for a moment. As thought came rippling back into his mind, he realized that whatever had hit him had done so with the intent to disable or kill him in one blow. As his vision solidified and the world around him became real once more, Nevick's eyes locked onto a pair of black armored boots.

"I knew that wouldn't be enough," a gruff but silky voice oozed in familiarity. "You're like me. You're not the same as the rabble." Nevick raised his chin to stare up at General Zouka, who glowered down at him. "I hadn't thought a human existed in this world like you. But I must say, it is not an unwelcomed discovery."

As Nevick struggled to one knee, the general reared back and kicked him hard in the chest with the sole of his steel boot. Nevick shot back two meters and hit his head on the roadway again.

"I've figured it out, you know," Zouka continued on, his tone light as if the two men had been meeting for lunch. "How you do it, I mean. Why you're so strong. You're funneling mana into your muscles to empower yourself."

Nevick's brow furrowed. "What are you…" he started to ask of the man who had put the final nail in the coffin of his home.

Zouka shook his head and cut him off with a laugh. "Remarkable. You don't even realize you're doing it, do you? You're a true savant! You know, many warriors of the Gorram Tribe tried and failed for years to master such a useful battle skill. And here you are, naught more but a mortal man, and you've mastered it without even knowing."

These words meant little to Nevick. Giving a name to his abilities changed nothing. He was still going to use them to cave in the general's face. Nevick's thoughts betrayed him as his eyes involuntarily swung toward the ramp and Deana, who still sat there, aghast at what was transpiring below.

Zouka's eyes followed Nevick's gaze and he smiled with a small laugh. "Ah, the cripple," the general observed. "Is she your woman?" Nevick snarled as he attempted to draw breath back into his lungs. "I always hate leaving a job half-finished. Perhaps before I take care of you, I'll finish her off. Or maybe I'll let her watch you die, and then have some fun of my own with her before snapping her neck. Is she still a real woman from the waist down, or is everything dead down there?"

Rage was precisely what Nevick needed at this moment. With a scream of fury, he erupted to his feet, muscles bulging with mana energy as he struck Zouka with such force that the armor plating over his stomach cracked. Zouka doubled over in pain and shot back, landing on his hands and knees, coughing blood stained slobber onto the ground. As Nevick advanced, his eyes smoldering with hatred, finally ready to end this foe once and for all. His kill rage broke as Zouka began to laugh.

The general stumbled to his feet, and Nevick sped forward, slamming his meaty fist into Zouka's face, solar plexus and chest, sending him sprawling back to the ground once more. But still the general laughed.

"Wonderful," he remarked once more, "simply wonderful."

"You have a sick sense about what's good in this world."

"I had thought the Rosintai was the only one on the planet capable of matching me." He rolled to one knee. "When I first encountered you, I was furious at your existence. But then I started to see the positive side of it. You match me, you challenge me, and defeating you has become a new goal to train for!"

"It's going to be hard to train when you're dead," Nevick said, the threat burning his throat with venom.

"Oh, I don't think so." Zouka shook his head as he stood once more. "You match me as I am now, and you are indeed a challenge. But you are not my equal."

"Agreed," Nevick replied. "I'm better."

Zouka's smile vanished instantly, with the crashing suddenness of mania. "You are going to regret saying that," he said slowly, enunciating every word. "You are not the only one who has mastered this skill, you know."

Nevick glared at him. He had a feeling their conversation was going to swing in this direction. "What're you waiting for then? Are we going to do this or are you just going to posture all night?"

Zouka did not answer this time. He closed his eyes and grunted in concentration. A yellow glow spread around the Gorram's arms. He screamed and slammed one fist into the ground. The armor and gauntlets that had contained his arms exploded as his muscles doubled in size, then tripled. His feet and calves bulged until his armored boots and greaves violently burst. Zouka's height increased as well. He rose past two and a half meters as his breastplate flew from his body. The black bodysuit he wore beneath his armor stretched until it, too, tore away from his arms legs and chest.

Nevick panicked and realized he had to stop this. He charged, ready to strike, until the general noticed his approach. The growing man raised one enormous hand and clamped his entire palm and fingers around Nevick's head and part of his chest. Zouka easily lifted the large man and stared at him, eyes alight with deranged triumph. This close now, Nevick could see a horrifying yellow glow of energy spreading along the tightly pressed veins in Zouka's arms and neck. Bursts of jaundiced light were flickering along his eyeballs.

Nevick kicked his legs pathetically, feeling utterly helpless in the grasp of this goliath. The muscles of Zouka's back and neck bulged up and out so much that his head appeared to sink within them. When the transformation ceased, Zouka stood over three meters in height, and his hand fit comfortably around Nevick's broad chest. He was a monster, a creature so massive and so demented, it made the Skirlack demons that had turned Nevick's wedding day into a nightmare look tame in comparison.

Zouka roared, blowing the skin of Nevick's face back in rippling waves. He brought his other mammoth fist up and pounded Nevick's body into the ground. As he smacked the stone, Nevick bounced like a ball back up into the air. Zouka unleashed a meaty backhand which sent him careening through the street, smashing through a still standing stone wall. As he lay there, shuddering in pain amidst the wreckage of a once very solid structure, Nevick felt a steady stream of warm gooey liquid pouring down over his right eye. He only needed a moment of clarity to recognize it as his own blood. He tried to rise, but the pain in his midsection bit at him furiously. He had broken some ribs, possibly sprained an ankle. His mind felt fuzzy.

"I had meant to save this for the Rosintai," Zouka said in a deeper, harsher sounding voice than before, "for the day when he truly decided to fight me with all he had. But you should feel honored. I've decided you've earned this. You won't be around long enough to tell your friend Valentean about it!" Zouka leapt into the sky and then came rocketing down.

Valentean flung the jagged ice daggers hovering over his left hand at Kayden who still sprinted toward him, large dueling boulders in tow. Kayden dropped his stony weapons and performed a graceful front flip over the lethal impalers. Before he had a chance to land, Valentean followed up his initial assault with a second volley of tiny jagged fractals.

The instant Kayden's boots touched the ground he leaped again, timing his avoidance just right and arching his body up, to twist out of the way. The frigid weapons shredded through the hanging portions of his robes. As he landed, Kayden drew the two large stones back to him and sent them hurtling at Valentean from both sides.

Valentean jumped straight into the air, just avoiding the crushing embrace of slamming stone. Kayden leapt up to stop him and struck Valentean in the chest with a mana-soaked fist. Valentean slammed into the street with enough force to shatter the roadway beneath him. With the emotional, energetic rush of his power fueling him, he rolled through the impact and came to a standing position, just in time to intercept his brother who was already closing in.

Kayden punched from all angles, but Valentean turned each blow away, connecting with a quick jab to Kayden's nose and mouth which staggered the larger Burai. Time seemed to slow around them as Valentean wound up and threw a punch from the hip into Kayden's stomach. The rainwater changed direction as he moved, following the trajectory of his fist. This added a surge of power to his punch in the form of a steady, strong burst of water which threw Kayden back, sending him crashing into a crumbling building before he tumbled out the other side.

Valentean realized his control over the water element was different from that of Seraphina or Aqua. He had no real knowledge of its magical properties, but it responded to his mind and worked like a weapon. As he waited for Kayden to rejoin the fray, he moved his left hand through the air, watching the water flow along with it, as though it were an extension of his arm.

Kayden skidded to a stop and slammed his hands through the road. When he pulled them back out, jagged grey stone spread along his hands, coming to tiny points on his knuckles. He closed the distance between them and swung at Valentean with precisely aimed thrusts of his rock-coated fists. Valentean dodged them as best he could, but Kayden was well-versed in all aspects of Valentean's defense and soon managed to score a blow along his smaller brother's kidney.

Valentean recoiled, chiding himself for being too slow. Kayden pounced and slammed his reinforced knuckles into Valentean's forehead, causing him to fall onto the slick street. Kayden attacked with hard punches to the face and chest as he pinned Valentean to the ground with a knee over his heart. Valentean was sure the orbital bone was shattered around his left eye. These punches fell with such overwhelming ferocity that the stone beneath the back of Valentean's head broke and created a deeper indentation in the street with every punch.

Valentean soon felt the torrential downpour beginning to fill the hole around his head with water. An idea quickly sparked in his mind as Kayden swung once more. Valentean jerked his head from the deadly path of his brother's fist. Kayden's hand fell to the bottom of the hole it had created, splashing into the puddle. Valentean, with a thought, froze the water solid into a pool of ice, entrapping Kayden's arm. He spun up to one knee and slammed his fist into Kayden's face three times. Each time he connected, the rain impacted along with him.

Kayden recoiled in pain but his arm remained solidly captive within the magically strengthened ice. Valentean erupted to his feet, smashing his knee into his brother's forehead. Kayden fell to the side, his hand still entrapped as Valentean moved in for the kill. He empowered a fist with mana energy. As it ignited, the water flowed around his arm with increasing intensity. Valentean punched down at his brother, but Kayden rolled back and to his feet, lifting a large chunk of rock and dirt from around his captured hand.

As Valentean stood, Kayden slammed him in the chest with the broken shard of street. Valentean fell back, slamming into the road and cracking it once more with the severity of his fall. Eventually, the white-eyed Rosinanti slid to a stop and rolled back up. His eyes met Kayden's through the wall of rain, and they charged headlong at one another. Kayden gestured, and a large rock tore from the ground and hurtled toward his incoming foe. Valentean rolled beneath it, coming up to summon the rain around him and send it shooting forward, thinking of Seraphina as he attempted to duplicate the complicated maneuver he had seen her perform many times.

The stream he sent was slow, and while it carried strength, it was clear to Valentean that he was not going to defeat Kayden with such tactics. The black dragon slid under the oncoming liquid and rose back to his feet, sprinting at his sibling, bludgeoning through the fat rain droplets.

Valentean turned and sped away in a mana-fueled burst of speed. A second later, he could hear the sound of Kayden following. They wound through and around buildings, down alleyways, and across abandoned roads. All the while, Kayden attempted to slow him down by heaving large shards of rock. Valentean nimbly dodged out of the way, sending slow-moving streams of water back at his brother, never hitting him but continuing to lead him away from the center of the city, away from the cannon, just as he had intended.

There was a moment of calm silence as Maura and Nahzarro stared, transfixed, at the twin speeding blurs that were Valentean and Kayden as they rocketed away. The Skirlack, as well, seemed to be following the epic conflict's trajectory, the spectacle cutting into their bloodlust and distracting them.

Maura knew Valentean was leading Kayden away, giving them time to fulfill their purpose. The same thought seemed to dawn upon Nahzarro, as she noticed his hand slowly moving toward the handle of one of his whips.

"Give the word," Nahzarro whispered just loud enough for Maura to hear.

It was an odd moment in which he was deferring to her judgement. Maura gave a slight, almost unperceivable nod of her head. "Now!" she cried out, dropping to her knees.

Nahzarro lashed out with both arms outstretched, summoning invisible waves of magical energy which passed over her head and flew out in every direction. The dozens of Skirlack demons who surrounded them were blown back by the unexpected assault, landing in a flailing pile of clumsy crimson flesh and intertwined bulky limbs.

Maura motioned toward the large steel staircase which wound up the scaffolding, and Nahzarro took off toward it. She followed at his back, looking over her shoulder to see the first of their enemies beginning to give chase. Once they reached the control platform, the staircase would serve as a beneficial tool which would funnel their witless foes toward her, one at a time.

As they reached the halfway point, far higher than many of Kahntran's buildings, Nahzarro stopped and motioned for her to continue ahead of him. Before she could protest, he shouldered past her and glared down at the oncoming demon horde.

Nahzarro extended his arms, and Maura heard him muttering more nonsense words. Suddenly, the staircase below them split and started to fall. The demons roared in the face of their own demise as the steel structure gave way, and they plummeted to their doom.

Maura laughed in astonished glee. Nahzarro panted heavily, now standing on the bottom step before a huge drop. He smiled slowly and tipped his hat to their fallen opponents. Maura grabbed the prince by his sleeve and continued to pull him along.

As they bounded up the remaining stairs, Maura felt a long-forgotten sense of hope blossom within her heart. They were so close, their pursuers were no more, and Valentean had things under control.

A few more steps took them onto the circular-grated, steel control platform. There was a large console at the far end, overlooking the base of the cannon's nozzle, which hung overhead. But standing between Maura and the damaged controls was Aurax. His red mouth was pulled back into a snarl and he glared at the two humans with hatred.

Maura drew her blades and ran at the frail cleric, leaping at him with daggers pointed for the kill. She passed harmlessly through the incorporeal demon, who stood affixed in one spot, neither moving nor flinching. He shook his head before turning to stare at Maura, lip curled in disgust.

"You again," he remarked, glowering down at her. "I find it astounding that one such as you has been blessed with such unbelievable luck. How else am I to account for your continued survival?"

Maura stood and attempted to slash at him with both blades, each weapon harmlessly passing through his body once more. The snap-hiss of Nahzarro's igniting twin whips filled the air with the smell of lightning. Maura dove back as the Grassani prince cracked both weapons around the creature and watched them pass harmlessly through, as though Aurax were naught more than air.

"Truly," he said slowly, shaking his head. "You humans never cease to amaze me."

Maura began to realize the futility of her tactic. Valentean had spoken of his most recent interaction with this annoyance, describing in detail how he had phased right through the demon's body as if he were a ghost.

"He's incorporeal," Maura cried across the platform to Nahzarro. "We can't touch him, but that also means he can't do more than talk at us."

Aurax's face fell.

"Well, then." Nahzarro smiled as he switched off his whips and placed them once more upon his belt. "If you'll excuse us, we have some repairs to make."

Before Aurax could respond, Nahzarro casually walked through him toward the console.

"Very good, humans," he said slowly. "Yes, I pose no physical threat to you personally, but I shan't allow you to repair this device."

"What, are you going to irritate us to death?" Maura said as she and Nahzarro arrived at the console.

The prince furrowed his brow and stared at the dirt-caked machine. Moving into a crouch, he roughly pulling a panel out from its side.

Aurax scoffed. "As you may have guessed by this point, I exist between realms," he stated.

Maura turned back to look at him as Nahzarro tinkered with the console's inner workings. "What's your point?" she asked, rolling her eyes.

"My … point is that the reason my people are able to cross the dimensional gateway into this world is because *I* have been holding the door open for them, widening it for centuries. I have forfeited a life of corporeal pleasures for the sake of my brethren."

"Let me know when I'm supposed to be impressed."

"I do not think you understand, girl." Aurax held his arms out, and the air around him shivered with a crimson shadow. Ten savage, snarling Skirlack soldiers appeared, fangs dripping with saliva as they glared impatiently at Maura.

Nahzarro tried to stand but she held one arm aloft to stop him. "I'll handle them," she whispered frantically. "Fix the cannon!"

"But…" he started to protest.

"Fix the cannon!" Maura held her blades before her chest. There were many of them, each one formidable. But she had killed their kind before, and she would do it again. There was no stopping her now.

From the center of the savage horde, Aurax smiled, his yellow teeth cutting through the darkness and rain around them. "Kill," he said to his subordinate soldiers.

Kayden was starting to get irritated. He weaved and raced through the empty, dilapidated streets of Kahntran, always just a tiny bit slower than his smaller brother. Valentean had been leading him on an infuriating chase for several minutes now, and the tactic was beginning to bore. For a moment, Kayden contemplated taking the form of the black dragon and overtaking his helpless brother, incinerating him and the city in one giant burst of energy.

Kayden's hand was, however, stayed by the authoritative commands of his Mistress. He could not simply destroy the city when Aleksandra had some plan for it. To do so would be tantamount to suicide. Kayden also wanted to show Valentean that he did not have to resort to such drastic measures to defeat him. He could best him here, now, in this place and in this form. That would truly be the final grand moment of his vengeance. It would be the sweetest justice ever doled out on Terran soil. But he could not defeat what he could not catch.

He reached out one hand, sending a shuddering rumble through the ground which caused Valentean to stumble. This afforded Kayden the added second it took to overtake his brother and smash him in the face with a mana-soaked fist, which exploded against his forehead. Valentean landed with a wet slosh on the rain-soaked ground. He rose quickly, coming at Kayden with a disoriented series of strikes, all of which the spirit of darkness turned away with ease.

Kayden responded with a solid punch to Valentean's kidney. As he recoiled from the blow, Kayden forced a rock to tear itself from the ground and smashed it into Valentean's chest. The white dragon fell back, and Kayden silently commanded a shard of black stone, two meters in height, to rise in Valentean's path. His brother smashed, back first, into this makeshift wall and paused to catch his breath.

That solitary instant was all Kayden needed. He burst forward with all the speed his addled body could muster. The black dragon began to pummel Valentean against the stone with powerful punches to the ribs, chests, shoulders, face, head, and anywhere there was an opening. Valentean was completely helpless, unable to so much as raise his hands to defend himself.

The darkness churned within Kayden as he slammed his fist of stone into his brother's soft flesh and bone again, and again, and again, and again. Each impact of rock against skin made his heart sing with a single-minded bliss that could only be obtained through dominant destruction. This was it, this was his moment. With a satisfying intake of breath, Kayden drew back a jade, crackling, energized fist and filled it with every last bit of his strength and power. His soul felt electrified as the world moved in slow motion, his fist poised for this moment of truth.

This is it!

This is it, Valentean thought as Kayden's fist rocketed toward his face. He had been drawing his brother away from the cannon, giving Maura and Nahzarro the chance to accomplish their mission. Valentean hadn't expected Kayden to catch him, and the offensive flurry he had unleashed was extensively battering. If this next strike fell, the battle would be over. He had to act now.

Valentean ducked his head and felt blistering heat on his neck as Kayden struck the stone causing a fiery explosion. Valentean's eyes glowed once more with the azure hue of order and he commanded the rain to aid him. The droplets of moisture converged upon them, freezing around Kayden's wrists and ankles, yanking him helplessly into the air.

Kayden cursed and thrashed, the disappointment of evaporated triumph still echoing in his purple gaze. Now, it was Valentean's turn. He unleashed a barrage of precisely placed punches, which fell with the full fury of his bottled-up rage. Flesh tore and bones fractured beneath his knuckles as the onslaught continued. But there was no joy to be found in this momentary advantage.

In Kackritta Castle, he had seen something in Kayden's stare. Some hidden, buried semblance of the brother he once loved. Despite his earlier posturing, he could not bring himself to end Kayden's life and snuff out that last shining hope for redemption. Kayden needed to be stopped. He needed to be subdued. But Valentean would not kill him. He needed to find some way to contain him and take him out of the battle. He decided to play his trump card, something Kayden would never expect.

His eyes turned from blue to white, and as the water released its hold on Kayden, Valentean lashed out with a stiff gust of wind that threw his brother up into the air. Valentean called on the wind to cradle him as he flew into the sky, grabbing Kayden around the waist with both arms and carrying him high into the upper reaches of Kahntran.

Kayden regained his composure and started slamming his fists into Valentean's back, but he could not find a strong enough angle of attack. Valentean soared up with his brother, rising above the tallest remaining building in the dilapidated city. It must have been seventy stories tall and would do nicely for what Valentean had in mind.

He flung Kayden down toward the top of the building and sent a gust of wind blasting at him, shooting him down with greater velocity. Valentean dove after his brother. He caught up to Kayden's plummeting body and grabbed him tight.

The spirit of light slammed into the roof, smashing his brother through it and the subsequent floor. He continued to pummel his sibling-turned-rival with tight fists as they crashed through floor after floor of the huge building. Kayden tried to fight back at first, but only at first. Each smashing crash took more and more out of him. Valentean was unrelenting in his assault, determined to render his brother unconscious by the time they hit the ground.

Kayden smacked into the floor of the building's base with a thud and a crack. Valentean landed atop him, relatively unscathed. As the smaller Burai climbed off his larger brother, he was astounded to see that Kayden was still moving, trying to get back to his feet.

"No..." Kayden said weakly, "...no. You ... won't ... ever..."

Valentean's eyes flashed back to blue and he motioned up toward the seventy-story hole their falling bodies had torn into the dilapidated structure. At his command, every drop of rain in Kahntran instantly changed direction and hurtled toward them. The flood poured into the building, merging together and slamming Kayden into the ground with the force of a tidal wave.

Valentean could barely see his dark sibling struggling against the full fury of his assault. He ordered the water to freeze into a giant column. Kayden was trapped inside, frozen in place at the base of this frigid tower. Valentean took a gasping breath of relief and fell to a seated position, spitting a small wad of blood onto the ground and rubbing the side of his aching face. His entire body hurt—from his limbs to his back, ribs, and head.

He stared at his brother, face frozen and contorted in indescribable rage. Valentean shook his head sadly, thankful that this ordeal was now over. He hoped that Maura and Nahzarro had made some progress with the cannon and resigned himself to head over there once the room stopped spinning. As he stood shakily through the pain, a sudden purple glare from within the ice drew his dread-soaked attention.

No...

Kayden's eyes were lighting up through the freezing embrace. A purple bolt of electricity tore out of the ice, and then another, and another.

No ... no... Valentean thought in a frenzy, trying to strengthen the prison and hold it steady to keep his struggling brother at bay. Soon the entire area was alight with Kayden's amethyst energy. It built to a blinding hue which Valentean knew could signal only one thing. He panicked and cursed loudly as a massive booming explosion tore the building to bits. Valentean was flung out as though he were nothing, battered, burned, and missing the right sleeve of his tunic and half of the fabric which covered his chest.

He slammed into the ground nearly a full kilometer from where he began, sliding along the roadway. Purple light shone throughout the city. His fear pushed upon him once more, and Valentean could not will himself to look up.

The animus warrior forced his resolve to harden. He slowly raised his head and looked ahead at his worst fear made flesh. Even from this distance, he could see Kayden standing tall, wings spread, hate-filled purple eyes locked onto him. The hulking black dragon opened its massive maw and shook the city with a thundering roar. It smacked the ground with its great tail and looked at Valentean with smoldering contempt.

Not good...

XXVII: ZOUKA THE UNSTOPPABLE

A purple explosion from somewhere far-off meant very little to Nevick. The past several minutes had been a frenzied fight for survival as the towering general pursued him through the streets. Nevick ran with all his might, but Zouka took leaping bounds which covered great distances, easily closing the gap between them.

Nevick had managed to remain unscathed since that initial shuddering strike, which was precisely why he still drew breath. That slam and backhand had fallen with so much power that he was amazed his body hadn't liquefied at first contact.

Zouka burst through the wall of a building and Nevick dove to the side as a fist wider than his torso broke the street with a punch. He diverted energy into his arms and pectoral muscles, striking the general with two fists to the chest. Zouka stumbled back. Nevick grabbed him by one arm, and flung him into a nearby house, the front of which fully caved beneath such force.

Zouka leaped back out of the dilapidated structure and swung at Nevick again. The warrior of Casid managed to duck underneath the strike and marveled at how, even with this incredible boost in strength, Zouka still had a weakness. He was slow and bulky now, and Nevick knew that if he could keep moving, keep dodging, he could wear the behemoth down with quick but powerful strikes.

He had never been the smaller man in a fight before, but took to it quickly, managing to bob and dart his way around the general's clumsy lashes. Nevick ducked beneath a wild backhand and struck into layers upon layers of muscle with four fast punches. Zouka tried to strike straight down at him with one hand, but Nevick blurred out of the way as the huge fist broke the street. He then kicked Zouka with all his strength right in the elbow before the giant had a chance to raise his fist again. He was satisfied when he heard a crunch and a howl of pain.

"You'll suffer for that!" Zouka screamed in fury.

He lashed out again, but Nevick ducked and gave a low drop kick to the monster's kneecap. Again, a crunching snap and pained bellow awarded his resilience. Zouka dropped to one knee and Nevick charged in, muscles bulging in his arms as he slammed his fists into the general's sunken face over and over again. Zouka teetered back, on the verge of falling.

Nevick, in his excitement, stayed just a shade too long in one place. A massive fist smashed into his chest, propelling him through a crumbling home, back within sight of the airship. Zouka leapt into the sky once more, trying to land on Nevick with both feet, but he managed to roll to safety at the last possible instant.

The monstrous Gorram reached out and grabbed Nevick around the calf, then flung him into the air and slammed his body into the stone, like an animal trying to open a coconut. Nevick kicked at Zouka's exposed wrist four times until he felt it give. The mighty grip released him and the ascendant general roared in pain. Nevick pounded punches into the goliath's ribs to drive him back. Then, he leapt up with both fists raised, ready to smash Zouka's face, when the hulking monster seized him around the torso with both arms and started to squeeze.

Nevick screamed as his bones began to whine in protest. It felt as though his insides were exploding from the force of this smothering embrace. He punched at the monster, but each time he felt as though he were starting to make progress, Zouka redoubled his grip.

"Now you see," Zouka said, his voice like stone scraping against metal. "You can see the fullest extent of my might! You were a fool to challenge me! No one can defeat me!"

Deana, Mitchell and Michael watched in horror. The sounds of Nevick's screams were like torture to Deana, and she cursed her inability to run to him in his time of need. Of course, even if she were healthy, how much aid could she possibly provide against something like that?

"We have to help him!" she cried out, desperately looking to Mitchell.

"Agreed, but how?" he pondered aloud, fidgeting nervously with his shirt.

"Doesn't this thing have weapons?"

Michael's face lit up. "The main cannon," he exclaimed. "As long as he stays in one place we can give him a good blast and be done with that monster!"

Deana felt the audacity of hope begin to rise in her heart, and she gripped the armrests of her chair with renewed focus.

"We'd take both of them out if we used that!" Mitchell said, shaking his head. "If Nevick could get clear, we might have a chance."

"What's the main cannon?" Deana asked impatiently.

"It's a big weapon installed in the ship's bow," Michael said as he moved across the command bridge, pulling out a large, long box. "It's something those Aleksandryan people added to the design. But the real interesting thing isn't the weapon itself, but what it fires." He grabbed a steel pipe from the floor and used it to pry the box open. Sitting inside was a pointed, thin metal cone.

"What is it?" Deana inquired, tilting her head at the oddity.

"It's some kind of projectile," Michael replied. "But the interesting thing is what's inside. When it hits, as far as we've been able to tell, it shoots…"

"Magic," Mitchell said with a scoff, rolling his eyes. The inventor was a man of science, and all things magical irked him.

"But do you think it will help?" she asked Mitchell, despite his derision.

"In theory?" he said, tapping his chin. "It's possible. We haven't tested it."

"Do it!" Deana roared.

Nevick's world was starting to darken around him. Most of his ribs were broken or breaking. A well of blood erupted from his mouth from internal injuries that were slowly killing him. He spat the crimson shower upon Zouka's face and the general grinned in response, his tongue erupting from his lips to lap it up.

His hazy eyes could just barely make out some movement coming from the direction of the airship. A large door swung open and a huge cannon pushed out through it. Deana, Mitchell, and Michael were trying to help. Maybe there was a chance after all.

Deana rolled up to the ladder which stretched through a tall chute. Mitchell sat in a seat on the bottom, moving levers and turning knobs, which would control the cannon's aim. Michael was up top, gently sliding the projectile weapon into its chamber, ready for launch. There was an audible click.

"Weapon is loaded!" Michael called down to his brother. From his vantage point at the cannon's base, Mitchell took aim.

"What is happening out there?" Deana asked, desperate for more news.

"More of the same," Mitchell said, a shuddering anxiety tinting his words. Deana could just barely see him turning a wheel on his left and pulling a lever on his right. In response, the cannon shuddered and slowly moved.

"Just a bit … lower…" Mitchell said in concentration. "There! Now Nevick just needs to break free."

Nevick watched as the cannon swiveled down to aim at Zouka's broad back. Clearly, if they were trying this, there was something about this weapon that he did not know. If the attack did not disable the general, then he would tear the airship apart looking for them. He was a savage creature bent on revenge, and Nevick hoped that his allies were not simply thinking with their hearts.

He had to trust his friends and the woman he loved. He needed to rely on their judgement. Whether the weapon was strong enough to upend Zouka or not, Nevick knew they would never fire it while he was still entrapped within the general's grip. He slammed his fists into the monster, trying desperately, once more, to loosen his titanic hold.

Zouka smiled as Nevick's weakening blows bounced harmlessly off his face. "Still some fight in you, eh?" he laughed, squeezing again, eliciting another pained shriek from his captive. Nevick rebounded, though, and continued to punch. "Can't you see how useless that is? I am mighty, and you are weak. That is the order of Terra!"

He squeezed Nevick and started to shake him back and forth, disorienting Casid's hero as he thrashed. Nevick continued to strike at Zouka with a determined flurry, blocking out the pain, blocking out the general's taunting voice, and soldiering on with mighty, hammering blows of his fists.

"You fight though you know you cannot win," Zouka said. "That is the most pitiful characteristic of you humans!"

Nevick's strength was waning. He needed to strike with everything he had. All his remaining energy. He needed to get away, or all was lost. He focused on the power within him, that power which had always answered his call. Zouka had called it mana, and Nevick's arms bulged with its power. It still would not be enough, though, and he thought back to last time his strength had failed him.

He remembered the intense heat of the flames, the silhouettes of monsters as they tore through flesh and stone. There were screams, there was blood everywhere, and Nevick could not stop it. Then, this very monster who so thrashed him now, had come, accosted the woman he loved, and finished the job. He remembered every face, every name, every special occasion his people celebrated. He had always greeted them with a smile, which they always genuinely returned.

He had been happy then. He had been content. His contentment led to weakness, and now, because he had chosen to smile so often, people were dead. It could never happen again. It *would* never happen again. The people of Casid were counting on him. He could feel them smiling at him now. Urging him to fight. It was in their names that his arms suddenly doubled in size, and his chest bulged as green energy lanced out over his veins.

Zouka had not even noticed. “You are weak! You are nothing! You are human and I am so much more! I am Zouka of the Gorram Tribe, and I…”

Nevick silenced the behemoth by smashing his fists together against his face with such force, the general’s grip loosened. Nevick vaulted back, creating distance.

A loud explosion resounded as Nevick’s boots touched the ground. He turned in the direction of the ship to see a ball of flaming mass soar through the air and slam into Zouka’s burly girth.

The resulting explosion tinted the area in green light and threw Nevick back from the blast’s epicenter. The general had not even the time to scream as the immense, unnatural hue engulfed him. The light was blinding, but once it subsided, Zouka lay in a smoldering crater, his form reverted to normalcy, unmoving save for the ragged rise and fall of his chest.

For a moment, Nevick thought about ending him. Simply picking up a rock and smashing him in the face with it until his chest stopped moving. But then, he recalled the faces of those he fought for. The men and women of Casid would have wanted better. They deserved better, and he wouldn’t murder a disabled opponent in cold blood, even out of vengeance.

Everything was quiet, save for the sound of battle from far off. The steady pounding of the rain cooled his flesh as he vomited blood onto the ground. The sound of footsteps drew his attention, as Michael and Mitchell crouched beside him, trying desperately to heave the big man up onto their shoulders. Nevick groaned and managed to rise with their aid, letting them carry the brunt of his weight back toward the ship.

As soon as they crossed the boundary into the cargo bay, Nevick pitched onto his knees and fell face-first to the floor. He could hear Deana’s chair racing toward him. One of the Duzels must have helped her from the seat, because soon she was beside him, hands alight with white healing energy. She placed a hand upon his back, filling his body with the warm rejuvenating glow.

“There’s a lot of internal damage,” she said softly, leaning down to kiss him gently on the head. “This is going to take some time, but I’ll have him up again soon.”

“V … Valentean,” he uttered, remembering the white and purple flashes of light.

“He can take care of himself, my love,” Deana cooed into his ear, her magic having a calming effect on him. “You’ll join him in a bit. But for now, just rest, and let me do my thing.”

His last thought before he slipped off to sleep was, *Hang in there, Valentean. I’ll be there soon.*

XXVIII: SERAPHINA'S STRENGTH

Seraphina arced her body out of the path of another of Sophie's red bursts of magical energy, fired wildly from the head of her staff. The two sorceresses flew through the air, unhindered by gravity's pull as the Pontifex pursued the princess in a desperate, mad dash for victory.

Seraphina had hardly fought back, wanting instead to embarrass Sophie before the masses. She needed her people to understand that they were not helpless in this struggle. There was a powerful voice that would answer their calls for help. They had to see their tormentor decimated before one infinitely her superior.

Sophie lashed out with another jolting red beam of destruction. Seraphina stopped and turned toward it, forming a circular shield of water which absorbed and dissipated the spell. Seraphina commanded that same water to slam into Sophie, smashing her once more into the unforgiving ground. Seraphina came to a gentle landing as the Pontifex struggled to her feet, leaning heavily on her staff for support.

"Your … evil … cannot win," Sophie panted, glaring at Seraphina.

"*My* evil? You corrupted the mind of a little girl. You manipulated and decimated an entire kingdom. You've killed and maimed and tortured innocents, solely because they do not follow your beliefs. And then you have the audacity to call me evil for trying to protect these people?"

"You're a fool," Sophie said. "We seek not to dominate, not to rule, but to strengthen this world! Chaos is the natural order of things. When a forest grows uncontrollably, a cleansing fire must destroy it so that it may live again, stronger and better than it was before. By coddling the weak, the world becomes weak. The goddess *embodies* this fundamental truth of reality. The goddess commands that the weak be culled from her world."

"This is not her world!"

"It always has been and always shall be!" Sophie unleashed another barrage of red energy, but Seraphina had been prepared. She took off into the sky, spinning out of the destructive light's path, continuing to draw Sophie's attacks toward her and away from the wounded rebels and citizens. There would be no reasoning with the Pontifex. She could not talk her way out of this conflict. She needed to get serious now before someone else was hurt.

Vahn watched the breathtaking encounter with wide-eyed fascination. He had seen magic many times before, but never to this degree, never with the mastery that was being displayed through the red sky of Aleksandrya. He had known Seraphina since the day she had been born. "The Princess Without Magic" she had been dubbed. Vahn felt a swell of pride rise within him, as though she were his own daughter.

He lay on his side, propping his body up with one arm. Sophie's assault had taken a toll on him. His arms and chest were covered in a multitude of burns and scrapes, and something within his left knee had popped. Still, he was one of the lucky ones.

Before Seraphina had stepped into the fray, Sophie had brutalized them. Many insurgents laid with missing limbs, others writhed in agony. Tiberius was very still on the ground, and Vahn crawled toward his friend.

When he arrived at the side of his former apprentice, he saw that Tiberius was wounded but not fatally so. Vahn's former apprentice watched the spectacle of sorcery unfolding above them in bewildered fascination that enraptured his face.

"The ice queen…" Tiberius whispered, giving voice to his astonishment.

"Indeed," Vahn said, patting his friend and ally on the shoulder. "I believe she is."

Seraphina dodged the bolts of super-heated hatred that Sophie hurled at her. She had settled into a routine of rising, falling, and darting about the crimson-colored sky, easily avoiding the dazzling, blood-colored bursts. Sophie was becoming enraged, now screaming in frustration as the power of her goddess repeatedly failed.

"Stand down, Sophie!" Seraphina called out to the Pontifex, "you cannot win!"

"The goddess lights our way in the dark!" she called out, her voice haggard and worn with mania. "Her blaze shall ignite the land, air, and sea! Her burning love shall cover the planet and give birth to the glory of humanity."

She unleashed a series of six magical bursts that erupted simultaneously from her staff, spinning through the air at Seraphina. The princess avoided all that she could but one managed to get through her defenses and struck her stomach, knocking her to the ground.

Sophie cried out in triumph, hovering in the air above Seraphina as she shot magical blast after blast to engulf the princess. The destructive spells slammed into Seraphina, exploding against her body, kicking up bursts of fire and clouds of smoke as the unrelenting assault continued.

Vahn could hear cries of sorrow all around him as the people of Kackritta watched their princess, their savior, their ice queen, buried beneath an avalanche of fiery magic. Sophie continued, screaming in furious victory with every bright bolt that careened out from the head of her staff.

Vahn watched helplessly as the daughter of his best friend was mercilessly beaten down, likely dying, within the horrid mess of flame-red energy and smoke. They had come so close, and yet The Faithful were still going to win this day. The sadness that struck his heart was more than the simple loyalty a warrior felt for his monarch. This was the daughter of his best friend and true brother. This was the woman his son had sworn his life to protecting. She meant so much to the people he loved, and he could do nothing to stop her destruction, frozen in place by injuries and uselessness. He cursed and looked away, still feeling the unrelenting heat of the magical inferno upon his skin.

Finally, whether it was from exhaustion or because she believed her point had been made, Sophie cut off her attack. She panted, the red light of her staff flickering weakly as she slowly wafted to the ground, smiling in triumph. Seraphina's body was still hidden by rising plumes of red smoke. Sophie turned back to them.

"Now do you see?" she raved, spreading her arms out and throwing her head to the sky. "The power of the goddess cannot be overthrown by the forces of evil. She will always prevail! See, now, the broken body of your Ice Queen!" Sophie swept a hand toward the smoke, summoning magic which waved it all away.

Vahn prepared himself mentally for the horrific sight of Seraphina's burned and broken body, but as the smoke cleared, he gasped in shock.

Seraphina stood, completely unscathed, bolts of blue electricity still crackling across her body. There was a collective buzz of excitement among the wounded onlookers as their ice queen remained triumphant.

The Pontifex screamed in fury and took a step backward.

Seraphina had surprised even herself with this newfound resilience. As she had fallen to the ground, she felt the dread that often came with such catastrophe. But as the magic fell upon her, pushing her into the street, she had been shocked to discover that there was no pain, no heat, no damage being taken. Each bolt of Sophie's magic sent a tingling tickle through her body, nothing more.

The Pontifex stared at her with a mixture of outrage and terror. Seraphina looked back at her, void of emotion. She simply allowed the moment to settle over Sophie and hoped she would see the error of her ways.

"No..." she said, taking another step back. "This can't be ... I am the chosen Pontifex of The Faithful ... I serve the one true goddess! I cannot be beaten by your blasphemous magic!"

"You *are* beaten Sophie," Seraphina said. "Surrender now and you will survive this to stand trial as Kackrittan tradition demands."

"Kackritta is dead!" Sophie screeched with the unraveling madness of shattered belief. She leveled her staff at Seraphina once more and shot a bolt of red energy. Seraphina made no move to dodge it. She simply walked forward slowly, allowing the weak magic to explode against her body as she stalked, unphased, through its destruction. Sophie snarled and fired once more. Again, Seraphina walked through, blue eyes narrowed as she drew closer to the backpedaling Pontifex.

Sophie fired, tears of frustration and disbelief cascading down her grime-caked cheeks as Seraphina came closer and closer. The Pontifex's strongest attacks could not even break her gait. When the princess was but a few paces away, she swept her hand to the side, forcibly tearing the staff from Sophie's grip. It clattered to the ground and the Pontifex watched it roll away with the sad, pathetic eyes of one who had lost all hope.

Seraphina reared back one arm and thrust it forward, sending a wave of water smashing into the Pontifex and knocking her to the ground. Another sweep of her hand called another stream of liquid which batted Sophie aside and sent her crashing into the base of her execution stage.

"Submit!" Seraphina commanded. Despite all the wrong that this woman had inflicted, the princess did not wish to end her life. There was no need to kill someone who was so fully beaten. In Seraphina's mind, there was a difference between taking a life to save another, and murder. Seraphina Kackritta was not a murderer.

"Never!" Sophie screamed, charging at Seraphina with her fists drawn. The princess held up a hand which summoned a spell that tossed the Pontifex down into the dirt. She used that same power to pull Sophie into the air.

"You have caused so much pain, so much suffering," Seraphina said sadly, as the Pontifex's legs kicked uselessly. "You corrupted my sister, filled her head with this fanatical nonsense and brought about the fall of a kingdom that has stood for one thousand years. My parents are dead because of the actions you set in motion. I should crush the life out of you for what you've done, but I will offer you mercy if you only surrender."

Sophie spat at Seraphina, the droplet of saliva and mucus hitting the ground between them. Seraphina grimaced and slammed Sophie face first into the road, then lifted her once more and, with a gesture, flung her toward the people she had wounded. The Pontifex rose to her hands and knees, staring at them through bruised and bloodied eyes

"Look at the faces of those you've hurt," Seraphina continued. "Look at what your fanatical cruelty has brought before these people! Beg their forgiveness, Sophie! Please, I know there must be a good person somewhere within your heart! Please, Sophie, submit!"

The Pontifex looked out over the people she had thrashed. There was a moment of silence that settled over the city square. Sophie took a long drawn out intake of breath, looked her victims in the eye and … smiled.

"As it shall burn!" she screamed, holding out an arm and summoning her staff to her once more. She pointed it directly at Vahn. The staff's head sparked and glowed to usher in the final spell she would call upon to finish the job she had started on these people. Seraphina panicked. There was no time to get between them and intercept the blast. That left only one option.

Seraphina pointed at Sophie's back with two fingers, summoning a thick, singular bolt of blue lightning that struck the Pontifex between the shoulder blades. The glow of her staff faded and Pontifex Sophie fell forward, dead.

Aleksandra sat still upon the skeletal throne as she had been for hours, lost in meditation, gathering the magic of the fortress to aid in her true body's escape within the Northern Magic. With alarming suddenness, a great sensation of loss ripped through her chest, as though a piece of her had been forcibly torn away. She screamed and opened her eyes, tears already spilling out over her face. She instantly knew what had happened.

Sophie ... she thought with alarming clarity. What had happened? How was this possible? With a snarl of rage and heartache, the empress leapt from her throne, disconnecting from the captive magic it contained. The mighty monarch sped toward the balcony, a black and red blur as she leapt down, encased in a crackling aura of crimson power toward the city's central hub.

A crushing sense of profound sadness struck Seraphina's heavy heart. She had not wanted it to come to this, but Sophie's single-minded fanaticism had been the true cause of her downfall. She shook her head and turned to her people who looked at her as though she were an embattled savior. The Princess Without Magic was no more.

As she opened her mouth to address those she rescued, a shrill scream erupted throughout the city with such force that it shook the ground beneath them. Seraphina ventured a guess as to the cause of it. With a feeling of dread reverberating through her, the princess sent an arcing dome of ice over the wounded people of Kackritta, covering them with its protective blue shielding.

As the spell solidified, a sparking beam of crimson rocketed down toward her, striking the street with the heaviness of panic. Aleksandra stood there as Seraphina had never seen her before. She was rattled, terrified, and filled with sorrow. Without so much as a glance toward her sister, Aleksandra fell to her knees beside Sophie's body, cradling it in her arms, rocking gently back and forth.

Seraphina was astounded to see the glistening streaks of tears falling along her sister's cheeks, and the sound of mournful sobs echoing from her throat.

"Please no..." Aleksandra wept bitterly. "Please, Sophie, no..." Seraphina took a step back in alarm. Even before the true extent of Aleksandra's mania had been made evident, she had never shown this manner of emotion, either privately or in public. "Please don't leave me ... Don't leave me ... mother."

Despite everything that had transpired between them, despite all Aleksandra had set in motion, all she had taken in her holy mission, Seraphina's heart still broke for her. Sophie had been more than a handmaiden, more than a nanny or servant. Sophie had been the maternal presence in Aleksandra's life, providing her with the love and attention their mother never seemed to have time for. Seraphina found tears stinging her eyes, as she watched Aleksandra mourn.

"Aleksandra," she said, causing the empress's head to snap toward her, eyes fully aglow with crimson energy, her tears sizzling on her cheeks.

"You?" Aleksandra asked, teeth bared, eyes narrowing as she laid Sophie down and rose to her feet.

Seraphina held up a hand as if to halt her sister's train of thought. "Aleksandra, she left me no choice."

"*You...* " she repeated with scarcely contained rage. Her face twisted, lips pulled back to expose a feral expression of utter hatred.

"Aleksandra..."

"*You die!*" she screeched, firing crimson bolts of lightning from her outstretched fingers.

XXIX: BROTHERS AND SISTERS

The Skirlack were rounding on Maura, pushing her back, attacking together. Her superior speed had been keeping her alive thus far, but it seemed as if each time a demon fell, Aurax summoned two more to take its place. She smacked into the floor's steel grating and looked through it to the ground below as the steady downpour abated into a drizzle. Maura quickly rolled to the side as a Skirlack demon attempted to slam its heavy foot down upon her. She slashed a gash across its chest, enough to wound but not to kill.

Another shudder rocked the entire platform as the cannon seemed to come to life around them. Nahzarro was doing it. Several creatures moved to intercept the prince, who had erected a blue shield around the console where he worked. They pounded upon the azure light, and Maura saw it flicker and weaken. They were being overwhelmed. This mission was about to fail, and then there would be no hope for Seraphina and the people of Kackritta.

Maura screamed in rage and charged at the creatures. In her zeal, she felt a familiar sensation: an eruption of green energy along her fists. In her emotional state, she had once again managed to pull the mana energy from her body, but this time, her Grassani daggers reacted and the green glow was channeled into the blades. She slashed along the back of the nearest Skirlack. There was an explosion and a shower of sparks as it fell dead at her feet, with a smoldering cauterized slash charring its skin. She turned to the next demon, and the next, lashing out with explosive cuts from her empowered weapons.

Aurax seemed to be straining as he summoned another four Skirlack onto the platform, motioning for them to attack as he stumbled. Was his power limited? It seemed as though the act of replacing the dead soldiers sapped the strength from the demonic specter. That was welcomed news.

"It's done!" Nahzarro yelled triumphantly from behind her as more Skirlack advanced on them. Maura breathed a sigh of relief. "I just have to feed it energy now!" Maura looked back and saw him stick both arms up to the elbow into two oval-shaped recesses in the console. A hazy green glow began to emanate around Nahzarro's body.

"Make it fast!" Maura spat.

A shuddering roar echoed through the city, and she knew the battle between Valentean and Kayden had taken a turn for the worse. She tried to tell herself that Valentean would be all right. He always found a way out of these messes. If anyone could stand against that monster, it would be him. Maura gritted her teeth and ran forward, sparking blades ablaze.

The black dragon spread its wings and lunged toward Valentean. Summoning the wind, he leaped into the air, flying up and away as Kayden's bulk slammed into the ground where he had stood just a fraction of a second earlier. He felt the displaced air kicked up from Kayden's massive jaws snapping shut just behind him.

Valentean dove further down, weaving around buildings, hoping to slow Kayden's advance by forcing him to maneuver. Instead, the black dragon bludgeoned its way through anything in its path, felling buildings with crashing finality. He attempted to throw Kayden off course with bursts of wind, but that too, seemed to do little more than irritate the ebony goliath.

Kayden let a burst of purple energy fly from his mouth, and Valentean dove to the side to avoid it. The sizzling energy stream passed so close, it left a red burn along his right side. Valentean landed on a nearby roof, rolled to his feet, and took off into the air as Kayden smashed onto it, crushing the building. He was so powerful, so aware of every movement Valentean made, and so terrifyingly fast.

As he fled through the air once more, Valentean realized with a shuddering moment of clarity that there was only one way to defeat this monster. He had to become a monster himself. The white dragon was his only hope. If he could somehow break through this mental block which kept him anchored in human form, then perhaps he would stand a chance. Still, though, no matter how he focused on the change, no matter how he begged the dragon to come forth, nothing happened.

How could he willingly take the form of a beast that had nearly killed Seraphina? How could he give himself over to that single-minded need for destruction? As he barely dodged another blast from Kayden's mouth, Valentean realized that he was making a mistake. The same mistake he had been making all this time. He thought of the dragon as a separate entity, a monster that took over his mind and body.

There is no dragon, the Rosintai had said. *There is only you.* When he had transformed once before, he allowed the base desires of the beast to take hold. But those desires for carnage came not from the twisted mind of some legendary Rosinanti monster, but from his own addled brain and heart. The dragon had not attacked Seraphina; Valentean had. It was a sobering thought, one that would haunt him for years to come, but still, this knowledge had unlocked something within his mind. Valentean suddenly felt very confident in his ability to keep himself under control.

Still though, he needed to concentrate for several seconds to trigger the change, and Kayden was not giving him any time. There was nowhere he could run or hide where his brother's hyper-sensitive dragon vision could not find him.

That's it! Valentean thought, realizing he had one trick still up his sleeve. Kayden's eyes were so sharp, taking in every detail, every shadow, every light. Valentean remembered it from his own transformation. A sudden flash of light could overwhelm Kayden's eyes and he could be temporarily blinded. All of this was, of course, pure theory and speculation. The time it would take for him to enact such a plan would allow the dragon to catch up to him, should it fail.

He gathered mana energy in both fists and turned, watching Kayden's monstrous face loom closer and closer. He closed his eyes and punched his two fists together above his head, causing a bright green explosion that burned his knuckles and neck. The dragon recoiled in pain as its purple retinas were scorched by the luminous flash. Valentean smiled and dropped to the ground as Kayden plummeted with a resounding slam that shook the street.

Valentean focused on the power that slept within him. There was no dragon. There was no monster that could take over his mind and heart. There was only his mind and heart left to guide this power.

"There is no dragon," he whispered, "only me." He felt the power welling up inside his chest. It was warm, inviting, and voluntary.

"There is no dragon," he repeated, a bit more forcefully this time, "only me." The power filled him, feeling so incredibly different from last time. Whereas in the Northern Magic, the power of the dragon had overtaken him, surprised him with its fury, this time Valentean kept it in check. He squeezed it out little by little. The light in his eyes shone brighter than before, and white bolts of electricity coursed across the ground and up the sides of dilapidated buildings. The power built to an incredible crescendo within his heart. He controlled the power. It bent to his will, and now, it was time to unleash.

White light exploded out of him, this time larger than ever before. The change was upon him, and he felt alive with tingling energy. His body grew and elongated, melting and reforming itself like clay. There was confidence, superiority, pride, and joy all mixing together as finally, Valentean Burai was complete.

Spreading his new wings, the light burst around him. Kayden looked up, and Valentean could tell his vision had returned. He drank in every centimeter of the black dragon, and it suddenly did not seem like such a terrifying creature. It was his equal. With his mental state under control, Valentean rippled the muscles of his new body. He opened his mouth and issued a bellowing roar of challenge.

Kayden snarled before returning the roar with a fury that Valentean could feel within every molecule of his being. The dragons spread their massive wings and leapt at one another, entangling in a mashing mess of teeth, tail, claw, and wing.

Their true battle had begun.

Seraphina held out her arms, trying with all of her might to turn away Aleksandra's dazzling bright bolts of crimson vengeance. For a moment, it seemed to be working. The lightning bent away from her outstretched hands, striking stone and buildings, while cracking the ice dome in which the rebels cowered.

Through the electric storm, she could make out the red pinpricks of Aleksandra's eyes, glaring at her in hatred. It was a stare void of the love and compassion her sister had always reserved for her.

The strength of the spell pressed heavily on her defenses. Aleksandra doubled its strength, and Seraphina had no choice but to break off and leap into the air.

"You cannot run from me, sister!" Aleksandra screamed, pointing two fingers at her. A thick powerful bolt of red lightning erupted from her fingertips, and Seraphina responded by firing off a blue bolt of her own. The two spells met and crackled against one another, pushing back and forth in a desperate bid for supremacy. Seraphina's magic began to press back that of her sister.

"What?" Aleksandra screamed.

The princess felt a thrill in the moment but reminded herself that Aleksandra was hobbled. This was not her true body and only a fraction of the power she commanded. She let the shudder that wanted to come over her evaporate as she kept her mind free and clear of such distractions, and doubled down.

Aleksandra cried out in her fury. Her spell leapt up with revised strength, cutting through Seraphina's lightning and blasting her out of the sky.

The princess hit the street hard and instantly sent forth a burst of water to intercept the monumental fireball bowling towards her. Fluid met flame and canceled one another out with a hiss of steam.

Seraphina climbed back to her feet as Aleksandra sped through the fog and hurled another fiery projectile at her. Seraphina flew up into the air to avoid it, simultaneously lashing out with another burst of water. Aleksandra leapt after her, a series of fireballs rotating around her body. She hurled them toward her sister, one at a time.

Seraphina took off, flying over buildings and down through alleyways to avoid the flaming orbs of Aleksandra's hate. All the while, she pulled water from the air which revolved around her in twin circles. She occasionally sent bursts of liquid at her sister, either to knock her off course or to block an oncoming fireball. No matter where Seraphina flew, or what route she embarked upon, Aleksandra was right at her heels, throwing spell after spell in an attempt to bring her down.

Much of the city's remaining buildings were caught in the crossfire. Seraphina tried her best to douse the flaming structures in water, but she could only divert her attention away from her enraged sister for so long before she came charging in once more. Soon, Aleksandra's assault became so heavy that Seraphina could no longer counterattack, instead opting to put all her energy toward avoidance and deflection. Eventually, one of Aleksandra's fireballs found its mark and singed Seraphina along her left side. As she recoiled, the empress let fly with another thick bolt of red lightning, which blasted Seraphina down. She crashed at the base of the giant statue of Sorceress Bakamaya which stood at the entrance to the city.

Aleksandra landed gently in front of her, fingers crackling with lightning. Seraphina searched desperately for something, anything that might prove her sister was still somehow the same person who, despite horrific actions, had loved and cared for her all her life. Within the smoking blood-colored orbs of Aleksandra's eyes, though, there smoldered only hatred.

"Sister," Seraphina said, coughing as she clutched her wounded burnt side.

"Do not call me that," Aleksandra said, rage and hate dripping from her tone. "After all I've done to protect you. After all the times that I stood there for you, this is how you repay me? You take from me the one person who ever truly loved me?"

"Aleksandra, please, you have to stop this! Look what you've done to our home! To our family!"

"Our home is stronger and more secure than it has ever been under the infantile leadership of our late mother. As for our family … well, we both know that never truly existed. I had allowed myself to believe that you and I shared a bond of sisterly love, but now I see you as you truly are, for what you truly are! You have proven today that I mean nothing to you!"

"That is not true! You're trying to destroy the entire world! You have to be stopped!"

"Silence!" Aleksandra shrieked. Her voice echoed throughout the trapped kingdom.

Seraphina lashed out with a ball of ice, trying to smash it into her sister's face, but Aleksandra caught it in one hand and shattered it. She sped forward, grabbed Seraphina by the throat and lifted her high overhead.

The princess struggled and kicked her legs. She tried desperately to call upon the magic of order but she was panicked, terrified, and the power would not respond to her commands.

Aleksandra slowly began to fly, bringing her face in close, until her eyes cast a red haze along Seraphina's face. "Now you shall die, *Harbinger*."

Wherever dragon met dragon, there was a flash of light and a shuddering pulse of energy. These twin gods hammered at one another, their epic struggle upending entire blocks of the ruined city in which they battled. Valentean was making a concentrated effort to keep Kayden confined to the far end of Kahntran, corralling him far from the cannon, where his friends worked to do their part.

As the titanic lizards rolled together in the destruction, scraping and biting at one another, Kayden managed to kick Valentean off and leapt into the sky, climbing higher with great beats of his leathery wings. Once Valentean found his orientation, he followed suit, taking off after Kayden who had a considerable head start. Valentean unleashed white bursts of energy from his mouth, but Kayden avoided them with ease.

It was astounding how easy and fluid his brother's movements were in this form. Valentean quickly realized just how much time Kayden must spend as a dragon. Whereas Valentean was clumsy, carrying all this extra girth, Kayden moved with the grace of a creature accustomed to such size and power.

As Kayden continued to climb, Valentean racked his brain trying to discern what he was doing. Then, suddenly, Kayden shifted his course and dove at him, teeth and claws bared as he smashed into Valentean. A spray of blood erupted from alabaster flesh as Kayden sank his claws into Valentean's belly and his teeth into his brother's neck. The white dragon roared in pain as the two titans plummeted back toward the ground.

They landed in a deafening explosion of power and bestial noises. Valentean could feel the steady berth of blood oozing from various puncture wounds. Kayden's teeth had only bitten down harder as they fell, and Valentean's sharp vision was beginning to blur from blood loss. Unless he did something fast, he was done for.

Aurax struggled to call another three of his soldiers through the dimensional tear. This human female had become too much of an annoyance, and he could tell by the confident smile she flashed in his direction that she had figured out his weakness. The strain of pulling so many soldiers through the veil that separated Terra from Lokhar was taxing, and he felt himself fading from existence.

He could sense the cannon gathering energy. It would not be much longer now. The fool Rosinanti had engaged the Shogai and was so engrossed in battle that he did not understand the very serious situation unfolding here. As the one called Maura carved through yet another of his soldiers, Aurax struggled one final time. Five more Skirlack stepped through the veil before Aurax pitched forward, his body evaporating in a red haze.

They would need reinforcements.

Aleksandra hurled Seraphina down onto a nearby roof. As her limp body smacked into the hard shingles, the empress raised one hand, gripping the princess on all sides with a crushing, invisible force and pulled her back up. Seraphina hovered just below her sister, eyes pleading through the blue tint of the magical shield which had saved her life just seconds before.

With another swipe of her hand, Aleksandra sent her careening down, cracking the stone wall of a building with her body, before falling to the ground several stories below. The chaotic monarch landed with a remorseless sneer, slowly advancing upon Seraphina as though she were wounded prey.

The princess breathed through harsh, pained gasps and attempted to call upon the order once again, but fear blocked the flow of power. She was nothing once more in the face of her sister.

The enraged empress extended her hand, palm out, calling upon a spell which dragged Seraphina through the air until her throat came to rest once more in Aleksandra's palm.

They slowly floated up again, Aleksandra effortlessly holding the princess before her with one arm. "This is not the end yet, Seraphina. Your punishment shall extend long after your death. Once you are dealt with, I will crack open that ice egg of yours and personally rip the neck out from every single one of your followers. Then, I will hang your body from my new fortress so that all might see the price that is to be paid for defying the will of the goddess.

"Then, I'm going to personally hunt Valentean down. I'm going to torture him slowly until he begs me to kill him, until he literally *begs* me to end the world you're both fighting so hard to defend. Then, and only then, will I split him open at the throat, tear the head off his shoulders, and hang it around the neck of your rotting corpse!" She threw Seraphina down toward the city's hub, and she impacted the ground next to the icy dome.

Aleksandra's words reverberated through Seraphina's mind. To think that her sister could say such things would have at one time been completely unfathomable. But here was the new reality. She would die here, alone and afraid. Then the rebels and Vahn would die. And then Val … her dear poor

Val … Thinking of the man she loved suffering such a heinous fate burned her far worse than Aleksandra's magic had.

She couldn't give up. To die here meant so much more than simply her death. It meant the death of the ideals she stood for. The death of the people she valued. The death of her home. The death of the man whom she loved with everything that she was. There would be no giving up.

She glared at Aleksandra as she formed a gargantuan fireball over her head with which to deliver the final blow. She had to let go of her fear. She had to recall her training. Aleksandra was the human embodiment of her dread, of her anger. She was the tether that held her to the flames of chaos. "You do not rule me…" Seraphina said, imagining her father's kind bearded face as he sat at her bedside, so long ago. "I rule you!" She began to let go, feeling the fear wash from her mind, stoic and steadfast in the face of Aleksandra's threats as she crawled to her knees.

"You do not rule me…" she repeated once more, making it up to her shaking legs, the glow of blue returning to her eyes. She thought of Valentean, broken, tortured and begging for death. She let this vision settle in her mind and used it to push her fear aside. The only way to protect the man she loved was to not be afraid. "I rule you!" The wind blew around her and a blue glow began to envelop her body.

"I am Seraphina Kackritta," she said up to the heavens and to the fiery, dark inferno that was her sister. The force of her power amplified her voice. "I am the crowned princess of the Kingdom of Kackritta and the Terran Spirit of Order. Chaos does not rule me, Aleksandra! You do not rule me! I rule you!"

Blue bolts of electricity jolted from her body along the ground. Soon, her azure light blotted out the entire surrounding area. Aleksandra let the giant fireball fly, but as it touched the borders of Seraphina's glow, it evaporated like a snuffed candle. An odd tingling spread throughout Seraphina's body, but she did not fight it. She embraced it with a clear and open mind, and the change occurred instantaneously.

As the glare subsided, what had once been a human princess now stood tall and proud as a massive blue dragon. The azure scales that covered her from tip to tail shone more like those of a fish than that of a reptile, and her long, thin tail ended in a fin. She stood on four webbed feet and, from the side of her head, two spiked fins moved out and in like gills.

She was power personified, mightier than she had ever dreamed possible. The blue and purple wings that spread to either side of her body stretched for the first time, and her glowing sapphire eyes locked onto Aleksandra's puny form, floating dumbfounded in the air.

Seraphina flexed her powerful leg muscles and leapt into the sky. Aleksandra attempted to stop her with several fire streams, but Seraphina's dragon body exploded through them as easily as she had Sophie's earlier attacks. Reaching Aleksandra, Seraphina drew back her great head and slammed the mighty empress with the side of her face, sending her temporary shell of a body smashing to the street. The empress erupted to her feet.

"No!" Aleksandra screamed, unleashing fireballs and lightning and anything she could muster at the blue dragon, but everything dissipated or bounced harmlessly off her cerulean scales. "No, I cannot be stopped! You are nothing, Seraphina! Even in this weakened form, you pose no threat to me!" Seraphina began to gather energy at the back of her throat as Aleksandra's magic continued to ineffectually fizzle against her flesh. "You cannot do this! You cannot win!"

Seraphina let a monumental beam of blue energy fly from her mouth. It pounded into Aleksandra who screamed in defiant fury. The explosion lit the shielded city as though it were once more exposed to the light of day and sent reverberating cracks through the ice dome which housed the rebels.

As the glow subsided, Aleksandra knelt amidst a circle of devastation, her temporary body reduced to stone, save for the eyes, which still glowed with crimson fury. Seraphina watched with trepidation as the light slowly faded from those murderous orbs, and her sister disintegrated before her eyes.

Aleksandra felt the now familiar biting cold of the Northern Magic as she awoke in her dragon form, still frozen in place by blasphemous magic. This time, however, she could feel how weak the spell had become.

The loss of Sophie still stabbed at Aleksandra's heart and rage gave her the added strength needed to thrash heavily against the icy bonds which barely contained her. There was a groan, then a crack, and then a resounding smash as the red dragon erupted from her confines, roaring and spitting fire into the snow-streaked sky.

The force of her unbound power washed over Aleksandra, and finally, she felt complete. The dragon began to glow with red energy and quickly dwindled back down to the sorceress's human body. She was still adorned in the long black-hooded robe and gloves once used to hide her identity. To feel the full rush of the goddess's power flowing through her true veins once more made her feel indescribably mighty.

Now her sister would pay. Now she would return and swat that blue dragon like a fly. She turned to leave as a spattering red haze appeared before her. It shimmered in the snow until it formed Aurax, on his knees, his form translucent, as though he were barely tethered to this realm.

"Aurax?" she asked, gazing down at her loyal servant. "What has happened?"

The demon looked up at her in a desperate frenzy. "Kahntran … Mistress … Matters grow … out of our control … the … Shogai…"

"Valentean is there now?" Aleksandra asked, an eyebrow raised in curiosity.

"He engages … your animus … fully empowered…"

"What has happened to you?" she asked, her face not showing a hint of the concern she truly felt. Aurax had always demonstrated fierce loyalty to her. He had been the one, so many years ago, to infuse her with the spark of the goddess's essence, thus beginning her true journey. She could not lose him as well.

"I was forced to … pull too many of the Mother's children … through the veil … I will recover but … my connection to your realm … has been disrupted … momentarily."

"Gather your strength, my loyal one," she commanded. Closing her eyes, she sensed the powers of light and darkness clashing on a grand scale relatively nearby. Seraphina could wait, for now. "Leave this task to me."

Valentean was losing blood. It spurted out from around Kayden's teeth. He gathered power in his chest, firing off a burst of white light from his mouth that connected with Kayden's flank.

The black dragon was blasted away, but a large chunk had been torn out of Valentean's throat in the process. The white dragon stood on four shaking legs, trying to steady himself. Kayden rose, with a burning, scorched gash taken out of his right side.

Both dragons were weary and hurt. A challenge settled between them, each begging the other to engage in one last pass, in which only one of them would emerge triumphant. They leaped forward, claws and teeth bared, energy shining within their mouths. This was it, their final moment. They were going to finally see who was truly superior between them.

Just as the two behemoths were about to collide, a red streak descended like a falling star between them. The crimson bolt smashed into the ground, stirring a massive eruption that threw both dragons back and away from one another.

The blood-colored energy ripped through Valentean's scaly flesh, and he heard a sound, like glass breaking. Suddenly, he was human once more, and his frail, tiny body smacked into the devastation he and Kayden had wreaked throughout the city.

He coughed several times, completely disoriented from his forced reversion. He brought a shaking hand to his throat only to feel the wounds that had torn through his dragon flesh absent from his soft human skin.

He noticed Kayden, equally haggard and human directly across from him, with something dark crouched between them. As the figure began to stand and his mind began to clear, Valentean realized what must have interrupted their battle. The only force on Terra capable of such a feat. He hoped desperately that he was wrong.

Looking up slowly, his vision traced a long black robe all the way up to a tight ebony braid and burning red eyes that shone from a face of milky white flesh. He took a gasping intake of terror and nearly fell back as Aleksandra stood to her full height and glared at him.

He could tell that this was Aleksandra in her true form, free of the magic which had contained her. Suddenly, all of his hopes and dreams of a mission accomplished vanished. This was no longer about victory. It had become a game of survival, and the odds were outrageously stacked against him.

"Hello, Valentean," she said sweetly, as though they were passing one another in the halls of Kackritta Castle. "I do so hope I have not interrupted anything of importance between you boys."

XXX: THE RAGE OF FLAME

Kayden was absolutely aghast. Right at his moment of ultimate victory, Aleksandra had stepped in, denying him the trophy that was so rightfully his. How could she justify this egregious intrusion on what was to be his finest hour? How could she treat him with such horrific dismissal?

"Mistress," he spat, his voice shaking and weak. She was rejuvenated now. This was her true form. He had to choose his words carefully, "I had this battle under control." She ignored him, keeping her eyes trained on Valentean, as though Kayden were not even present. "Mistress Aleksandra, please!" He was silenced as a bolt of red lightning descended from the sky, striking him and transporting him away from the battlefield.

Valentean struggled to his feet, trying to remain stoic and calm, but his ragged breathing gave away the extent of his fear.

"Well," Aleksandra said, dusting off her hands in the wake of Kayden's forced departure, "now that that's taken care of, we can continue with the business at hand, shall we?"

"What might that be?" Valentean asked through clenched teeth.

"Your princess has taken something very dear to me, and now, I am going to return the favor." Valentean tensed and dropped into a ready stance. "I am not going to kill you yet, Valentean. I'm going to incapacitate you and return you home. I shall present to my goddess a united world, trembling in fear of the Rosinanti, bound together by faith. For that, I need you alive for now, but not in one piece."

Valentean ran forward, determined to catch her off guard and overwhelm her. She was so blindingly, maddeningly fast, though, and turned in a dark blur of movement, planting a solid kick to the center of his chest which sent the animus warrior soaring back. He struck the road with such intense force that he left a trail of upended stone where he landed. He stood again and charged, throwing a series of punches at her face and torso, but the empress bent her body away from each with such extreme ease, Valentean felt it was almost comical.

She responded with a flat palm-strike to the center of his chest, and Valentean's body shattered the wall of a nearby house. He stood amidst the damaged interior and leaped back out through the hole he had created, but Aleksandra was nowhere to be found. He scanned the city streets with a shaking gaze, but there was no sign of the all-powerful sorceress.

Valentean felt a displacement of air behind him, and he lashed out with his elbow. Aleksandra easily caught the oncoming limb and kicked his leg out, sending the Rosinanti to his knees.

He attempted to swing his head back into her stomach, but Aleksandra caught him by the hair and threw him into a crawling position. She gave one mighty kick to Valentean's torso, sending the spirit of light spinning up through the air. As his body reached her eye level, Aleksandra lashed out with a fireball that exploded against Valentean's chest and knocked him breathless to the ground, smoldering and smoking in a heap.

"Truly, Valentean, this laborious exertion you put yourself through is not necessary. Simply acquiesce and cease hostilities and this will all be over. Do not force me to degrade you further."

Valentean's eyes glowed a bright blue and he lashed out with the power of order, sending every bit of gathered rainwater on the ground rippling through the air at her. Aleksandra held up one hand, conjuring a shield of flames which cancelled out every last bit of Valentean's attack. Then she responded with a jolting blast of red lightning which threw him violently back across the street where he fell to the ground, body still sparking.

"I see my sister has shared her blasphemous abilities with you," Aleksandra said, slowly stalking toward him. "I find that offensive on every conceivable level."

The rage of Aleksandra's flames could be felt in every attack. Valentean's entire body ached with the echo of her fury. He needed to create some distance, perhaps try to transform into the white dragon once again and overtake her that way.

White light found his eyes and he attempted to take off into the air. His momentum was completely halted as the empress reached out and wrapped one hand around his ankle. She then swung him downward, smashing him face first into the street. She pulled up on his leg, yanking him back into the air before smacking him down once more. In panicked desperation, he called out to the power of his transformation. He tried once, twice, and finally on the third burst of energy, the light enveloped him.

The white dragon loomed large over the tiny sorceress, roaring down at her. Valentean unleashed a beam of destructive white light from his mouth, and Aleksandra stood her ground against it. She reared back with one arm and swatted it away as though it were nothing. Valentean heard the far-off sound of his energy exploding somewhere in the distance.

Aleksandra pointed two fingers at him. "As it shall burn," she said, and an explosive nova of flame engulfed him. The sound of shattering glass could once again be heard and Valentean's body deflated into the form of a human. This was an unreal nightmare. He had known she was powerful, but this was on a whole other level. She had defeated the dragon with absolutely no effort, and now he thrashed on the ground, burnt, bloody, and disoriented in the wake of his sudden change.

"I trust we understand one another now," Aleksandra said, haughty superiority emblazoned upon every immaculately enunciated syllable. She raised one arm into the air and a giant red representation of her hand surrounded Valentean, holding him in its grip as though he were but a toy. She squeezed her fist, and the hand of magic constricted around the animus warrior. Valentean screamed in agony as his bones creaked against the confines of those crimson fingers.

"It is within my power to snuff the life from you right now, you pitiful insect. I could usher in the return of the goddess here in this place. But it is with the truest extent of my restraint that I settle for simply shattering every bone in your weak, pathetic body!"

Valentean shrieked as she squeezed tighter, his ribs and arms cracking under the force of her pressure. His vision began to haze over. The sound of his screams became hollow, as though he were hearing them from underwater. Then, suddenly, the pressure vanished.

Aleksandra dropped her arms and turned to intercept an incoming shard of debris, three times her size. She raised one hand and the entire massive projectile burst into flames, crumbling to dust before it had so much as grazed her. Valentean looked up and saw Nevick, arms still following through from a mighty throw with which he had intended to crush the sorceress.

"Well, the warrior of Casid, is it?" Aleksandra said with an amused smile and a raised eyebrow. "Word of your impressive prowess has reached my throne room on more than one occasion, sir."

"I'm not here to impress you," Nevick spat back.

"You don't," she replied simply. "I was being gracious. It is an excellent quality in a ruler."

"You're not a ruler. You're a witch."

"I am the most profound leader this world has ever known. I am shaping an entire world to my whims. Perhaps if you had exerted more of your own will upon your people, your village might still be standing today."

Nevick roared in rage and charged at Aleksandra. Valentean winced in dread. She casually raised two fingers and a fiery explosion erupted from the ground beneath the big man. But an instant later, Nevick dove out from the flames, unscathed save for a few burns and launched into a furious, swiping onslaught against the empress.

Aleksandra placed both hands behind her back and bent her body easily from Nevick's path, toying with him in the same manner as she had Valentean only moments ago. Nevick's lumbering, powerful punches began to fall with increased intensity and speed, but still, the nimble sorceress could not be scratched. Finally, tiring of this game, Aleksandra ducked beneath a punch and buried a knee in Nevick's midsection. The big man was tossed up and back, where he landed on his side in a puddle of water.

He rose again and punched at her, but Aleksandra caught him at the fist with one hand and roughly bent his wrist back, causing Nevick to scream in pain. She lashed out with a high kick, striking the shoulder of his captured arm which dislocated with a sickening pop.

Nevick recoiled as Aleksandra released his arm and swept his legs out from under him. As he rose back to his knees, she appeared behind him, squeezing his wounded shoulder with such force, Valentean could see the muscles of Nevick's neck and arm bulging between her fingers. Nevick's screams urged Valentean to stand, shaking feeling back into his aching joints and limbs.

He charged at Aleksandra from behind, but the sorceress heard him coming. She released Nevick and struck Valentean with a hard fist across the face, continuing to move past him as he fell. Both Valentean and Nevick rose to their feet, and Aleksandra turned to face them, one arm neatly tucked behind her back, the other held on the defensive as red lightning crackled along her fingers.

"Well, gentlemen, shall you try again, together this time?"

Valentean looked over at Nevick as he cradled his arm. The two warriors made eye contact, and Valentean tilted his head, asking Nevick if he would be able to continue the fight. Nevick grunted in response and gave a hard yank to his dislocated arm, popping it back into place with naught more than a grunt of discomfort. He wound the wounded limb in a slow circle, moving feeling back into it, and nodded to Valentean.

"Let's do this," Valentean said.

"Right," Nevick replied.

Aleksandra stood perfectly still, save for the jolting miniature bolts of energy that crackled along her fingers. Valentean advanced first, with Nevick trailing behind. He attempted to strike the empress with a leaping roundhouse kick which Aleksandra ducked beneath just in time to bend her body away from one of Nevick's powerful arms as it hooked at her head. Valentean ran in once more, firing off a series of punches which were casually avoided or blocked by Aleksandra's left arm. He dove at her waist, attempting to tackle her, but she vaulted over his head with a twisting flip that took her into Nevick's path, back turned to the big man.

She ducked and spun as he punched down at her and bent back to avoid a wild elbow to the head. Aleksandra kept the same infuriatingly amused smile plastered upon her face throughout the encounter, so as there was no mistaking the fact that she was simply playing with the two warriors. She had kept her right arm locked behind her back for the entirety of the battle, sending a clear message as to the level of effort she was exerting.

Turning from Nevick, she nearly ran into Valentean's crackling fist, which she easily batted aside with one hand and kicked the animus warrior in the sternum. Valentean fell back, skidding through the pooled rainwater. Every casual smack from the sorceress fell with such incredible strength, he believed that a fully powered punch might separate his head from his shoulders.

Nevick charged in once more. Aleksandra ducked under his lunging arm and hit him with another knee to the abdomen, which sent the big man reeling backwards. As he fell, Aleksandra's long ebony braid came to life like a snake and reached out, elongating across the battlefield and wrapping around Nevick's neck. The chord of tightly wrapped hair yanked him toward Aleksandra, and she elbowed him in the face.

As Nevick fell, Valentean charged. Aleksandra's braid came disentangled from large warrior's throat and pointed threateningly at the oncoming Rosinanti. It swiped at Valentean several times, like a chain or whip. The animus warrior ducked and leaped out of its path. Then, Aleksandra ramped up the speed of her attacks, and Valentean found the black braid to be everywhere. He barely kept out of its path when the blade-shaped tip slashed down his face, cutting his cheek.

As a slow trickle of blood began to flow, Aleksandra smiled sweetly at him. "Come now, is that truly all the two of you are capable of?" she asked, spreading her arms out wide. "I expected more from the two most capable warriors on Terra."

Valentean fought to stave off a crushing feeling of hopeless depression at their inability to so much as touch the powerhouse sorceress. Frustration and fatigue were taking a toll. He was fighting with every bit of his Rosinanti power, and she was simply playing. It seemed as though she were drawing the fight out intentionally, goading them on as she tested her newly liberated body. Valentean wiped a splotch of blood from his lip and glanced at Nevick. The big man nodded to him, though Valentean could see the beginnings of desperation forming in the eyes of his ally.

They rushed at her from both sides, attacking together in a whirlwind of fists and feet. Both Valentean and Nevick threw everything they had at Aleksandra with as much speed as they could muster. But still, she managed to dodge every last blow. She maneuvered herself so as to place both warriors in one another's path. This forced them to retreat from each other several times before redoubling their attacks upon her.

It seemed as though Aleksandra had grown bored with the games. She very subtly shifted from defense to offense and chopped Nevick in the throat, causing him to fall back. She blocked a punch from Valentean with so much force he thought his arm might have shattered against hers. As he recoiled, she grabbed him by the shirt, lifting him effortlessly. Aleksandra punched him once in the face with enough strength to raze a stone wall and flung him at Nevick, who was nearly on his feet.

The big man caught his companion, but as he did so, Aleksandra pointed to the sky with two fingers, and the ground beneath them exploded in a fiery blaze. The detonation hurled both warriors into the air, shooting them off in separate directions. Aleksandra faded from view, moving so quickly around the battlefield, even Valentean's heightened senses had no way of tracking her.

She attacked them at such a breath-taking speed, Valentean never saw what hit him. Hammering blows fell upon his chest, legs, abdomen, face, neck, and back, all in such rapid succession that he hadn't even the time to fall. From the corner of his eye, he could see Nevick flailing with equal difficulty. She was pummeling them, and they were completely helpless.

Finally, the heinous torment wracking Valentean's body eased and he fell onto his back. Aleksandra stopped in front of Nevick and floated into the air. The empress grasped him around the throat and lifted him up. Aleksandra caught Nevick's arm as he attempted to strike her. With a smirk and a twist, she snapped the bones in his forearm. Shards of white splintered skeleton tore through flesh. Nevick screamed in agony as Aleksandra punched him down to the ground.

She floated back slowly, taking in the sight of their battlefield. "I sadly require Valentean's continued existence," she said, glaring at Nevick through burning red eyes. "You, on the other hand, are expendable."

She raised her fingers like claws. Valentean gasped, knowing what was to come next. She was through playing games. She was going to kill Nevick. The crimson lightning erupted from her fingertips, tearing through the air, ready to carve through the last warrior of Casid and end his life. Valentean moved without thought, leaping between Aleksandra and his friend, absorbing the bolts of her hate and letting the now familiar burning pain tear through him.

"No!" Nevick screamed, rising through the pain and running at Valentean. A stray lightning blast ricocheted off his convulsing body and struck Nevick in the chest, throwing him to the ground, dazed.

Valentean's insides were boiling as the arching rage of chaos forced him to his knees. "Fool!" Aleksandra said with a giggle, "did you truly think you could liberate your ally from my wrath simply by absorbing my magic in his stead?"

Valentean had felt the sting of her lightning many times. As a child, it was a sensation that ate him alive with fear. Even now, with all he had accomplished, all the training, all the personal growth, he was still susceptible to the very same spell which had incapacitated him so many years prior.

He thought of Seraphina, of the people of Kackritta, and realized with a mournful moment of clarity that he was letting them all down. Seraphina, his father, they would all be made to suffer at the hands of this demented lunatic unless he did something. Valentean clenched his teeth together and looked up through the electric storm at the face of his tormentor. Despite the agonizing, searing heat and intensity of the lightning, he planted his right foot on the ground and rose.

"What?" Aleksandra hissed in disbelief. She ramped up the energy, eliciting a scream from Valentean as he crumpled back to his knees. But once more, the kind eyes of his father flashed through his mind. He slowly stood, this time taking a shaking step towards the sorceress as the lightning blistered his skin.

"No!" she cried out, and more energy crackled along the destructive spell.

Valentean screamed in agony but caught himself as his knees began to buckle, glaring at her through sweat and blood. The light in his eyes intensified and bathed Aleksandra's rage contorted face. He took another step, and another, imagining the good people of Kackritta who had smiled at him, accepted him, and now suffered under the lash of the Skirlack. He pictured a world on fire, engulfed by the flames of chaos, and onward he walked.

"Im … possible!" Aleksandra choked out, voice heavy with exertion. The intensity of her spell nearly doubled.

Valentean fell, screaming, to the ground, hands braced beneath him, holding him aloft as he continued to glare at his ultimate foe. *She will not win this*, he thought.

As the last Skirlack fell, Maura looked back at Nahzarro, still aglow with a jade-colored, magical haze. His posture was slouched and he leaned heavily upon the console. As Maura turned toward him, now free from the deafening noise of combat, she heard something else. An electric sizzle, like crackling lightning, and her stomach dropped. She ran to the side of the platform and looked down. There, she saw her worst fear realized.

Aleksandra was there, pouring that horrible red lightning of hers into Valentean, who seemed to be struggling valiantly within a whirling storm of chaos.

There had to be something she could do to help. A cry of exertion from the direction of the control console drew Maura's attention. The glow around

Nahzarro had faded and he staggered back. Maura rushed to him, catching his falling body beneath the arms and gently eased the Grassani prince to the ground.

"Are you all right?" she asked as the top hat tumbled from his head.

"It's … finished … the weapon … it's ready!"

Maura's eyes came alight with drive and hope. There was something she could do for Valentean. Exactly what he wanted. She could finish the mission. She looked back down at Nahzarro. "What's wrong with you?"

"Had to … put a lot of my energy into it … More than … I thought." He kept trying to rise from her arms, reaching a gloved hand toward the console's levers and knobs.

"Hold on, tough guy," Maura said, holding him down. "You've done enough, and you can barely stand. Let me handle this."

"Are you … kidding? You expect me to entrust something this delicate to a…"

"To a what?" she asked, looking at him sternly.

Nahzarro sighed and he nodded slowly. "You aim with the wheel on the … right and the large … lever to the left. I'll give you … the coordinates."

Maura smiled and laid him on the steel grating. She rose to her feet and stalked towards the controls. With shaking hands, she gripped the heavy wheel. The sound of sizzling magic could still be heard throughout the still night.

Hang on, Valentean, she thought.

The lightning was beginning to split his burning skin, with long gashes along his arms, legs, chest, and back. Valentean felt his scorched flesh beginning to ooze. Looking down, he saw the blackening skin on his exposed right arm. The pain was perhaps the most intense he had ever felt in his life. His body was ready to give in, to shut down, to die and let the torment simply end. But something deep within Valentean's essence, beyond his heart and even his soul, would not abide surrender.

"He's the light I hold onto in my heart. He has the strength within himself to control that power and to not give in. I will never give up on him. I believe in him. He's … He's the love of my life."

Valentean recalled Seraphina's words from the dreamscape. She believed in him. She was counting on him. He breathed in the superheated air that surrounded his burning body, held that humid breath within his lungs, and pictured her face as she had looked in that moment. Her eyes had connected with his in trust and longing. He could not let her down. She needed him. She was trapped within that crimson bubble, working hard to oppose the Aleksandryan regime. That was all the motivation he would ever need.

Screaming in agony, Valentean slowly rose to his feet, eliciting a gasp of horror and frustration from Aleksandra. For a moment, he stood there as the powerful lightning tore through him, learning to bear its fury upon him without falling. He blotted out the pain, ignored the smell of his cooking flesh, and winced through the feeling of his cheeks and forehead beginning to blister.

He raised one foot slowly, deliberately, with utmost care, and slammed it down in front of him. Placing all of his weight upon that leg, he swung his other foot forward, repeating the process one step after another.

"Just one more step, Valentean," he said through cracked, oozing lips. "Just one more."

Each plodding stomp forward was his fixation, and after each one, he urged himself on. "Just one more." Time and time again, he stepped forward. No matter how much power Aleksandra pushed into her furious onslaught, he continued on.

Valentean held his hands up as he approached the empress, now less than a meter between them. Every smoking centimeter of space sizzled with the furious lightning storm.

"This can't ... be!" Aleksandra screamed, sounding like a spoiled, petulant brat being denied something she desired for the first time in her life. "You ... can't ... match ... me!" Her final blast nearly succeeded in sending him tumbling backward. The pain was so incredibly severe, but the sorceress was within striking distance at last. Valentean felt too weak to throw a punch, too taxed to call upon the wind or mana, so he did the only thing he could do. He grabbed Aleksandra by the sides of her head with both hands, and every arching bolt of lightning that conducted through him rounded out the circuit by passing back into her.

Aleksandra threw her head back and did something that shook Valentean to his core. She screamed. She cried out in pain as the scorching, burning rage of her own hate rebounded into her body. She did not break off the attack, seemingly obsessed with the idea of stopping Valentean, of proving her superiority. And so, she suffered by her own hand, crying out in agony like any other human being.

Valentean's robes burst into flames which chewed at his flesh as his insides cooked. The fire engulfed him, burning through fabric and leather and skin and muscle. The hair on his head seared away as his flesh blackened and charred, like the burnt-out husk of a used campfire. The flames spread onto Aleksandra and the mistress of all fire cried out as the rage of the flames discriminated not one iota between them. They screamed together. They thrashed together. They burned together.

Through the hazy murk of agony, their eyes met. White and red collided in a mixture of wild light, their hatred burning hotter than the lightning and fire which engulfed them.

"You will burn!" Aleksandra screamed desperately at him.

"And you will burn with me!" he spat back in her face. In that instant, he felt something pass between them. Some deep, prickling, oozing sensation that spread up his arms and through his chest. Aleksandra gritted her teeth, clearly feeling the same pain, and looked into his eyes. Her gasp of terrified astonishment overpowered the aching bite of the flames.

Just then, from the direction of the cannon, a bursting blast of green magic erupted from the weapon's nozzle, sailing off across the horizon and cutting a swath on its path toward Aleksandrya. The empress gasped again as she turned her pained expression to stare at the burst of mystical might, watching helplessly as it soared toward her home.

Valentean smiled, content that their mission had succeeded. Now, he just needed to survive this.

There was a sudden explosion between the two of them, which threw Valentean's charred, bald husk of a body onto the street. Aleksandra smashed back through a crumbling building, hidden from view. The evening air felt like the biting winds of the Northern Magic against his cooked flesh, and Valentean crumbled, his eyes closing for what he feared would be the final time.

XXXI: HOPE

A profound sense of relief washed through Seraphina as she shed her dragon form, standing once more in the city's central hub as a human princess. The superior girth and power had felt strange to her, an unwelcomed necessity needed to attain victory. But she was herself again and breathed a sigh of gratitude for that. She still could not believe what had just transpired. She had defeated Aleksandra. She had transformed into a dragon. What had become of her life? Albeit, she had defeated a depowered clone of her sister while struggling to control the wild power of her new body, but still, it was an accomplishment she had never fathomed as a possibility.

She raised both hands parallel to the ground and dissolved the dome of cracking, melting ice which housed Vahn and the rebels. As the protective surface dissolved, her people looked upon her with a variety of emotions. There was joy, pride, but also hesitancy, fear, and uncertainty. Vahn stood at the head of the crowd, favoring one leg. He gave her a reassuring smile and nod, motioning to Seraphina, silently asking her to address her city.

Seraphina nodded as her limbs shook. She had never given a public address before, but now was the time. With Aleksandra elsewhere, her forces scrambled, and Sophie dead, Seraphina could address the whole of Aleksandrya uninterrupted. She ascended into the air, hovering below the red dome of energy which concealed the stars. As she spoke, the magic within her carried her words throughout all corners of the city.

"Good people of Kackritta." She tried to sound authoritative, but instead, only sounded like Seraphina, a normal girl. That, she decided, was not a bad thing. "I look upon what has become of our once fair and proud home, and it breaks my heart. You have been deceived. You have been taken captive in your own city. But I swear to you all that the subjugation of Kackritta ends here and now. My sister will return, more powerful than ever. She will reclaim this city and strike down upon us with renewed anger and vengeance. But please, my friends, I urge you to be strong! Hold onto your pride, hold onto the memory of Kackritta, because as long as our kingdom lives on in our hearts and minds, then it shall never die.

"This barrier will fall, and there will be a battle for your liberation. When the heroes of light emerge, do not fear them. Support them and embrace them. They fight for our way of life. You've been told that the Rosinanti are evil, and while it is true that the dragon that assaulted our city and butchered your friends and family did so with wickedness in his heart, know that it was Aleksandra herself who orchestrated the attack.

"Valentean Burai, Champion Animus of Terra, my animus warrior, is indeed a member of the Rosinanti race. But he is a force for good, a force that fights for us, even now, at the ends of the world. He is the Dragon-Lord, who will bring justice and freedom back to this land; and so will I!

"I have never desired to be a queen. I never thought that the responsibility of ruling a kingdom would fall on my shoulders. But I do not fear it. I do not shirk it. I will fight with every last burst of who I am to see what we have lost restored. I swear to you all, in the name of my parents, your queen and king, that I will never stop fighting for you. I will never stop fighting for the ideals that Kackrittan life has been based upon. And I will never stop fighting Aleksandra, the Faithful, and the Skirlack, because they seek nothing less than our annihilation.

"We are going to live on, we are going to persevere and survive! Together, we are going to bring order and light back to Terra. Together, we will bring Kackritta back from the dead and drive The Faithful from this world forever!"

A still silence settled over the kingdom. She needed to make some kind of statement. There needed to be a grand punctuation to her speech. She looked with contempt at the statue of Sorceress Bakamaya, which stood tall over the enclosed city.

This statue and this historical figure represented the lie which had sparked the blaze the Faithful used to burn the world. It would do. She pointed two fingers at the monument and fired a concentrated bolt of blue lightning at it. Her spell struck the mighty stone sorceress in the back, and the entire statue exploded in a flash of cerulean light. As it fell, a monumental surge of energy careened towards the city. Had Aleksandra returned so soon? Seraphina readied herself, trying to peer through the veil of crimson shielding, trying to ascertain what exactly was heading toward them. A deafening explosion shook the entirety of Aleksandrya.

There was a green flash along the red sky, a jade glare that forced an entire kingdom to look away. As it subsided, Seraphina gasped. She could see the sky. The perfect clear night sky, with the pinpoint lights of stars and an illuminated full moon all capped off by the glowing churning dance of magical energy that meandered through the heavens. It was a miracle. It was amazing. It was…

"Valentean…" she whispered, knowing that her animus warrior had somehow orchestrated the removal of Aleksandra's barrier. As she floated back down to the rebels, a small smile danced upon her face. The people gazed up in wide-eyed wonderment at a sight they had likely never expected to see again. Vahn looked upon her and smiled wide. He turned to his people.

"All hail the Ice Queen!" he screamed, his voice carrying throughout the square. His bellow echoed through the silent streets, until a tall dark man at his side raised his fist high.

"All hail the Ice Queen!" he cried out, mirroring Vahn.

The cry of allegiance began to spread, first among individual warriors, and then to large groups, until the entirety of the rebellion stood with one arm raised in deference and respect.

"All hail the Ice Queen! All hail the Ice Queen! All hail the Ice Queen!"

Seraphina smiled in the warmth of their acceptance. She had an army now, or at least the beginnings of one. She suspected the Faithful had spread throughout the city, indoctrinating many by playing on their long-held superstitious and fictitious view of history. But there were many, she hoped, that would rally to her cause. Many who would fight by her side.

A prickling heat pulled her from this moment of optimism and spread throughout her body. Sharp pain ripped through her chest. Seraphina stumbled, but caught herself, remaining upright. Tears found her eyes as she instantly knew what this sensation meant.

"Val..."

The sound of the cannon's blast had momentarily deafened Maura. She lay on the metal grated floor beside Nahzarro, the only noise she could hear was a steady, high-pitched whine. Eventually, sound trickled back into her brain and she began to stir.

"Are you all right?" she asked Nahzarro. The prince pushed himself onto his hands and knees, shaking his head back and forth in an apparent attempt to clear his mind.

"I'll be fine," he said, catching his breath and reaching over to help Maura to her feet.

"Do you think it worked?"

"There's no way it didn't."

A large explosion sounded from below them, and Maura rushed to the side of the platform, suddenly remembering Valentean's struggle against Aleksandra which had bought them the time needed to fire the cannon.

She saw him below, thrown back as Aleksandra flew off in another direction, smashing through the remnant of a building. From this height, she could just barely make out the tiny form of his body smacking into the road, where he lay, unmoving. She squinted through the darkness. Something did not seem right. What had happened?

"We have to get down there," she said to Nahzarro, suddenly remembering the destruction of the staircase on their way up.

The Grassani prince laid a hand on her shoulder. "Let me handle that," he said, wrapping one arm around her waist. He closed his eyes and muttered something unintelligible under his breath. The hazy green cloud of his magical aura flickered on and off four times before finally solidifying around his body. They lifted gently into the air and wafted toward the ground below.

As they approached the roadway, Maura saw a large man on his knees slumped over Valentean. She had no idea whether he was friend or foe, and mentally reminded herself to be prepared for anything. As the scene below her grew larger at their descent, she took in a sight that nearly stopped her heart. Valentean was unrecognizable. He lay there, a blackened, hairless, smoldering husk. Nahzarro gasped beside her as the full extent of the Rosinanti's injuries became plain to see.

As soon as their boots touched the ground, Maura pulled away from Nahzarro and sprinted to her friend's side.

"Valentean!" she screamed in mounting horror as she threw herself down beside the large man, grabbing her friend by the shoulders, desperate to see some semblance of life within him. There was nothing. The stench of his cooked flesh sickened her stomach. She tried to breathe through her mouth to avoid such morbidity, but it was such a powerful aroma that she could actually *taste* it.

"You must be Maura," the big man beside her said, cradling one arm against his broad chest.

"Who are you?" she snapped, hardly even glancing at him. She was afraid if Valentean left her sight for even an instant, he would die. *Protect him, Maura*, Seraphina had begged. Maura cursed her foolish weakness. Once more, it had been Valentean who had to protect her. This time, he and the world as a whole would pay the ultimate cost for her shortcomings.

"I'm Nevick," he said, "I'm a friend of his."

"A likely story," Nahzarro said beside them, standing tall and glowering down at the man. "How do we know that?"

Nevick stood beside her, rising far up to an intimidating height that towered over Nahzarro. She did not look, but the uncomfortable silence that permeated the encounter seemed to indicate some form of ridiculous macho stare down between the two men.

"I guess you'll just have to take my word for it," Nevick said slowly, with more than the hint of a threat. She felt his great shadow envelop her. "We need to get him back to the airship."

"What good will that do?" Maura said, her eyes never leaving her friend's body. "When he dies, you know what happens, don't you?"

"I do," Nevick replied. "Which is why we have to get him back aboard the ship. My fiancé is there. She's a healer. She can save him."

Maura's eyes snapped up to his and she found kindness and a sad desperation that belied his imposing stature. Looking down, she saw that Nevick's arm was horrifically broken with bits of bone stabbing through his skin.

"Your arm…" she whispered.

"She can patch me up after she saves his life." Nevick wrapped his one good arm around Valentean's waist and effortlessly heaved him up onto a shoulder.

"Maura, you can't be serious!" Nahzarro exclaimed. "We know nothing of this … barbarian. How do we know he isn't leading us into an ambush?"

Nevick seemed to brush off the comment and inclined his head to her, as if to ask for her decision.

"What choice do we have?" she asked. "If he stays here, he dies. And then we all die when Ignis is released!"

Nahzarro took a step back, grimacing in annoyance. Finally, he nodded his head and gestured forward with both arms.

"Come on," Nevick instructed. "We need to move fast. We have, maybe, seconds." He took off running; Maura and Nahzarro trailed after him.

Nahzarro still stumbled in his weakened state, but adrenaline kept him upright. "Seconds until what?"

Violent flames erupted behind them, and Maura glanced over her shoulder as they sprinted away, watching the building Aleksandra had crashed into start to melt into a liquefying flow of molten red sludge. The empress burst into the sky, red aura blazing around her and lighting the entire city in its blood-colored hue.

"Infidels!" she screeched. The ground beneath them began to shake. Maura looked up to see dark, swirling clouds converging on Kahntran. "You cannot run from me! You cannot escape from me! I will hunt you! I will eviscerate you! I will burn you to ashes!" Bolts of red lightning fell from the clouds, striking the ground and igniting much of the jungle vegetation which spread throughout the city.

"This is unreal!" Nahzarro cried out.

The rumbling beneath them grew to such an extent that Maura nearly lost her footing several times.

It was not long before the Aleksandryan airship could be seen in the distance. With destination in sight, she tried to push all thoughts of Aleksandra's terrible power from her mind and focus on her goal.

"Where are you?" Aleksandra bellowed into the air. "If I cannot find you, then I will destroy it all!"

The red light surrounding them instantly brightened, and Maura stole a glance back to see the glare's epicenter explode outward. Where there once had been a woman, now hovered an immense red dragon, more than two times larger than the one which had destroyed Lazman.

Nevick cursed loudly and Nahzarro gasped as the dragon began to beat its wings. The lightning from the sky upended buildings, vegetation and ground alike. Maura ran through an exploding red field of horrors until they reached the miraculously unscathed airship. She followed Nevick into the battle-scarred vessel, knowing that they were far from safe.

Deana could not believe what she was seeing. The dragon which was visible through the command bridge's viewport was terrifying in its immensity. She had not heard Nevick right away as her lover stormed into the chamber along with two others. Deana, Mitchell and Michael turned in relief, but the healer screamed in horror when she saw the hideous, scorched corpse that Nevick carried over his shoulder. Was it Valentean? What had happened?

"Is that…?" she started to say, while the Duzels looked on in horror.

"Do your thing, Dea," he said, laying what was left of their friend on the wooden floor. Deana pushed up out of her chair, throwing herself at Valentean's side. It was a miracle he was still alive. A blonde-haired girl knelt beside her, while an extravagantly dressed, tall, thin man hovered over them.

"Can you help him?" the girl asked.

Deana realized this must have been Maura and Nahzarro. She tried to give her the bravest look she could muster. "I'm going to do what I can," she replied, holding her palms over him and humming softly.

"Mitchell, get us in the air!" Nevick screamed as both Duzel brothers sprinted toward the control console.

White light began to emanate from Deana's palms but her magic bounced off his dying body. He might have been too far gone. She opened her eyes in a panic. She knew what would happen should Valentean's life end. So, too, would end the entire world.

"Can you do it?" Nahzarro insistently demanded.

"Hold on," she replied, placing her palms flat against his cracked oozing chest, trying to feel the pathways of flowing energy within his body to discover the extent of the damage. "His energy is hardly flowing. We have no time…"

She heard Maura gasp beside her. Deana knew the life of her new friend and the entire world's existence depended on her in this moment. She had to revive him. She needed to get the Rosinanti energy flowing through his body once more.

"Maybe if I…" she thought aloud, holding her palms together as energy gathered between them.

"Mitchell, why aren't we moving?" Nevick roared as another tremor rocked the universe around them. The floor lurched roughly to the side.

"The engines aren't responding!" Mitchell cried out. "I warned you this was likely a one-way trip!" Jolts of impact jostled them as the cascading lightning impacted the ship.

"And this lightning isn't going to help," Michael added.

"So, we're stuck?" Nahzarro exclaimed, turning from Valentean's body and rounding on the control console. Another strong lurch nearly threw Deana back. The world seemed to be rocking back and forth.

"No..." Michael groaned in utter shock.

"What is it?" Maura yelled.

"The city..." Nevick said, his voice dying as it left his lips.

"She's ripping it out of the ground," Nahzarro finished in astonished bewilderment.

Deana stole a glance out the viewport and, indeed, the entire city was rising toward the hovering dragon, pulled from the ground like a weed as lightning continued to fall with greater frequency and strength.

"The ground is cracking!" Mitchell exclaimed, pulling levers, throwing switches, and turning wheels, but still nothing seemed to work.

The energy within Deana's palms vibrated and she quickly pressed them into Valentean's chest, releasing them in a super-concentrated burst of healing light. His entire body bucked upwards at the sensation, but there was no change. She grunted in frustration and began to gather the energy once more.

Maura covered her mouth with both hands, keeping her attention on Valentean and not on the devastation occurring just outside.

Stealing another glance out, Deana could see heavy chunks of land and buildings tear into the sky. The massive cannon crumpled in the wake of the dragon's power.

As the energy reached its zenith again, Deana pressed her palms into Valentean's chest and released the healing light again. His body jumped, as it had before, but still no reaction.

"No, no, no," Maura said into her hands, already beginning to grieve for her friend. Deana could hardly feel even the faintest echo of energy from the husk that once been the Champion Animus of Terra. He was going to die. As she built up what was to be her final attempt, she saw the dragon, so close now she might have reached out through the viewport and touched it. The creature's glowing red eyes locked upon the airship, and a burning red glare began to gather at the back of its throat.

Deana's terrified adrenaline empowered the energy gathering between her palms, and it glowed with a vibrating shudder. She screamed in terror as she slammed her hands hard against Valentean's chest, feeling the power pound into his heart with a final fury. Valentean's body jerked violently and he took a massive sudden intake of breath as white light exploded from his charred eyes and mouth.

Maura cried out as Deana fell back, feeling as though every ounce of her strength had been sapped. The white glow enveloped the ship as the red dragon's maw flared with intensity. The red beam of destructive hate-filled chaos ripped past its throat and teeth, and just as it was about to impact them, the entire airship blinked out of existence in a flash of alabaster hue.

Nevick had no idea what had happened. One second he was staring into the face of their death, the next there was clear night sky glimmering above them. The airship was suspended in the air, but with no power to the engines, it spun wildly as it plummeted a short distance, smashing into the ground with a resounding crash.

The force of impact threw Nevick and Nahzarro to the ground. The fall jostled Nevick's wounded arm and nearly forced the big man to cry out in pain. Mitchell and Michael remained strapped into their seats at the console, while Maura, Deana and Valentean lay off to the side.

Nevick crawled over to Deana, whose unmoving form unnerved him to the point of near hysterics. She was pale and gaunt with a cold perspiration spread over her skin like a film. Nevick pressed two fingers to her neck and felt a weak but steady pulse beating beneath them. He sighed in relief and held her in his one good arm, looking over at Maura.

"Is he…" he trailed off.

"He's alive…" Maura said in overjoyed wonder. "She did it!"

Nevick smiled and hugged Deana closer to his chest. He was so proud of her in that moment. She had saved the entire world by saving Valentean, and Nevick was so overcome with relief that he laughed in joy. Maura joined him soon after as the two threw their heads back and enjoyed the moment.

"We're alive, too," Nahzarro said, picking himself up off the floor. "That white light of his … it sent us somewhere."

Mitchell gasped as he straightened the spectacles upon his nose. "It sent us home!" he exclaimed.

Nevick gently laid Deana down and rose to his feet, still favoring his mangled arm. "I'll be damned," he said, looking through the viewpoint at the ruins of Casid. "He must've teleported us here somehow." He gazed back at Valentean. "What a guy."

Below the dragon lay a smoking crater that had once been a deserted city. Despite her power, despite the ability to tear an entire community from the ground and rip it to shreds, her prey had eluded her. They had vanished without a trace, in her stolen airship nonetheless. The dragon roared a bellowing rage-filled, hate cry, hoping that wherever the Rosintai was now, he would hear it, and he would feel her resolve to end him.

The crimson dragon landed roughly in the crater, instantly engulfing itself in a red haze until it once more stood as Empress Aleksandra, fists clenched at her side.

"M ... Mistress..." a weak but all-so-familiar voice uttered. She turned to find Aurax, his translucent body lying prone on the ground, as though gravely wounded.

"Aurax," she said, looking down upon him, too enraged and engrossed in this latest humiliation to care about his condition. "What has happened?"

"The Shogai ... and his ... allies have ... escaped. To where ... I do not ... know."

"Then use your powers to find him. He shan't escape my vengeance. Not after he..."

Aurax's body nearly faded from existence before solidifying again. "I ... cannot ... Mistress. Please forgive ... me. My powers are ... depleted. I will need ... time to gather them ... once more before I can ... interact with this plane."

"Unacceptable! The Goddess's power is without limitation!"

"There are ... limits to ... everything..." Aurax said as he faded away, leaving Aleksandra alone to stew in her failure. That sensation she had felt ... it had been pain. She had not experienced true pain since childhood, and she liked it now far less than she remembered. Her sister and Valentean had caused her extreme humiliation on this night. And with her barrier destroyed, Seraphina and those damned rebels would be lost to the wind and far more difficult to weed out.

And then there was that moment, when she and the Shogai had stood nose to nose. Had she truly seen what she believed? Her mind raged, trying desperately to deny what she knew in her heart to be the truth. He had taken it... She clutched at her chest as the chaos storm within her body churned. But it felt different now.

This had been a failure of utmost proportions. It was unthinkable. She was Aleksandra Kackritta, empress of Aleksandrya, prophet of Ignis, lord of the Skirlack. She did not suffer failure. She was better than that. Sophie, Zouka, Aurax, and especially Kayden, had failed first, leaving her in such a vulnerable state. They had allowed the enemies of Aleksandrya to use deceitful tricks to undermine her power, causing this defeat.

There would no longer be any games. There would be no more waiting. She had to act. She had to strike back. She would take the world as her hostage. The hour of her vengeance awaited. Valentean would die, slowly, intimately, and Seraphina would suffer as she watched him bleed out. Or maybe it would be the other way around ... It did not matter. The rage born of chaos flowed through her as a tingling, reverberating shudder and she allowed it to fan the flames of her detestation.

Kayden stood, hunched, upon the balcony of Aleksandra's floating fortress. He'd listened intently to Seraphina's impassioned speech and watched as the blast from the Kahntran cannon dissipated his mistress's magic. He had gazed down at the city square in the wake of this momentous happening and saw the princess standing amongst the rebels. He also saw the smiling face of his father as he moved in to hug this "ice queen."

Kayden scoffed at the irony. His father seemed so desperate to be rid of him that he now took on surrogate children to wash away the stench of his shame at having a son such as he. Kayden could have leapt down and taken the wounded and fatigued princess apart. He could have dived into the fray of rebels, slaughtering every single one until only he and Vahn remained. He could have then torn the old man's still-beating heart from his chest cavity and bitten it in half, spitting the pulpy chunks back into his face as he died.

He could have done all of this. But he did not. Instead, Kayden turned and walked away, giving the rebels a much-needed head start in order to vanish. Aleksandra had interfered in his moment. In that instant, his existence was to be defined. But alas, here he stood, banished from the battlefield like a child.

He would show her. He would show his father. And, the next time he stood face-to-face with his brother, there would be no surprises. The next time they met in battle, it would be the final time. He was through with battling Valentean to a standstill. He was tired of wondering as to the result of their glorious final battle. It was coming. He could feel it. Aleksandra had failed where he might have succeeded. He had no idea how, but his brother had evaded her. Even from this great distance, he could sense it.

Valentean had foiled Aleksandra. He would not be so lucky the next time he faced Kayden.

Four days had passed since Seraphina had saved the rebellion and revealed herself to the populace of Aleksandrya. Four days had passed since she had taken on the form of a massive blue dragon, and still, she could feel the aftershocks of that powerful burst of might echoing through her body. She stood alone in a tiny room within the filthy run-down guardhouse which the rebellion called home.

She had walked among them as they reveled in her victory. She had smiled with them, learned their names, conferred with them, and hid with them. Aleksandra had, of course, returned to the seat of her empire's power. Seraphina could sense her in that floating monstrosity which hovered over the grave of her home. It was known that Aleksandra and The Faithful were scouring the city for them, for her, specifically. Rewards were being offered for her head. There were many throughout the city who called her "Harbinger." But still, her words had inspired hope in the hearts of those willing to listen. According to the reports she had seen, unrest began to gather throughout Aleksandrya.

Her powerful magic aided the already impressive concealment spells which kept the rebellion's location a guarded secret. But Seraphina knew this location would not hide them from Aleksandra's wrath forever. In the last four days, this had been a hanging topic of discussion passionately debated amongst the elite warriors who now deferred to her lead.

Vahn had been instrumental to her adaptation. She was thankful to have him there because her mind was often elsewhere. She could feel Valentean's pain throbbing through the air, choking her with sobs in those rare moments she had been able to steal away for herself. He was hurt, and it was bad. But there was something else troubling her in what she could sense from her animus warrior.

It was as though something about him had changed. Some deep, bubbling presence shifted the light of his soul ever so slightly. What had happened out there? She needed to know. She wanted desperately to leave, to selfishly abandon this mission of rebellion and return to his side, where he needed her. But she could not. She had a duty here, to her home and to her people.

A small rap echoed on the door to her chamber.

"Enter," she called softly. The door creaked open and Vahn Burai limped his way inside, smiling gently at her, as though she were his own child.

"How do you fare, your highness?" he asked, inclining his head in respect.

"Vahn," she replied, shaking her head, "he's in pain."

"I know," he replied sadly, gazing down at the floor. "Since you told me of your connection, my son's condition has been weighing heavily on my mind. But, you must be strong now, my Queen."

She had asked Vahn not to call her that several times, but his oath as a warrior demanded it. That was what they called her now—a queen. The concept rattled her nerves and dredged up uncomfortable memories of her deceased mother. It was bothersome, but a queen was what was now needed, so a queen she would be.

"It is not easy," she replied, a tear glistening in the corner of her eye.

"I know," Vahn said, taking a step into the room and laying a strong, reassuring hand upon her shoulder. "I have often struggled with the duality of the warrior's life. We are drawn in two separate directions at all times, between what we want and what is required of us."

"How do you deal with it? How do you turn these emotions off and focus?"

"You never turn them off," he replied, a calm strength in his voice. "You simply must remember what it is you fight for. You hold the things you want in your heart. You never let go of those emotions. Love is not weakness, Seraphina. It is strength. So, you soldier on, and you embark upon the journey that is your duty because it is undertaken to defend the people we want and love."

She nodded in recognition of his wisdom and stood, brushing herself off and taking a long slow breath. She reached down onto the small table before her and lifted a silver tiara which had been given to her by the rebels a day prior. It had been constructed by one of their ilk: a blacksmith who sought to thank her for saving his life. A small blue gemstone shone in the center of it, surrounded by a web of silver designed to look like shards of ice. She placed it gingerly upon her head and turned, nodding to Vahn.

The Captain Elite led the way out of her chamber, and she followed him into the large circular meeting place which served as the rebel council's war room. Seraphina walked calmly to the table, donned in light black body armor, over which she wore a long blue coat that billowed behind her.

The elite warriors, Vahn included, stood at attention before bowing their heads.

"All hail the Ice Queen!" they cried in unison.

She smiled at her warriors and motioned for them to sit. It was time to get to work.

The sound of light footsteps caused Valentean's head to throb. It was an irritating, grating thump that forced him to grunt in frustration. He tried to move but found himself completely paralyzed with pain. What had happened? Where was he? It was then that he had remembered the chewing sting of the flames, the electrocuting mania of the lightning, the sound of Aleksandra's screams. That last part was as pleasant a memory as the others were horrifying. Her scream was like the sweetest symphony to his ears. He wanted more. He wanted to feel her burn again. To relish in the…

Valentean stopped his train of thought. What was happening? Why was he thinking like that? Where was Seraphina?

"Seeerraaaa," he groaned through black cracked lips.

"Shhh," he heard Maura's voice say from the other side of the room. She slowly entered his field of vision and placed a soft, cool hand upon his scorched flesh, forcing him to recoil in agony. She immediately pulled back. "I'm sorry!"

The idiot girl! What had she been thinking? She deserved to pay for causing him pain. Were he only able to, he would leap up and see that…

He stopped himself again. What was happening to him? Where was he?

"You're on *The Heart of Casid*, in one of the main crew quarters," she said, as if reading his thoughts. "You nearly died four days ago, fighting Aleksandra. Deana … well, she's a wonder. She brought you back. I was sure you were done for. But when she did it, something happened, and you teleported us here, to Casid. It looks like it was beautiful once.

"We're going to be stuck here for a bit. Mitchell and Michael are fixing the airship. Nevick and Nahzarro are helping as best they can, but they are understandably not the best of friends.

"All that aside, Deana expects you will recover, but it's going to take a lot of time, even at your rate. She's been giving you healing sessions every few hours for days, and she said that things seem to be progressing. So, thank goodness for all that."

He was getting irritated again. He had asked her a question and she fumbled about, talking about other things he had no interest in. "Seeeerrraaa," he moaned once more, hoping the idiot girl would finally understand.

Maura shook her head. "I'm sorry, I have no idea. We don't know about anything that's going on out there. Nahzarro said, though, that the cannon should have taken out the barrier, so hopefully, she's all right…"

Valentean took a deep calming breath, trying to keep the vitriolic sting of this newfound frustration and anger down. He nodded his head to Maura and tried to smile at her, but even such a tiny movement shot pangs of pain echoing through his face.

"Try to get some rest, Valentean." Maura reached out to touch him but stopped short. She leaned over to the table beside the bed and lit a small candle which spread some much-needed light through the room. Maura smiled at him one last time and turned to leave.

Valentean was transfixed by the candle's flame for several minutes, watching the subtle beauty of it as it swayed and danced along the wick. The ease in which it melted the white wax upon which it sat, sending super-heated dribbles of gooey liquid running slowly down the candle, collecting into a puddle at its base.

Everything dies, Valentean, came the distorted voice of his father. *No flame can burn forever.*

Those words had haunted him for most of his life. But he had come to accept them as the truth of Terra, the one constant that could not be overcome. He needn't fear the candle nor mourn the burnt-out wick that it left behind.

Love can burn forever, the Rosintai had said. He thought of Sera, of the love they shared, and the sense of profound happiness that it dredged up within him. But with that, there also came another burst of frustration. The woman he loved, that he pledged his life to, was a world away from him. There was nothing he could do save lay in a bed and wait to be tended to by those infinitely his inferiors.

Seraphina needed him, and he needed her. He would be back with her again soon, no matter the cost; no matter how much blood he had to shed in order to do it. He was done playing around. Results were needed, not happy thoughts.

He made a silent vow to himself as he quietly raged. *As I shall wish it, so shall it be*, he thought. *As my enemies shall gather, so shall they fall.* The wrath of The Faithful had perverted his world for too long. It had crawled its way up through the centuries, twisting the minds of the weak, and it was only getting stronger. *As it shall rise...*

He stared at the flickering flame upon the candle and felt his rage blossom throughout his body in a warm, tingling reverberating shudder that only served to empower this selfish burst of ambition. He smiled at the flame, as though it were an old friend, ignoring the searing pain in his face the expression birthed. As he concentrated on it, the fire responded to his silent command and jumped, extending toward the ceiling like a miniature inferno.

Its red flame echoed the crimson glow which now emanated from his eyes...

As it shall burn...

Valentean and Seraphina Will Return in Rosinanti: Rise of The Dragon-Lord

OTHER WORKS IN THE ROSINANTI SERIES

Rosinanti (book 1)

Rosinanti: The Decimation of Casid (a Rosinanti Novella)

ABOUT THE AUTHOR

Kevin J. Kessler lives in Orlando Florida, where he owns the White Dragon Podcast Network, which puts out weekly podcasts on a variety of topics from Walt Disney World, to movies, television, comic books, video games and more. A lifelong geek, Kessler can often be found at the many theme parks and local attractions in Orlando. He developed the story for Rosinanti as a sophomore in high school, sixteen years before the release of the series.

OFFICIAL WEB SITE: www.authorkevinjkessler.com
FACEBOOK: www.facebook.com/kevinjkesslerauthor
TWITTER: @KevinJKessler
INSTAGRAM: @WhiteDragonPN
OFFICIAL ROSINANTI FAN GROUP: www.facebook.com/groups/rosinanti

Made in the USA
Columbia, SC
09 May 2017